To Pete
Matt and yan_el

Hannah & Horatio Pea

Bless you.
With my love,
Sally

Hannah & Horatio Pea

Sally Noble

ATHENA PRESS
LONDON

Hannah & Horatio Pea

Copyright © Sally Noble 2006

ISBN 1 84401 673 0

First Published 2006 by
ATHENA PRESS
Queen's House, 2 Holly Road
Twickenham TW1 4EG
United Kingdom

Printed for Athena Press

Acknowledgements

I Would like to publicly thank Sarah Checkley, Barbara Harrison, Guy and Ann Harrison, Ian and Rosemary Johnson, Edwina Lloyd, Sandy and Barbara Noble, Janet Tuckett, and Andrew Wall.

Without their generosity this book would not have been published.

For the real Hannah – Hannah Pagram –
the inspiration behind the book.

Introduction

I would like to tell you about some people who live in a village above Stroud. I have known them for a long time. They are very important to me and I am going to share them with you. Many fascinating and extraordinary events have occurred in their lives, and no doubt more will occur in the future.

They have all known Hannah. She has helped them to survive. She has made living easier for them. Sometimes we lose our way and fall heavily, but when Hannah was around it became easier to climb back onto the path, to stay in this world.

She helped four children do this. Andrew, Joseph, Bess and Bibi – with the assistance of Horatio Pea! Maybe you have wondered why this book is called *Hannah & Horatio Pea*? Well, sit back and I'll tell you.

My story begins in 1988…

Chapter One

*H*annah held the seeds in her hand. The ground was ready. She had prepared it so carefully, digging the expectant soil and sifting it with her firm, gentle hands. The pea sticks were standing by the wall of her garden shed and the water butt was full of sparkling rainwater. 'Must make sure you little ones are watered,' said Hannah.

It was spring, early spring. Hannah's garden was full of green; the air was clear and warm.

'Hannah?' There was a question in the voice. 'Hannah, why are you standing, staring at the ground?'

'Oh, hello, Andrew!' Hannah was always pleased to see Andrew.

'Hannah, were you speaking to the ground?'

'Yes. I was telling the earth that Artie and I are about to sow the peas.'

Hannah's eyes crinkled up as she looked through her glasses at this child, so serious and a little worried.

Andrew was nine years old and tall for his age. He wore spectacles, large ones that covered up his beautiful brown eyes, which was a pity because there was such feeling in those eyes. Hannah loved him as much as he loved her, and that was heaps and heaps!

Hannah touched his shining hair. 'Would you like to help me?' she asked.

Andrew, after a clear moment of thought, said, 'Yes, but

I would like Joe and Bess to help as well.'

'Well then, you run off and find them. Hurry back! I'll wait for you!'

Andrew was away, running towards Hannah's back gate, which led to the orchard where the old pony lived, and then on over the meadow to his home. Andrew lived in a house at the top of the village called The Oak Tree House. 'What a wonderful oak tree!' people would say. Andrew loved the tree… it was always changing its face. He spoke to it every time he passed it.

The Oak Tree House was large and friendly with lots of nooks and crannies and stairs leading to interesting rooms of all sizes. 'Our house was born in the middle of the seventeen-hundreds. It is very old,' Andrew told his friends.

Andrew lived in The Oak Tree House with his parents, Jan and Chrissie Leigh, and three other children, Joseph, Bess and Bibi.

Hannah's face was full of pleasure and her eyes shone. 'Artie! We're going to have helpers. We shall need something to keep us going,' she called.

Artie knew what his wife meant. He called back, 'Do you need me down there?'

'Any time you want to come, we shall be pleased to see you!' Hannah's face was full of life and energy.

Dear Lord, I am so thankful that you helped me find this lovely little lady! thought Artie.

Horatio Pea was about to be planted, to be made real. Horatio Pea. Of course, he was just part of a seed-pea at this moment in time, but soon he would be in that welcoming earth; life was about to begin.

Hannah, Andrew, Joseph, Bess and Bibi were hard at work planting the pea seeds. The children loved being with Artie and Hannah. Chrissie, Andrew's mum, was constantly saying, 'You really should allow Artie and Hannah time for themselves, now come home!'

Hannah had been Chrissie's nanny. She had looked after Chrissie and her brothers, Fred and Kel, from the time they were babies. Chrissie knew exactly why her children wanted to be with Hannah: she treated them like real people, never making them feel unsafe or silly. Mind you, Hannah did not stand for any nonsense; everyone was expected to use their minds and be kind and careful.

Andrew was always telling his parents how they spent the time at The Cottagey House where Artie and Hannah lived. 'We laugh and laugh and talk and talk... and then we're silent and we think.'

Jan liked to hear laughter. He had been a sad little boy. He didn't have a home, only places he stayed in with people who were always 'on the move'. Refugees, he called them. Andrew wanted to know more about these refugees, but Jan did not find it easy to tell him, and Chrissie said, 'Just wait, darling. One day Daddy may tell you.' It was a truly dreadful time for Jan. His memories were full of night and daymares, like Joe had.

Maybe I should tell you about Joe, Bess and Bibi, who lived with Jan, Chrissie and Andrew at The Oak Tree House. Joe was not able to see very well. His eyes had been damaged in a car accident when his parents were killed. Chrissie had always wanted lots of children, so when Hannah told her about this little boy, Joseph, whom she had met in the children's hospital during her storytelling time there, she had rung Jan at once and asked him if Joe could come and live with them. 'We may be able to love him back to health... with Hannah's help, naturally.'

Naturally! thought Jan, and he said, 'Yes.' Joe arrived, so frightened in his dark world. He was able to see faces and some objects, but there was confusion and everything went past him 'fast and furiously', Hannah said. But gradually Joe became safer and surer and could see more. Of course, he had lots of advice from the doctor, who also lived in the village, and the vicar, who had lots of children and people in his house all the time.

Mind you, Joe still hid away in unusual, quiet places and Andrew had to look for him carefully, making sure that he did not make him jump or frighten him. The two boys became great friends... they still are.

Bess. Now, what can I tell you about Bess? One very certain thing: she was 'found' – yes, found! 'Thank the Lord,' said Artie, and Hannah repeated, 'Thank the Lord!' When Jan and Chrissie brought Bess home and Andrew and Joe saw the ragged head and curled up body wrapped in a furry rug in Jan's arms, they thought it was an animal.

'Ah! Another creature,' said Joe, and Chrissie smiled and said, 'Yes, you're right. She is a little girl creature.'

They were very surprised. Andrew said, 'Has she a face?'

'Oh, yes, a beautiful face, but she doesn't want to show it to us yet.'

The two boys were fascinated with this 'little girl creature'. She never talked to them, never talked to anyone. Hannah seemed to know what she wanted and seemed to understand some of her feelings. Chrissie said, 'When we first met her she said a word that sounded like – "Bess". It might have been her name or it might have meant something else. The word certainly seemed to be important to her. We'll call her Bess.'

Bess had been found wandering the streets in a small Cornish Town. Jan and Chrissie had been down to Cornwall for a few days' break. From time to time, Hannah would suddenly say, 'Now, it's about time you two had a

Chapter One

break, so away you go to the sea.' This meant Cornwall, a very special place for Jan and Chrissie.

Anyway, some friends told them about this little girl who was continually noticed walking the streets and the beach. She didn't seem to belong to anyone, so she had been taken to a local children's home. Chrissie and Jan had just looked at each other. There was no need for words. They went straight to the home and now Bess had been at The Oak Tree House for about eight months. Bess settled into the family quite easily. Andrew became even more caring, and perhaps even too attentive. Joe was very wary. He found it difficult when Bess did not answer him or join in the 'table talks'. The family always had exciting talks after they had eaten their meals. Invariably, there were lots of people sitting at the big round table. Sometimes the vicar's children dropped in, and stayed... and stayed! Sometimes actors and actresses arrived for lunch or tea because they were in the area, touring a play or filming for the BBC or other TV companies. Jan was a film director and Chrissie had directed plays before they had moved to The Oak Tree House. There was always a variety of animals in the house as well. Animalia, Andrew called them. They didn't mind. They smiled at him... or wagged tails... or purred.

Suddenly, one day after Bess had been with the Leighs for about six months, she began to make sounds. There was a great deal of excitement. 'Now, try not to keep at her; Bess will speak in *her* time not ours,' Hannah advised. Darling, darling little lady... she knew... 'Han has a direct line through to God,' Artie had told them.

I should tell you that police and social workers are looking for Bess' family, in Cornwall and all over the country.

Yes, I am going to tell you about Bibi. She is a very important little person. She stays with the Leigh family whenever Laura, her mother, is working. Laura is an actress and has to work – indeed loves to work! So, Bibi comes to her 'other home' as she calls The Oak Tree House, and is such a joy. She is now two years old, with long, white blond hair and astounding violet eyes. Andrew tells everyone about the violet eyes. She laughs and sings most of the time. In fact, she is hardly ever quiet.

'Surely she is quiet when she's asleep?' queried Joe, and Chrissie said 'No!' Joe was surprised. 'She talks in her sleep… real, clear words?'

Chrissie laughed before she answered, 'Oh, yes! Really clear. She talks continuously!'

Joe was even more surprised. 'Oh dear!' Then he added, as an afterthought, 'Perhaps she could give some of her words to Bess!'

'That's a splendid idea, Joe,' said Hannah, 'You go and suggest it to her.'

So he did and now Bibi is often seen 'feeding' words to Bess. Andrew told Artie once, 'Look! Bibi is using a dessert spoon to feed words to Bess!' Bibi is staying with the Leighs until September, but Laura will come and see her as much as possible.

Anyway, Andrew rushed into the kitchen at The Oak Tree House just as Bess said, 'Veggie.'

He shouted, 'Hannah says we can help her sow the peas! All of us! Come! We must hurry, the earth is absolutely ready!'

Joe was painting. He jumped up and knocked the paint water over. It ran over the edge of the table, onto Pippin the golden retriever. She shot to her feet and the three of them ran of out of the room. 'Wait! Wait! Joe, come and wipe up the water,' called Chrissie catching Bibi as she began to slither around in the watery mess on the floor. Bibi was shrieking with pleasure. Bess stood very still and kept on repeating, 'Veg... Veggie.'

Joe returned, grabbed a cloth and wiped everything and everyone in sight! *Such excitement over planting peas*, thought Chrissie. But, then, Hannah made everything in this wonderful world exciting. Chrissie remembered her own childhood and chuckled. 'Would you two girl creatures like to plant peas with the boys? Shall we show them how it should be done?'

Bibi said, 'Peassssss?' She made the word long, the 's' at the end sound like a buzzing bee. 'Peassssss. Yesss, pleasssssse!'

Bess nodded, and put her hand into Chrissie's, and they left The Oak Tree House and made their way across the orchard towards The Cottagey House, with Bibi skipping and chattering and Bess walking quietly beside Chrissie.

As they arrived at the pea patch, they heard Artie saying, 'I thought you might need something to keep you going, so here is some orange juice... yes, freshly squeezed, Andrew... and the SBT.' SBT? Special Biscuit Tin. Initials can be confusing at times, can't they?

But first seed-peas were handed around to everyone – oh, yes, two-year-olds are able to sow seeds! We are able to do anything if we know how and why, and there is always time to find out about all the hows and whys! Hannah had told them, 'There is always time... If you *make it and use it.*' This was one of Hannah's 'Wise Sayings', sometimes called HWS. Andrew regularly used initials – he still does. It saves time, he says.

Artie gave each of them a dibber, a tool for making holes in the earth. 'When you've made your hole carefully, drop the seed-peas in and then come and look at all the others.' Artie showed them how to do this. Soon there was a long row of sown pea seeds waiting for their 'bedclothes', as Artie called the earth, to be placed cosily round them.

'Lovely, warm soil… oooh!' said Joe. He loved feeling the earth. He loved the feel of leaves and grass, animalia coats and skin and so many different – there was a word… Different what? 'The word is "textures",' Chrissie had said. Bibi had spoken *that* word for hours!

'Now, how many are there of us?' asked Hannah. Andrew and Joe counted, with Bibi joining in with the numbers she knew.

'There are seven of us,' said Andrew, and Joe added in a worried voice, 'What about Jan Dad?' Joe knew that Jan was not his real father, which was why he called him Jan Dad.

'One of us will sow his seeds for him. We'll each hold his seed-peas in our hands for a few seconds and then Artie can put them in the earth for him,' Chrissie said.

Joe looked sulky; he wanted to sow Jan's seeds. 'Why Artie?'

'He's the eldest and wisest gardener,' answered Andrew.

'How many years have you, Artie?' asked Bibi.

'I think I have about one hundred and seventy-four,' said Artie seriously, and then he winked at her.

Joe saw the wink and grabbed Artie's hand, saying, 'Oh, Artie! You told me one hundred and eighty last week!'

'Did I now? Well, I must have lost some of them since then!' Artie squeezed Joe's hand and said, 'You are seven years old, Joe, so touch your seed-peas seven times very gently and think of seven special things – no, no, don't tell us! They are your own specials… and as you're seeing them in your mind's eye–' he tapped his head– 'place the earth around and on top of the seeds. They will be safe and warm and feel at home.'

☙ Chapter One ❧

'Mmm,' said Andrew, 'you're quite old, so you will have to take lots of time. I'm nearly ten, Bibi is two, and Hannah is… I think you said one hundred and seventy-eight, didn't you, Hannah?'

Hannah laughed and said, 'Oh dear, Andrew, I've dropped a lot of years since I told you that! However, I shall have a large number of special things to think about when I tuck in my seed-peas, won't I?' and she laughed again.

'What about Jan Dad?' asked Joe. 'How old is he? About the same age as Chrissie? Is that right?' and he looked up at Chrissie.

'Yes, we're about the same age,' she said, ruffling his hair. She looked at Bess, who was standing looking at her seed-peas. Her little face was wet with tears. Chrissie went to her, and, kneeling, took the child's cold hands and said quietly, 'Shall we think of lots and lots of special things for Jan?' (Chrissie always called him Jan and herself Chrissie when she was speaking to Bess.) 'Bess, oh, dear Bess!'

Chrissie saw a strange, dark look come across the child's face whenever Chrissie said daddy or mummy to her. The other children seemed to cope quite well when speaking to her. They just said 'Jan and Chrissie' quite naturally, and Bess' face did not darken.

Bess now looked at Chrissie for a moment, and then she went to Artie and put out her hand for the seed-peas. He touched her cheek, placed some seeds in her hand and folded her fingers over them. Bess stretched out her other hand to Chrissie and they went back to her seed hole. They both knelt down and the others watched in silence as the Bess' seed-peas were sown. Then everyone became very noisy and busy.

Soon all the seed-peas were comfortably settled in their homes and Artie said, as he mopped his brow, 'Juice and biscuits?'

Chapter One

Now there was another silence – well, there weren't any voices, just the sound of crunching and slurping! Finally, there was a wonderful nothing.

'A silence is a time when the brain wheels are being oiled.' This was another HWS. You know what that means, don't you? Yes, that's right: Hannah's Wise Sayings!

Suddenly Bibi said, 'Does Bess have years?' Everyone looked at Bibi and then at Bess. She did not seem to have heard the questions, but it was clear that Bibi needed an answer.

Andrew was the first to speak. 'I think Bess has had nearly six full years.' He went to her and helped her smooth down the last piece of bedclothes over her seed-peas. She smiled at him. He looked hard into her eyes, in fact, he took off his glasses and looked hard into her eyes! 'Yes, she has had six years, nearly, and her birthday is close to mine. In July. It is April now, so she has three more months being six and then she will be seven.'

No one said a word... even Bibi was silent. Then Bess spoke: 'Six, then seven.' And then she said, oh, so clearly, 'A pea is a veggie.'

Hannah clapped her hands and hugged little Bess close to her heart. Bess told Andrew when they were older that, 'Hannah always had such a strong, comforting heartbeat.'

They had sown their peas and some more for the animalia: one for Dog Pippin, Smudge Cat – she belonged to Artie and Hannah – and a new kitten called Bossie; she lived with the Sophia Lady up the road in Merlin Cottage. The 'Sophia Lady' was a great friend to everyone in the village and Bossie stayed with all her friends. She moved around a great deal – Bossie, I mean! When Joe first heard the 'Sophia Lady's' name, he thought it was the *Severe Lady* and was very concerned. He couldn't see her easily. She was tall, with lots of beautiful red hair, and she radiated life and colour and used many extraordinary words. 'No, Joe, she is not severe, but she likes us all to use our brains and not to be foolish,' said Andrew when he and Joe had been to visit her with a message from Chrissie.

Sophia and Chrissie talked together a great deal. 'Oh, what a full of wonder talk I have had with Sophia this morning, Jan! She makes me feel really alive!' Andrew had heard his mum say this; he wondered what it would be like to feel really dead...

Those seed-peas were not dead, although they appeared to be wrinkled and dry when you held them in your hands. Joe spent a long time feeling his seed-peas. One of them had lots of grooves and, yes, it seemed shrivelled – how strange! Artie and Hannah assured him that with careful 'nurturing' – 'Get the dictionary, Andrew. Now lets have a look – nurturing... feeding... watering... It will soon change its shape in the earth and begin to put down roots and to shoot upwards, like us human beings... we have to be nurtured and loved and then we will begin to grow. You have all been nurtured and loved and see how you have all changed and grown.' Hannah's voice and face were full of her joy of living and giving.

Joe said proudly, 'My eyes have been growing very well.' Hannah glanced away and thought of the time when he would have to go into hospital to have an operation on his poor eyes. Her heart jumped for a second as she thought about the pain 'we shall all feel for him and with him'.

'Bess' words have grown. I like her sounds, her noises,' Andrew said cheerfully. He loved Bess very much.

'Why doesn't Bess speak like us, Chrissie?' inquired Joe after Andrew and Bess had walked up the path to the kitchen to fetch watering cans.

'We don't know yet,' answered Chrissie, and her eyes clouded. Joe was beginning to know more about Chrissie every day. He was able to see her fair hair and deep-set eyes as long as he was close to her, but he knew her better by her quick movements and her touch. She touched him often. He seemed to relax when he felt her hands on his body. She often knelt down and put her arms round him. She was always very aware of his insecurity. Joe waited for Chrissie to continue. She spoke again.

'I am going to London soon, Joe. I shall be seeing people who are looking for Bess' family. Perhaps they will be able to give me some information.' She gave him one of her quick smiles and he smiled back.

Hannah, Artie and Bibi had finished their refreshments and Bibi was talking about the seed-peas in a loud, clear voice. They had decided that everyone should write their names on a label and put the labels in front of their sown seed-peas. Each one of them would look after their own seeds – with help, if it was needed, from whoever was around and free. 'I hope we don't get a May frost,' said Artie, 'Remember last year Hannah?'

'Oh, dear, yes! What a nightmare! We lost so many veggies and flowers!' replied Hannah.

Joe thought about *his* nightmares. He wondered if the frost had given Artie and Hannah the same fearful feelings he had... or maybe the word nightmare had another meaning... *I'll ask Andrew*, he decided. Suddenly, he saw Andrew and Bess. They were each carrying watering cans. They all filled the cans from the water butt and with instructions from Artie, who had soaked the peas for a short time before they had been sown, they gave them their first drink in the earth.

'They're quite comfortable now.' Hannah smiled as she spoke. 'Let's go and write their labels.'

Chapter One

The children rushed off to The Cottagey House, leaving Chrissie and Artie together. They sat down on the long wooden bench and Artie sighed. Chrissie patted his hand and said, 'Is that a good sigh or a bad sigh, Artie? Maybe we've made you tired – Bibi is so noisy!' This time Chrissie sighed. She didn't find Bibi easy.

'Certainly a good sigh, my maid. Ah yes! A very good sigh!' Artie said reassuringly.

They sat quietly in the spring sunshine. From the house came the sound of laughter as voices rose and fell. Chrissie was about to ask Artie a question, but as she turned to him she noticed that his eyes were closed and his lips were slowly moving.

She had not known Artie for long. Hannah had told Chrissie and her two brothers, Fred and Kel, a long time ago, that she was going to marry a lovely young man, but he had been killed in the war. 'No, there has never been any other man for me. No, no one could measure up to Henry.' Hannah had looked after Fred, Kel and Chrissie until they were old enough to leave home and go to university or college. She then went back to her birthplace, which was Hay-on-Wye in Herefordshire – or was it Monmouthshire? Nobody seemed to know when they had talked about the little town. Anyway, Hay-on-Wye is *now* in Powys.

'Then Hannah is *now* a Welsh lady,' said Andrew. 'I have never seen her in a high hat and a cloak, have you?'

'I am never able to understand why county names in Great Britain are changed,' Jan said.

There was a silence full of thoughts. Andrew eventually said, 'I will ask the Sophia Lady to take me to the library in Stroud. We will find out.'

'Thank you, Andrew,' said Jan, with a faint trace of a smile.

Hannah had taken care of her mother until she died and had lived in the Hay-on-Wye house by herself for some months after her mother's death and then she suddenly decided that she would go on a holiday to the Cotswolds, having lived with a family in Malmesbury when she first became a nanny. She said, 'Yes, I shall take a coach tour to all the places I knew when I was a young girl. Lovely!' She had a wonderful time. There were so many memories. She laughed and smiled, and cried too. One day the coach driver told them he was going to stop in Cheltenham for tea. He would like to see an old chum, so, 'Be back in an hour, ladies and gents.'

Hannah walked up and down the Promenade lost in memories of pushing a pram with a cheeky faced baby in it. She was recalling how she nearly tipped the baby out, when she heard her name: 'Hannah Lovejoy?' She turned round. There stood a big chunky man with a thatch of white hair and navy blue eyes. He said again. 'Hannah? Are you Hannah Lovejoy?'

'Yes. Who are you?' she stared up at him. He was quite tall and she was a tiny lady. Suddenly she laughed and clapped her hands. 'Oh, dear Lord! Is it Arthur Best? Artie, is it you?'

He beamed and answered, 'Yes, it is.'

'When did I last see you?' exclaimed Hannah.

'It must be over thirty years ago!' replied Artie.

Hannah looked at his tanned, lined face and she said to herself, *What a gentle, dear boy he was. I remember him at School. He always carried the small children on his back.* Suddenly the years rolled away and she was back at the village school in Hay. She saw her brothers and sisters, her friends and... Artie. Artie had been a very good friend to her and her family, and now here he was, looking down at her!

Chapter One

They went to Artie's favourite coffee shop and they talked and talked and laughed and laughed, sharing memories. Time went by and when Hannah glanced at her watch, she realised that she would have to run back to the coach station. It was well over the hour that the driver had given his passengers!

'Oh dear! What shall I do? The driver will be worried about me!' Hannah had gone very pink and seemed most distressed.

Artie smiled. 'Now, don't fret. I'll go back to the coach and tell them to go on. You just sit here... I'll be back. I have a small car and I can quite easily take you to your next stopping place to meet the coach. Now, be peaceful, m'dear.' He stood up, bent and kissed her on her cheek and was striding off towards the coach station. Hannah watched him. She felt quite breathless. She thought, *Oh, dear Lord, this is a special day. What have you got in store for us?* She felt surrounded by warmth and love. Everything – and everyone – seemed to be sparkling. People smiled at her and she smiled back. Her own face was full of light and her eyes were shining. She saw Artie coming back, walking towards her. He looked so happy and people were smiling at him as well!

Artie said later, after they had been married at the tiny church in the village and were living in The Cottagey House, 'Do you remember that afternoon we met in Cheltenham, little Han? When everyone was smiling at us? Well, one of my old mates saw us and told me that I was walking around with a large grin all over my face. And so were you. No wonder people were smiling!'

Hannah had laughed. 'Oh, what a wonderful afternoon it was! The Lord certainly has our lives in His hands. Here we are in this dear little house close to all the folk we love the most and with so much to do! Lovely! Lovely!'

Artie's eyes crinkled and he said with a twinkle, 'And you always said no one could ever measure up to Henry...'

Hannah reached up and patted his cheek, saying, 'He was fatter than you, and not as tall!' Artie put his own hand up and covered hers.

It had happened so quickly. Their meeting, the decision to be together and live in this village where Chrissie, Jan and Andrew had lived for many years. Artie and Hannah had arrived about five years ago. Artie knew the area and someone had told him about The Cottagey House, which was for sale. Hannah had rung Chrissie and there was such excitement! Chrissie had said, 'Oh, you'll love this cottage, Hannah!' The vicar, Jay Bond, was sitting in the kitchen at The Oak Tree House at the time and Chrissie had asked him if she could borrow his car. 'I need to fetch some keys so that Hannah and Artie Best can look at this cottage they are going to live in!' she told him. Chrissie was absolutely certain that this was the house for the couple; she was right!

Chrissie's mind jumped back to the bench. She and Artie turned to look at each other at the same time. Chrissie said, 'Artie, you're good to us, so patient.'

He smiled, then said quietly, 'I love you all very much. It's easy to love folk like you.' He patted her cheek and his hand was cool and reassuring.

Hannah and the children were back with their labels. Bibi had run all the way down the path. Her voice was full of jumbled sounds and tunes. 'I can't understand what you're saying, Bee!' laughed Chrissie.

Andrew had been finding Bibi very annoying. He looked hot and he was frowning. 'She's just a silly baby!' He sounded angry and stressed. 'Why doesn't she keep quiet for a few minutes? She's ruined my label... she spat on it! Look!' Andrew held up a soggy-looking label. It was indeed a mess!

Hannah understood Andrew. She had to intervene before he burst into tears. She said quickly, 'Andrew, I've a spare label in my apron pocket. You go find a safe, quiet place and write another label.'

'Thank you, Han,' Andrew mumbled. He turned away from the others and walked towards the greenhouse. He had a secret place there, behind some pots. Bibi never came into the greenhouse.

Every seed-pea now had a comfortable bed and a label. They belonged to someone. 'Do they need to have three meals a day, like Jan Dad?' asked Joe when they were all eating their tea.

'I'm not sure,' answered Chrissie. 'That's something we shall have to find out.'

'Tomorrow,' said Joe.

Bibi shrieked, 'Tomorrow! Tomorrow! Tomorr—'

Joe yelled, 'Hush up, Bibi!' and Bibi repeated, 'Hush up, Bibi, hush up Bibi!'

Hannah put her hands over her ears. 'Oh, dear! What a pandemonium!' she said, and closed her eyes.

Bibi immediately stopped shouting and said, 'Pan-de-mon-ium.' She spoke the word in bits, gradually making it into a tune. She began to dance round the room, chanting the word and waving a piece of bread and butter.

'Well, well!' exclaimed Hannah. 'That little girl is rather special. Maybe you should consider sending her to dance classes.'

Chrissie had also recognised Bibi's special creative qualities. She said, 'You're right, Han. Dancing would soak up some of her remarkable energy. I'll contact Soozie in Bristol. Bibi will like her. Another job for—'

'—tomorrow!' interrupted Joe.

Andrew thought, *What a relief! We can all have a few hours*

of peace if Bibi goes to Bristol! Actually, he liked Bristol. There were so many places to see, including the best toy shop ever! He heard Chrissie saying, 'This has been a good day. Let's be still and remember all that's happened.' Andrew closed his eyes. The pea sowing day. His seed-pea was safe. He was safe.

Chapter Two

It was the beginning of May. The seed-peas had changed. They'd had plenty of water, and compost had been placed on the earth above them. Lots of goodness had filtered through and they were growing.

'Look!' said Artie. 'Shoots of green! They've rooted and are strong. Now they'll send their shoot stems up through the soil and into the air... they want to show themselves to the world and have a look around!' Artie chuckled.

'We must look out for a May frost,' Andrew said quickly.

Artie became serious, 'Oh yes! Oh dear, yes! Frost is cruel. It can fatally damage young plants.' He looked worried. It had been cold recently. Suddenly, after a warm spell, the wind had changed and there had been snow in the air. 'I do hope we're not going to have a difficult spring!' murmured Artie to himself.

Andrew ran off up the path to meet Hannah. He called out, 'Hannah, green peas shoots are showing!' Hannah had on her favourite cuddly coat. She looked warm, but Andrew noticed that there seemed to be something troubling her. He asked, 'Are you all right, Hannah?'

She replied in a steady tone. 'Yes, Andrew, I'm fine, thank you.'

But Andrew was unsure. He was a sensitive boy. Ever since he was a little boy, he had noticed when people were feeling concerned. He was aware that Hannah was feeling –

what? Unsettled? Maybe it was the cold weather… However, Andrew was right; Hannah was beginning to have one of her 'feelings'. Something significant was about to happen. She had woken up feeling trembley – that was her name for this feeling. May the third; yes, it was going to be quite a day.

Andrew took Hannah's hand and gently led her towards the pea area. Her hand was cold. He rubbed it and put it into the pocket of his own coat. Hannah smiled at him. 'It's all right, Andrew. Don't worry about me. My, isn't that a fine sight to be seen!' She gazed at the pea shoots. 'We should have a strong crop this year. We must look after them…' Suddenly she stopped speaking and turned around quickly, towards the narrow road that ran past their garden gate. Andrew and Artie were watching her. They suddenly heard a car approaching, moving fast. It was Jan's car. Stones scrunched under its wheels as it came to a halt. Jan opened the door and jumped out, calling to them, 'Is Chrissie here? I've just had a call from Joe's eye specialist. He says that Joe will be able to have his operation at the end of June. Isn't that good news?'

Andrew spoke with excitement. 'Oh, Dad! That means that Joe will be able to see properly again! Great!'

Hannah was standing very still. She was staring up into a hawthorn tree that was full of blossom. Artie, Andrew and Jan were talking nineteen to the dozen and Hannah was staring at a tree. Artie was saying, 'Hannah, do you think that Chrissie and you will take it in turns to be at the hospital with Joe?' Hannah did not answer. Her eyes were closed and she was whispering words. Andrew went to her and he heard her say, 'Not the end of June. Oh, Lord, please not the end of June!'

Andrew touched Han's arm and asked, softly, 'Why Hannah? Why shouldn't it be the end of June?'

Chapter Two

Hannah jumped and her eyes met his and then moved to look at Artie and Jan. There was a strange moment of silence. Then Artie said, 'Have you one of your feelings, little lady? Is there going to be trouble?'

Hannah moved to Artie and took his hand, holding it tightly. 'I hope not, but I have known that something was going to happen today ever since I woke up this morning. Perhaps the date will be altered. We mustn't let this upset us. The news about the operation is good. We must prepare little Joe gently. Yes, we must be very gentle and choose our words carefully.' Hannah kissed Artie's big, strong hand and walked away from them, through the garden gate and past the car, talking to herself. Nobody moved or spoke for a long time.

It could have been a full minute, or maybe longer, Andrew thought later when he was by himself, recalling that scary time when Hannah had taken herself away from them. 'She was in another place... she wasn't with Dad, Artie and me,' he told Chrissie when she'd questioned him. It had left Joe feeling very uneasy. He knew all about Hannah's feelings. You should know more about these feelings, then you will understand why Jan and everyone who knew Hannah well were anxious.

Hannah came to look after Fred, Chrissie and Kel when they were babies. First, there was Fred and then, four years later, Chrissie was born. Finally, after nine years Kel arrived. Hannah had been with their family for about thirteen years before Kel was born and during those years, as in all families, a great deal had happened, good and bad. It had become absolutely clear to the children and their parents that Hannah seemed able to know about future happenings. She had often warned the children about certain roads and pathways. She used to say, 'I wouldn't go that way. Choose another way.' And, sure enough, there had been a nasty accident during the time they would have been passing down the road or the path. One day she had warned Fred about a bridge over a river. He hadn't taken any notice and there had been a near disaster. The bridge, weakened by a storm and gale-force winds, had collapsed and three little boys had fallen into the seething waters below and had nearly drowned. Hannah had been so worried that she had persuaded some men to go to the river. They had arrived just as the bridge broke apart. The boys had been rescued because the men had been there. There are many other stories – not all bad! Hannah knew that good things were going to happen as well. The point is, no one who knew Hannah took her feelings lightly!

When Jan told Chrissie about how strange Hannah seemed when he had called at The Cottagey House that morning, she decided to visit the old lady as soon as possible. Chrissie had also experienced the feelings. She wondered about the last week in June. Why was Han so concerned? What could possibly happen to Joe? To one of the family? 'I must go to see Hannah *now*.' She spoke quite loudly. The children were having lunch with the vicar, Jay Bond, and his family. Then they were all going swimming in Cheltenham and would be away for hours. Yes, she would go *now*!

The door of the living room opened and there stood Hannah. 'I knew you were thinking about Joe's operation,' Hannah said. 'I've come to talk with you.'

Chrissie's heart missed a beat. She said, rather breath-lessly, 'Han, darling, come and sit down. I'll make you a warm drink. You look worried.' Hannah's usually bright eyes were clouded and her face was pale. Since she had left her garden and the others at the pea sowing place, she had walked through the village and down to the stream. She felt a feeling of peace and a depth of quietude there. She knew that she would be near her Lord.

Hannah had sat on a seat underneath a willow tree and waited. Maybe she would be told what might happen in the last week in June, or maybe it would become clear as the days went by. It was only the third of May, after all. Plenty of time yet until June... When she finally looked at her watch, she realised that she had been sitting by the stream for nearly an hour! Her mind snapped into gear again. She had seen Chrissie's face. In her mind's eye, Chrissie's face was as clear as crystal.

Hannah and Chrissie sat at the round kitchen table drinking coffee. Their minds were working away but they didn't speak. Joe was about to go through a vital time in his life. They both knew that he had a marvellous talent; an ability to paint, to draw, to use colours like no other child that they had met. They knew that without eyes Joe could become a desperately lost little boy. The car accident had been horrific. There were times when Joe had shrieked out descriptions of his parents' bodies, the blood, the twisted shapes on the ground. Mr Sanders, Joe's father had lost control of the car and it had swerved off the road and down an embankment into a small copse. The police had had great difficulty getting to the car. Joe had been thrown clear, but had lain unconscious. When the paramedics finally managed to get him to hospital, the doctors found that there were no bones broken or internal injuries, but he had a deep gash on the left side of his face; the right side was unmarked. Later, he complained of pains in his right eye and the doctors found that it was also damaged. They would need to investigate the eye further when Joe was stronger. The pain gradually went away, but Joe was in deep shock for many weeks. When Hannah first met him in hospital he was a thin, sad little boy. He was having his nightmares *and* daymares frequently and was in the middle of one when she walked past his cubicle. The sounds were frantic! She told Chrissie about them. 'He sounded like a terrified little animal! He was thrashing round his bed with two nurses trying to hold him down. Poor girls! He stopped screaming and felt around the air for my hand. I stroked his face and he found my hand and held it, oh, so hard! He managed to say, "Please stay… don't leave me… they always leave me!"

' "Sit down," I said to the nurses. "Just sit down and let him know that you are here with him. I can stay as long as he needs me." So I did. Remember when I stayed with you, when you had pneumonia – you were only a wee thing. Do you remember?' (Chrissie remembered that Hannah had always stayed with her and her brothers as long as they had needed her – sometimes all day and all night.) 'The nurses had to go, of course, to other children in the ward, but I stayed with Joe. I talked to him and stroked his poor face. Gradually he began to relax and finally he slept. I visited him every day and stayed for hours. There were problems, however: he wouldn't eat. Perhaps he couldn't eat. You were like that when you were desperately unhappy – you still are.' Hannah paused. 'He liked me to tell him stories. He liked to hear about the village and all the folk who live here. The doctors suggested that I fed him. It slowly began to work, thank the Lord. Stories and a spoonful of his favourite food.'

Joe became stronger and began to be part of the world again. Everyone knew that it was Hannah who had brought him back to life. Soon he was living with Jan, Chrissie and Andrew at The Oak Tree House.

Chrissie stood up and moved to Hannah. She put her arms round the old lady. Neither of them spoke. They understood each other. All at once Hannah chuckled. Chrissie knelt down by her side. 'What is it, Han? Has something been made clear?'

'Well now,' replied Hannah, 'all I know is, that we shall be able to cope with "whatever it will be" – just as long as our lines through to the Lord are working. Where's Joe at present?'

'He's gone swimming with Bess, Bibi and Jay's brood. Janice is with them.' (Janice was Jay's wife, the brood's mother.) 'They won't be back before four o'clock. Shall we have a bite to eat and chat over how we're going to tell Joe about the operation?'

Hannah's eyes were twinkling again. 'Yes. Oh, and we must tell them all about the pea shoots. Have you seen them? D'you know, Andrew is becoming deeply interested in peas!' And she laughed and gave Chrissie a hug.

Chrissie said, 'I think Jan ought to be here when we discuss Joe, don't you? I can imagine that the house will be full of strange, unsettling comings and goings during Joe's time in hospital. Maybe you could come and stay here, Hannah? It will help the children to have—'

The door shot open and Andrew rushed in. He looked stricken. 'Something terrible has happened! Her peas… her shoots… they… they've!'

As Andrew took a breath, Hannah said, 'Whose peas shoots, Andrew? Tell us clearly, slowly now.'

The lad was certainly very upset. He sat down by the fire. Andrew had always done this when he was upset; warmth seemed to comfort him. 'Why should it be *her* peas? It's so unfair!' He began to cry.

Chrissie looked at Hannah. Hannah mouthed, 'You go to him… he needs you.' She gathered up the empty mugs and took them to the sink. Later Chrissie recalled the 'sounds' in the room. She found sounds curiously calming. The sound of Andrew crying and the sound of running water and in the background the tick of the clock. Andrew never cried loudly, not like some people. He just sobbed and his whole body shook. Chrissie stood close to him and stroked his shining head. He was beginning to get back his normal breathing pattern. She said, 'Tell us, darling, as soon as you can. It must be very important.'

He told her, 'Artie and I were… looking at the… row of pea shoots. Some of them… are strong and tall… yours are climbing around the hazel stick and they have white flowers. The we stopped at Bess'—' his voice cut off. He got up and started to walk around the table. His words were clear and his eyes were full of pain and love. Hannah was holding a mug in one hand and the drying-up cloth in the other. Chrissie was kneeling by Andrew's chair. She realised that in some way what was about to be said would affect them all.

'Bess' pea shoots are dying.' The ticking of the clock was louder. 'They have been… frosted.'

Chrissie felt a small twinge of a giggle rise inside her. Hannah looked at her sharply. She *must not laugh*! It was all enormously serious! *Poor Andrew. He really loves that little girl*, thought Chrissie.

A voice from the open back door said, 'Now, now, my little man, it's not quite as bad as all that. I think we may be able to do something to help.' Artie was taking off his large muddy boots. His face was alive with smiles. 'Would you get me a drink, Andrew? You know what I prefer.' The atmosphere changed. Everything became lighter. Hannah finished drying the mugs and Chrissie got up and fetched Artie's tankard. Andrew hesitated for a moment. Then he breathed out and ran to the fridge. He took out a bottle of

Artie's Light Ale and gave it to him. Artie winked and Andrew smiled. 'What a drama we've had,' Artie said as he sat at the table and opened the bottle. Andrew was close to him, holding on to his sleeve. Artie was using the knife with all the gadgets. Andrew was going to have one like it for his birthday. He loved watching Artie's hands. They could do anything. He had forgotten the desperate situation for a moment.

'I'm going to have knife like yours, Artie, for my birthday.'

'Then I must make sure that you know all about it, mustn't I?' Artie closed the bottle opener gadget inside the knife's outside jacket and put the tool into Andrew's hand. 'Now, the pea shoots. I've thoroughly inspected little Bess' injured plants and I think we can save some of them. They may be slightly damaged, but I think we can help them to go on growing. Of course, we won't know about the actual peas until we have picked and smelled them. I can't promise that they'll be all right, Andrew, but we'll do our best. You'll help me to tend them, won't you?' His voice was soothing and as he spoke he touched Andrew's shoulders and arm and hand. Andrew was listening intently. The only person in the room for him at this moment was Artie. Chrissie and Hannah were forgotten. They were always amazed at Andrew's concentration!

'What can we do?' he asked.

'Hope and pray that the weather gets warmer,' said Artie.

'Can we cover them with anything?' asked Andrew.

'Ah, well now, I'll put my mind to that.' Artie finished his ale in the silence that followed his words. Oh, those silences! They were so important and so full of energy and ideas! 'I love silences,' Andrew told Bess when they were older, 'so much goes on in them.'

Tea time again! The Leigh family and Jay's Brood were gathered around the table. Joe, Bess and Bibi had shining faces and their hair was still damp from their afternoon at the swimming pool. Hannah and Chrissie had cut tons of 'arnies'. Have you heard of 'arnies'? No? I thought not! They are sandwiches – sarnies! – called 'arnies' by Andrew when he was a very small boy. He found 's' sounds difficult. Now everyone calls them arnies! There was also chocolate cake made by Chrissie with help from Bess and Bibi. Andrew and Joe had fallen about laughing when Hannah told them all that Bibi had 'helped'.

'Helped? Bibi helped you? Never!' Joe just could not believe that Bibi had helped.

'It's a wonder that we have a cake at all,' said Andrew, his deep brown eyes gleaming behind his specs. 'She didn't spit in it, did she?' He was not being nasty; he just had a very good memory!

Bibi said carefully, 'Bee does not spit any more. She tastes.'

They all looked from Bess to Bibi. The tiny girl was in the middle of an enormous mouthful of cake. She beamed and closed her eyes. They were all laughing, their faces alive and radiant.

There was a knock on the kitchen door. It opened before anyone was able to say 'come in'. It was the Sophia Lady. She also looked radiant. 'Hello, hello, you lovely people! Jan is parking the car. He tells me that Joe is going to have his operation in June. How marvellous!'

Oh, how a few words can change an entire roomful of people! Sophia immediately realised that Joe had not been told about his operation – nor Bess, nor Bibi. Eyes were moving from one face to another. Chrissie heard the clock again. It seemed to be ticking faster. *It certainly understands everything that happens here*, she thought. *Maybe it is alive as well.* Jan came into the room carrying lots of bags. 'Ah! Just in time for my favourite family tea. May I have some…'

Chrissie went to him and whispered, 'Ssh!' He understood the situation at once – he'd heard Sophia's words as he came down the path. He gave Chrissie the bags and said in a clear, ordinary voice. 'Yes, we have had great news! Joe, do you want to know more about it? Now? Shall I tell you all about the phone call that I had today?' There was a sudden burble of voices, words tumbling around. 'When, when?', 'Which day?', 'Which hospital?', 'Will Joe have to wear dark glasses?', 'Yes, that's right. I saw someone wearing them the other day and tapping the road with a white stick,', 'Can we visit Joe in hospital?' and many other thoughts. Jan clapped his hands once, a strong, ringing command. 'Hush!' And they did. They knew when Jan clapped his hands and said 'Hush!' like that, no one must make even a small sound.

Chrissie listened for the clock. It was loud, but it was not ticking too quickly. Jan reached out to Joe. He stood up, pushed his chair back slowly and went to Jan. They were all looking at those two important people – that is, all except Bibi, who was still munching away at her cake. 'Bibi—' began Andrew, but Hannah signed to him not to go on. She put a finger to her closed mouth and Andrew nodded solemnly and did the same. Hannah came to Andrew and he gave her his chair and stood close to her, his hand resting on the back of her neck. Jan took Joe's hand and led him to the fireplace. He turned his back to the fire and smiled at his family.

Jan told them all he knew. That the eye specialist was going to look at Joe's 'good eye' to find out if he could make the sight better; that this was going to happen at the end of

June; that it would be an exciting and happy time, also quite a worrying time, because no one really knew what might happen. Chrissie was about to interrupt Jan, but he looked at her and went on. 'I have to tell you that it will be worrying. It is the truth. We should know the truth. However, the specialist is optimistic. Where is the dictionary? Ah, thank you, Sophia. Will you tell us what that word means?'

There was a pause while Sophia searched the book. 'It means that the doctor has a "hopeful view of the situation, that he is full of hope, expecting a good happening, a good result",' said Sophia cheerfully.

Bibi had finished her piece of cake and was stretching out her hand for more. She was standing on her chair, leaning across the table. *Crash!* Her chair slipped backwards and she fell onto the table, onto the food, the plates and cups and mugs! What a mess! Her face had landed in a bowl of Fruit Salad and her hands, attempting to push herself up, were scrabbling around, knocking over anything they came into contact with. Poor Joe was forgotten! Bibi was rescued and taken off to the bathroom by Hannah. Sophia was organising a clearing up operation with Andrew, Jay's brood and Chrissie. 'Operation? This time it has a different meaning, Andrew,' Sophia was saying. 'When we've finished we will look the word up and find out all its meanings.'

There was so much going on that they hadn't noticed that Bess was not with them. She had left the kitchen and gone to get Bear. When Bess was found in Cornwall, she had Bear with her. He was an old teddy bear and she was never without him. Gradually, over the months that she had been at The Oak Tree House, Bear had been left sitting in special remembered places. He had to be found quickly, however, whenever he was needed. He was needed now.

Chapter Two

Jan was talking to Joe. They were still near the fire. Jan said, 'Chrissie, Joe and I are going to the orchard. We would like you and Hannah to join us when you have finished here.'

Gradually, the atmosphere changed and everyone became slower and quieter. Jay's brood went home to the vicarage; Andrew sat down in the living room with Sophia and the dictionary. Bibi was given a bath and persuaded to get into her bed, as long as Hannah told her a very special story about all the animal toys! Chrissie let out a long sigh. 'Ohhhh! At last... a little moment of peace!' But she had forgotten Bess. Bess had found Bear. He was sitting under the beautiful grand piano in the music and television room. Bess and Bear often sat under the piano. It was Jan who played the piano and she used to creep in and sit there with Bear, listening to the extraordinary sounds. Nobody minded. She appeared to be in another world, with the music swirling round her. Usually her eyes were closed and she cradled Bear in her arms. Her lips moved at times, but no sound came out. Andrew used to watch Bess for ages, wondering where she could be and what she was saying inside her head. He did not let her see him. He always tiptoed from the room and often went to his secret place in the greenhouse. He had a notebook there, hidden in a huge flowerpot. He wrote notes on Bess. They could be important clues for the detectives who were trying to find out about her family, her parents.

Bess was not under the piano now, however. She had picked up Bear and had run fast, out of the room, along the corridor. She was under the stairs in a large cupboard full of brooms and brushes, Hoovers and dustpans and dusters. She felt safe here. She was very frightened. They had said a word

42

that had caused her head to go 'all swimmy'. The word was important, but she did not know why. She felt cold and began to shiver. She sat in the darkness of the stair-cupboard and held Bear tightly to her. She could hear her heart thumping. She also heard the sound of voices coming nearer. They belonged to Sophia and Andrew. 'Will Joe be in the hospital for a long time, Sophia?' Andrew's voice! The *word! Hospital. Hospital?* Bess didn't know what it meant. Her head had lost its swimmy feeling, but she did not know what hospital meant. She jumped up and opened the door just as Sophia and Andrew had passed it. 'Andrew!' she called. 'Andrew, what is hospital?' Her voice sounded strange. After a few moments, Andrew said, 'I'll take you to Joe's hospital when he's there, Bess. I think you should see it then. It is a good place for making us better when we are not well.' He realised that Bess was disturbed and that he should not describe the hospital to her at this moment. He knew that she must not be alone so he smiled and said, 'Hey! Bear looks fine! Hannah gave us lots of clothes for the animal toys. Let's go and find him some new trousers. Excuse us, Sophia Lady, won't you?' Andrew took Bess' hand and he guided her quickly to the nursery room and the clothes.

Sophia watched them disappear through the door. *Strange, lovely child*, she thought. *Who are you? Are your really called, Bess? Who could possibly have just left you, wandering? What kind of person could have done such a terrible thing?* She heard the phone ringing. She called, 'Chrissie, shall I answer that for you?'

'Please, Sophia. Hannah and I are off to the orchard to join Jan and Joe. Keep an eye on everyone here, will you? I wonder what will happen next.' Chrissie's voice sounded strained.

Hannah was walking steadily down the path that led to the orchard. Sophia could hear her footsteps. She said her thoughts out loud and she moved quickly to the phone. 'Little Hannah, you are really going to be needed in the days to come?' The phone stopped ringing, but had started again. Chrissie would have known, had she been there, that this could be a special sign. Her very best friend could be phoning her from the other side of the world, Nah Cox. Her name was Anna, but she was always called Nah! Chrissie and Nah had been friends for a lifetime. Hannah said this was a friendship made in Heaven. It certainly felt like it! The children were thrilled when Nah came to stay. Andrew was always saying that the house was full of warmth and colour and great comfort when Nah was there. This was true; Nah was another special person.

Sophia shrieked when she heard Nah's voice. 'Nah! Where are you? In America? Coming home? When?' The questions went on and on. Andrew and Bess came out of the nursery room to listen. They'd found Bear some brightly coloured trousers, which he was wearing. A door crashed open upstairs and Bibi appeared, dragging bed-clothes behind her. She was shouting, 'Is it Nah? Where? Where? I want her now! Nah! Nah!' Andrew ran upstairs to her just as she tripped over the blanket and toppled over. He caught her before she could come to any harm, but she would not stop saying, 'Nah? Where is Nah?'

'Hush up, Bee!' said Andrew, holding her very tightly. 'Sophia can't hear what Nah is saying. She's not here now. She's speaking from America. She's coming to us soon.' Bibi was struggling so much that Andrew could not hold her. She wriggled free and rolled down the stairs. Bess tried to catch her but Bibi managed to get to her feet and run to Sophia. Bess put her hands over her ears and closed her eyes. She could hear Bibi screaming and Sophia's shrill voice. She hated high, shrieky voices. Her head was becoming swimmy again. She felt for the floor, and keeping her eyes closed, slowly crawled with Bear back to the nursery room, where Andrew found her later, curled up on the window seat behind the curtains. She'd covered herself and Bear with a patchwork woollen rug. Bess felt safe in this rug. We all need something or some place that makes us safe, don't we? Poor little Bess. She was so quiet and in the background that she was often forgotten. Andrew felt guilty when this happened. 'Why do we forget Bess? *I must remember her, I must remember her.*' He used to repeat these words to himself, and indeed, it was Andrew who usually found her. They used to walk together, hand in hand, not saying anything – just being safe.

While the telephone call was causing intense excitement, Jan had been explaining to Joe that some time in June he would be going to have his right eye explored. He was telling him about the retina, a thin, skin-like tissue. 'I will show you a large picture of a tissue. There is also a model of the eye at the hospital. You will be able to feel it, and look at it, very, very, carefully.' Jan told him that Joe's retina had been damaged in the accident. It had become detached. It had broken away. This retina was not doing its job properly. 'Retinas are light carriers. They are sensitive to light and light is not getting into your right eye, Joe, not the way it should do. The doctors need to look behind the eye. They need to find out if they are able to make it—' Jan thought for the best word— 'to make it stronger.'

Joe was listening intently. He was very pale. Hannah and Chrissie arrived as Jan was saying 'stronger'. Hannah looked at Joe. He turned his head towards her and put out a hand. Hannah smiled and settled herself down on the grass under an apple tree. Joe came to her and nestled close. She smoothed his cheek and he guided her hand to his right eye. He closed the eye and pulled her fingers over it, shutting out all the light. The old lady felt the little lad shudder and she held him to her with great love. She tried to take her hand away from his good eye, be he wouldn't let her. 'No light, no light,' he said.

Chrissie said, 'Joseph, let the light in now.' He took his hand from Hannah's and she moved her fingers. He opened his eye slowly and blinked at the beam of light that was coming through the leaves of the tree.

Hannah said, 'There is always light, Joe, if you want light. Inside your head.' Joe nodded.

Jan went on: 'No one knows about the back of your eye yet. This is why you need to go to the hospital. Maybe the doctors will find that your sight will get better, that they will be able to mend the retina. We should think – what was the word Sophia looked up in the dictionary?' Jan waited for a reply.

Joe turned towards him and said, 'Optimic… Optimis…' Chrissie helped him and all at once the four of them were playing around with the fine word 'optimistic'. Finally, they all shouted, 'Optimistically!'

'Yes, yes! That's the word, that's the way! We shall all be full of hope!' laughed Hannah. Joe threw his arms round her and gave her a large, wet kiss, and then Chrissie and then Jan. He rushed over to where the pony, White Star, was quietly munching away at the grass and gave him a great hug. The pony whickered and nudged him with his head. Joe fell over into the long grass and lay there looking up at the clouds scudding across the sky. A wind had got up and the sounds were wonderful. He wasn't frightened any more. He had been, but he knew now that his family, his friends would be near him always, no matter what happened. He remembered Artie and the peas. 'May I go to The Cottagey House and tell Artie what you have told me, Jan Dad?' he asked, still lying in the grass.

Jan said, 'Of course you can. That's a very good idea.'

'Find out about the frosted peas as well,' Chrissie added. Hannah pulled Joe up and they walked off together, chatting happily. Their voices were alert and there were many chuckles.

'Thank you, my darling.' Chrissie reached up and kissed Jan. 'Thank you for being so gentle.' Jan held Chrissie and they watched the little old lady and the boy until they were through the orchard and out of sight.

Artie was sitting on his wheelbarrow, mopping his brow. He'd been working hard and fast, trying to find out how much damage had been done to the young pea plants. The frost had been quite severe. Bess' plants were a sorry sight. They'd been growing so well with the beginning of flowers showing here and there, but now there were a number of blackened areas and Artie knew that they would die. The sheltered plants seemed safe, but he had noticed more damage to some of Andrew's and Bibi's. The animalia ones looked all right but, well, he wouldn't know the full damage until they had grown some more. 'Oh dear,' he was speaking his thoughts out loud, 'Oh dear! So many problems coming all together, just when everyone seemed so happy. Isn't it always the way? Oh well, I expect we'll be able to manage. We shall… now what is it that little Andrew says? Ah, yes. We shall have to put our minds to it!' He laughed.

'I think we'll need a lot of heart as well as minds Andy, my little mate!' He felt that he needed to talk to Hannah, Chrissie and Jan and that it must be soon. Artie had an un-wavering belief that the Lord would help. 'All we have to do is "hand the problems over and do our best",' he said loudly as he stood up. Hannah and Joe saw him move away from the peas.

'Artie! Artie! Joe has come to tell you about his opera-tion,' called Hannah. 'It's very interesting. We have decided to look at all the eyes we meet and Joe is going to draw them.'

Joe added, 'And will you tell me about the eyes inside our minds, Artie? I may need those.'

Artie looked at the expectant faces gazing up at him. His own eyes filled with tears. He reached out his arms to the two dear people and gathered them in. They never forgot those moments when they cried together. They were exceptional moments and we don't forget exceptional moments.

When Artie brought Joe back to The Oak Tree House later that eventful day, there seemed to be a different atmosphere in the house. Andrew was still awake, probably reading in his bedroom. Joe saw the glimmer of Andrew's desk light. All the people who lived in The Oak Tree House had desks and lights. Jan and Chrissie were in the music room listening to piano music. He recognised it. It was Mozart music. He had been told that. Jan and Chrissie were going through a 'Mozart phase'. Joe wondered if they would ever get out of that Mozart phase! The house was full of music. 'I can't live without music!' Chrissie said often. 'I can't live—' Anyone who heard her would say— 'without music!' Joe smiled. He said goodnight to Artie and waved him down the path and then stood for a while outside the music room listening to the tunes. He couldn't hear any voices. He closed his good right eye. The left eye without the sight closed also. Joe was not disfigured. He looked as if he'd had an accident, but his face was amazingly undamaged. The scar down this left cheek under his eye had faded considerably. Of course, it would never really disappear, but it was not as livid as it had been even two months ago. The doctors at the hospital had done a 'marvellous piece of mending!' Someone had said that it sounded as if Joe was a piece of clothing, a sock or a torn coat! They'd laughed and inspected his face with a magnifying glass. Indeed, the doctors had done a fine job. Joe was a handsome boy. His looks, his bone structure had not been impaired. As he stood surrounded by the surging sounds, he had an urge to look at himself in a mirror. He opened his eyes and walked up the stairs and into the bathroom. He switched on the light over the mirror where Jan and man visitors shaved, and leant forward until the blur that was his face cleared. He saw the chin, the mouth, the cheeks... all the various colour shades of his skin. He saw the eyes. He said to his reflection, 'I can see you now, Joseph Sanders Leigh. I am going to look at you so hard, that I shall never forget you. Then I shall go and draw you and put the drawings in my suitcase. After I've had my operation I shall take you out of the case and look at you again. You will be different. I shall draw you again!' He sounded strong and he wasn't frightened.

He knocked on Andrew's bedroom door. 'May I come in, Andrew?' There was no reply. He knocked again. Silence. He put his ear against the wood and held his breath, but there were no Andrew sounds. Should he go in? Andrew was a private boy. His room was his refuge, a place of protection from danger or trouble. There was a notice on the door saying this: 'Andrew's Refuge'. He called through the keyhole. 'Are you in there, Andy?' No reply. *That's very odd*, thought Joe, *very odd indeed. His lamp is on, I can see the brightness.*

He heard footsteps coming up the stairs and turned round. Andrew and Bess were coming slowly nearer up the stairs. They had something over their eyes. It looked like bits of cloth, or maybe it was a scarf or ribbon? They were holding hands and their other hands were feeling for the banisters and the wall. Joe had excellent hearing. He recognised Andrew's heavy breathing and Bess was counting. 'Fourteen, fifteen...' The two children were indistinct at first, but sometimes they became bright and they seemed to shine. Joe rubbed his right eye and was about to say something, then stopped as he heard Bess say, 'The dark is thick, Andrew. My daddy went into the dark.' Joe quickly moved and crouched down against the wall next to the bedroom door.

Andrew said, 'Your daddy, Bess? Can you tell me about your daddy?' Joe waited for the reply.

'Soon. Yes, soon.'

The music boomed and a long shaft of light came from an opened door downstairs. 'Real coffee or a cappuccino? Would you like a chocolate biscuit with it?' Chrissie was going to the kitchen. She glanced up the stairs, stopped and whispered, 'What are you doing up there? Andrew, Bess, have you covered your eyes?'

She walked up the stairs and touched their faces. Joe was still by the wall watching. Andrew said, 'We're finding out what it would be like to be without eyes, Mum. I think we should know just in case Joe doesn't have his sight made better. Bess and I have been all over the downstairs and we're about to try out the bathroom. You don't mind, do you?' He was holding on to Chrissie's skirt and had let go of Bess' hand.

Bess suddenly said, 'Joe is near us.'

Chrissie looked beyond the two blindfolded children and was aware of a shadowy shape by the wall. 'Is that you, Joe? How long have you been back from The Cottagey House?' Joe stood up and came over to them. Andrew and Bess put out hands to feel where he was. They still had their eyes covered.

Joe spoke carefully and calmly. 'I've often covered my good eye to see what it would be like to be quite sightless. It's OK if you know where all the furniture is. Would you like to come up to the top rooms with me? I go there to practice being without eyes. I have a room up there all carefully arranged!' He pointed up through the ceiling. The heads of the others turned up to the ceiling also. Chrissie put her arms round Joe and drew him to her. She knelt with him, her lips on his warm, soft cheek. Dearest Joe. He was being very brave.

Bess had moved to Andrew. She always knew where he was. She slipped her hand into his. *Oh, another silence,* thought Andrew. Suddenly there was a small thud. Bess said, 'Bear!' Chrissie picked him up and guided Bess' hand so that she could hold him. Bear had been in Bess' overall pocket. He looked very dashing in his new trousers! Joe peered at them. 'They're great! The colours are so bright... they make him look like a topless, half-dressed soldier bear!' They laughed.

Chrissie said, 'Do you know what time it is? After eight.'

Andrew broke in, 'Mints! May we have one, Mum?'

Chrissie touched his tussled hair. 'I don't see why not. Tell you what, you two take off your...' she hesitated for a split second and then said, '...eye covers, then come down

52

to the music room and I will go and get us all some drinks and After Eight mints.'

She ran downstairs just as Jan called, 'Hey! Chrissie, where's my drink? What's going on?'

Joe pulled off Andrew's eye cover and they rushed downstairs, leaving Bess and Bear at the top. She sat down and tried to take off the scarf she had over her eyes. Jan was in the hall and realised that Bess was by herself and went up the stairs. 'Bess? Little Bess, do you need me?'

Bess was saying quietly over and over again, 'My daddy, my daddy.' Jan gently undid the knot in the material and gave Bear to the little girl. She crept into Jan's arms and buried her hot, pale face in his neck. 'My daddy, my daddy.' But Jan knew that she did not mean him.

Much, much later that evening Jan said, 'Chrissie, darling, I believe that Bess is about to tell us more about herself. She keeps saying "My daddy" and that is certainly not me. I must watch and listen – we all must.'

Chrissie came out of their bathroom and climbed into bed. She was exhausted. 'Yes, yes, we must be...' she leant over and kissed Jan gently... 'vigilant, Jan, that's the word Andrew would use.' Soon they were fast asleep, worn out with the day's happenings.

The weather had improved, thank the Lord. Artie and Hannah, and anyone who happened to be around, had been taking care of the peas. The pods had formed and were growing! 'Beautifully!' Artie was heard to say, 'Beautifully!' each time he looked at them. The first crop would be ready for picking in a couple of weeks. May had gone by and it was now June. The gardens in the village were looking splendid.

The Cottagey House garden was a wonderful sight to behold. There was an enormous amount of growth. Bibi spent most of her time there, hiding amongst the tall flowers and grass. Sometimes you could only hear her voice. She sang and talked non-stop! Hannah gave her lots of jobs and she did them all without grumbling or complaining. Bibi hardly ever complained. She was a very happy child but she was never quiet!

However, the family had had a meeting about Bibi. She irritated them and they found it difficult to get the important things done. Andrew was having a bad time. He spoke to Jan one Sunday as they were going to church. 'What are we going to do about Bibi, Dad? She's invaded my room every day for the last week. My special books are not in their homes… she's scribbled on some of them! I get so angry with her and I hate getting angry! Is she going to be with us all summer? Surely, Laura can come and take her off our hands!'

Jan looked down at his son. Andrew was very serious and quite upset. Something had to be done, so a family meeting had been arranged. It was a proper meeting. 'Like Jan Dad has when he has his film-making meetings,' said Joe. Finally, it was decided that Chrissie should speak to Laura and take Bibi back to London where they lived. Chrissie told them that Nah was due any time. She'd had to stay in New York to record some voice-overs for the film she had just finished.

Jan clapped his hands and everyone looked at him. Jan spoke in a pleasant, positive way. 'Good. Our problem is solved! We will phone Laura and Nah and ask them the questions that have been discussed. Hannah and Artie, would you have Bibi to stay with you until we hear from the two ladies?' Artie lifted his eyes to heaven, but he was smiling and he winked at Andrew as he said, 'We'll get that little Bibi into shape! We'll highly organise her!'

And Hannah added, 'She needs a lot of attention, that little miss.'

'Fine,' said Jan, 'the meeting is closed.'

The children went their various ways, happier now. The four grown-ups sat in silence for quite a while. Suddenly Jan said, 'I'm going to ring the hospital.' The others watched as he stood up, carefully pushed his chair under the table and walked out of the kitchen. Chrissie, Artie and Hannah sat, waiting for the 'ting' as Jan picked up the telephone receiver. The minutes ticked away. They could hear Jan's muffled words, then another 'ting' as he replaced the receiver. Jan came back into the kitchen. He looked at their expectant faces gazing up at him, and then he spoke. 'Joe's operation will be at the end of the last week in June.'

Nah had arrived. She had flown back to England and driven down to The Oak Tree House from London. She was with Bibi.

'More tea, Nah?'

'Yes, please, Bibi.' There was the sound of liquid being poured into a cup – or could it be a mug? Suddenly there was a tinkle of laughter and then a shriek. 'Oh, Nah, I've spilt Pippin's tea! Look, she's licking it up!' Hannah was walking up the path from the veggie patch. She paused for a moment, wiping her hot face with a big white handkerchief. Then she called, 'Where are you both?'

'In our garden house, Hannah,' said Bibi, and a face appeared through the tall grass. It was a very grubby face and it was shining with fun and enjoyment. Another face joined it… a Nah face! Hannah smiled down at them. 'Oh my dears, you *are* having a happy time! Is there room for me in there?'

Nah answered excitedly, 'Yes, Yes! Come and join our tea party, dear Han! We've plenty of food and we can make you a lovely cup of tea!' She disappeared into the grass and Bibi helped Hannah into the garden house. The special place had been built for Andrew by Chrissie and Nah when he was about three years old. There was a great fir tree in Artie and Hannah's garden and they had allowed the grass, which was full of wild flowers, to grow very tall all round the tree. Chrissie, Nah and Andrew had cleared an area near the trunk and every year they kept it clear, the only way in to the garden house was through the grass and under-growth. It was cool inside the garden house. There were rugs and cushions and a small chair for Bibi. Hannah had made herself comfortable.

'Oh! This is better than picking veggies.' Hannah sounded weary. 'It's too hot today and everyone seems to have lots to do. Jay and Janice are giving a dinner party this evening and they've asked Artie and me to supply the veggies. Artie and I were working away when suddenly the phone rang and Artie has had to go and help a friend with a problem. I've managed to pull up the carrots and pick the courgettes... the potatoes are ready... but I haven't started the peas yet. Oh dear!' Hannah closed her eyes, running her fingers through her hair. 'I feel as if I could sit here and not move for a long time!' Hannah sighed.

Nah said cheerfully, 'Well then, you do that very thing! Bibi and I will go and pick the peas.'

Bibi shot to her feet. 'No, we won't,' she yelled. 'I want to stay here and have my tea party! I'm not going to pick peas!'

Hannah and Nah looked at each other. Oh no! Not one of Bibi's rare tantrums. Hannah began to get up. 'Never mind, then, I'll go back—'

Nah interrupted her. She looked calm, but her eyes were as hard as stone. 'No, Hannah darling. You're not going back to the veggie patch. Bibi and I will go and pick the peas and then we'll shell them.'

Bibi shrieked, 'No! No! Noooo! I won't! You can't make me! I want—' Hannah put her hands over her ears, shutting out the noise.

Nah caught hold of Bibi and said in a clear, strong voice, 'Either you come with me or I leave you on your own. Hannah is going up to The Cottagey House to have a rest.'

'But I want—'

Nah interrupted. 'Yes, that's what you always say, "I want"! Well, you're not going to have what you want!' Nah helped Hannah to her feet, saying, 'Off you go, Hannah. Bibi and I will cope.' Nah was guiding Hannah through the tall grass and on to the pathway when there was a loud, crashing sound… in fact, there were many loud, crashing sounds coming from the garden house! Hannah stopped and began to go back, but Nah said quietly and firmly, 'No, Hannah! I will deal with this.' Hannah nodded, squeezed Nah's hand and continued her journey wearily towards her kitchen, a cup of tea and… peace!

The noise coming from the area behind the tall grass and undergrowth grew louder The child was crying and repeating, 'I hate you all! I hate you all! All of you! All! All!'

Nah crawled carefully back towards the obvious chaos. She marvelled at the small child's vocabulary and speech. *Just over two years old*, she was thinking. *She handles language like a four-year-old! Amazing!* Now she was back in the garden house – well, what was left of the garden house! Bibi had smashed everything she could. She'd poured water and milk over the cushions and the rugs; the small chair that the child had loved, for as long as she could sit on it, was broken, with the seat amongst the cakes and bread, and a leg about to be thrown up into the branches of the tree.

Nah did not say a word. She just calmly looked at the havoc. What a sight! Bibi was holding her breath staring at Nah. Nah's eyes slowly moved round until they were looking directly at the child. What a child! She was covered in dirt, mud, grass... her face was streaked with tears, her hair was tangled and wild, but oh, she was magnificent! Her eyes were shining and her body was alert and poised, ready for... what? That was the question. What was going to happen to her?

At last, Nah spoke. 'Well, well, well! What a pity. You've destroyed our garden house. Did you enjoy yourself?' Silence. 'Did you enjoy yourself?' Still Silence. Nah bent down and picked up an odd looking shape. She brushed off bits of food and earth. It was Bibi's favourite soft toy rabbit. He was ruined. Nah held him out to Bibi. The child didn't take him. She still seemed to be holding her breath. Her face was pale. Nah wanted to gather the child into her arms, but instead she said in a clipped, hard voice, 'And you've even destroyed Baby Thumper. Just because you "wanted" to have your own way, and then you "wanted" to destroy what you love. My sweet, darling little Bibi, you've learnt a lesson this afternoon!'

Nah went to the statue holding its breath and gently kissed her burning cheek. There was a sudden, immediate outrush of air and the statue collapsed onto Nah, sobbing and holding on to her. Nah quickly knelt and cradled the little creature, rocking her in her arms. Very gradually Bibi began to relax and Nah began to talk to her, telling her that she need not have gone through that fearful time, why couldn't she just have 'thought'? Yes, of course she'd been disappointed that they would have to postpone their tea party for a while ('postpone' was explained). Nah told her that people are more important, are the most important. They could have picked and shelled the peas for Hannah and then come back to the garden house and had their lovely time together with Pippin Dog and Baby Thumper.

'Oh, by the way, what happened to Pippin Dog?'

A strangled voice managed to deliver these words: 'Pippin ran away when I began to destroy things.'

Nah quietly and gently said, 'Oh, what are we going to do about that?'

Bibi answered at once, 'I will go and look for her... will you look for her too? With me?'

The exquisite little face gazed up at the older woman, who also said, at once, 'Yes, now!'

Hannah was carrying her tray of tea out of the back door as two figures hurtled round the side of The Cottagey House and through the gate into the orchard. 'We're looking for Pippin Dog!' called Nah and Bibi at the same time. There was a shriek of laughter and they were gone. Hannah thought, *Well, it sounds as if everything is back to normal, but what about those peas?*

As it happened, 'those peas' were being picked by Artie, with help from Andrew and Bess. The two children had turned up as Artic had returned from his helping mission. He'd found the bowls for the peas but nobody else! 'Right! Come along you peas! Time to leave your stems!'

A voice said, 'Hello Artie. May we help you?'

'Yes, you may, my little mate! And you as well, my maid!' Bess gave him one of her rare smiles, and Artie smiled back and said, 'What a splendid face! You've given a bit of extra light to the world. Are your fingers ready for those pods?' They picked three bowls of fine peapods, very green and shiny. Hannah came back just as Bess had put her last pod into the bowl. 'Oh, how lovely!' The old lady looked radiant and, thankfully, rested. 'Thank you so much, all of you! Now all we have to do is to sell them!'

They did not appear to like this last remark. Andrew said, 'Oh, I'm afraid that we must go back home now, Hannah. We are going to see Joe. He is going to have his operation tomorrow. Tomorrow is Friday. Remember?' Hannah's stomach jumped. For a short time she'd not been thinking about Joseph. He'd gone into the hospital the day before, Wednesday. It was the last week in June. Oh yes, and the next day would be Friday...

It had all gone smoothly. Joe was quietly confident and the whole family had gone with him, on Wednesday, to get him settled into his ward. He was in a small side ward in the hospital with three other boys. He'd taken his special bits and pieces with him: his crayons, paints, lots of different coloured paper and his soft toy animal – a bear with bells in his ears. Chrissie had given Bells to Joe when he first arrived at The Oak Tree House after his accident. Bells, like all the other soft toy animals which belonged to the children in the family, was an essential companion. They'd stayed with Joe for a short time. Artie and Hannah had gone with them too. Bess and Andrew held hands all the time. Andrew was keenly aware that Bess seemed strangely tense and she'd held on to him tightly.

The Leighs had gone into the hospital by a special 'In-patients' door. There was another door marked 'Casualty' nearby and Andrew noticed that Bess had walked very quickly past this door. In fact, he had had to run to keep up with her. She seemed to recognise the word 'Casualty'. *How strange*, he had thought, but he was soon thinking of other things.

He'd never been in a side ward before. It seemed quite cosy. The nurses were very pleasant and kind. Bibi had insisted on trying out each bed to find out if there were different – harder of softer, she'd said. Nobody seemed to mind. Only one boy was actually lying on his bed. He had broken his leg badly and seemed to be all 'Trussed up like a poor dead chicken,' said Artie. The two other boys were sitting in big comfy chairs outside their beds. They would be going home soon, they said. There were curtains around each bed, which intrigued Bibi. However, she didn't have time to draw them too often. Joe stored his bits and pieces in a roomy side table. Then he was told to put on his pyjamas and dressing gown.

A nurse came in with a warm drink and some biscuits. Of course, Bibi had to have a couple of biscuits as well; she always had to have whatever one of the others had. Joe gave her all of his biscuits. Hannah said to him in a low voice, 'I'll make some of your "specials" for you, Joe, and bring them in when I come tomorrow.' Joe smiled at her and reached for her hand. Soon, Chrissie said that they should go, but Joe still held tight to Hannah's hand. 'You go back to The Oak Tree House and I'll stay with Joseph,' Hannah said. 'I'm going in to tell him a story.'

Chrissie gathered the rest of the family and after lots of cheery goodbyes and hugs, they were all packed into the Land Rover and zooming off down the hospital drive.

Bess was still holding on to a piece of Andrew's clothing; his jumper or his trousers. He was becoming deeply concerned. On the way out of the hospital and to the car park, where they had left the Land Rover, Andrew suddenly said to Jan, 'Bess and I are going out of this door.' He spied another door saying 'Exit' and this door was before the 'Casualty' sign. Before Jan could argue with him, he had taken Bess quickly out of the door and then she'd dragged him across a kind of courtyard. For a moment he was unable to see any sign saying car park and became fearful, but Bess spoke quickly and clearly. 'This way, Andy! This way!' Sure enough she was leading him to the large green Land Rover! 'That was clever of you, Bess,' he said with a grin. She gave him a hug and he saw that her eyes were full of tears, which brimmed over and ran down her little white face. He took out a hanky and was wiping the tears away when all the others arrived, talking nineteen to the dozen.

'Isn't Hannah coming with us?' inquired Andrew.

'No, she's staying with Joe until he's gone off to sleep,' answered Jan. 'She'll phone me then and I'll come back for her. It is very important that Joseph feels safe.'

Artie winked at Andrew and Bess. 'Han will make sure that he is well and truly—' and Bibi finished the old man's sentence— 'OK?' Everyone laughed, even Bess smiled.

Now it was Thursday and another visit to the hospital had been planned. Tomorrow was Friday, the day of the operation. Hannah's stomach did another jump. She heard Andrew's voice. 'Han, did you hear what I was saying? We are going to see—'

Hannah replied, 'Yes, yes, Andrew, I know, of course, it's getting late. You must go and have your tea before you go to the hospital.'

Bess carefully placed her bowl of peas on the garden bench, looked at Andrew with a straight, deep look, turned and ran off up the path. Andrew called, 'Bess, Bess, wait for me! Please! Hannah, I don't think Bess should be on her own; there's something seriously worrying her! Bess! Bess!'

He gave his peas to Artie so forcefully that some of them

fell out of the bowl and onto the floor. Artie said, 'Hey, little mate! The peas!' He bent down to pick them up, but Andrew had run off after Bess calling her name. 'Andrew!' called Artie. 'Look, I've found some more pods under the bench.' But Andrew was out of earshot. Artie sighed. 'Well, well! Oh, never mind! I'll open these pods for my little Mate. He clearly has more important things to think about!'

Hannah was gazing up the path, watching the two children. She could just see Bess as she ran through the trees in the orchard; Andrew was gradually catching her up. He was still calling the child's name. 'Bess! I'm here. Don't be worried. I'll take care of you. Bess! Bess!' The voice was becoming quieter and quieter. She stood holding her bowl of freshly shelled peas. 'I think I'll stay at The Oak Tree House this evening. You go with the others to see Joseph. Nah is going down to Merlin Cottage to see the Sophia Lady. I'll ask her to come to The Oak Tree Ho after she's had her supper.' (They often called The Oak Tree House 'The Oak Tree Ho'.) 'Please telephone me from the hospital if you feel that I should be with little Joe.' Artie was watching his Hannah carefully. *Her mind is full of everyone*, he thought. *Never herself... other souls, small and large.*

'All right, me dear. Never you fear.' He gave her a wide grin and his navy blue eyes were big and so, so kind. 'Now, let me just finish emptying these two pods... I found them under the bench just before Andrew raced after Bess.' He sat down on the upturned bucket and opened up a large, shining pod. 'Well, bless my soul. Hannah girl, look at this pea!' He spoke the words so loudly that Hannah jumped.

'What is it? Where?' She moved to his side and looked at his hand holding the pod. Sure enough, there inside the pod was the biggest, most perfect pea she had ever seen! 'Oh, my! I've never seen such an amazing pea!' she exclaimed.

'Andrew will be delighted! We shall have to keep that pea. He must stay here in his house-pod until I see Andy again. Oh, Artie, have you noticed all the tiny peas as well? They must be the big one's relations!' Hannah began to laugh. 'What a wonderful sight!'

The old couple were still chuckling as they carried the dinner party veggies up to The Cottagey House. Jay would be along at any minute to fetch the peas together with the carrots, courgettes, and potatoes. Artie felt quite peckish just looking at them; he hoped that there would be time for supper before he went to the hospital. He opened the back door for Hannah and she crossed the threshold. He popped a couple of peas into his mouth. 'Now, don't you take any more, Arthur!' Hannah said without turning round.

'How did you know I had?' Artie was regularly astounded by Hannah.

'Oh, you always sneak a couple after you've shelled them, you know you do. Can't say I blame you. They're crisp and sweet this year. Good thing I've the big one in my apron pocket – you'd have eaten him for sure.'

'Oh, no, not him, he's special,' replied Artie.

Now, what had happened to Nah and Bibi? As you know they had hurtled off to look for Pippin Dog, who had herself rushed away from the garden house when Bibi had lost her temper and destroyed it. Pippin knew a place of safety: the small shed in the orchard where White Star, the pony, usually slept. It was warm and dry and Pippin often slept there in a corner, on some hay… and that's where Nah and Bibi found her. 'Nah, she's here! But, oh, listen! She's making a funny noise!'

Nah joined Bibi. She was hot and getting very tired. They both listened. The noise was Pippin's teeth chattering. Nah spoke quietly. 'Poor Pippin Dog, you're scared! Your teeth are making a very odd sound and you're shaking all over. Go up to her very quietly, Bee; it's *you* she's frightened of after all that crashing in the garden house!'

Nah pushed the child forward and Bee walked slowly towards the dog. Nah talked gently to Pippin and gradually the teeth stopped chattering and she began to settle. Bibi knelt down and put a small grubby hand on the dog's shoulder. She could feel the trembling under the fur. Bibi started to cry. The sound was not loud and Pippin began to lick the little girl's bare arm. Nah stood and watched as the animal and the child comforted each other. *What an afternoon!* she thought. She said, 'Come along, Bee. Tell Pippin to come with us. It's getting late and you need to have a bath and some supper. Then, bed!'

Bibi looked up at Nah. 'I'm going to see Joe this—'

Nah was shaking her head. 'No, you're going to have bath, a sandwich and a warm drink and then you're going to bed.' Nah watched expressions pass over Bibi's face. There were no words, just expressions. There were intakes of breath and she thought there were going to be a lot of words, but they didn't come out of the child's mouth. Finally, Bibi spoke, 'I'm not going to see Joe 'cos I've been bad!'

'You've been rather silly. You haven't used your brains,' said Nah, very gently. 'Hannah would say that you haven't "put your mind to it". Yes, that's right, you just stopped using your mind and everything went wrong, didn't it, sweet soul?'

Bibi nodded. Nah took her hand and led her out of the shed. She called Pippin, who got up and trotted behind.

Chapter Two

The three of them went wearily through the orchard and up to The Oak Tree House.

Andrew did not actually catch up with Bess: he had to stop to take a tiny stone out of his sandal and when he looked up, Bess had disappeared. *I only looked away from her for a moment*, he thought, *and she's gone! I know her safe places, though, so I will look for her there*. However, he didn't find her. She was not in the music room or the nursery or even under the stairs. Andrew was baffled. Where was Bess? He finally went to the kitchen where Chrissie was preparing their high tea. She noticed that he seemed preoccupied. His face was set – solid, Hannah called it.

'Do you need help, Andrew?' Chrissie asked. He didn't reply. He seemed far away, in another world. She tried again. 'Can I be of any help, Andy?'

He said, 'Bess is very concerned about the word "casualty". We saw a sign in the hospital yesterday and she rushed past it… wouldn't look at it. Now she's gone.'

'Gone? What do you mean, "gone"?' Chrissie was suddenly alert. Andrew told her about Bess' strange behaviour down at the pea picking place and how she'd run ahead of him and had just simply gone. Chrissie made a decision.

'You sit down and have your tea. I'll go and search her out. She must be somewhere around. We have to leave in about three-quarters of an hour. We mustn't be late getting to the hospital.' She moved quickly, getting the cakes from the tin and pouring a glass of milk for Andrew. 'Andy, give Dad a call. He's in the work room.' Chrissie's voice sounded just a trifle tense. She hurried out of the kitchen and wondered which room to look in. The music room door was open, so she went in and called quietly, 'Bess! Are you there?' There was no response. Suddenly she was aware of a shadow under the piano… she bent down and saw that

Bear was sitting there, all on his own. Bess wasn't with him. She heard the sound of footsteps and turned to see Hannah standing in the doorway.

'I've come to find Bess,' Hannah said.

Chrissie smiled. 'You knew that she was missing?'

'I watched Andrew run after her when she left us in the veggie patch,' replied Hannah. 'I knew that he hadn't found her, so I thought that I would stay in The Oak Tree House whilst you went to the hospital to see Joe. Nah and Bibi have just come back.' The tone of Hannah's voice was 'loaded'. Chrissie realised that a great deal had been going on since last she had seen this part of her family. She would have to have a word with Nah.

'Hannah, you are being very deep! I'll speak to Nah now.'

Nah and Bibi were going upstairs. They both looked dishevelled and tired. 'Just going to run a bath for Bee,' Nah said, smiling at Chrissie and Hannah. Bee's eyes were on the floor. She wouldn't look up. She was very quiet. 'Nothing to worry about, Chrissie, I'll catch up with you later, after you've seen Joseph. All right?'

Chrissie nodded.

The hospital visiting party left calmly, on time, and Joe was trying to be brave when they arrived. He'd been painting, lots of vivid colours – not shapes, just colours. Everyone had been kind to him, he said. He'd had tests. He had had his eyes examined by different doctors and had been asked to read letters and numbers. No, it hadn't hurt. They told him that Hannah would be coming later if he really needed her. They told him some of the afternoon's happenings, but not that Bess had taken herself away. They didn't want to worry him. Joe introduced them to his favourite nurse, Charlie. 'Her name is Charlotte, but I'm

calling her Charlie. She likes me calling her Charlie.'
Charlie brought them a cup of tea and said that Joe had
been a 'fine, plucky wee lad'. She came from Scotland and
spoke with a lovely accent. Chrissie liked the way she
touched Joe's head. She seemed gentle and caring. Her eyes
were full of lights and they twinkled when she talked.
Chrissie was relieved that Charlie was going to be with Joe.
She sat back in her chair and breathed out. Jan, Artie,
Andrew and Joe were telling Charlie about The Oak Tree
House and The Cottagey House and all the animalia and
veggies and… Chrissie had a chance to think about Bess and
Hannah, Bibi and Nah. She wondered what was going on
back at the house…

A great deal was going on as it happened. A great deal was
always going on in The Oak Tree House, it was that kind of
house. Hannah was busy going into each room. She had
decided to walk around all the rooms on the ground floor,
stopping and listening for sounds. She didn't call Bess'
name or appear to be looking for her. She had just come out
of the cloakroom when Nah came downstairs carrying
Bibi's grubby clothes. 'What are you doing, Han?' Nah
inquired.

'Hush! Talk quietly, Nah dear. Come into the kitchen
and I'll tell you,' whispered Hannah. They went quickly
into the warm room and Hannah told Nah everything she
knew. 'I'm trying to be casual… if Bess is hiding in one of
the rooms down here, I want her to think that I am just
tidying up, not searching for her. She's obviously disturbed
about the hospital. Maybe at last we're going to find out
about her. Oh, I do hope so. Poor little soul!'

Chapter Two

Nah put an arm round Hannah's shoulders and hugged her. 'That sounds like a very wise plan. Call me if you need help. You're staying here, aren't you? Bibi is in bed. I'm just off to Merlin Cottage to have supper with Sophia, but I'll be back soon. We'll have a good chat then.' Nah kissed Hannah's soft pink cheek and went out through the back door, calling loudly, 'Goodnight, Bee. Sleep well.'

It was quiet again. Hannah went to the bottom of the stairs. She stood absolutely still, straining her ears for any tiny sound that might tell her where Bess was. But nothing. She began to climb the stairs. Suddenly Pippin barked. Hannah stopped on the stairs. Then Pippin barked again and went on barking. 'I wonder what's bothering her... I'd better go and see.' Hannah found the dog standing by her feeding bowl, which she had placed near the fridge. 'Oh my dear Doglet! Have they forgotten to feed you? We can soon put that right.' Hannah opened the fridge and took the special dog food out. Pippin's tail became quite dangerous... it was wagging so fast! 'Now, stay away from me, Pippin Dog, or else all your supper will be swept over the floor! You *are* hungry.'

Upstairs in Bibi's bedroom, the sound of singing was heard. Bee was giving her toys a concert, every song she knew! She stopped in the middle of a slightly unusual version of Little Boy Kneels at the Foot of the Bed. 'Where are you, Baby Thumper? This is your fav'rite song.' Bibi threw the bedclothes up in the air, trying to find the small rabbit. She jumped off her bed and looked under it. Then suddenly she spied Baby Thumper, or BT as she liked to call him, sitting in her little armchair. She grabbed him to her and hugged him. 'Oh, you smell nasty... you're dirty and smelly... you must have a bath! I'll give you one now.'

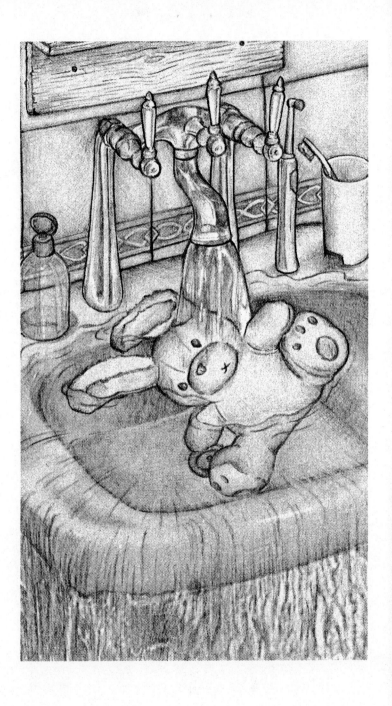

Chapter Two

Bibi opened the door and ran quickly to the bathroom. Hannah didn't hear her: Bee always moved so quietly. She put BT in the basin, dragged the stool over to the basin and climbed up. She turned on the taps. Water ran over the grubby toy and became brown. Little bits of twig and leaf made their way down the hole. 'Soap!' she said. 'I'll wash him in the new soap that Nah gave me from 'Merica. It will make him smell like her!'

Bibi climbed off the stool and ran back to her room. But she'd left the taps on! The water rose higher and higher until it spilt over the rim of the basin and gushed on the floor. Bibi, of course, couldn't find her new soap. Her room was in such a muddle! She hurtled around, throwing everything about. She had completely forgotten about the water! At last she found the soap and ran with it along the corridor. She saw the water creeping along the carpet outside the bathroom! 'Oh!' she squealed. Then she shouted, 'Someone! Come quickly! Water!'

Hannah heard the squeal and hurried out of the kitchen, Pippin's bowl in her hand and Pippin following behind. She put the bowl down in the hall and climbed the stairs as fast as her old legs would let her, all the time saying, 'What is it, Bibi? What's happened?' She arrived, breathless, and was appalled at the soggy sight!

'Oh, Bibi, quickly! Help me turn off the taps.' They squelched through the open door, up to the basin and stopped the water. Everything was sodden. Bibi picked up Baby Thumper. 'I was going to give him a bath. He was smelly,' she said in a tiny, high voice.

'Oh dear, what a day you've had, haven't you?' Hannah sounded tired and she sat on the side of the bath. Bibi began to cry very, very quietly. *Poor little mite*, thought Hannah. *I mustn't be angry with her, but we are going to have a bad time drying the carpets and all the other bits and pieces*. Bibi sat down on the floor and got up again. Her nightie was wringing wet. Hannah sighed.

Suddenly a voice said, 'I'll help you, dear Hannah. Tell me what I can do.' It was Bess. She stood in the doorway, her sandals in her hand. Bibi stopped crying. Bess' face was white and there were deep shadows under her eyes but she was calm and her words were steadily spoken and clear. Hannah looked at the mess and then at the two dear children. Her mind clicked into action. 'We shall need lots of towels to mop up the water. Bess, dear, run to the airing cupboard and bring back as many old towels that you can manage – you know, the ones on the shelf nearest the floor.'

Hannah bent down to speak to Bibi. 'Now, Bee, you go with Bess and she'll give you some of those towels. Bring them straight back here.' The old Lady patted Bibi's bottom and gave her a firm, but gentle push. Her hand came away wet. She wiped it on her apron and smiled. *Here we go again*, she thought.

They worked so hard. The children did all the fetching and carrying while Hannah crawled over the landing and bathroom floors, pressing the towels into the carpets. Gradually it seemed that most of the surface water had been soaked up. Hannah sat back on her heels and wiped away a stray piece of hair. She was very warm! Bess and Bibi looked down at her. Bess said, 'Han, may I go to the kitchen? You need a strong cup of tea. May I fill the kettle? I'll be careful.'

Hannah said, 'Yes, what a good idea. Bibi will need another short wash and change of nightie. We'll be down soon. There's good children. I couldn't have done all this without you.' She reached up and kissed them. 'Come along, Bee. Help me to my feet.'

72

'I'll get BT,' said Bee. The little rabbit was wrapped in a towel. Bess had looked after him.

Nah walked up the road from Merlin Cottage towards The Oak Tree House. She'd had a very stimulating talk with the Sophia Lady and a splendid supper. Actually, she had listened a great deal! Sophia really enjoyed a 'good chat'… she was such an interesting person. Nah had finally managed to tell her about the work in America with Kel. He made documentary films. This one had needed an experienced, sensitive actress to handle the commentary. The film was going to be entered in the film festivals. If the critics liked it enough, it could be 'invited' into the important festivals all over the world.

Kel and Chrissie were similar in many ways. They seemed to have an inner energy that drew people into their circle. Nah thought of Chrissie. What a wonderful friendship they had! Soul mates, Hannah called them. *Yes, soul mates! Well, I need to see my soul mate soon… we must talk… on our own*, thought Nah. *But when?* So much was happening!

She arrived at The Oak Tree House and went into the kitchen, making sure that she didn't make too much noise. Pippin would be sure to bark! However, no one was in the kitchen. She called, 'Hannah?' Then a little louder, 'Hannah! Are you there?'

'We're upstairs… in Bess' room,' came the reply. 'Come on up. The children are having a story.' Nah's mind started to race. 'Children': Hannah had found Bess. She went quickly upstairs and, sure enough, there they were, the three of them! Hannah was deep inside the big armchair in Bess' room with the two little girls on her lap. Bibi was asleep, but Bess seemed wide awake. Hannah put her finger to her lips and then indicated Bibi. Nah scooped Bee up and carried her to her room and put her into her bed. She looked at the chaos, her mind full of unspoken questions, found the sheet and blankets and covered the sleeping child. Bee shifted and put up her arms. Nah knelt down and stroked her forehead. 'Nah,' it was a small, sleepy sound. 'Nah, stay with me.'

Nah said, 'Yes, I will. Be peaceful, little Bee.'

When Nah went back to Bess' room, she saw a large pile of wet, crumpled towels. She wanted to ask Hannah what had happened, but realised that it was not the time to ask questions. Hannah was standing by the chair. She looked weary. 'Bess has gone to get Bear. She left him in the music room. Would you like a drink, Nah?' Han's voice was low and she looked at Nah as if to say, 'I've got a great deal to tell you.'

Nah answered quickly, 'Yes, please. Let's go to the music room. Would you like a whiskey and warm water, Han?' This was a special Hannah drink; she only had it when there were exceptional goings on.

'Clever Girl,' was Hannah's response.

When they entered the music room, they saw Bess standing by the piano. Bear was sitting on the piano and Bess was talking. The child must have heard the two women come in for she turned slowly and looked at them. No one spoke. Nah's throat seemed to close up. She just stared at the eyes that were gazing into hers. Hannah cleared her throat. 'Bess, we're going to have drink, Nah and I. Would you like some juice?'

Bess shook her head. There was a trace of a smile. 'No thank you, Hannah. Bear and I are going to sleep now. Thank you for taking care of the water, and Bibi.' She walked over to Nah and looked up at her. 'Nah, Hannah is very tired.' Then she walked out of the room, closing the door behind her. 'She wants to be on her own again,' said Hannah. 'Oh, how I wish I could get through her wall!'

'I certainly can't,' murmured Nah.

'I think the only person who is going to make a chink is Andrew,' Hannah said. 'Why, oh why can't we find out more about her? It makes me very unhappy to see her so distressed. Oh dear!' Nah guided Hannah to the small settee and they both sat down.

'Now, tell me what's been going on, Han.' It took quite a time. Nah was amazed, but they both found the situation very amusing and in the end they laughed and laughed. 'This is better than crying,' chuckled Hannah and Nah agreed. She threw her arms round the little lady and hugged her. 'Oh Han! I do love you.'

Suddenly the telephone rang. Nah jumped up and ran to answer it. It was Chrissie from the hospital. Joe had asked for Hannah. *Poor Hannah*, thought Nah. *There'll be a place reserved for her in Heaven*. She said to her, 'Han, darling, Joe has asked for you. Jan will be here to take you to the hospital in about fifteen minutes. He'll think we've been boozing all evening!'

Joseph enjoyed his chat with the men. He was glad that they seemed to like Charlie. He found her Scottish voice soothing. He wanted her to talk to him all the time. He didn't want to hear Chrissie say that they would have to go soon. He knew that they would go. Charlie touched his head.

'Joseph? Hannah said that she'd come and read you a story. Would you like that? We only need to telephone her.' Joe listened to the tunes in her voice and the funny 'R' sounds. They rolled round her mouth. He nodded and held onto her hand tightly. 'Right. That's fine then… I'll go and ring her.' And Charlie went quickly from the room.

Chrissie watched little Joe. He was sitting quietly, with his hands resting on his thighs, palms up. She was aware of a certain peace. Just Joseph and herself, waiting, listening, thinking. She knew that he didn't need her to touch him or even speak. There was this peace, so real and comfortable. She suddenly realised that Joe had moved… he had left his bed and was walking to the door. He clearly wanted to be alone. Again, the stillness, the calm. Chrissie breathed out and closed her eyes.

Artie and Andrew watched Jan drive away. Then Andrew said, 'Oh Artie! A huge pea? And lots of little relations? Where are they?'

Artie laughed. 'I think Hannah put them in her apron pocket. Yes, they should be safe there, but we must get them out before she washes the apron, mustn't we?'

Andrew didn't laugh. He was wondering what would happen to the pod with its family if they didn't rescue them from the pocket! Washing powder and hot water can't be good for peas! 'We need to give that pea a name,' said Artie, as they walked back to the hospital. 'Put your head in gear, Andy, and come up with a fine name.'

'We must tell Joe about him,' Andy said quickly. 'Hmm, but not this evening, old mate. Look! There he is standing in the doorway waiting for Hannah. He needs her now. We'll keep our news about the pea until a little later. Come on. I think we'll go back to the car park and wait for Jan to return. Now come on, Andy, start thinking… names for an outsize pea.'

Jan drove carefully through the main gates of the hospital and parked the Land Rover. 'Dad! Dad! I'm glad to see you…' called Andrew. 'Hannah, Artie told me about the pea. We're trying out names for him!'

Jan swung round and saw Andrew running towards

them. 'A pea? What pea?' he asked.

Hannah chuckled. 'I didn't tell you about him, did I?' she said. 'I'll leave Andrew to do that... Artie, will you take me to Joseph? I have an idea he's becoming worried. I feel all trembley inside.'

Artie and Hannah walked into the hospital, hand in hand, chatting. Andrew began to tell Jan about the Pea. He was clearly very intrigued about it. Jan noticed the boy's eyes shining behind his specs, and he was talking very quickly... too quickly for Jan! 'Steady, steady, Andrew! I would like to take all this into my head! Say the words carefully, and slowly! Let's sit in the Land Rover and you can tell me all about the enormous pea.'

Joseph saw Hannah and Artie as they walked down the long corridor. He ran to her, but his eye was hurting; it hurt when he moved suddenly, so he stopped and put his hands out to her. She left Artie and hurried to the boy. Taking his small hands in hers, she knelt down in front of him. 'Hello, little Joe. My, that was good, seeing you there waiting for me. Where's Chrissie? Oh, I see her. She's in your room. Let's go and show her that I'm here.'

Chrissie rose to greet Hannah. 'Ah, now, there you are. That was quick. I'd better go... Jan will want to get home. I'll be sending out lots of thoughts, Joe. We'll all be sending out thoughts, all the time, even in our sleep. I love you, Joe.' She stooped and kissed him. He put his hand and patted her cheek. This was his sign for Chrissie. She knew what that pat meant. 'I'll be here tomorrow. Han will stay as long as you need her.' Chrissie smiled at them both and moved away, down the corridor. She was so thankful that they had Hannah and Artie. 'Blessed, we are,' she said to herself as she shut the front door of the hospital. 'Truly blessed.'

'What's that you said, my dear?' It was Artie. He'd been waiting to take her back to the car park. 'Truly blessed, Artie. That's what I was saying. Having you and Han. What should we do without you both?'

'A great deal, no doubt, my girl. You do quite a lot already, actually. Now, look sharp! I could do with one of my specials from the fridge! I'm rather "thirsday", as Bibi would put it.' They laughed and hurried to the Land Rover.

Chapter Three

Nah was on the telephone when the four of them arrived at The Oak Tree House. Chrissie's elder brother, Fred, had rung from Scotland. Fred was a teacher. He taught outdoor pursuits, riding and sports of all kinds. He was always 'on the go' and always involved with hundreds of people, especially with the ones who had 'problems'. He was big and bouncy and had a large laugh.

Fred was coming to the Cotswolds to look at a pony that he thought he might buy, and could he stay at The Oak Tree House for a couple of days? Nah knew Fred well. She went to stay with him and his family, a large family, quite often, 'to unwind and laugh', Nah used to say. Sure enough, that's exactly what she did – unwind and laugh!

Fred, Trub (that's what Fred calls his wife – her real name is Fiona!), Hannah, Flora, Duncan and Mollie, lived on the edge of a loch – Loch Awe – in an amazingly beautiful old Scottish stone house. They were surrounded by great trees and heather and gorse. There were boats – and animalia, of course. The whole family went Scottish dancing and ran weekend parties and just invited 'everyone' from miles around to join them. They had a barn that had been made into a small theatre and touring companies arrived and presented plays and music. They were a huge Christian family. Nah used to tell such stories about her visits to Scotland: 'You're made to feel as if you have been part of the family from the moment you came into the world,' she used to say every time she returned to England. 'The safety! The closeness! If you feel like screaming, then you go out and scream! If you want to cry, then you cry and someone is always there to hold you or be near. A very extraordinary place, very extraordinary people!'

Chrissie took the telephone from Nah. 'Fred... How lovely! Yes, do come and stay! You'll certainly be needed here!' and she told him all about Joseph and the next day.

Nah took Andrew, Artie and Jan into the kitchen. She laid out the cheese, biscuits and other bits and pieces on the round table. Chrissie came into the kitchen and sat down and sighed.

'A difficult time?' Nah enquired.

Chrissie nodded. It was clear that she did not want to talk yet – in fact no one seemed to want to talk.

Artie and Andrew had fetched the specials from the fridge and Jan had gone upstairs to look at Bess and Bibi. He liked to creep into their rooms and watch the sleeping children... sometimes he sat on their beds and looked at the ever-changing expressions that crossed their faces. If they stirred and woke he used to whisper to them until they slept again.

The kitchen was warm and cosy. It welcomed them and gradually the tension in their minds and bodies fell away and they began to eat. The sounds were fascinating... clinking of glasses and mugs and knives on plates... scrapings... tappings... munchings! Then Jan came back and smiled. The silence was over. Andrew's words came first. 'Joe will be OK now. Hannah will stay with him all night.'

'How do you know that?' asked Jan. 'Did she tell you?'

'No, I just know she will. Do you think they'll let her sleep in a bed in Joe's room, Mum?'

'I'm not sure, Andrew,' replied Chrissie. 'She'll be very near him, though. Perhaps she'll sit in the armchair next to his bed. She did that when I was very ill… I think I was five or six… I had pneumonia and she stayed up with me all through the night. Whenever I woke, she was there.'

'Truly, a splendid lady,' said Jan, as he helped himself to his favourite stilton cheese. They went on munching and thinking.

Nah suddenly said, 'Would you like to hear the story of Bess and Bibi?'

'Yes, very much,' Chrissie chuckled. 'I'm looking forward to it. Andrew, you can stay up and hear it, if you wish.' Andrew's mouth was full, so he just nodded furiously and Nah told them.

Joe was nearly asleep. Hannah had told him his favourite stories – the Pooh and Rabbit one, when Pooh gets stuck in Rabbit's front door, and the very, very special one about himself, when Hannah first met him. He had to hear every detail. Hannah was not allowed to leave anything out! Joe would stop her sometimes, saying, 'Han, no! You've missed out the eating bits… remember? The spoon?' Dear Hannah! She realised that this evening of all evenings it all had to be right. She finally noticed that Joe had closed his eyes. She wondered if she should tell him about the pea.

He felt for her arm, and said, 'Tell me a new story now, Han, please.'

Well, I have my answer, Hannah thought, so she told him about the pea.

Joe listened intently, then said, 'Will you bring the pea to see me tomorrow – no! not tomorrow, the day after?'

'Of course I will. Andrew is probably thinking of a name for him this very moment.'

Joe suddenly opened his eyes. 'He must be called Horatio. It is a big, strong name… the sounds are round sounds and he is round, isn't he?'

'Oh, very round! And he needs to be strong and brave, he has all those tiny relations in his house-pod. They need caring for. Horatio? That's a grand name, little Joe,' said Hannah.

Joe said softly, 'Hannah, I don't think I shall be little after tomorrow. Could you find another name for me?'

'I will, oh yes, I will!' Hannah stroked his face and kissed his head. 'Joe, I must go and find Charlie. We need bedtime drinks. You just lie quietly and think of colours. Tell me about them when I get back.'

'My colours are not very bright at the moment,' Joe said.

'That doesn't matter.' Hannah was at the door. 'Just see colours. They're all good and there are so many shades.' She walked briskly down the corridor. Joe could hear her feet. He saw clear pictures when he heard sounds and noises. *I think she's going into Charlie's small office*, he thought. *Ah, now Han has stopped moving.* He heard muffled voices and a short tinkle of laughter, the Charlie's 'r' sounds.

'Righty-ho, Hannah my dear. Let's take these drinks to the wee boy and the other lad, Jamie. Will you carry the biscuits for me? Thank you.' Footsteps again, but now four feet.

I can see them in my head… their clothes, their faces, their hands, Joe thought.

Chapter Four

It was six o'clock on Friday morning, the day of Joseph's operation. The oak tree was… holding its breath. *How odd*, thought Chrissie. *The house is full of tiny sounds.* They seemed to change according to the time of day, but this morning Chrissie was only aware of her heart beating. Jan lying beside her shifted and turned towards her, putting out a hand, touching her shoulder. He whispered, 'Don't get up yet. Stay close, my Darling.' She kissed him gently and they both lay there waiting. For what they didn't know.

'We just lay and waited,' said Chrissie when she recalled that waking time. But now it was nearly ten o'clock and Chrissie was with Nah at the hospital, sitting in the recovery room, waiting again. This time they were waiting for Joe to come round after his operation. His head was swathed in bandages. Just a nose and mouth were visible. Hannah had been ordered to 'go and sleep'. She was quite put out, but she'd gone!

She'd hardly closed her eyes all night. Joe had been very restless. She'd cradled him in the armchair for many hours. He managed to sleep when he was close to her, all snuggled in. He whimpered in his sleep. It was such a sad sound. He'd tried to be brave when the doctors, nurses and the anaesthetist had arrived at eight o'clock. Hannah had told him about the anaesthetist. He understood that this man was to make him sleep and that he wouldn't feel any pain…

but he wouldn't let go of Hannah's hand as she walked at the side of the trolley when they took him along the corridors to the operating theatre. After his injection, Hannah felt his grip loosen and she carefully withdrew her hand. She left him then and paced up and down outside the operating theatre. This was where Chrissie and Nah had found her and had gently and firmly escorted her back to Joe's room.

The Sophia Lady and Artie were in charge at The Oak Tree House. Andrew had gone to school and Bess and Bibi had gone shopping in the Sophia Lady's noisy, old car. They'd gone to Stroud; there was a favourite grocer's shop there. It sold special biscuits. The SBT needed filling up – someone had eaten most of the biscuits! 'Now, who could that have been?' Sophia Lady had asked.

Bibi immediately cried, 'That was me! I was hungry, so I invated the SBT.'

Sophia gently patted Bibi's tiny bottom and said, '*Invaded*, Bee, not *invated*.' Andrew sighed. Bibi was always using his words, but they were hardly ever right. Sophia said, 'Now, Andrew, try to be patient. You're older than her, remember.'

They bought some scrumptious biscuits and lots more food. Sophia had invited Artie to lunch. She thought it would be a good idea to have the children at Merlin Cottage for the day. 'Goodness knows when Chrissie and Hannah will be home, and Nah has to be at an audition this afternoon. Better come to me.' And that's where they were when the telephone rang. They'd just finished eating. Sophia hurried to the phone. When she came back to the kitchen she looked worried. 'There have been problems at the hospital, Artie. Chrissie has asked me to keep the children this afternoon and fetch Andrew from school, and would you go to The Oak Tree Ho. Jan is not there at the moment. She would like you to wait for him and tell him to get in touch with the hospital.' Sophia sounded distressed. Artie squeezed her hand and left.

There were indeed problems at the hospital. It had all happened in the recovery room. Joe had been lying peacefully, sleeping off the anaesthetic, and Chrissie and Nah were talking quietly. Suddenly Nah glanced at Joe and noticed that he was stirring. 'I think he's coming round, Chrissie,' she whispered.

Joseph was awake, but he could not see. He called out, 'Daddy! Mummy! Where are you? The car! Where are you, oh! Where are you? Mummy!'

Chrissie managed to catch his waving arms and said, 'It's all right, Joe! It's all right! I'm here! It's Chrissie!' But Joe was struggling to sit up. He was screaming and Chrissie couldn't hold him. He fell out of bed and before she could get to him, he was tearing at the bandages round his head and eyes. Nah had rung the bell for the nurse and was calling, 'Hurry, hurry! Please, help us!' Joseph's nurse Charlie came in followed by a young doctor.

'Quickly!' he said, 'get hold of his hands! He mustn't tear off those bandages!' But such was Joe's panic, that neither Chrissie nor Charlie was able to stop him ripping off the cloth over his eyes. The doctor caught hold of Joe and pulled his face in towards his chest to shut out the light! Joe's body suddenly seemed to go limp. The doctor said, 'I think he's fainted! Nurse, quickly! Help me to put him back on the bed!' Joe looked white and he was so still. His eyes were closed and his breathing was shallow.

Chrissie said in a shaking voice, 'What's the matter with him?'

'I don't really know, but we must move him to intensive

care immediately.' More people arrived and Joe was put onto a trolley and rushed off surrounded by nurses. Hannah was with them, holding Joe's thin, lifeless hand.

How strange, Nah thought. *When did Hannah arrive? I didn't see her.* Then she looked for Chrissie and saw her standing, gazing out of the door, tears running down her cheeks. She spoke, 'Oh, Nah! What's wrong with him? He didn't know me… he seems to be back at the accident.'

Nah went to her and gently took her arm, saying quietly, 'He'll be fine… try to stay clam, Chrissie darling. The doctors will do everything to find out what's happening. I'll get us a cup of tea.'

Chrissie nodded. 'All right. I'll stay here in case they need me,' and she sighed.

Hannah was talking to God. 'Lord, Joe needs your help. Please, please let him be strong so that he will come back to us. Be in his head, Lord, and make it clear again.' Charlie stood, watching the old lady. Hannah was sitting outside the intensive care room, her hands in her lap and her eyes closed. Her lips were just moving. Her lovely face was troubled. Charlie waited and Han opened her eyes and looked at her as if she knew that she was there.

Charlie said, 'Hannah, Joe is unconscious. We're doing all we can, but he seems to have gone into deep shock. Maybe the feeling of darkness behind the bandages was so intense that it brought back the accident and he just switched off. We shall have to be patient and see what occurs from minute to minute. Would you like to see him?'

Hannah shook her head. 'I must find Chrissie… she should be with Joe.' Charlie said quickly, 'I'll find her. You sit there now.'

Charlie left her and Hannah shut her eyes again. She whispered, 'Where are you, Joseph? Are you a long way away? Your body is here, but where is your spirit? Your mind?'

Suddenly she heard her name being called. It was Joseph's voice. Her eyes snapped open and she moved rapidly into the intensive care room. Joe was in bed surrounded by machines and wires and tubes. His face was ashen and his hair looked jet black. His eyes were closed. Hannah said, 'I heard Joe's voice... did he ask for me?'

The nurse standing beside the bed looked surprised. 'No,' she said sharply. 'He hasn't said anything.'

Hannah stared at the little boy. She bent over him and whispered in his ear, 'Joseph, why did you call me?' She looked into Joe's face. She was very close to him. 'Joseph... Joseph.' It wasn't a question. It was rather like a command. But there was no sound. Joe said nothing. However, when Hannah straightened up, her face was lighter. She said, 'He's still with us, but he's a long way off. He'll come back when he feels safer.'

The nurse spoke again. 'How do you know? And *when* will he come back?'

Hannah smiled, 'Only the Lord knows that, my dear.' They looked at each other. This nurse had heard about Hannah's feelings, but she didn't believe them. She laughed in a scornful way. Hannah said, 'I know you don't believe what I believe. That's quite reasonable, but you do want Joseph to get better, don't you?'

The nurse stared at Hannah. 'Of course we want him to get better!' she said in an angry, shrill tone. 'And we shall do our best to care for him.'

Hannah smiled again. 'I'm sure you will. By the way, what's your name, my dear?'

There was a slight pause, and then nurse answered, 'Amanda.'

'Ah! I shall call you Mandy,' said Hannah, picking up Joe's hand. She began to rub it gently. There was another silence, and then Amanda turned to the doctor who had come into the room. 'Dr Miles, shall I stay with Mrs Best?'

The doctor looked at Hannah and Joe and said, 'No, I think they'll be better on their own. We're used to Hannah here. She needs to be with children by herself. She'll call us if she thinks she needs help.' He beckoned Amanda to go with him. Now the room was empty... Well, of course, not actually empty! The sounds of the machines, the feelings coming from Hannah, Joe lying in the centre of it all. The room was full of love, and hope – and yes, some fear. Hannah lowered Joe's hand onto the blanket, walked round to the other side of the bed, picked up the other hand and began smoothing it. She closed her eyes and wondered again. 'Where are you, Joe? Why have you gone from us? Is it safer there?'

Chapter Five

*A*ndrew had had a difficult day at school. He went to the junior school in the village called Misserden. There were only eighteen pupils in the school and three teachers. They were lucky to have three teachers. Mrs Avery, the head teacher, was about to have a baby and a supply teacher, Mrs Champion had joined her. So, in fact, there were four teachers! It was a fine school. Each child was given individual care and tuition. The youngest boy was five and the eldest girl was ten years old. Andrew told Mrs Avery about Joseph. She had spoken to the children and teachers at their morning meeting, saying that they should 'Put out thoughts for Joseph as often as possible.' Mary Ann had said, 'You mean, we should pray for him?' And Mrs Avery had replied, 'If that is what you and your family would do if you had someone you knew with his problem, yes, you should speak to your God.' Mrs Avery had children from Pakistan and Africa in her school; they had different religions. She had explained these religions to them all.

'Joseph needs many strong, good thoughts. You remember him, don't you? He's visited us many times.' Certainly the children remembered him. They'd found him fascinating. The way he drew them with his crayons and pencils and felt their faces and hands. Joe could see them well at times, but at other times his eye went misty, and anyway, he liked to feel faces and hands and clothes. 'Much more exciting,' he said.

Most of the time Chrissie, Hannah, Artie and other friends in the village taught Joe. 'I've lots of schools,' he had told Nah when she asked if he went to school. 'Sometimes I stay with Andrew at Misserden, but often I go to see my village people. Jay, at the vicarage, teaches me heaps. He's very clear, and Janice paints the way I like painting... lots of colours!'

...Yes, Andrew had had a difficult day. He could not concentrate. Mrs Champion asked him to listen, to pay attention, again and again. In the end, she became irritated and quite cross with him. Poor Andrew. Mrs Champion noticed that his specs seemed full of water... oh dear! Not tears? Andrew crying? She was sorry that she had spoken sharply to him. She went over to his table and asked if he would prefer to sit in Mrs Avery's room until it was time to go home. She went on, 'It's nearly three o'clock, so it won't be long until someone is here to take you home or to visit Joseph.' Her voice was kind. Andrew nodded. He didn't trust his voice to come out. 'Off you go then,' said Mrs Champion. 'I'm sorry I upset you, Andrew.'

Andrew cleared his throat, 'You didn't upset me, Mrs Champion... God has upset me.' Lots of eyes left their books and stared at Andrew. He gathered his pencils and papers and went out of the room.

'What did he mean? Does God upset people?' asked Mary Ann.

'I'm not sure what he means,' replied the teacher. 'We must talk about it some time.' She felt quite distressed. Andrew was obviously very deeply worried.

Andrew stopped outside Mrs Avery's door. It was open and he could see her sitting in her armchair. She was reading the paper. She looked up. Mrs Avery had a round, bright, cheerful face and a beaming smile. She smiled at Andrew. 'Hello, Andrew. Did you want to see me? Come in.' She folded the paper and rose to greet him. She saw tears on his face. 'Right!' She crossed the room to the cupboard where she kept drinks and biscuits. 'I think you and I are going to have a little something.' Andrew began to shake his head, but Mrs Avery went on quickly, 'Oh yes! Certainly a drink. I need one if you don't!' This lady was very, very good at giving tender loving care without anyone knowing it.

Andrew felt light, as if he were going to float away. He wanted very much to go home. *If only I could fly*, he thought, *I would be back at The Oak Tree House in minutes*. His mind was everywhere – with Joe, with Bess, with Chrissie and Hannah. He could see their faces. They flitted in and out of his mind's eye. Mrs Avery had poured the drinks and was standing, holding them, watching the boy's stricken face. He looked transparent and he was very pale. She knew all about Andrew's depth of concern for other people and animals. He was an unusual boy. He seemed to have the ability to think so deeply that he went far away into worlds that no one else could reach.

She spoke very quietly. 'Andrew, come and sit down. It's very hot today, isn't it? Would you like me to talk to you? Maybe you'd rather just sit and look at some new books that have arrived from Bristol. There are some plays here, look. We're going to do a play next term for Christmas... doesn't the year go quickly? Perhaps you could choose a play for us... you'll be at senior school then, won't you? But I'm sure you'll be back to see our play... with your family, of course. Here, have a search through these.' She gave him a pile of interesting looking books.

Andrew took them to Mrs Avery's armchair and sat down. It was a large, comfortable old chair. He felt safer when he was in it. 'Thank you, Mrs Avery,' he said. His voice was OK. He had wondered earlier if his voice would ever work properly again. When he was frightened, it became trapped in his throat somehow… very weird! But it was back again – good! He smiled at Mrs Avery. She was so big. He wondered about the baby inside her tummy. 'When will your baby be born?' he asked.

Mrs Avery laughed, and rubbed her stomach. 'Any day now. He's very busy inside here. I wish he'd hurry up… he makes me weary.'

'*He?*' said Andrew. 'Do you know it's a *he?*'

'Yes – well, no! Not for sure. I think he will be a he!' Another laugh. Andrew loved Mrs A's laugh! She had such twinkly eyes. He felt better. 'Will you be going to the hospital in Stroud? The one Joe is in?' he asked.

'Yes, everything happens in that building.' Mrs Avery was walking carefully around the room taking sips from her glass of orange juice. Andrew got up and followed her, sipping his juice.

Nicholas and Sarah were running across the playground. Nicholas stooped and said to Sarah, 'Look, Sarah! Mrs Avery and Andrew are walking around her room.'

'Oh, yes, one behind the other, how funny!' Sarah crept forward until she was near the window. They began to giggle, it looked so peculiar. Andrew and Mrs Avery appeared to be in step, marching slowly around and around the furniture! Mrs Avery spied them peeping over the window sill and said with another large rolling laugh, 'Dear me! We must look very odd, Andrew. Don't worry, Sarah and Nicholas, we're trying to settle our brains, they're not balanced at the moment.'

☙ Chapter Five ☙

Andrew looked at the clock: nearly 3.30 p.m. already! Sophia Lady would be here at any minute with news from the hospital. He didn't know that Joseph was unconscious or anything about the fearful happenings. Neither did Sophia. She had had a wonderful day with Bibi and Bess. They'd bought some very special biscuits and filled not only the SBT at The Oak Tree Ho, but all the other SBTs at Merlin Cottage and The Cottagey House as well! Pippin had eaten two cream biscuits and White Star had been given a butter cookie. Sophia had to ration Bibi, but Bess had refused to eat. (She'd had a 'minute lunch', Sophia told Chrissie later in the evening when everyone was gathered in the music room to discuss the day.) They had driven to Cheltenham and been to feed the ducks in the park. Bibi had never stopped talking. She'd danced on the grass; there had been a band playing and Bibi adored music! People stopped what they were doing and came to watch her. Sophia noticed that Bibi smiled and laughed and spoke to her 'audience'. *Well, well!* mused Sophia. *We have a little show girl!'* But Bess just sat on the grass and made a daisy chain and put it around Bear's neck. He was with her, of course. Then she collected lots of small pebbles and made a circle and put Bear inside it. She did not say one word. Sophia was anxious about her. She stayed close to her, talked to her, but there was no reply. Bess nodded or shook her head. Now and then a slight smile crossed her face. *I have to talk to Chrissie and Jan*, thought Sophia. *The little mite is closed in; anything might happen. Oh dear!*

Sophia was driving to fetch Andrew from school. She glanced in the mirror... the two girls were in their car seats in the back. Bibi was asleep, thank God! Bess was holding Bear close to her face. She seemed peaceful. Sophia said cheerfully, 'Are you comfortable, Bess darling?'

'Yes, thank you, Sophia Lady,' a clear voice answered.

The first time today, a reply, thought Sophia. 'Good. We're nearly at the school.' Sophia did not know that Bess had been talking to Bear, making plans and her mind had quickly switched towards the problems at hospital. She needed to know what had really happened. Chrissie had just said that Joe had pulled off his bandages. Poor Sophia! All she could do was imagine.

Artie had gone to The Oak Tree House after the telephone call from Chrissie earlier that day, to wait for Jan. He liked being in this house. It was a fascinating place, full of atmospheres. He washed up the cups and saucers, swept the kitchen floor and wondered what to do next. He noticed a script lying on the table. He turned the page and found that it was a television play. Jan was directing a new play for the BBC. He had been in Bristol discussing the casting. The play was going to be filmed on location in Cornwall and Devon. When Jan was directing he was away a great deal. Artie hoped that everything would soon settle down, for he felt certain that Jan would be in an awkward dilemma. Chrissie would need him, but he was under contract to the BBC. Another problem! Artie wondered why so many difficulties came together… it had happened to him all through his life. He decided to ask other folk if this had happened to them. He was reading the script when he heard the sound of a car coming up the drive. He looked up and saw Jan getting out of his sports car. He went to the back door to meet him. Jan was surprised to see him. 'Hello, Artie. What are you doing here?'

'There's been some trouble, old mate. Come in and I'll tell you all about it.'

Andrew was standing outside the school waiting for Sophia. She saw him there as she turned the corner. She wound down the window and waved and he waved back. *He looks quite relaxed*, thought Sophia.

Bibi had woken up and was shouting, 'Andy! We've been feeding ducks and dancing! We're very happy! Andy, come and sit in the back!'

Andrew laughed. 'I'm too big, Bibi. I shall squash you. I'll sit in the front with Sophia. Hello, Bess. Have you had a good day? Bear looks OK.' Bess gave Bear to Andrew. His fur was damp, all around his face. Oh dear, thought Andrew. *Bess has been crying.* He knew that whenever Bear's fur was wet that Bess had been crying into Bear's head and ears. He decided that he would talk to Bess that evening to try to find out what was really worrying her. He climbed into the front seat and said, 'How's Joe? Have you been to the hospital, Sophia?'

'I'm going to drive us there now,' replied Sophia. 'It's on our way home.'

'Good, good! I can move the curtains again and lie down on Joe's bed!' shrieked Bibi. 'Good, oh, good!'

'I don't think you'll be able to see Joe, Bee,' said Sophia. 'We'll ask a lot of questions and make sure that he's peaceful. Sometimes it takes a long time to come round after an operation. The anaesthetic can make you feel all woozy.'

'What is ana-anaset-hik? And woothy?' Bibi repeated the two unknown words, making them sound different each time she tried to say them. Sophia and Andrew laughed.

'Oh, do stop, Bee.' Sophia was laughing so much that she stopped the car. 'I can't drive, I'm aching with laughing!' But Bess was not laughing. She touched Andrew's shoulder and held out her arms. He gave Bear to her and she cuddled him, burying her face in his fur and closing her eyes.

Finally, they arrived at the hospital. It was now just after four o'clock. The sun was bright and it was very still. Not even a breeze. Sophia parked the car near the Land Rover. She said to Andrew, 'I'll take Bibi with me. You stay here with Bess. I won't be long.'

Andrew got out of the car, opened the back door and said, 'Bess, shall we walk around the car park and count the cars? There are so many. Maybe we'll see some interesting foreign cars.' But Bess shook her head and took Andrew's hand. She began to pull him towards the hospital. Andrew realised that she was taking him to the door past the 'Casualty' sign – the door that they had used when they left the building the day before.

'Bess, tell me why you don't like the "Casualty" sign? Do you know what the word means?' Andrew spoke quietly, but Bess did not answer… she just kept running and pulling Andrew. At last they were inside the building and they both stood still, breathing heavily. Bess looked quite calm, but she was very hot. Andrew said, 'Do you want to see Joe?'

Bess nodded but she didn't move. She suddenly sat down on the floor and buried her face in Bear's fur. Andrew heard footsteps coming towards them. He looked up and saw a tall woman in uniform walking down the corridor. She was wearing black shoes and her hands were holding some papers and a small bottle. Andrew looked at her face. She was tall and thin. Andrew felt that she wouldn't be friendly. Her eyes seemed hard and they were green and far away. However, he knew that he had to speak to her. 'Please, could you tell me where Joseph Leigh is? Do you know him?'

The nurse stopped in front of him. She was silent for a moment. Then she said in a high, cold voice. 'Are you another member of that peculiar family? Can you hear voices?'

Andrew was confused. What a strange lady... she seemed to be scared of something. 'I'm not sure what you mean. I'm Andrew Leigh and this is Bess. We're looking for Joe. He's had an operation—'

'—on his eye and is now in deep shock,' the nurse finished the sentence with this extraordinary information!

Bess stood up quickly. 'Where is he?' she said in a loud, strong voice.

The nurse replied at once, 'You can't see him. He can't see you.'

Bess looked hard at the nurse and said, 'Yes, we can see him... we belong to him! We'll find him!' And she grabbed Andrew's hand and pulled him down the corridor.

They rushed round a corner and collided with someone.

'Och! My! You nearly floored me! Oh! It's Andy and Bess! Where are you going in such a hurry?' It was Charlie.

'We're looking for Joe!' said Bess.

'He's in that room there, but you can't go in—' replied Charlie, but they were already inside the room. Charlie opened her mouth to say something, but closed it again. She watched the two children. They were standing absolutely still... they seemed to be holding their breath. Then Andrew let go of Bess' hand and walked slowly towards the bed where Joseph was lying. Charlie heard him say, 'Joseph? Why are you surrounded by wires and electricity? Can you hear me? Are you asleep?' Bess was still standing just inside the door. Andrew went on talking to Joe. 'Joe, what have they done to you?' He turned round and looked at Charlie. 'Please tell us, Charlie. Tell us what has happened.' Andrew's eyes were huge behind his specs.

So Charlie told them all she knew. Finally, she said, 'Hannah believes that Joe is a long way off, but that he will come back to us when he feels safe.' There was a sudden scuffly noise behind them. All heads turned towards the doorway: Bess had gone!

Andrew called out, 'Bess! Wait! Wait!' He pushed past the others and ran down the corridor that led to the front door of the hospital. Charlie ran after him. 'Andrew! Andrew!' She was aware that Sophia and Bibi were standing in the corridor... she said urgently, 'Bess has run off and Andrew has followed her! I must find them! Please, Sophia, go to Joe and stay with him...' She was still moving. 'If he shifts, ring the bell for help!' She was suddenly out of sight.

Bibi began to jump up and down, asking lots of questions. Sophia said, 'Hush, Bee darling! We must go quickly to Joe! Come on!'

They arrived in Joe's room to see Amanda bending over him. She straightened up sharply when she heard them. She had something in her hand. Sophia was not sure what it was, but it looked like a cloth of some kind, or a face flannel? Amanda said brightly, 'Oh, hello, I was just listening to Joe's breathing. He's fine.'

Sophia did not answer and Bibi was also silent. There was a strange atmosphere in the room. 'Where's Chrissie and Hannah?' asked Sophia. Amanda did not reply. She began to walk out of the room, past the two people as if they were not there. She seemed to have completely forgotten them. Bibi said, 'Where is Hannah and Chrissie?' But Amanda just walked on, looking neither right nor left.

'That is a very unhappy lady,' said Sophia. Bibi stared at Sophia's face. She did not speak. Sophia was holding Bibi's hand and she pulled her gently towards Joe. He hadn't moved at all... the sounds in the room were clear and positive. Joe's face was serene and he was breathing in a regular way. In... out, in... out.

Bibi put her small hands on the blanket and gazed into

the little boy's face. She whispered, 'He's not here in this room. He's in a different place.' Suddenly, she heard a voice. It was Hannah's.

'That's right, Bee. He'll be with us again soon.'

Sophia was delighted to see her. 'Darling, Han! What *is* going on? We're really confused!'

Hannah looked at them for a short time and then she picked up Joe's hand and began to smooth it. Sophia and Bee could hear Han whispering to Joe. They couldn't hear the actual words. Gradually, Sophia became aware of a warm glow moving through her body. Hannah turned and spoke. 'Joe is nearer us. He will open his eyes soon. Now he is going to sleep.'

'How do you know that, Han?' said a voice behind them. It was Nah. She had been there for quite a while and had watched Hannah closely. She had also had had the amazing feeling during that time that Hannah had been stroking Joe's hand and whispering to him.

'Joe told me,' said Hannah. 'I'm going to get a cup of tea. Would—'

Sophia interrupted her. 'Hannah, do you know that Bess has run off? And that Andrew has gone to look for her?'

'No,' said Han in a tense voice. Her mood had changed completely. They caught the sound of footsteps and in came Chrissie and Andrew. Andrew had been crying and his face was ashen. Chrissie was clearly very shaken. She was breathing heavily as if she had been running fast. She managed to tell them that she had phoned The Oak Tree House again and that Jan was coming to fetch Bibi, Andrew and herself. Bess had just disappeared!

Hannah said, 'I'll come with you; Joe will be quite safe.'

Sophia added, 'I'll take Nah back in my car. We'll make a thorough search for Bess. Do you want us to notify the police, Chrissie, or have you already done that?'

Chrissie shook her head. 'No, that sounds a little drastic, she must be quite near the hospital, she can't have gone far.'

Andrew said, 'Please, please can I go with Sophia and Nah, Mum? Bess trusts me. I know some of her special places.'

'But we're such a long way from the village,' interjected Nah. 'She doesn't know her way around this area, Andy.'

'Has she Bear with her?' asked Hannah.

'Yes, yes, she has. Why?' Andy was puzzled.

Hannah went on: 'I think she has gone to the place where you parked the Land Rover when we brought Joe here last Wednesday. I think she is waiting for the Land Rover to come to the hospital, then she will be able to go home.' Andrew turned and ran past the others once again. Chrissie started after him, but Hannah caught her arm.

'Let him go, Chrissie.' She appeared to be very calm and controlled. 'Let him look for her. He knows where the Land Rover was parked.'

Nah touched Sophia on the sleeve. 'We'll go down to the car park, Sophia. We will be able to keep an eye on Andrew; in fact we can stay with him until Jan arrives.'

'Yes, that's a good idea, Nah,' replied Sophia and the two of them moved quickly. Now it was quiet again. Chrissie sighed and Han smiled at her. 'Try not to be too concerned. Bess is safe. She has Bear and she's not far away. Andrew has probably found her by now.'

Sure enough, Andrew *had* found Bess! He had gone to the parking space where they had parked the Land Rover. Another car was parked there now, but he had found Bess sitting on the ground in front of it. She was gently swaying and holding Bear close to her face. Andrew stood a little way from her and said very, very softly, 'Bess?' She stopped swaying, but did not answer or even turn her head. Andrew spoke again. 'Bess, Jan Dad will be here soon. Then we can go home.' Bess stood up and came to Andrew. She slipped her hand into his and pulled him to where she had been sitting. He held onto her hand firmly and she turned her eyes towards his. 'I won't run off. You are here.' Her voice was steady and her hand felt cool. Andrew wanted to cry, but he swallowed, and smiled at the little girl.

Nah and Sophia saw the two children standing in front of the car as they made their way to Sophia's parking spot. 'Look!' whispered Nah and she grabbed Sophia's arm. 'Look! There they are! Andrew *and* Bess!' Sophia began to move through the lines of cars, but Nah called out in a low, urgent voice, 'No! Wait, Sophia! They seem perfectly all right. Let's get into your car. We can see them from there and I'm sure that Jan will be here soon.'

So, when Jan finally drove into the car park Nah was silently watching two children standing, also silently, by a large red car and Sophia was asleep. Andrew saw the Land Rover and waved and shouted. Jan saw him and called back: 'I'll park. Wait for me there!' Nah carefully opened the door and edged her way out of Sophia's car. *Good*, she thought, *I haven't woken her!* Suddenly they were all together: Andrew and Bess, Nah and Jan. Andrew began to talk, very quickly, but Jan said, 'Hush now, Andrew. Let Nah tell what has been going on.' And Nah told him.

Back in Joe's room in the hospital, Hannah was talking to Charlie. 'So you see, Charlie, it will be quite all right for me to go back to The Oak Tree Ho and find Artie. We need each other now. Certainly, I need him and I expect he is feeling concerned, not knowing anything about the goings-on here. Please phone me if anything unusual occurs, won't you?'

Charlie had been listening carefully to Hannah. She

nodded and said, 'I will, Hannah, I'll tell Dr Miles that you have gone back to The Oak Tree House. It sounds, well, somehow, a special place.'

'It is a *very* special place, Charlie,' replied Hannah. 'Special people live in that house.'

Bibi spoke, 'I live in The Oak Tree House... am I spechul?'

Hannah chuckled. 'Oh, yes! *You* are "spechul", all right! Have you been talking to Joe? In your head, little one?'

'Yes, I've been telling him all about today, when we were with the Sophia Lady in that place where we fed the ducks on the water and I was clapped by lots and lots and lots and—'

Chrissie said quickly, 'Come on, Bee, we must go home. Artie is there all by himself! I expect he is wondering and wondering what we're all doing!'

Bibi touched Joe's face and whispered, 'We'll be back soon, Joe. You'll be awake then.' She hopped the distance between the bed and Hannah, Charlie and Chrissie.

'Och! You're a funny wee creature, Bibi!' laughed Charlie. 'Now Chrissie, Hannah – you won't worry too much, will you? I will take great care of the little lad.' She paused for a split second, then impulsively, kissed Hannah, then Chrissie and then gave Bibi a hug.

'Bye, Charlie!' Bibi was yanking on Chrissie's hand. 'Come on, Chrissie Mum! Hurry! Hurry! I'm hungry, hungry!'

When they found the Land Rover, Andrew and Bess were inside and Jan was listening to Nah and Sophia, who were both telling him all the details of the extraordinary day. Chrissie called out, 'Jan! Oh, I'm so pleased to see you!' She reached up and kissed him. 'Can we go as soon as possible. My head feels as if it were about to burst!' Truly, poor Chrissie looked as white as new snow.

Jan held her close to him and said gently, 'Yes, we are going now. Nah, are you coming to The Oak Tree Ho straight away, or will you take Sophia home first?'

Sophia answered for Nah. 'May I come back with you? Maybe we all ought to talk further.'

'Yes, that's a good idea.' Chrissie sounded weary, but positive.

'Our brains need feeding as well as our bodies,' added Hannah, and everyone smiled.

'See you at the house... drive carefully... I couldn't bear it if anything else happened!' said Chrissie.

Chapter Six

$\mathcal{A}$rtie was mowing the stretch of lawn in front of The Oak Tree House. He had decided to do this as he would be able to see the car come up the drive. He was getting increasingly disturbed. They had all been away from the village for such a long time. Before he started cutting the grass, he had opened tins of soup and found some brown rolls. There was also cheese, butter and lots of biscuits sitting on the round kitchen table, all covered with cloths. *They'll be very hungry*, thought Artie. He had looked into the fridge and noticed that there was a selection of juice and plenty of milk. *Good*, he thought.

Artie was bending over the mower, about to empty the grass container when the heard the sound of engines. He looked up just as the Land Rover turned into the drive, followed by Sophia's ramshackle old car. 'Thank you, Lord!' said Artie, and immediately ran back up the lawn to where the cars had come to a halt. 'Am I relieved to see you all!' he gasped. 'How's Joe?'

'He's probably asleep right now,' answered Hannah, as she clambered down from the Land Rover, Artie helping her. They moved away towards the kitchen, talking nineteen to the dozen.

Nah and Sophia had hurried off to the kitchen to start the meal. 'We all need food,' called out Nah. Nah had always been able to make a meal appear in what seemed seconds – miraculous! Jan and Chrissie looked at each other. What a day – and it wasn't over yet!

Bibi had jumped down from the Land Rover as soon as had stopped, and had run on ahead to let Pippin out of the back door. The dog came out barking with her tail wagging so hard that they had to avoid it. Her tail could be quite dangerous! Bibi came running back to the Land Rover, shrieking, 'Andy! Bess! Quickly! I want to take Pippin into the orchard to find White Star!' Bibi was not allowed into the orchard by herself; in fact she was hardly ever on her own; things happened when she was by herself! Remember the water and BT? But Andrew did not seem to hear her words. He was walking hand in hand with Bess towards the kitchen door. 'Andy!' Bibi shrieked again.

Jan appeared in the doorway and said very firmly, 'Bibi, stop screaming like that! You are to come back at once. No, don't argue, please. *Come in now!*' Bibi stopped her leaps in the air; thought for a second, opened her mouth, then shut it again. She walked to Jan's outstretched hand, took it and trotted docilely at Jan's side. They disappeared into the house. Silence.

Andrew and Bess had stopped walking. Now they moved on again, through the kitchen door and up the stairs to Andrew's room. Bess stood quietly whilst Andrew opened his door, but didn't go in. He turned around. 'Are you coming in, or are you going to your own room?' Bess was not looking at him. She was stroking Bear's furry back and her eyes were down. She hadn't heard Andrew's words. He wondered where she was. Oh, he was worried about her. She hadn't been so cut off for ages. He went to her and touched her face. 'Bess, would you like to come into my room for a while?'

She said clearly, 'No thank you, Andy. Bear and I have

lots to do in my room,' and she walked off up the landing, went into her own room and closed the door, quietly yet firmly. Andrew stood for a moment, knew he could not help Bess and went into *his* room and shut *his* door. He switched on the bedside lamp and his desk lamp, took off his sandals and lay down on his bed to think.

Jan and Bibi had gone into the music room. He had explained to her carefully that everyone was tired and needed his or her own space. He was going to listen to some music. Would she like to stay with him? She could lie under the piano and look at books, but she must not talk… she must be like a small mouse! Bibi said that she would like to stay with Jan and yes, she would be mouse-like. And that is how Chrissie found them about ten minutes later when she came to tell them that the meal was nearly ready. Suddenly the round table in the warm kitchen was a very busy place. Lots of people, all eating and drinking; no words, just eating sounds. Thinking time as well, of course.

What was going on inside Bess' head? What had she been doing in her room? She had taken her small suitcase out of her cupboard and had put into it some special pieces of clothing. Also, clothes for Bear. She had taken her money-box out of a drawer and emptied it into her blue purse – it was a big purse, it had belonged to Hannah. Bess had looked at her watch – all the children had a watch, even Bibi: it said 5.30 p.m. Bess had thought deeply for a moment with a frown, and then said, 'I have to ask questions.'

'Jan Dad?' It was Bess. Suddenly, all the minds tuned into the voice, except Bibi. She was munching away, totally absorbed in her knife and fork and the food that was being put into her mouth. Nothing disturbed Bibi when she was hungry and able to eat! Jan put down his knife. 'Yes, Bess,' he said.

'Jan Dad, will you be going away?' No one spoke.

Jan picked up his knife again and began to butter a cheese biscuit. 'Why do you ask that, little Bess?' he said. Everyone had gone back to their food, but they were all waiting for Bess' reply. It did not come, however. Jan asked the question again. 'Bess, why do you want to know if I am going away?'

Bess looked at her plate of food... she wasn't hungry. Hannah was aware that Bess hadn't eaten like the other children, but, then, Bess had never eaten as much as them. Hannah could only hear the chink of cutlery and various munching sounds – oh, and Bibi breathing noisily. Bess didn't speak. Jan shot a quick look at Chrissie and Hannah and both, at the same time, shook their heads. Jan did not ask the question again.

Andrew's brain was racing along. *What on earth had Bess meant, 'Are you going away'? Did Bess want to go with him? Was she planning something? No! Surely not! It was such a strange question. If I ask her what she means, I'm sure she won't tell me. Oh, dear! I wish I could really know what is going on inside her little head! It's all very disturbing!*

However, no one referred to the question again and the meal was finished in comparative silence. At last Jan spoke. 'Hannah and Nah, would you be angels and organise the children's bedtimes? Perhaps Sophia would also help? I need time to talk with Chrissie.'

Artie said cheerfully, 'I'll do the washing up and clear the table – I like doing that – then I'll walk home.'

Hannah added, 'I must remember that, dear Artie, when you sneak away to watch the television after our meals at the cottage!' But she was twinkling at her husband and the dimples were evident. Everyone laughed. The strained atmosphere had been broken.

Good, thought Nah, who had been becoming very tense. *Now we shall be able to get on with the ordinary jobs,* and she began to think about bedtime stories. 'Shall I read to Bibi, Chrissie?' she asked. Bibi replied quickly, 'Yes, yes, yes. Nah reads the best!'

'Every one of us "reads the best",' smiled Nah. 'Come along, you funny creature, as Charlie so aptly called you!'

Bibi said, 'Funny, *wee* creature, Nah. I'm a funny *wee* creature,' and she hurtled up the stairs. Sophia stretched her eyes and looked up to the heaven.

Gradually the kitchen emptied and Jan and Chrissie were alone. 'Oh!' sighed Chrissie, and she moved wearily to the armchair by the fire. It had been a warm day, this last Friday in June, but now it was becoming chilly. Jan struck a match... the tiny flame made Chrissie's eyes shine in the twilight and Jan bent over and kissed her lips. She stroked his face and pulled him down to her... the match went out. Jan drew away and laughed. 'There now! Look what you've done!' But he struck another match and lit the paper underneath the wood chippings. Small, short flames leapt and there was a pleasant smell. 'Lovely!' murmured Chrissie. 'Now we can talk.'

Chapter Seven

The Oak Tree House had five bedrooms on the first floor and there were three bathrooms. Actually, there were four bathrooms, but the fourth one was attached to the master bedroom and that belonged to Chrissie and Jan. The children used the other bathrooms, but for a treat or if one of them was not well, Chrissie let them use the 'M Bathroom' as it was called: Master Bathroom! Some clever person wondered why it wasn't named the Miss Bathroom, but this name never stuck somehow.

The sounds of voices and water came from the various places and then at last there was just the murmur of voices as stories were told and read. Hannah had been helping Bess, talking quietly and calmly to her. The little girl was so beautiful, with jet-black hair and expressive eyes that changed colour when her thoughts and feelings changed. Her eyes became clouded when she shut herself away from people. This had happened often recently and Hannah understood why Andrew was worried. But Andrew worried a great deal. *Perhaps he cares too much – no, you can't care too much*, thought Hannah. She turned and smiled at Bess who was in bed cuddling Bear. Hannah had been telling Bess about her own childhood. Bess liked to hear about Hannah when the old lady had been six or seven years old. Life was very different then, and especially for Hannah who had had three sisters and four brothers, all of whom had worked in big houses as maids, footmen, gardeners and cooks. Chrissie, Fred and Kel had loved these stories. They each had their favourite. Hannah noticed that Bess looked sleepy. She whispered, 'I'm going along the passage to look in on Andrew and Sophia and Bee and Nah. God bless you, little one. Say your prayers after I've gone.' Hannah bent to kiss Bess. 'I'll leave the door ajar.'

'No, please shut it, Han.' Bess spoke quietly and quickly. 'I shall be all right.' *That's unusual,* thought Hannah as she left the room and closed the door, but the thought went away as she heard giggles coming from Bibi's room.

She tapped on her door and at once, two voices said in American accents, 'Come in, won't you!' Han pushed open the door and her face creased into a smile at the sight that met her. Nah and Bibi had dressed up as cowgirls. Bee was sitting on her rocking horse and Nah was sitting astride the back of the armchair. They looked so funny!

'Hannah, Hannah, Nah has been telling me about the time she went to a ranch and rode ponies and fell off and lay in the mud and wet and...'

Nah had 'gotten off' her chair/pony and began to shush Bibi. 'We've had a wonderful time, Han! This is a very intelligent little soul! We've had such a laugh!'

'I'm not little, I'm *wee*!' shouted Bee.

'Yes, I'm sure you've had a fine time,' chuckled Hannah, 'but don't you think you ought to settle down now, Bee? The night will go so fast and then you'll be able to see Nah again.'

Bibi jumped off her 'pony', ran to Hannah, threw her arms round her, gave her a smacking kiss, then did the same to Nah and leapt into her head. She slithered down under the sheet and blankets and all that could be seen of her was a strand of blonde hair lying on the pillow! Nah tucked in the bedclothes and switched off the lamp.

The two women said goodnight to Bee, and had muffled 'Goodnights' in response. Then they left the room. The door was left open; Bee didn't like the dark. She liked to see the landing light, which was left burning all night.

Nah closed her eyes and breathed out. 'Whoo! What a child! She is really quite something!'

Hannah was looking at Nah's clothes. 'Don't you think you should become English again, my dear?' Nah had found some boots and had tucked her trousers into them; her blouse was open at the neck and she had turned up the collar and put on a scarf. 'Where on earth did you find that marvellous sombrero?' enquired Hannah.

'Oh, Kel gave me this as a goodbye present just before I left the States. He said it suited me.'

Hannah laughed. 'You could be American!' she said.

'Bibi can sound American as well. She has an amazingly good ear,' added Nah.

They were walking along the passage towards Andrew's room. They could hear Sophia's voice. She was saying, 'Yes, that's a good idea, Andrew, but try not to crowd her… give her space. I know that you want to make sure that she is safe, but give her space.' Andrew's bedroom door was open and Sophia was sitting on his bed. The boy was propped up on the pillows. He had taken off his specs and his eyes were troubled. Sophia turned as Nah and Hannah opened the door. 'Good,' Sophia said, 'now we can tell Nah and Han what we've been talking about.'

'No, it's all right, Sophia, I'll try to get some sleep. You tell them. Thank you for your help. Goodnight.' And Andrew patted his pillows, snuggled down and closed his eyes.

The three women looked at each other in surprise. Hannah said, 'Goodnight, Andy. God bless.' She beckoned to the others and they left the room. Nah and Sophia also said their 'Goodnights' and followed Hannah.

'He *is* an odd soul,' said Nah very quietly.

'No, he's just a very deep soul who needs to be on his own to put his mind in order at times,' explained Hannah.

Sophia nodded and added, 'Yes, that's absolutely right. Andrew has to have his head organised. Come on, let's go down to the music room and I'll tell you what we've been discussing.'

Back in the kitchen, Chrissie was saying, 'Hannah seems sure that Joe will regain consciousness soon. Jan, I find it quite amazing how Han knows these things. She's always right. All we have to do is to believe what she says.'

'And hand it over to God; we must remember that,' Jan said. He sounded very serious. Chrissie had told him everything about the day – well, as much as she knew. She did not know about Amanda. Only Hannah, Andrew, Bess, Sophia and Bibi had really seen Amanda. Of course, Charlie and Dr Miles knew her, worked with her. *Did they find her odd?* Hannah was thinking this last question as she walked into the music room with Nah and Sophia, and Chrissie suddenly said, 'Jan, Hannah has something important to tell us. She's in the music room. Come quickly! And she got up from where she had been sitting on the rug leaning against Jan's knees and ran out of the kitchen.

'Ah, Chrissie,' said Hannah sharply, 'I was just telling myself that you should know about a sad nurse I met today, called Amanda. She is a very unhappy person. Something must have made her like she is, her eyes are hard and cloaked.' Jan came into the music room. 'I'm concerned for Joe. This Amanda watches him with a very peculiar look on her face. I am not clear about what may happen, but I think someone ought to speak to the matron at the hospital and to the other nurses and doctors who have worked with her.'

Nah and Sophia were listening intently. Hannah went on: 'Amanda is fascinated with little Joe—'

Sophia interrupted the old lady. 'I saw this Amanda this afternoon bending over Joe. She had a piece of cloth or towel in her hand. Bibi and I had just come into Joe's room and there she was, as I said, bending over his bed.'

'Do you think she'd touched Joe?' asked Chrissie in a tight voice.

'No, I don't think so. Nothing seemed to have been disturbed.' Sophia looked worried. 'Does Charlie know her well, do you think?'

Jan said, 'I'll phone the hospital now and ask to speak to Charlie. If she's gone off duty, I'll ask for her home telephone number.'

'Oh, she should be in the hospital,' interjected Nah. 'She told Chrissie, myself and Hannah that she would make sure that Joe was safe. She told us this before we left to come back here.'

'Good,' said Jan, as he went down the passage to the telephone.

There was a silence in the music room for a split second, and then Hannah stretched out her hands to Chrissie, who went to her. 'Now, now, Chrissie, don't look so frightened. Joe is going to be all right. I told you he would be earlier, didn't I?'

'Oh, Han, we don't *really* know.'

'Yes, we do,' Hannah said in a firm voice and she patted Chrissie's cheek. 'Come along, we could all do with a drink – a strong one!' Hannah was smiling again. 'You get me my special whisky and warm water, and I'm sure Nah and Sophia would appreciate their favourites. Oh, and please tell Artie that we are all here. Tell him to come and join us.' Hannah breathed out, 'Ah!'

Chapter Seven

Nah hurried towards the door. 'I'll tell him,' she said, 'Sophia, will you help me with the drinks? Do we need some crisps?'

Chrissie replied, 'Yes, you'll find them—'

'I know where they are. This is my second home, remember?' laughed Nah.

Chrissie crossed the room to Hannah, sat down on the floor and rested her head against Hannah's legs. Hannah ran her fingers through Chrissie's hair. There was silence. Finally, Chrissie said, 'Han, I love you so much.' Her voice was low and shaky.

'Yes, my dear, I know you do,' Hannah said quietly. 'I love you very much too. I always will. You are my life. All of you. Let's just be still and talk to God. He needs us to tell Him our worries and troubles. He'll take care of us.'

Chrissie moved quickly and kissed Hannah. 'Don't ever go away from us, Han,' she whispered.

'No, I will always be close. Just call me,' Hannah whispered back and she patted Chrissie's cheek.

Sophia and Nah found them sitting in the twilight when they came back carrying trays of drinks – Nah signalled to Sophia not to speak and the two ladies put the glasses on tables and were aware of the extraordinary atmosphere around them. Suddenly, Artie came bustling in, still wearing an apron. He looked so funny that Sophia had to chuckle and the silence was broken.

'Darling Artie,' Sophia said, 'you *do* look domestic! I shall have to borrow you some time, to help in Merlin Cottage!'

Artie threw a twinkly look at his beloved Hannah. She was also twinkling. 'All right, Sophia,' said Hannah. 'When Artie gets difficult, I'll telephone you and you can have him!'

Chapter Seven

It was as if a cool, gentle breeze had blown the troubles out of the music room. Everyone in the room was smiling or laughing. 'Is Jan still on the phone?' asked Nah.

'No, I heard the ting of the receiver a few minutes ago,' said Hannah. 'He may have gone upstairs to check the children. He'll be here soon.'

Jan walked in as they were all sipping their drinks. He said, in a light cheery tone, 'I spoke to Charlie. Everything's fine at the hospital. Joe is sleeping peacefully and Amanda has gone off duty. Dr Miles seems pleased with Joe's condition. He thinks he may wake soon and will phone us when this happens. Oh, a glass of wine. Good, good! Sophia, do you like this wine? I was given it in Bristol when I was at Broadcasting House. A friend of mine works at a local wine merchants. He recommended it.' And the five of them were talking freely again. Joe was pushed gently out of the forefront of the minds, as they chatted about food and drink and other people's likes and dislikes.

But, upstairs in Bibi's bedroom? Hmm, an amazing scene was being acted out by Bibi and her toy animalia. Actually, Bibi was doing all the talking, as you may guess. Three rabbits were sitting on the bed, numerous bears were being moved from place to place. They were dressed in various bits of clothing; some were wearing hats, others scarves. Each time Bibi picked one up, she spoke for it – or was it him or her? Certainly all the voices were different and any listener could make out if the animal was male or female! Bibi was having a wonderful time. She was not at all sleepy! Jan had been in to see that she was all right, but Bee had been under her bedclothes then, and Jan had not seen the toy animalia strewn around the room.

Bibi was acting out her day. And what a day it had been! She was sitting on her bed surrounded by the animalia. BT wasn't there. Hannah had wrapped the small, dishevelled rabbit in a baby's towelling nappy and put him in the airing cupboard to dry thoroughly. Bibi had watched Hannah do this so she knew where he was. There were other rabbits on her bed or in her bed. She had begun to tell them about the park and the ducks and how she had loved singing and dancing and hearing the people clap their hands. She had wanted to sing and dance for ever!

She suddenly jumped off the bed, ran to the door, and pushed it open, slowly and ever so quietly, holding her breath. Was there anyone around? Coming up the stairs? She looked carefully and listened, still holding her breath until she had to let it all out. She ran fast to the airing cupboard, opened the door and saw BT lying on a shelf just above her head. She reached up, standing on tiptoe, and pulled the little animal towards her. He fell on the floor. Bibi whispered, 'Oh dear, poor BT! Don't worry, I'll take you to my bed. You'll be safe there with the rest of your family!' The little girl didn't realise that she sounded just like Hannah... she was speaking in Han's voice! Nah had been correct when she said that Bibi could copy accents. Bibi raced backed to her bedroom and jumped back onto her bed. She began to tell the animalia about the hospital and Joe.

'I saw Joe with lots of wires in him. I did! I did! You must believe me!' Bee's voice sounded like Sophia's this time, very dramatic! The story went on and on. Bibi was having a fine time. She was so involved in the words and changing voices of the people who had spoken them that she was quite unaware that Bess had been standing in the doorway listening to the story.

Bess had heard a lot of unusual sounds and had opened her door. She was holding Bear. Her face was expressionless. She watched Bibi for a while, then turned around and began to walk towards the staircase that led to the attic rooms. She knew that Joe had often visited one of the rooms up there to practice being 'without eyes'. She climbed the stairs and went into Joe's attic room. She sat down on the floor underneath the window. It was nearly dark outside now. She stared at the sky and there was the evening star. It was so bright! Bess was making plans. She had decided that she must find her father. She remembered the hospital in Cornwall. She remembered going into the hospital, through the door with the sign that said 'Casualty'. She had asked her father what the letters said. He had told her, 'The word is "casualty". It means a place where you can get help if you are suddenly hurt or ill.' She remembered thinking that her father's voice sounded strange; weak and foggy. She felt frightened. Her tummy had jumped and she had felt sick. He had told her to sit on a bench and wait for him to come back, but he had never come back! Now she had to find him; she couldn't wait any longer.

Bess was not as young as the Leigh family thought. She was eight years old, but small for her age, very small. Bess gazed at the star and tried to recall her mother. She couldn't. Her father had always been the one person who looked after her. He had told her that her mother had left them when she was a tiny baby. Bess had seen photographs of her. 'This is your mother. Isn't she beautiful?' her father murmured. 'You are beautiful. You are like your mother.' Bess had looked at her father's face and had seen a far away look in his eyes. 'Your mother was called Elizabeth, like you,' her father had gone on. 'But, she always called you Bess.' But whenever Bess had asked him to tell her more about the beautiful mother lady, her father had said, 'No!' in a stern, hard voice. She missed her father. He had been kind and gentle, and they had been together all the time, except when she had been at school. Bess had loved school.

Her father was a writer. He worked from home but had sent Bess to a playgroup when she was three years old. She had always been a friendly little soul and the two young mothers who ran the group had spent time with her, realising that she didn't have a mother at home. Bess had a quick, alert mind and loved words. She began to recognise letters and sounds and was reading quite fluently within weeks of being at the playgroup. She was often found sitting in a corner surrounded by books. Of course, she had had plenty of books at home and her father had encouraged her to look at pictures and had read to her whenever he had time. He was aware that he had a great responsibility, looking after Bess on his own, but he loved her dearly, although each time he looked at her he saw her mother, in the colour of her skin and her hair and her eyes. It was very hard for him. Bess' mother had left him when the baby was just over a year old to return to her own country. She was French. She had left a letter saying that she didn't love him any more and that she was going home. However, when he had contacted his wife's parents they told him that they had not heard from her or seen her. She had just disappeared. He was desperate at first, searching and questioning, to no avail. Then he made up his mind to try to forget her and concentrate on looking after their small daughter.

After his wife had left, Bess' father found that he was unable to write, but gradually his mind became clear again and he sat down one afternoon and realised that he was able to go on with the story he had been writing, that terrible day when he came back to an empty house.

He had met his wife in Verona, when he was researching the story of *Romeo and Juliet*. He was only eighteen years old and was about to start university. He had a place at Cambridge to read English. Someone bumped into him in one of the narrow side streets and he looked down to see this lovely girl, about his own age. She was tiny, with jet-black hair, which was covering her face. She had fallen onto her knees and was leaning against his legs for support. Suddenly she tossed her head back, the hair fell away and he saw her eyes. Oh, those eyes! He brought her back to England with him after the long, tempestuous summer and they were married by Christmas. She came from a large family. They lived in Provence, but she had never been part of the family, she wanted to be free. She told him that she would leave him if he ever tried to tie her down. He adored her and for about two years they were idyllically happy. Then she became pregnant and she changed… he noticed that she was restless and very tense, and was increasingly out when he came back from lectures or other university activities. He was a busy young man and popular with the members of the college. His wife said she was shy and nervous when they went to his friends' parties. Finally, she refused to go anywhere with him and after Bess was born, she spent all her time with the baby, taking her out in her pram in all weathers. Sometimes she took her to London in the train and was hardly ever at home. Then came the day when he had a free afternoon and he had taken Bess to the swings in the park, the day he came back to an empty house. That day had been in June. Bess had overheard her father telling a policeman. June… June…

Bess and her father were forever going into police stations to ask questions about her mother. The child had wondered about 'June'. Of course, as she grew older, she found out that it was a month of the year, the sixth month, a summer month.

⚙ Chapter Seven ⚙

Bess, sitting on the floor under the window in the attic room in the dark, said out loud, 'It is June again, I must find my daddy.' She also knew that her father had taken her to Cornwall; that the hospital that they had walked into was in Cornwall. Jan was going to Cornwall. Bess had overheard a telephone conversation between Jan and one of the people he worked with at the BBC. She had heard Jan say, 'That's a good idea… Cornwall would be ideal. We should go down and look for some suitable places to film those scenes.'

On hearing heard the word 'Cornwall', Bess had instantly recalled the whole situation. When she sat on the bench waiting for her father to come back to her; the time when she had left the hospital and wandered down the long hill into the town and on and on until she had reached a beach with rocks; the time she had curled up near a wall as it became darker and darker. She recalled her fear and how she had sobbed; how people had looked at her as she wandered through the streets the next day and how a kind lady with a big round face had knelt down and taken her hand and said, 'Where's your mummy, my dear? Are you lost?' She had tried to get away, but she was weak with hunger and so thirsty. She had just sat on the pavement and sobbed into Bear's fur. Then what had happened? She couldn't remember the next bit. It was a blur in her mind, but she certainly remembered being in a big bedroom with other children who stared at her and asked lots and lots of questions. It had been a very bad time. Then a tall gentleman who spoke in an unusual way and a lady with short fair hair and blue eyes had come into the bedroom. The other children seemed to disappear; all she could remember were the gentleman and the lady who told her that she would be going with them to a house where she would be safe and where she would meet a boy called Andrew and a dog and a

121

pony and a cat, and a lovely kind little lady called Hannah. Bess had opened her mouth to say, 'Where is my daddy?' but no sound came out. She had tried again, but she could not make her voice work. She had managed to say, 'Bess,' when they had asked her name but nothing else. That had been such a long time ago – or it felt a long time ago. But now, now, she knew what she must do.

Bess picked up Bear and held him tight. She couldn't do anything more tonight so she must go back to her bedroom and go to sleep. Actually, she was feeling calm and thought she would be able to fall asleep quite quickly. Her father had explained to her the ways of relaxing her mind so that her little body could become floppy and her eyes would close. He had made himself do this during the years he had been without his wife. It had been such a lonely time for him. After he had left Cambridge, he had moved to London, taking Bess with him naturally. They had lived in a small flat, south of the River Thames. There were two bedrooms and they each had their own space. Her father had helped Bess make her bedroom into a home, a special place where she was able to be herself completely. She had her bed, of course, and lots of bookshelves and cupboards for her soft toys and other favourite 'bits and pieces', as her father had put it. Her father had his room too, with all his bits and pieces. They had a sitting room and a warm, cosy kitchen, and a dear little bathroom and a lavatory. Her father insisted that they called it a lavatory. He had said that the correct words should be used, if you knew them. There were other names for 'lavatory', and, of course, she would hear them. Bess loved words, but she had stored them inside her head after, the time her father had not returned to the bench in the casualty department. She had stopped speaking. She didn't want to speak.

☺ Chapter Seven ☺

Bess got off the floor of the attic room. She walked out of the room, making sure that nobody could hear her footsteps. She was repeating, in her head, over and over again, 'Where are you, my daddy? Where are you, my daddy?' She passed Andrew's bedroom, stopped for a tiny moment, listened, and then ran soundlessly into her own room and climbed into bed. She lay there holding her breath so that she could hear if anyone was coming upstairs, or along the corridor. No, it was all quiet now; even the funny sounds from Bibi's room had stopped. She closed her eyes and thought her floppy body thoughts. Soon she was asleep. She did not know that Andrew was still awake. He was writing his journal.

Andrew's journal was like a diary. He wrote in it all that had gone on during the day and, sometimes, when he was unable to sleep, he would write down his thoughts and feelings. He found sounds very interesting, in the night when he was awake, he used to listen and then write all about the sounds. After he had asked Sophia to leave him, he had tried to go to sleep, but found it quite impossible. There were hundreds and thousands of thoughts zooming around his head. Nothing for it but to get up and write in his journal. And that's when he heard a minute sound as Bess passed his door. He stopped writing and sat there, motionless, pen poised, as he heard her door open and close. *Now, where has Bess been?* wondered Andrew. He sighed. There were so many unanswered questions. *I have to find the answers*, he thought. 'Yes!' he spoke out loud. 'I have to find the answers! I'll go to sleep now,' and he yawned and stretched. He looked at his watch: *Nine o'clock. Hmmm, I'll set my alarm clock to go off at seven a.m. Then I will get up and start to search for answers.* Andrew scrambled into bed and very soon he was fast asleep.

🥚 Chapter Seven 🥚

Now all the children were sleeping. Nah was on the landing listening. She could see a lump in Bibi's bed; the tiny child's bedroom door was open. Nah could hear chattery sounds at times and little chuckles. *Darling Bee*, thought Nah, *she never stops talking!* Nah moved slowly along the corridor, stopping at Andrew and Bess' door. These doors were both shut, but she put her ear to them and heard only breathing sounds. *Good*, thought Nah, *I'll go downstairs again and finish my drink!*

The telephone rang. Nah jumped. The music room door opened and Chrissie rushed out and picked up the receiver. 'Hello, Mrs Leigh speaking… Yes! Oh, thank God! Do you want us to come? Are you sure… all right, I'll tell Hannah. Thank you, Charlie. We'll come to the hospital tomorrow morning early… God bless you. Goodbye, Charlie. Oh, tell Joe we all love him! Thank you. Bye.' Nah had run downstairs and was standing near Chrissie. 'Joe is awake? Oh, Chrissie!'

Nah was nearly crying and she hugged Chrissie. 'Come on,' she said, 'we must tell the others!'

Chapter Eight

Charlie was talking to Joe. He was certainly very much awake. He still had a bandage over his right eye. Dr Miles and Charlie had managed to re-bandage the eye after Joe had torn the other bandage off. He had become unconscious quickly and of course they could re-bandage him easily. He was lying very still, but he had spoken various words, in a whisper. Charlie had been sitting next to him reading a book. She had heard him say, 'Chrissie? Hannah? Anybody? Please, anybody?' and Charlie had dropped her book and had said. 'Joe? Little Joe? It's me Charlie! You're back with us! Och! The Lord be praised!' Charlie took the hand that was groping for hers. It was cool and dry. She held it firmly and then began to stroke it. She had seen Hannah do this. Joe let out a long sigh. He withdrew his hand and put it up to his right eye. Charlie watched him, but she didn't tell him not to touch the bandage.

Joe moved his hand all around the material of the bandage. At last he said, 'Charlie, will I be able to see or will I be blind?' Joe had never spoken the word Blind before. Perhaps it had been used at The Oak Tree House but not recently. Everyone avoided it, it seemed so final, somehow. Charlie didn't know what to say. She was thinking about the best words to use, when she heard someone come into the room. She turned to see Dr Miles. He answered Joe's question. 'We can't tell you that yet, Joe. We were concerned when you tore off the bandages – after you came round from the operation. We bandaged your eye again, as you have felt, but we must leave the eye to rest for a while. We will be able to tell you what is going to happen in a couple of days.'

Joe stretched out his hand again. This time the doctor took it. Joe said, 'Thank you for looking after me. Will you always tell me the truth?' The doctor replied, 'Yes, old man, I will. You're a brave fellow. Are you scared?'

Charlie was surprised by the question. She thought it was rather soon to ask the lad such a straight question, but Joe seemed very calm. He said, 'No, I'm not scared. I have lots of people at The Oak Tree House who will help me. I would like Charlie to stay with me until the morning comes.'

Charlie said at once, 'Och! My, I don't think that...' but she was interrupted by Dr Miles.

'Of course, Charlie – um, Nurse Charlotte – can stay with you, but she needs to phone your father and mother – ah, I mean...'

Joe's face, what could be seen of it, creased into a smile. 'It's OK. They are my new dad and mum. I call them Jan Dad and...' he thought for a moment, then added, 'I call Chrissie, Mum. That's odd, isn't it?'

The doctor smiled and squeezed Joe's hand. 'No, not at all. You call them what you like. They're special folk, aren't they?'

'Yes, yes!' Joe's voice was strong and full of life. When Dr Miles signalled to Charlie to go and telephone the Leighs, she noticed that the man's eyes were full of tears. She swallowed hard and ran off.

The doctor lifted Joe's hand with his fingers on his wrist.

He was making sure that the boy's pulse was steady. It was. Joe did not have a temperature. His forehead was cool and his breathing was normal. 'Would you like a drink, Joe?' Doctor Miles stood looking down at him.

'Yes, please. I would like some juice. We have real orange juice at home. Do you have it here?' Joe's voice sounded sleepy now, but he went on, 'Would you ask Hannah to bring Horatio to see me tomorrow?' He turned over on his side, placed his right hand over his right bandaged eye, sighed and was asleep.

The doctor bent over him and realised that he had fallen asleep in a split second. Amazing! These people really are special; he made a mental note to find out more about them all. Each one of them had been full of – what? He couldn't put it into words. Horatio? Was this another boy? Or a man? What a name! He must certainly find out more about Horatio.

Charlie came back into the room, 'Everything is fine,' she told the older man. 'Chrissie and Hannah are coming in tomorrow morning, early.'

'Hannah must bring Horatio with her,' said the doctor and he went quickly out of the room, leaving Charlie staring after him. *Horatio? Who's Horatio?* she wondered.

Chapter Nine

*B*ess woke up. She lay in her bed with her eyes shut, listening. She could hear many muffled sounds… the walls of The Oak Tree House were thick, but there were always sounds. Her room was next to Andrew's. She stretched her ears towards the wall on her right. Was he awake as well? She would like to be with him, but she didn't want to disturb his sleep. Bess sighed. She sat up and slowly got out of bed. Her mouth seemed very dry, so she went to her washbasin and poured herself a glass of water.

Then she heard a tiny sound… it was a door in the corridor opening. Bess waited for the tap on her door, Andy's tap. Three taps with his fingernails – yes, there it was… good! Bess had wanted Andrew to be with her. She knew that she would be leaving The Oak Tree House soon. She knew that Jan would be leaving in the Land Rover to drive to Cornwall. She had to speak to Andrew. Bess said in a whisper, 'Come in, Andy. Oh, dear Andy, you always know when I need you.'

Andrew took her hands; they were quite cold. He said, 'I just woke up and got out of bed and here I am. Are you OK?'

'Yes,' answered the little girl. Andrew noticed how large and beautiful her eyes were. She was so tiny and so thin. The boy's heart was full of concern and love. Oh, yes, you don't have to be grown up to love someone.

Bess was gazing into the middle of Andrew's eyes... she seemed to be looking into his mind. The silence was deep, but not scary. This was a very, very important silence.

Finally, Andrew said in a gruff, shaky voice. 'Bess, are you going to tell me what's wrong? I know that there is something terribly wrong. Please, please tell me.'

Bess did not answer at once. She shook her head. Then she spoke. 'Andrew, you are not to worry, not to be frightened. I have to do a difficult job. It may take a long time to do it.' She paused, then continued. 'I will always be near you. I will always come back to you.' Bess withdrew her hands from Andrew's and kissed him gently on the cheek. She turned away from him, saying, 'You must go back to your room now.'

Andrew knew that he must not stay or say another word. His throat felt tight and his eyes pricked and smarted. He turned round and walked out of Bess' bedroom. He closed her door and stood in the passage. He was not really scared but he was worried. *What was the little girl going to do? Was she going away? But how could she? Where would she go? Did she have a family somewhere in England? In Great Britain?* He was confused, but he realised that he must not tell anyone else in The Oak Tree House. He must wait until the next happening, whatever that might be!

So, back he went into his own room and took out his journal and wrote in it all that had just happened. *I have to keep a record of events*, he thought, *just in case they are needed, like in a mystery play or book.* Andrew looked at his clock. It said nearly seven o'clock. *Ah, it's Saturday. Good*, he thought, *no school.*

The house was slowly waking up. Nah lay in her comfy bed, thinking. There were so many thoughts, all swirling around her head. She would have to put them in boxes.

While Nah was doing this, Chrissie was out in the garden. It was the last Saturday in June and the sun was shining, the sky was clear and new. Chrissie was picking flowers. She found the garden peaceful and calming somehow. A new day. She decided to list all the jobs that had to be done in her mind and then when she returned to the kitchen with her flowers, she would write them down.

Jan was looking out of their bedroom window. He caught sight of Chrissie walking towards the rose garden. *My darling girl*, he thought. Jan always spoke of Chrissie as his darling girl; she seemed eternally young to him. *There she goes, to fetch the flowers, to bring beauty into the house, into our lives.* He opened the window wide, leaned out and called, 'Chrissie, pick some white and pink roses, will you? Pick lots and lots. We need to take them into the hospital. Here, catch this!' And he blew a kiss to her.

Chrissie laughed and caught the kiss. 'Thank you,' she called, and tried to blow a kiss back to Jan, but dropped the scissors and some of the roses that she had cut. They both laughed.

'Would you like some coffee, my darling?' Jan called.

Chrissie was picking up the flowers. She nodded her head. 'Hmm, lovely!' was the reply, and Jan disappeared from the window.

Bibi was still asleep. Strangely enough, she needed a great deal of sleep, especially after one of her mad, glorious days.

Nah had put her head in order, had a bath and dressed. Now she was walking along the passage past the children's bedrooms. All was quiet in Bess' and Andrew's rooms. She stopped outside Bibi's door and listened. Good, not a sound – well, a few snuffly noises and a couple of unintelligible words. *I'll go down and have some breakfast*, thought Nah, and that's what Jan found her doing when he came into the kitchen.

'Everything seems very peaceful this morning, Nah.' He smiled as he spoke these words.

Nah smiled back. 'Yes, great, isn't it?' She had laid the table with fresh fruit, marmalades, jams and honey. There were the serviettes in their rings, a different ring for each child and grown-up. There was a small vase with tiny flowers in it. A wonderful smell of coffee and toast hung in the air.

'I love breakfast,' said Jan.

'So do I,' answered Nah.

Chrissie walked in through the open door. You couldn't see her face, her arms were full of roses. Wonderful roses! A mass of varying shades of pinks and whites. What a sight it was! Jan crossed to her and took them from her.

'Come, sit down and have breakfast. It seems quiet at this moment. Let us share this quietness. Hmmm?' He smiled at the two women and took their hands. He kissed them both, sat down and said in a chuckly voice, 'Women, serve me my food and drink!'

Chrissie ruffled his hair. 'No,' she said, '*You* told me that you were going to make me some coffee.'

She sat down at the table, stretched and let out a long breath. 'Oh, it's so good to have you here, dear, dear Nah! And, look, no children! Just the three of us!'

Artie was carrying a tray laden with more breakfast at The Cottagey House. He was whistling a tune. Hannah didn't recognise it, but then, she often didn't recognise Artie's tunes. He seemed to be whistling nothing! It was quite a pleasant noise, however. It was unusual for them to have breakfast in bed on a Saturday, but Hannah had been so exhausted the evening before when they finally arrived back in their own home, that Artie was determined to make her stay in bed until ten o'clock the next morning. It had taken some persuading, but Artie was a strong-minded man when he believed that he was in the right, so Han had agreed to 'Breakfast in bed, my maid, tomorrow, and no arguing!' So she didn't, and now she could hear his slow, sturdy footsteps on the stairs. Hannah lay back on the pillows, relieved that she didn't have to get up. The sun was glinting through the half-drawn curtains and it was warm and cosy. Artie's and Hannah's bedroom was such a friendly little room.

It was very quiet and Hannah felt peaceful, sitting in bed, propped up against her pillows. She smiled as she imagined Artie preparing her breakfast. He was always so caring and particular, taking simply ages to cut the bread for toasting and making the coffee. The tray would have an embroidered cloth on it and there would be a small vase full of country flowers from the garden. In fact, she had heard Artie outside in the garden a little earlier, just after she had woken up. Maybe he had been picking the flowers then. Now she could see him through the open door. His dear, weather-beaten face was wreathed in smiles. He said, 'Oh, my dear soul! Those stairs are getting steeper! No! I'm getting stiffer. Here you are, me darlin', your brekkie.'

Artie put the tray down on a table by the side of the huge bed and then he sat down in a comfy chair near the window and breathed out. 'Phewww! I'm hungry, real hungry. I've brought up a lot of your favourites. Look.' And he waved his hand towards the tray. Sure enough, Artie had found different flavoured marmalades, all made by Hannah, he had made a basketful of toast, white and brown bread. There was orange juice and apple juice, chopped apples and pears, a steaming jug of coffee and another of hot milk, and finally, some cream for his coffee.

Hannah clapped her hands. She was thrilled. 'My darling man, thank you, thank you! It all looks marvellous. All the colours and the smells! You are such a kind soul.' She stretched her arms out to him and he left his chair and came to her. Hannah wrapped her arms around him and buried her head in his chest. He smelt warm and soapy. Their love was deep and full of comfort, a love made in Heaven and they knew it.

Suddenly, the telephone rang, breaking the moment. 'I'll go,' said Artie. He kissed Hannah gently and was off down the stairs to the phone. Hannah picked up a jug of apple juice and a glass and listened carefully. She heard Artie say: 'Hello, The Cottagey House? Oh, hello, Chrissie... Yes, we're fine thank you... we've just had a kiss. You've rung the hospital? Yes... Good... Yes, I'll tell Han. God bless. See you soon. Goodbye.' Artie replaced the receiver and came back upstairs. 'Han, Chrissie says that Joe has slept well for most of the night and would like to see us this morning and could you bring Horatio. Where is Horatio? Is he still in your apron pocket?'

Hannah gasped, and put her hand to her mouth. 'Oh, yes! I must get that peapod out of there and put into a box!'

Artie sat down again, but this time he had a plate piled with delicious food. 'We'll have our brekkie and then we'll get ready to go to see Joe. There's plenty of time, me dear. Chrissie says she'll pick us up at a quarter to eleven. The others are not coming this morning, they are going to visit Joe this afternoon, when Bibi is less energetic – those were Chrissie's words. I think I might have used the word "nutty"!'

Han laughed. 'Each day is a nutty day for that little girl. She is remarkable!' Hannah looked so pretty with her serviette tucked into her nightie and her eyes sparkling.

Joe was also having some breakfast and he too was sitting up in bed. His eye was still bandaged but he looked better. His skin had a little more natural colour. Charlie was helping him to eat some warm, creamy porridge. He liked creamy porridge; he had told her when she had asked him what he would like to eat, 'Creamy porridge, please.' So off she went to the kitchen. She had insisted on making the porridge herself. She found some cream in the fridge. She knew very well that this cream was for the doctors, but she thought that they could do without their cream this morning.

Joe had insisted on feeding himself, although Charlie had told him that it would be quicker and less messy if she fed him. He had said that she could start him off, but he must do it himself. Actually, he managed very well. Charlie only mopped up a couple of times.

Doctor Miles had come in and had stood in the doorway watching. Joe realised that someone was in the room. 'Who is that? Are you a friend?'

The doctor thought it sounded as if a war was going on – 'Are you friend or foe?' He said, 'I'm a friend, Joe.'

'Doctor Miles,' Joe said, after he had swallowed a mouthful of porridge. 'I like that name… Doctor Miles.' He spoke the words as if he were tasting them. 'What is your first name? What are you called at home?'

'Oh, Joe, I don't think it is very polite—' Charlie was interrupted by the doctor.

'My name is David. You can call me David.'

'Thank you. I will,' replied Joe. 'Horatio is coming in this morning. Will you be able to meet him?'

Charlie looked at David Miles. He was smiling. The he answered Joe, 'Yes, I hope so. I'm rather busy this morning, but if Charlie lets me know that Horatio has arrived, I will endeavour to be here to meet him. Joe, we are going to leave your bandages on until tomorrow at least. We have to be sure that light does not get into your eye. The nurses will help you to do everything you need to do, but I would like you to rest as much as possible. Do you like music? There is a radio attached to the head of your bed. You could fiddle around with it and find different programmes.'

Joe said, 'Oh, yes, I'd like that. I listen to the radio at home. What day is it?'

Charlie quickly said, 'It's Saturday, Joe. We'll fix you up with the radio after you've had a wash, etc. Come on, now. Finish your porridge.' David Miles moved across to Joe's bed. He lifted up Joe's left hand and felt his pulse. 'Good,' he said, 'you haven't a temperature. Would you like a bath, Joe?'

'If it isn't too hot,' replied the boy.

'What did he mean by "et cetera", Charlie?' Before Charlie could reply, the doctor touched Joe's visible cheek and said, 'Bye, Joe, I'll see you again soon.'

'Goodbye, David.' Joe tipped his head up as if he was trying to locate the man. He felt for David's hand, found it and held onto it. 'Come back and meet Horatio, please.' The doctor left the room. 'Now, Charlie, what did he mean when he said we were going to do "et cetera"?'

That's a fascinating lad, thought Doctor Miles. *Now, I must get back to meet his Horatio!*

It was very busy back at The Oak Tree House. Andrew, Bess and Bibi had had their breakfast and were being organised by Nah. She was telling them that they were not going to the hospital until after lunch. Hannah, Artie, Jan and Chrissie were going at about eleven o'clock and were taking Horatio Pea with them. Artie had told Chrissie about the outsize pea. He really was very large! Artie certainly had never seen one as huge as Horatio! *I wonder what made him grow like that, inside his pod-house?* he had thought.

Chrissie had laughed and laughed. 'Now, there will be some special Hannah stories!' she had told Artie.

Chapter Ten

The three children were going into the village to do some important shopping: food for the weekend! They were also going to visit the vicar and his family and perhaps, if she was calm and fairly quiet, Bibi could drop in on the Sophia Lady. Nah wanted to go into the church. She would like to just sit there and talk to God. Andrew and Bess were going with her. Bee had told Nah that she did not want to sit in the church. She wanted to run up and down the 'passages'. Andrew sighed and said, 'Oh, dear. Must we have Bee with us, Nah?'

Bibi was hurtling in and out of the kitchen, yelling, 'I'm going to run and run and run and—'

Nah looked up to the heavens and said in a low, but penetrating voice, 'Don't worry, Andy, I'll divert her. I'll take her over to the Sophia Lady with Pippin Dog. I'm sure that Sophia will be there… she'll get her into line.'

'Poor Sophia,' muttered Andrew.

'Come on, my jolly folk!' called Nah. 'It's nearly ten o'clock. We've a lot to do!' Bibi shot past her and rushed towards Nah's little car, which she had parked in the yard behind the house.

Andrew looked around for Bess. He saw her standing in the middle of the yard. She was holding Bear by his paw. He noticed that Nah was watching him. He looked at her and said, 'I'll go and tell Bess to get into the car. I don't

137

think she heard you.' The boy and the older woman looked hard at each other. There was so much not being said. Nah nodded her head and touched Andrew's shoulder. She smiled, but he didn't smile back. He just turned away and walked over to Bess. Nah picked up her bag and list of shopping, called 'Goodbye' and hurried to the car.

Inside The Oak Tree House, Jan and Chrissie were preparing to go to the hospital to see Joe. They were taking the Land Rover. There was so much room in the Land Rover, and goodness only knows whom they would bring back or deliver to their own homes. It was a hectic time. However, their first trip was to The Cottagey House to pick up Hannah and Artie. Jan came into their bedroom where Chrissie was putting on her sandals. 'Are we going to take anything special for Joe, darling? Will he need extra clothes or pyjamas?' Jan asked her.

'No, don't worry, Hannah will have made sure that Joe has everything that he needs,' Chrissie replied. 'Just pop downstairs and phone Han and Artie. Tell them we're on our way and will be with them in about ten minutes.'

Hannah was singing in the bathroom, the only place where she ever sang – well, sang loudly! She said that her singing voice was not for others. She was singing a special song of her own, a Hannah song, made up of lots of well-known hymn tunes and special Hannah words. The words this morning were hopeful, happy words, 'For little Joe,' she had told Artie. 'Because he could do with some hopeful, happy words!' Of course, they sounded most peculiar when she began to clean her teeth! She had heard the telephone ring and left it for Artie to answer. He had called up to her that she had better get a move on as the Land Rover would be arriving for them soon. Han had chuckled to herself. She imagined the Land Rover driving up the lane on its own, no driver or passenger! She'd also wondered what kind of voice this vehicle would have. A booming, rumbly voice, perhaps?

☙ Chapter Ten ❧

She liked the Land Rover. It was full of friendly smells and always felt warm and cosy. It seemed to belong to the land and the countryside. A comforting kind of character. *Yes,* thought Hannah, *the voice would be deep and rumbly and smiley.*

She suddenly stopped thinking about the Land Rover because she had left the bathroom and was at the top of the stairs. 'Oh, dear Lord! I've forgotten Horatio! Now, where's my apron, oh, where is it? Artie, dear! Have you seen my apron? I must rescue Horatio!' She caught the sound of a deep, chuckly laugh from the kitchen.

'It's all right, my maid. I have the pea here. I've put him in a box.' Hannah was coming down the steep stairs quite quickly as Artie came out of the kitchen, holding a small box in his large hands. He saw her and said, 'Be careful, me dear. Those stairs are dangerous! You always come down them so fast... one day you'll fall! Let me help you.' Artie helped the old lady down the last few steps and put the box he was holding in her hand. 'Look, I found this little wooden box in the shed. It is just the right size for Horatio's pod. It fits in very neatly.'

Sure enough, when Han opened the box, there was Horatio inside his pod! Artie had put some cotton wool in first, then had placed the pod with its large pea and tiny relations on top. The lid slid on grooves and closed smoothly.

'What a fine home,' chortled Hannah. 'They'll be safe and sound in there. Joe will be pleased! Now, I'll get my coat and I'll hold the box in my hand until we get to the hospital. Oh, Artie, here's the Land Rover now... good!'

Chapter Eleven

*A*manda stood by the side of Joe's bed. She was staring at an empty bed. Joe was having a bath. Amanda was about twenty-eight years old. She was tall and very thin. Her face seemed shut. The eyes were dark brown and large, under beautiful arched eyebrows, but they were dead eyes. Amanda began to pull the sheets and blankets off the bed. She pulled them slowly and very carefully, then let them drop to the floor. She then picked up a pillow and held it close to her, swaying backwards and forwards, as if she were cradling a child. A sobbing sound was coming from her throat and her eyes were closed. Then, with savage movements, she tore at the pillow, ripping off the outer case and digging her nails into the material. The sobs grew louder and she crumpled to the floor.

Hannah stood in the doorway and watched the extraordinary scene. Her heart was beating fast and she was holding her breath. Suddenly there was silence. Amanda had somehow realised that someone was near. She got up, smoothed her apron, put her hands up to her cap and turned to look at Hannah. Hannah let out a long breath. Neither of them spoke. Amanda finally picked up the pillow, replaced its pillowcase and placed it on the chair. Han moved to Amanda, picked up the sheet and held it out to the nurse. They made up the bed together without

Chapter Eleven

uttering one word, and when Joe and Charlie returned from the bathroom, the small room was neat and tidy again. Amanda stared hard at the little old lady and left.

Joe looked pink and smelt of soap. 'Han, my dear, dear Han! Here you are! Have you brought Horatio?' Joe was so excited and eager. The right side of his face was newly bandaged, but the left side was visible and the skin glowed. He was full of energy. Hannah went to him and took his waving hands in hers. She leaned over and kissed him.

'Joe, I have Horatio and his family here in my pocket. He's in his pod in a box. Do you want to see him now?'

'Oh, yes, yes… but David needs to be here to see him too!' Joe moved his head to where he thought Charlie might be. 'Charlie, could you find David?'

'Well, I don't think I can do that, Joe,' answered Charlie. 'I believe he's working on another ward at this moment. You see, other children need him also,' Charlie continued.

'Joe means Dr Miles, Hannah. He lets Joe call him David. Maybe you could see Horatio now, Joe. The doctor is very busy.'

Joe replied quickly, 'All right, but please tell David that Horatio has arrived when you see him, Charlie. Han, let me feel Horatio.' Hannah placed the wooden box in Joe's outstretched hands. Immediately, the boy felt all round and over the smooth wood, finding the lid and sliding it back. He felt inside and took out the pod very carefully. 'Ooh, what a shiny skin! Is Horatio inside?'

'Yes,' said Hannah. 'Just open the pod and you will find him. He is very large!'

Joe's fingers found the pea and realised the size of it at once. 'Has there ever been a pea as huge as Horatio?' he whispered.

141

'Well, I've never seen one.' Hannah was smiling as she spoke. 'And I've lived a very long time. Horatio is a strong, gentle, handsome pea. He laughs a lot and is always having adventures. At the moment he is looking at you with a solemn face. He is hoping that you will like him. Meeting new people is a little strange, isn't it?'

Joe looked towards Hannah. 'Oh, I liked him as soon as I saw him,' said Joe. His face was rapt. 'Tell me, Han, does he like me?'

'Certainly! Most surely, little Joe. I'll ask him. Here, give me the pod house.' Hannah took the pod from Joe and spoke in a low voice. No one could hear what she said. Charlie was fascinated. She watched everything that went on with a growing sense of wonder. She was aware of the closeness of the two people, the young boy and the old lady. She breathed out, realising that she had been holding her breath. Joe heard her and said, 'Charlie, come and see Horatio… Han is talking to him.'

Charlie came near and stood with Joe as Hannah walked round the room with the pod held close to her ear and then to her mouth. She was smiling and chuckling. Then she stopped walking, sat down in the chair and said, 'Joe, Horatio says that you are a brave, fine young man. He would like to stay with you. He has a number of relations in the pod house. They need to have their mid-morning break, so would you please put him back in his box. He would like to stay on the table beside your bed. Come and get him now.' Joe moved directly to Hannah. He could not see where he was going, but he went straight to the chair and stretched out his hand. Hannah put the pod into his right palm. She took the box from her pocket and placed it in Joe's left hand. Joe moved to his bedside table and as he moved he was tucking the pod back into the wooden box. Charlie was amazed. The blind Joe walked with such confidence. He did not bump into the various pieces of furniture. He stepped over a pillow that was lying on the floor. He knew exactly what to do.

Chrissie and Jan arrived in the doorway. Hannah and Charlie glanced their way and Han put her finger to her lips, then indicated Joe. He said, 'Hello, people in the doorway. Who are you?'

Jan said quietly, 'It is Jan Dad and Mum, Joe. You look well. I like your bandage... very smart!'

'Have you seen Horatio and his relations, Mum?' Joe came round the bed to the doorway. Chrissie knelt down and kissed Joe's left cheek.

'Oh, yes, Joe, I've seen him. Isn't he splendid? Are you going to look after him now?'

'Well, for a short time. He may have to go with Hannah, but she'll be here now for a while.'

Hannah said, 'Joe, Horatio belongs to you now—'

Joe turned so fast that he nearly fell over. 'No, no, Han! He belongs to *all* of us! He should live with all of us, in our rooms. When can I come back to The Oak Tree Ho?'

Dr Miles heard the last words as he came into the room. He said, 'I don't know when you can go home Joe. Possibly early next week. We have to keep an eye on you over the weekend.'

'Do *you* only have one eye, David?' Joe asked. The Doctor laughed gently. 'I have two eyes, Joe, but I wear glasses, so maybe I should say I have four eyes!' Everyone laughed. 'Now, show me this extra ordinary Pea.'

'Oh dear!' said Joe. 'Horatio and his family are having their mid-morning Kit-Kats and orange juice. Could you wait a minute?'

David Miles was aware of the seriousness of the moment and he said having glanced quickly at all other faces around him, 'Yes, Joe, I'll come back in about half an hour. I would like to talk to your dad and mum, anyway. Now, you get up onto your bed and have a short rest, while the peas are finishing their snack. Would you like a drink and a chocolate biscuit?'

Charlie was speechless. She had always admired Dr David Miles; had known that he was a brilliant doctor, but she had never seen him smile much or even show the least sign of a sense of humour. She was staring at him with her mouth open when he looked at her and said, 'Charlie, close your mouth, dear, and pop off to the kitchen. There's some real orange juice and chocolate biccies on the table. Bring them back here. Quickly now!' And Charlie obeyed, at once!

David went on, now speaking to Jan and Chrissie. 'Shall we go to my office? We can have some coffee, etc. and talk.' He patted Joe's bottom and turned and walked out of the room. Jan and Chrissie followed. Hannah said, 'Up onto your bed now, Joe. Charlie will be here directly with our mid-mornings. How exciting! I wonder what kind of chocolate biscuits Dr David has brought us.'

'Oh, I do like that name, Hannah, Dr David. Oh, yes, indeed!' Joe sounded so grown up, Hannah thought. She was still sitting in the chair watching Joe and listening to him chattering on about the hospital, his bath, how hard his bed was, when Charlie came running in. She was quite out of breath. 'Och my! I really am very unfit! Blowing away like a Grampus – I'll tell you about a Grampus after you have had a drink and a wee snack,' said Charlie quickly, before Joe could ask the obvious question.

Chapter Twelve

Nah and Andrew were in the grocer's shop in Stroud, the one they always visited, owned by Mr Harding. It was a truly excellent shop, full of everything you could ever need, and lots more besides. Bess was with the vicar, Jay. The four of them had met in the church. They had been sitting and looking and listening when Jay had crept up and sat down behind them. Bess had suddenly turned round and had seen him. She had jumped and grabbed for Nah's hand. Jay had whispered, 'It's all right Bess. Don't be startled. It's only me.'

Nah had turned and smiled, and then the four of them had left the church. 'Where are you going?' asked Jay.

'Shopping,' said Andrew.

Bess was holding Jay's hand. She looked up at him and said, 'May I spend this day with you?'

The vicar looked inquiringly at Nah. She nodded, saying, 'What a good idea, Bess. It will be hot in Stroud.'

Andrew was surprised and said, 'Bess, don't you want to—'

Nah interrupted him. 'It will be exciting to spend the day at the vicarage with Jay, Janice and the brood. Have you anything planned for today, Jay?'

'Oh, yes,' answered Jay. 'We're going to attack the garden and clean out the rabbit hutches and runs.' (The vicar's family owned about ten rabbits.) 'You like the rabbits, don't you Bess?' Bess turned her beautiful eyes towards Jay. She looked so sad and withdrawn, but then she smiled at him and said, 'I love rabbits. May I help?'

'Of course you can, we could do with another pair of hands.'

Andrew added, 'And legs, if one of the buns gets away!' They all laughed and after lots of 'Goodbyes' they went their separate ways and now Nah and Andrew were in the grocer's shop. Inevitably, it was taking a very long time to do the shopping. Mr and Mrs Harding were great talkers. They knew all that went on in the village and, sure enough, they knew all about Joe and his operation.

'How is the wee lad?' asked Mrs Harding. 'Has he survived the ordeal? Can he see? Is he in pain?' The questions went on and on and on. Other shoppers had stopped choosing their groceries and were listening to Nah and Andrew as they tried to answer the enquires. At last the two of them staggered out of the shop with their shopping bags full, and scrambled into Nah's car.

'Oh dear, oh dear,' gasped Nah. 'I'm worn out! Let's go to the coffee shop and have a drink.'

'Oh, what a beautiful morning, oh what a beautiful day…' Artie was singing as he picked the veggies for lunch. He was proud of his veggies this year. They had come on well after the late frost and the carrots, potatoes and peas looked splendidly fit. He was working hard and fast, knowing that the Leigh family and Hannah and Nah would be back at The Oak Tree Ho at about one o'clock and lunch should be well on the way by then. He was going to cook lots of fresh veggies to go with special mince. Special mince had been

introduced into the family by Hannah years and years ago.
Then when Chrissie was old enough to cope with all the
various ingredients and the stove – when Chrissie was about
eight years old! – Han had taught Chrissie how to make it.
Special mince was a great favourite. It was sitting in the
fridge waiting to be taken up to The Oak Tree Ho.

Artie was talking to himself. 'Mashed potatoes, carrots
and peas – wait! Are we going to be able to eat peas? They
are clearly most important now that Horatio is with us. Ah,
well, I'll take them with me up to the house and wait for
Han to come back. I'll ask her. I'm feeling hungry already! I
love special mince!'

He picked up the basket of veggies and bounded up the
path just as the postman's van came up to the front gate. He
turned as he heard Tom, the postman, call out. 'Hey there,
Artie my old friend! I've some mail for you.'

'Have you any for Leighs?' called back Artie.

'Yes, I have. Are you seeing them today?' Tom opened
the gate and ran up the path. Tom ran everywhere!

'I'm going up The Oak Tree Ho directly. I'll take them,'
Artie said. He liked Tom. 'Have you time for a cuppa?' he
asked.

'Thank you, my friend. I would like a cuppa coffee,
made your way.'

Artie was a little puzzled. He frowned.

Tom went on: 'You know, all frothy on top.'

Artie's face cleared. 'Oh yes, surely! A poor man's cappuccino! I like them too!'

It seemed to be mid-morning snack time everywhere!
The two men disappeared into The Cottagey Ho nattering
about the state of the village cricket team and the pitch.

'We need more young players in the team,' Artie
sounded enthusiastic. He loved his cricket and the village

team was most important to him, and, indeed, to Hannah. She spent most of Sunday afternoons up at the ground, helping with the teas in the summer months. The children joined her to play their own game beyond the boundary with The brood and other village friends, and helped her and the other ladies to serve the teas to the players and spectators in the club house. Andrew said that he would like to join the village men's team when he was old enough. Andrew played a 'rare old game'. Artie had been training him for a number of years now.

Tom said, 'Maybe we ought to have a junior team and bring on young fellas like your Andy and his pals.'

'Yes, yes! A very good idea, old mate!' The voices died away as the two men disappeared into the kitchen and the breeze blew the back door shut.

Amanda was standing just inside the big gates of the hospital car park. She was standing behind one of the stone pillars. It seemed to her that this was a safe place, no one would be able to see her. She was wrong. Hannah was slowly washing and drying mugs and plates used for mid-mornings. She had been going through all the morning's happenings in her mind. Musing over some of them, she had moved to the window and looked out at the trees and up at the amazing blue of the sky and the few white wisps of cloud. The expression on her face was constantly changing as she recalled the reactions of the folk who had been Horatio and his family. Already, she had many stories about Horatio and his family running around her head. *Oh, how lovely it's going to be*, she thought, *how lovely! They'll be able to have marvellous adventures!*

Suddenly, she caught a glimpse of a movement by the pillars of the gate into the car park. She stopped drying the plate she was holding and stared hard at the gates. Yes, it was someone standing against the stone and her face seemed to be buried in her hands and arms? Hannah realised that the woman was deeply disturbed... she watched, standing absolutely motionless, willing her eyes to see what was happening. Was it Amanda, the nurse? Hannah put down the plate and tea towel and hurried out of the little kitchen, making her way as quickly as she could out of the building and across the car park towards the gates. It was surprising how fast Hannah could walk. She was not a young woman any more, but her mind and her spirit took her across distances as rapidly as anyone years younger than herself. She slowed down as she neared the gate pillars; yes, it was Amanda, and, yes, she seemed to be very disturbed. She was scraping her hands up and down the rough stones of the pillars. Hannah could hear small, sharp intakes of breath and cries as the jagged bits in the stones cut into her flesh.

'Amanda! Stop doing that!' It was an order. Hannah's words were clear and as sharp as those stones. 'Stop doing that, *now!*'

Amanda stopped. She did not turn around. Hannah moved quickly, took hold of Amanda's arms, turned her around and held her. Amanda was a tall woman and Han was very small, but this did not seem to matter. The poor, sad soul seemed to crumple, and if anyone had been watching this extraordinary incident, they would have seen the taller woman on her knees wrapped in the arms of this dear, gentle little lady, who seemed to be stroking her rumpled hair and talking quietly, yet quite urgently to her.

Hannah was saying, 'Dear, dear girl... try to breathe out

and be still... come now... try! No one is going to harm you... hurt you... be still... I'm here... I'm not going to leave you...'

Hannah felt Amanda tighten inside her arms, as the fearful woman pulled away from them. Hannah went down on her knees to get nearer to Amanda, but Amanda managed to avoid her. She scrambled to her feet and began to run towards a car, which was parked a few yards away. Han was left sitting on the ground without much breath left in her lungs. She had been cruelly jolted when Amanda had dragged herself away. She was unable to speak for a few seconds. Finally, she said in a strange, tiny voice... 'Oh, oh! Oh dear! Amanda, Mandy, let me help you...'

But Amanda did not hear her. She had started the car and was now driving towards the open gate of the car park.

Chapter Thirteen

'*H*e will be blind. It won't be easy for anyone, least of all Joe himself. There'll be help, of course. Would I be welcome if I came to The Oak Tree House?'

Chrissie had taken Jan's hand. They were both speechless. The news about Joe's blindness was still in their ears. Dr David had said, 'I'm sorry. I shouldn't have asked you about my visiting you. You must be shocked about Joe… I'm sorry.'

Chrissie got up still hanging onto Jan's hand, so he had to get up too. She said, 'Please, please come to see us, we need you.'

She suddenly began to cry and Jan held her close to him. He spoke over her shoulder. 'Dr David, you are a good man. Visit us whenever you wish. Yes, all of us will need your help. We shall need a great deal of guidance in the days to come. Blind… blind.' And Jan closed his eyes and buried his face in Chrissie's hair. When he opened them again and looked up, Dr David had gone.

Charlie met David Miles as she was coming out of another room down the corridor. 'Doctor, I need to speak to you…' Her voice trailed away as she saw that the man's eyes were full of tears. He just shook his head and walked swiftly on. She watched his back and wondered. 'What now?' she said, out loud, and hurried on, as she heard a voice call her. So much had happened in the last twenty-four hours – or was it more than a day? Or less? But she was now deeply involved with the Leigh family and all the other folk whom she had encountered and she vowed that she wouldn't lose them. She needed them in her life. She was not to know it then, but the Leighs and their friends needed her too, needed her very much!

Charlie heard the voice again. There were other children that needed help as well as Joe Leigh. She hurried into the room where the voice had come from. 'Now, now, Flora, here I am! Oh, look at you! Why are all your blankets on the floor? Come now, let's tidy you up. Did you think I'd forgotten you?'

Oh, dear! Charlie thought as she gave little Flora a hug. *That's exactly what I have done: forgotten the other wee patients! I must not think about those Leighs for the next few minutes!*

Chrissie stood in the doorway of David Miles' office watching Jan as he walked briskly down the corridor. He was going back to The Oak Tree Ho. She was calmer now. Jan was always able to make her feel more balanced. She knew so well that she had to be balanced. If she allowed herself to become unbalanced – if the extremes took over – it could be very disturbing for everyone, especially herself. All through her life she had had to cope with extreme feelings: extreme happiness, fear, anger, love. Extreme feelings had caused a great deal of trouble in her life. But it was not easy to stay balanced. Hannah used to say, 'Keep your scale equal, balanced, my dear. Look at every side of the problem. Just be still and think it all through carefully. I will help you… God will help you.' But it was so difficult! Where was Hannah? Chrissie realised that she must tell her about Joe. Where was she? Who else should she tell? Nah? Of course… yes, Nah. She hadn't seen Artie this morning. Oh yes! Hannah had told Jan and herself when they had gone to fetch the two old folk from The Cottagey House that Artie was going to stay and prepare the lunch for them all. He would probably be at The Oak Tree Ho now. Chrissie glanced at her wristwatch. 11.30 a.m. She must make a plan of campaign: find Hannah; phone Artie to tell him that Jan was on the way home. She couldn't get in touch with Nah – she could be anywhere – but that was all right as Nah would be going back to The Oak Tree Ho for lunch. Andrew was sure to be with her. Chrissie stopped writing her list. The children were in safe hands… they had such good, kind friends. *Andrew, Bess and Bibi are fine. First, I must find Han.*

Han was still down by the gate of the car park. She had been trying to get up. When Amanda had pushed her away, Hannah had jolted her back quite badly and every time she struggled to get to her feet, her spine hurt. Way back, when she was younger, she had hurt her pelvis. She had slipped on some ice outside a shop, fallen and broken her pelvis. She had been in hospital for a long time. It was an extraordinary time for the little lady. She had been very frightened and had become very ill. So much so, that everyone thought the she might die. Hannah had seemed to lose her faith, her will to live. Chrissie had been directing a play and had not known about the accident until Jan managed to track her down. The days spent at the hospital, sitting by Hannah's bed watching her slip away from them were desperate. Finally, when they all thought that there was no hope, a ward sister had come into the room and had suddenly said, in a crisp, no nonsense way… 'Are you just going to let her go? I think she wants to go on living in this world. There is still a great deal that she has to accomplish. Talk to her, coax her spirit and mind back to you and your family. Go on! Don't just sit there gaping at me, girl! She has done everything for you all through your life; help *her* for a change!'

And that's exactly what Chrissie had done. She picked up Hannah's hand, her beautiful, gnarled, work-worn hand, and began to smooth and stroke it, all the time talking to her, gently, yet with increasing energy, just as Han had done so often in the past to herself and Kel and Fred, her brothers. Gradually, gradually, Chrissie had felt the little hand in hers move and return the pressure, and gradually Hannah had come back into their world, into a world that was even more important to Hannah than it had been before the accident. It was after this fearful time that Han had met Artie in Cheltenham.

Hannah was hanging onto the gatepost, forcing herself to stand up, when she heard someone say, 'Here, old girl, let me help you. How on earth did you manage to be down there? Up you get!' And a couple of strong, warm hands were under her arms and lifting her to her feet! She was then picked up and carried to a shining sports car and carefully placed on the bonnet. 'Ooh,' squealed Hannah, for the bonnet was hot. 'Ooh, that's warm!' She was looking into a handsome, tanned face. A smiling pair of eyes was looking at her. Han forgot her precipitous position on the car bonnet and smiled back. The young man was continuing to hold her... she felt safe and a bubble of a laughter burst out of her. They laughed together... laughed and laughed. The man picked her up from off the bonnet and put her into the passenger seat. He said, when he could speak. 'You were having a rare old time, trying to stand up! I wondered if you had been on the bottle. You haven't been boozing, have you old dear?' But before Hannah could even shake her head, he added, 'No, of course you haven't!' His face became more serious. 'Tell me what happened. How did you fall? What made you fall? I can't imagine that you wanted to be on the ground!'

Hannah blew her nose on one of her sparkling white hankies, took a breath or two, and answered. 'I just… just tripped and fell.'

'Oh, come now… that's not the truth, is it?' chuckled the young man.

'No. However, it is a private matter and I don't know who you are, and if we are going to be friends, let's have less of the old girl, please!' Hannah twinkled up at the handsome face. The man knelt down and looked deep into Hannah's eyes. She felt very safe with him. She seemed to recognise him. 'Who are you?' she asked.

'I'm a doctor. I'm visiting the hospital. I have to see a lad who has had an eye operation. A pal of mine asked me to see him.'

'Why?' asked Hannah.

'I seem to be able to help people who are blind, or will be blind.' The young doctor stood up and closed the car door. He walked round to the driver's side, opened the door and slid in. Hannah noticed the length of the legs; he was a very tall man! Then, Hannah shivered; it was a strange kind of shiver, a complete body shudder, and she seemed to gasp.

'What is it?' The man turned towards her and took her hands.

'Is the lad's name Joe Leigh?' she asked breathlessly.

'Sanders-Leigh,' answered the doctor. 'Do you know him?'

Hannah sighed. 'Yes, I know him. So, he will be blind.' It was a flat statement. No emotion. She looked steadily at the man. 'Tell me your name, please. I believe that you and I are going to become friends.'

'I am Benedict Taylor.' The voice was deep and warm. 'Shall I drive you up to the door of the hospital?' Hannah replied, 'Thank you, but no. I must walk… will you walk with me? I have to talk with you.' Benedict opened the door and got out of the car. He came round to Hannah and lifted here bodily from the low sports car. 'You are an exciting man!' she gasped. He put her down onto her two feet, but held her very carefully. 'A lovely man as well,' Han added.

Chrissie saw Hannah being lifted out of the sports car. She had been told that Hannah had been seen going down to the Gate of the car park – what had happened? Her heart seemed to miss a beat… No! Not Hannah! Nothing must happen to Hannah! She called out: 'What are you doing? Is Han hurt?'

Benedict looked up to see a figure running towards them, with wild eyes. 'No, no, don't worry, everything's fine!'

But Chrissie took no notice of him. She ran to Hannah and knelt down reaching for her hands. 'Han, Han, are you all right? What happ—?'

Hannah spoke quickly, 'Chrissie, hush now! Benedict has been taking care of me. Come along with us. We are going to see Joe. Benedict is going to help him. Does Joe know that he will be blind? Now get up and help me back to Joe's room.' Chrissie stood up and looked up at Benedict and then down at Hannah. She suddenly felt exhausted… so much was going on around her. *I can't cope*, she thought.

Hannah patted Chrissie's cheek. She said calmly, 'Now, Mr Benedict, help me to walk back to the hospital and we will introduce you to Joe Sanders-Leigh. Chrissie, Benedict is going to be very useful…' and she told Chrissie what Benedict had told her.

Chapter Fourteen

*B*ess was sitting in the vicarage garden, surrounded by rabbits. Rabbits: large, furry ones; small, silky coated ones – all shapes and sizes. The brood had asked her to look after the little animals. Jay had told them when Bess had been walking around the rabbit run and carefully counting the buns, that they should 'be careful' with Bess. 'Organise her gently… be sure that one of you is always near her, but try not to hassle her. OK?' They said 'OK' in answer and winked at their father.

The brood consisted of four children; two boys and two girls at that moment. Two more boys, twins, were away at camp. They were older than the others – fourteen – and wanted to do grown up things.

Janice was calling: 'Brood! Bess! There's a cold drink and some biscuits here in the kitchen!'

Tom the elder of the four, called back, 'OK, Ma, we're coming!' He looked at Bess. 'Would you like a drink and a biscuit, Bess?'

Bess shook her head. She had picked up a jet black rabbit and was slowly stroking it. Bear was sitting on the grass next to her. 'No, thank you, Tom. It's nearly lunch time and I must be getting home.' Tom had never heard Bess say so many words before.

'I think you're staying with us for lunch… aren't you?'

Bess again shook her head. 'No. I have to be back because I have to do lots this afternoon.'

Tom was confused. He said, 'I'll go and ask Ma... she'll tell me. OK?' He ran off and Bess wondered why they all kept saying 'OK'.

The rabbits seemed to know that their run had been cleaned and they were moving back there. Bess watched the creatures as they hopped and jumped along. She stood up, still holding the black bunny. She talked quietly to them...

Tom had stopped and turned round to look back at this strange, private little girl and he saw her leading a long line of animals as they wound their way through the trees, back to their run. 'Wow! What do yer know! I've never known the buns to follow us like that!' He shut his eyes and opened them again quickly. Bess and the rabbits were now out of sight! He scratched his head, and then ran into the kitchen.

Nah enjoyed the last drop of coffee, then said to Andrew, who was finishing his chocolate biscuit, 'Now then, Andy dear, I think I shall phone the hospital and find out what's going on. Chrissie may need a lift home. Do you think that's a good idea?'

Andrew looked at his watch. 'It's nearly a quarter to twelve. We seemed to have been here for ages. I really like those biscuits, Nah. I wonder where they bought them... Oh! Sorry! You asked me a question about Mum. Shall I telephone the hospital?'

Nah thought that was a very good idea, so Andrew went to the phone box which was not far from the coffee shop, whilst Nah took the groceries to her car. She was just closing the boot when she heard running feet and Andrew arrived. He gasped, 'Yes, Mum and Hannah would be glad of a lift home as Dad has taken the Land Rover. He has to make plans for tomorrow... I wish I were going with him, I love Cornwall. And he's going to my favourite place: Falmouth!'

Nah smiled at him. 'You and I will go, as soon as everything becomes more peaceful, Andy. It will do us good to get away. I think we keep each other calm!' They laughed and Andrew felt very happy. He loved Nah dearly.

They arrived at the hospital to find Chrissie and Hannah waiting for them. They saw the two ladies standing on the steps by the front door. They were deep in conversation. Andrew said, 'Look, Nah, there they are, still talking. I expect we shall hear all about their morning... I wonder if we will be able to get a word in!' And again they laughed.

It took them about twenty minutes to get home and, strangely, not much was said on the journey. It was now the hottest time of day; the sun was at its highest. It blazed down on the little car as it bowled along the road back to the village. Andrew had managed to tell Chrissie and Hannah about the shopping and the coffee shop, but then silence descended on the four people. There was a great deal of thinking going on inside that car. Nah drove smoothly and the silence seemed soothing.

'Joe will be blind.' The words had been spoken by Hannah. They dropped into the silence so easily. There was no response from the other three for minutes – it seemed like minutes. Then Nah said, 'Does Joe know that he will be blind?'

Chrissie said, 'Yes.'

The car purred down the hill into the village, on to the oak tree at the gates of the drive and up to the old house. Nothing more had been said. As they slowed down on nearing the garage area behind the house, they saw Jan and Artie walking out of the back door. Artie waved. Andrew realised that his legs had gone numb with tension. The car had stopped and the others had got out, but he was unable to move. Artie opened the door and said, 'Come on, me old mate, let me help you. Legs won't work, eh?' And Andrew felt himself being lifted out of the car and carried into the kitchen. He felt so weak and silly. 'I'm sorry, Artie…' His voice did not belong to him, it was all croaky.

Artie settled Andrew in the armchair by the fire. The boy felt as if all his bones had gone floppy. He felt filleted, like a fish without its bones! He looked around for Hannah. She was sitting on a stool opposite him. She looked far away. He stared hard at her, willing her to look at him and suddenly, she lifted her hand to brush away a stray piece of hair from over her face. She smiled and said, 'Now then, my dears, it's special mince time. Come along! I don't know about you people, but I'm very hungry. What about you gentlemen looking after us ladies?'

The atmosphere changed in an instant. Andrew glanced towards the kitchen table. He saw the gleaming glasses, the jug of water, the plates and brightly coloured serviettes. He closed his eyes and when he opened them again, everything seemed lighter and clearer. The voices were steady and the words spoken were bright and cheery. *I think Hannah must be an Angel sent from God to the world*, thought Andrew. He joined the family and the meal began.

Chrissie put down her fork and took in a deep breath. She held it for a second or so and then let it all out slowly. She looked at the faces around the table. Dearest Hannah finishing a carrot, chasing it as it slithered on the plate, then finally helping it onto her fork with a finger. Bess had eaten her minute amount of mince, mashed potato and carrots.

Chapter Fourteen

She looked relaxed, but she looked isolated, as if she were in a box. Andrew was talking to Artie about Horatio; Nah and Jan had eaten in silence, as had she. Chrissie spoke silently. *Oh God, how I love these dear people! Please let us be strong and be able to help Joe when he comes home. He will need such care and gentleness.* She heard Nah say, 'Coffee? Or have you a surprise afters for us, Artie?'

'No, no afters, just some special chocolate biccies. Hope that's OK.'

It was Jan who answered first. 'Certainly it is OK, my friend, very OK!' Jan was very fond of chocolate biscuits.

'Right, then!' Artie stood up and went to the fridge. He took out a plate of very interesting-looking biscuits.

'Wow! They look great, Artie!' squeaked Andrew and even Bess looked interested.

It had been a good meal… a good time for everyone. Nah and Chrissie were sitting in the garden, in the shade of a maple tree. They had been quietly discussing future plans; the return of Joe, naturally, but they had also talked about Jan's work in Cornwall. He had told Chrissie that he would have to leave about three o'clock the next day. It would be a long journey. Jan was due to meet his producer and other members of his team on Monday. They had a great deal to talk about and many decisions had to be made. Jan was to direct a new play for BBC 2. The writer would be arriving as well. It would be a busy time. Jan was becoming well known; he had also been offered a film.

'It all happens at once. I wonder why?' Chrissie looked at Nah, expecting a reply, but Nah was asleep. 'My dearest friend, you do so much for us. I love you.' She bent and kissed Nah's cheek, put their empty coffee cups on the tray and began to walk back up the path to the house.

Gradually she was aware of a kind of whispery sound coming from behind a clump of bushes. She stopped to listen. It was Bess! She strained to hear the words, but Bess must have seen her or heard her footsteps, for the voice stopped and there was a rustling sound as the child moved from behind the shrubs. Chrissie watched her run across the grass and away into the orchard. She had Bear with her. He was wearing a jacket and trousers, his travelling clothes. Hannah, Chrissie and Nah had made lots of clothes for Bear. He had his own small suitcase where they were kept. Chrissie stood and watched the tiny figure disappear into the trees. Then she heard a whicker. It was White Star welcoming Bess. *Oh, that's fine*, thought Chrissie, *Bess will be safe with the pony*, and she walked on up to the house.

Jan was in his study making final travel plans. Chrissie tapped on the door and heard him say, 'Come.' She was never sure about the way he said 'Come' in this flat, stern voice. It made her think of school. Her headmistress had always used this word whenever any of the boys and girls had knocked on her study door. It was really quite scary! But Jan was not Miss Rees, the headmistress; he was her dear, dear man and he was going away and she needed to be near him as much as possible before he went.

Chrissie pushed the door open, and there was Jan sitting at his beautiful desk, his head bent forward, his right elbow resting on the polished wood. His blond hair had fallen over his hand. Jan had let his hair grow quite long and Chrissie loved the way he tossed his head and the hair flew. Often, when he was seated, his hair fell in different directions as he moved this way and that, picking up books and pens and pencils and changing his position. He was not aware that

Chrissie had come into the room and was watching him. She heard him sigh and say, 'I wonder why everything happens at the same time. I don't want to go away tomorrow.'

Chrissie closed the door and Jan turned around sharply. She smiled at him and said, 'That's just what I said – why does everything happen at once! Darling, I don't want you to go away tomorrow. However, it has to be, so let's make sure that you have all you need. We'll be fine here. Nah is staying until the end of July and you know how marvellous Hannah and Artie will be. Maybe the five of us should have a special meeting this evening after dinner in the music room. We can discuss the days ahead of us. Joe should be home by the middle of next week. It won't be difficult looking after him and I know that there'll be a great deal of help coming from the hospital. Dr David and Charlie are splendid people and they seem to like us. I'll be in touch with them each day. I must know that *you* are all right, that you are safe and well. Please phone me as often as you can.'

Jan took her hand and pulled her to him, holding her close. Chrissie slowly ran her fingers through his hair. She felt the strong softness and there were sudden tears in her eyes. This lovely man was so important, so dear. They had been through many problems and difficult, fearful times together over the years and their love was deep and was growing. They had vowed that they would always try to talk and tell each other their joys and fears. They laughed and cried together. There had been a time when they had nearly lost this love… a time when there was darkness and panic, but that is another story.

Jan lifted his head and gazed into Chrissie's brimming eyes. He gently covered them with his hand and then touched her lips with his fingers. He spoke so quietly that she only just caught the words. 'I'll be sending you so many thoughts when I'm away. I shall send strength and laughter to Joe and Han and the children and, well, everyone. You are so special to me… don't worry, I will be back very quickly!' Jan was looking deep into Chrissie's eyes, into her soul, it seemed. She pulled his face closer and they kissed, full of keen awareness of each other.

Suddenly, they heard a car coming up the drive and the sound of singing. Jan took Chrissie's hand and they moved to the window. Looking out, they saw the Sophia Lady and Bibi. The car was moving very slowly, the windows were open and the sounds were pouring out into the evening sunshine. Bibi had seen Jan and Chrissie and she waved and sang even louder: 'Frarer Jacker, frarer Jacker, dormay voo, dormay voo! Hello, you two, up there! We're back! I'm hungry!'

Jan looked at Chrissie and raised his eyes to heaven. 'So, here is Bibi again. I had quite forgotten her. You go down and try to organise her, darling. It's nearly her bedtime, isn't it?' He smiled at Chrissie and pushed her carefully towards the door. She kissed him again and then left the room and ran downstairs.

The Oak Tree House was resting. The children were in bed, or certainly, in their rooms. The sun was hanging in the sky; it looked weary of the day, soon it would disappear. There was such stillness. A near perfect evening.

Nah was gazing out of her window. She was leaning on the windowsill, gazing out in the distance. She loved this house and as for the people, well, they were hers. That's how it seemed. She knew them well, loved them so much! She was aware of peace around her, but somewhere deep inside her, there was a strange feeling of concern. *How silly*, she thought. *Everything will be fine. Hannah and Artie are here. Joe will be coming home, the other children seem to have settled. We shall be able to cope with whatever happens.* But still Nah felt a pang of worry. *Oh, come on, you daft woman! Get on down to the music room and have a drink. The special meeting will be starting soon.*

Nah met Hannah at the bottom of the stairs, carrying a tray of glasses. Nah said, 'Oh, Han, I'll take those for you. Are you going to have your usual, whisky and warm water?'

'Thank you, Nah,' answered Han, 'but just a small one, please. I'm rather tired and I shall fall asleep, if I'm not careful!' She twinkled up at Nah and went back to the kitchen. Nah found the others, Jan, Chrissie, Artie and Sophia, in the music room. Nah was pleased to see Sophia. Sophia was a very wise person. She understood about the problems of living because she herself had had many problems. Nah put down the tray of glasses on the drinks' table and crossed to Sophia and gave her a hug. 'It's so good to see you, Sophia. Are you still in one piece after having Bibi all day?'

Sophia laughed. 'We had a grand day... what an amazing child! She needs a lot of attention and that is what I was able to give her. She also needs to sleep. The energy she uses when she is awake! Phenomenal!' And she laughed again.

Nah adored Bibi, but she found her exhausting. 'Sophia, may I come and talk to you about Bee? I find her fascinating, but I am never really sure how to handle her.'

Sophia patted Nah's cheek. 'Oh, you just need to love her and treat her like an equal. But she needs to know that there are good ways and bad ways of behaving and that she is not the most important person in the world. She is special, though, isn't she? Come to lunch tomorrow.'

Chapter Fifteen

The meeting went well. They exchanged information and suggestions. Jan told them that he would be away for about four days, that he was leaving after lunch the next day, Sunday, July 1st. Sophia agreed to take over Bibi as much as possible. Hannah and Artie said that they would be around to cook and tend the garden etc, etc. Chrissie would be free to do whatever was needed. Nah would do all the driving, taking Andrew to school and fetching him in the afternoon. The next day, Sunday, would be a splendid day. They could all go to church in the morning, then go to visit Joe in the afternoon after a family lunch. They must find out when Joe was coming home. If he continued to get stronger and his eye was stable, he should be back on Wednesday. Nah and Hannah would go to the hospital and bring him back to The Oak Tree House... *and then it will be Thursday and Jan will be home*, thought Chrissie.

There was a sudden silence. Chrissie looked at all the faces in the room. It was gradually getting dark and there were shadows in the room. She sighed and Nah glanced at her. She smiled and sighed also. Maybe she had no need to worry. Pippin pushed the door open and ambled across the floor. She lay down on the rug and stretched, making squeaky sounds. Hannah chuckled and fondled Pippin's head. Pippin always lay close to Han whenever possible. Artie stood up. 'Come along, my maid. It's time you laid

Chapter Fifteen

your head down. It's been a very, very long day – no, don't argue. Off we go.' And he helped Hannah out of her chair. They wished everyone a goodnight, a peaceful night. There were lots of 'God blesses' and then silence reigned again.

Upstairs, Andrew was writing his journal. Bibi, surrounded by bears and rabbits, was fast asleep and talking now and then or singing. Bess was standing in the middle of her room checking that all was prepared for her journey to Cornwall. Her small case was packed. Bear was ready, dressed in his travelling clothes. Bess had laid her clothes on the end of her bed. She crossed to her table where she kept her moneybox and slowly opened it and took out the money. *There is enough here*, she thought. *I shall have to be careful, but I think I shall manage.*

Bess had so many secrets. Nobody really knew anything about her. They were beginning to find out some things, and the police and other authorities were constantly searching for her family… parents? Andrew felt certain that he would be able to start asking more questions soon. Bess seemed to be trusting him. She held his hand now and even allowed herself to be hugged at times.

Little Bess was much more capable than anyone realised, however. When she had lived with her father, she had looked after him well in her own way. She could prepare him easy meals – that was the name he gave to boiled eggs and toast, tea and a piece of cake or a chocolate biscuit or cereals. She could travel by bus by herself and shop in the local shop near where they had lived. She knew about money and that she must be sure that she never spoke to strangers or accepted lifts from strange people. Bess was capable of a great deal and now she was determined to find her father. She picked up the letter that she had written for Andrew. It had taken her a long time to write:

Please do not worry.I shall telephone you.

Using a telephone really worried her. When she decided to stop speaking to people, her throat seemed to close up. There seemed to be a kind of barrier that made her voice stay way down in her throat. Speaking on a telephone was very difficult, even now that she had begun to talk again. Sometimes she had picked up the receiver on the phone downstairs, but she just could not make the words come out of her mouth. So she had put the receiver back. But now that she had told Andrew that she would telephone him she would have to make the words clear. She looked at the letter. She read the message out loud.

'I will telephone you when I have arrived.I will be safe.I know where I am going. YOU MUST NOT TELL ANYONE.'

She thought the big letters looked fine and she smiled and smoothed them with her fingers. She looked at the last words she had written. These were special words for Andrew. He never forgot them. Bess spoke them in a whisper. 'I love you.' She spoke them again. 'I love you, my Andy.' She folded the letter. She then wrote, '**Andrew**', in small letters on the envelope and went to the boy's room and slipped it under the door. Andrew, by this time, was asleep and did not hear the scuffly sound as the paper slid under the wood of the heavy door.

The next day was sunny again. The family awoke to the most beautiful morning. The sky was cloudless and the birds were singing as if to say, 'Oh, please get out of bed and look at the world, our world, your world!'

It was six o'clock and Artie had been up for about an hour! He loved the early mornings, no matter what season it was or whether it was cold or hot or raining or snowing. He loved the feel of the new air on his face and often he was to be found standing in the garden of The Cottagey House or in the lane – anywhere really. It was the time he had a chat with his Lord. It was a 'pure time' he told people. 'Our pure time. God's and mine.' This morning, he was leaning on the gate leading into the lane that led up to The Oak Tree House. He watched a squirrel race up a tree and he was aware of two magpies staring at him. He said, 'Good morning, my friends, have a fine day. I'm looking forward to my day – so much to do. I'll see you again.' And he turned and walked jauntily up the path to the kitchen door, singing quietly as he went.

The Oak Tree House was also awake, but the people were still in their rooms. The house was full of little sounds; it was awake, and very busy. Bess was also very much awake. She was standing in the middle of her room, and like Artie, she was looking at her special friends. She loved this room, it was her safe place. She could be herself here. She was a neat little soul. Everything had to be in its own place. Her father had taught her to be careful, to organise her mind. The only way that he could live was to be organised, so that he did not have too much time to think about his beautiful little wife. This had rubbed off on to Bess. She looked at Bear. He was standing with a paw on her case. Bess smiled and said in a whisper, 'I'm going to put on my old play clothes for this morning, Bear. After lunch, I will change into my travelling clothes. Nobody must know that we are going away. You won't tell them, will you?' It was extraordinary, but Bear looked as if he were smiling.

The morning passed quickly and before Chrissie could think too much about not having Jan at home it was the afternoon and everyone was outside ready to say goodbye to him. Bibi was jumping up and down and singing, 'See you soon, come back soon, see you soon!' On and on! Hannah suggested that she mouthed the words, and, thankfully, Bee thought that would be fun.

Andrew and Artie had helped Jan pack his belongings into the Land Rover and they were all standing on the driver's side. They did not see Bess climb carefully and, oh so quietly into the back and crawl under the rugs. She was behind the back seat. Lots of rugs and cushions were kept here. The rear door had been left open. All the doors were opened whenever anyone or the whole family was going away. Then the doors were closed by various travellers.

'So,' Jan sighed, 'I must leave. I will phone you from different places.' He kissed Chrissie and Han and Nah. Lifted Bee high in the air and finally gave Andrew a hug. He did not notice that Bess was not there. During the time that the little girl had been with the Leighs, she was often not there. She was such a quiet, still person that, unfortunately, others didn't always register her. Today, it was fortunate for her that they did not think about her! She was holding her breath under the rugs and it was very hot. She heard the engine burst into life and the voices calling, 'Goodbye! Goodbye! Safe journey.' The Land Rover moved forward and they were off down the drive. No one had seen her. 'Thank you, God!' Bess whispered into Bear's furry head, and breathed out.

Bibi ran after the Land Rover, waving her arms and rushing around in circles until she fell and hurt her knees.

Artie said, 'It's all right, I'll rescue her!'

Nah, Chrissie and Hannah looked at each other and said, practically together, 'Tea!'

Andrew and Pippin were walking in the orchard. He was telling her about the visit to Joe that afternoon. The dog's ears moved and she kept looking up at the boy as he told her that Joe was a brave fellow and seemed to be managing his bandages and his blindness well. Hannah had told Joe the first Horatio story. Andrew had listened, it had been fascinating. Han had described Horatio and his Relations and his pod home, the colours, the shapes, but Joe had known the shapes; he had felt the pod and Horatio thoroughly!

The story had been wonderful! 'Hannah is brilliant at telling stories. She talks to *you*, doesn't she, Pippin Dog?' Pippin smiled. 'Han is going to tell a daily Horatio story to Joe. I need to hear them as well. I must tell Bess.' Bess had not gone to the hospital to see Joe. Chrissie thought it would be wiser if she went to church with Janice and the brood and stayed to lunch with them. They had brought her back to The Oak Tree House just as the rest of them arrived back from the hospital. He stopped. Where was Bess? He hadn't seen her for ages. 'Come on, let's find Bess! She must hear these stories as well!' Andrew turned and began to run back to the house, closely followed by Pippin. But although he searched and searched he couldn't find Bess. You see, there was a small rug inside the door of Andrew's bedroom and Bess' note had hidden itself under this rug! He had not found the envelope!

Andrew ran into the kitchen where Hannah and Nah were chatting over a cup of tea. They looked up at him. He was breathless and his face was red. 'Have you seen Bess?'

Nah shook her head. 'No. Why? You're very hot, Andy.

Is there a problem?' Nah's heart had missed a beat. She recalled her concern earlier in the day. Bess! Had something happened to Bess?

Hannah stood up and carefully pushed her chair under the table. She put her hand into her apron pocket and took up a small white envelope, which she held out to Andrew. 'I found this under the rug in your room. It has your name on it.' Han's voice was steady and gentle. Andrew opened the envelope. The two women watched him. His face was tight. He raised his eyes and they saw fear in them. Han said, 'Please read us the note, Andrew.'

The boy didn't reply. He was staring into space, then he turned and rushed out of the kitchen. Nah and Hannah heard his footsteps on the stairs, they heard him running along the upstairs passage and then there was a bang as Andrew shut the door of his bedroom.

The boy was leaning heavily on the door. He was reading the words out loud:

> 'Please do not be concerned. I shall telephone you. I will telephone you when I have arrived. I will be safe. I know where I am going. YOU MUST NOT TELL ANYONE. I love you. I love you, my Andy.'

Andrew's legs seemed to crumble under him. He slid down the door and sat heavily on the floor. Nah and Hannah heard a dull thud. They had not spoken when Andrew had hurtled out of the kitchen. Nah was still sitting at the table and Hannah had washed up the two cups and saucers. They both looked up. There was silence, but not for long. Hannah spoke. 'It's best that we don't go near Andy for a while. Yes, there is a problem. It appears to be his problem at the moment. He will need us when he has decided what to do next.' She dried her hands, walked to the backdoor and went out into the yard. Pippin lifted her head, stood up, stretched and followed Hannah.

Nah sat transfixed. She realised that she felt absolutely calm and that her head was as clear a crystal. She listened to her own voice. 'Crystal.' She spoke the word aloud. 'I must polish the glasses for dinner this evening. Yes, crystal.'

'I love you, my Andy…' The words kept repeating themselves inside Andrew's brain. He was till sitting on the floor with his back to the door. Gradually, he moved onto his knees and scrambled to his feet. *Where is Bess? Where has she gone? She could be anywhere! Oh, God! God! What am I going to do? What shall I do?* He fell towards his bed and lay there sobbing. His specs had fallen off and he could not see for tears.

After what seemed like hours, he stopped crying and lay there exhausted. *I am going to find you, Bess. You've made me angry… angry because I love you so much. You should have told me where you were going. I would have helped you.* Andrew stopped the flow of words. No, he wouldn't have helped her to go away. He would probably have asked Jan for advice. Bess clearly needed to do what she was doing, she needed to do it desperately. Andrew was breathing in a regular, controlled pattern again. His mind was beginning to clear. He went to his desk and picked up a pencil. He carefully wrote:

PLANS

Search in Bess' bedroom for clues.

Think hard where she might have gone.

'Hospital… casualty… hosp— she was frightened of the hospital casualty area.' Andrew was talking, out loud. 'Why was she so scared? What about her family? Mum will know about her family – has she a family?' What a puzzle Bess was!

There was a tap on Andrew's bedroom door. 'Andrew? Are you in there?' It was Chrissie. 'May I come in?'

'Oh, yes! I need to talk to you, Mum! Please come in!' and he quickly opened the door and said, 'Have you found Bess? Have you seen her?'

Chrissie could tell at once that Andrew was extremely worried. 'No. We have looked everywhere and we haven't found her.' Chrissie waited for a reaction from the boy; he was staring at his lists of plans. She went close to him and looked over his shoulder at the paper. 'What are you doing, Andy? Do you know anything about Bess? If you do, you must tell us.'

Andrew's face was stricken. 'I can't tell you... I don't know anything. Just that she will be safe... she has gone away, but I don't know where she's gone.' He put his hand into his pocket and felt the envelope, the secret note. He mustn't say any more; Bess had asked him not to tell anyone. He had already said too much. Before Chrissie could speak, he went on, 'Mum, do you know anything at all about Bess' mum and dad, about her family?'

Chrissie had been watching her son closely. She was very concerned, but she felt that she must answer the questions that Andrew had asked her before she did anything else. 'We only know that she was found wandering about Falmouth. She could not, or would not, tell us anything about herself, where she had come from, or if she lived in Falmouth, why she was there; nothing. We did meet a lady who said that she thought she'd seen Bess walking up Church Street with a man. She had noticed the way the man was talking to the little girl with him, how they were laughing and seemed so happy. She had also registered how beautiful the child was, it was her eyes, she said.'

Andrew interrupted her. 'Where did you meet this lady?'

'At the police station. After we went to the children's home to see Bess, back here we popped into the police station to have a word with the policeman who had taken Bess to the home. The police in Cornwall have been looking everywhere, trying to find out more about her. We were in touch with them every day. They've found out nothing. If the man with Bess was her father, do you think she has run away from here, to look for him?'

Andrew did not reply, but he was thinking fast. *Yes, yes, maybe! Dad was motoring to Cornwall... was she in the Land Rover? When did she get in? No one had seen her, but then, sometimes they forgot her! Oh God!*

Chrissie was shaking him. 'Andrew! Andy! Look at me! What are you thinking? Tell me! We must find her!'

Andrew pulled away from her and rushed out of the room, nearly colliding with Hannah who was standing in the passage outside.

Chrissie called, 'Andrew! Stop! Do you hear me? *Stop!*'

Hannah moved to her and took her hands. 'No, Chrissie, darling! Leave him! He must do what he has to do. He must do what Bess has asked him to do. The little girl is all right... safe. I don't have a bad feeling about her. Let the boy alone. He will find her.'

Chrissie was appalled. 'Hannah! What are you saying? He can't find her on his own!'

'No. He will come to us. When he's ready,' replied Hannah.

But Chrissie was not listening. She turned and began to run down the stairs. She was calling, 'Andrew! Where are you going? I *must* talk to you... please, wait for me!'

However, Andrew had rushed out of the house and was

making his way through the orchard. He had to be on his own to decide what he had to do. His breath was coming in gasps now and he suddenly tripped and fell heavily into the long grass near an apple tree. He lay there sobbing. *Why did he have to react like this? Why couldn't he be calm and just discuss everything with the others? Because he loved Bess so much? Because she had written in those big letters? 'YOU MUST NOT TELL ANYONE'.* They seemed to be such important words.

Andrew had gradually begun to realise that Bess was not as young as the others thought. She seemed to be very positive. Positive was a word that Jan used often. He had told his son that to be positive was to be really grown up. *Oh, all these words! It was so difficult to understand sometimes! So difficult to know what to do and how to do it!* He buried his face in the long grass and felt little insects move across his cheek. He smelt the sweet, tangy smell of the grass. He breathed steadily and he whispered, 'Father God, help me, please tell me what to do, somehow, tell me.'

Hannah stood still with her eyes closed. She heard Chrissie's words, she heard her running down the stairs and she heard her feet on the gravel outside the back door. She stood where she was for a long time.

Nah had heard everything as well. She had seen Andrew rush out of the house and run into the orchard. She had been in the shed where the Leighs kept the garden furniture and lots of bits and pieces. Nah was worried. So her concern earlier in the day had been right. The disappearance of Bess was most disturbing. Certainly something must be done, but what? Another meeting? Oh dear! She felt suddenly weak and tired. She spoke out loud, 'Good for nothing, I am, at the moment, I must sit down.' And that's what she did until Artie came into the shed to get a spade; he found Nah asleep on a pile of sacks!

'Oh! My dear soul! What have we got here?'

Nah opened her eyes and smiled at the old man. 'Hello, Artie. How are you?' Nah sat up quickly. 'Oh! What am I doing here? I should be looking for Bess!'

Artie took her hand and helped her to her feet. Nah staggered for a second but Artie held her in his strong arms and her mind cleared. He said, 'What's going on? What about Bess?' And when Hannah walked into the shed Nah was telling Artie all she knew about the Bess happenings.

Actually, Chrissie had not looked for Andrew. After she had rushed after him, she had decided to look for Bess in the village and the lanes. She took her car and was still searching and asking questions. She was, at the time of Nah's awakening, driving slowly up the lane leading to the riding stables. Bess had always found horses friendly. She spent a good deal of time with animals, her quiet, gentle nature attracted them, they felt safe with the little girl. Chrissie had been frightened, but she had settled and her mind seemed to be in control again. 'We will find you, Bess… we will find you.'

She caught sight of two figures in front of her. A tall, elegant lady, swinging a scarf and a small child skipping along by her side. Chrissie heard singing as well. Sophia and Bibi! She banged the horn. Sophia and Bee swung round and saw her. Bibi began to run back towards the car. Sophia waved her scarf and called, 'Hi, there! Where are you going? Do you want us?'

Chapter Sixteen

Jan was driving fast. He was near Exeter and he thought that he should stop soon. He was thirsty and hot. Although the windows of the Land Rover were open, he felt sticky and quite weary. Yes, he would stop at some tea rooms that Chrissie and he knew. He would have tea and scones. Why not? He was very fond of Devonshire cream and jam and scones. *Right*, he thought, *now, how long to a cup of tea?* He guessed about four or five miles. Good!

In the back of the Land Rover, Bess and Bear were wide awake and also very thirsty and very warm. She had felt that it would be safe to push the rugs and cushions aside and there they were sitting on the floor out of Jan's eye line! She needed to go to the lavatory, this concerned her a little. Would Jan stop soon? He had been driving for hours and hours – well, it seemed like hours and hours! She heard Jan say, 'Ah! There it is!' and the next moment he had swung the Land Rover to the left and stopped. Bess immediately burrowed under the rugs again and waited while Jan got out and slammed the door. She caught the sound of the key in the lock. Then, Jan's feet as he walked away. He did not realise, however, that the rear doors were still unlocked. Bess slowly emerged from the woolly rugs. She crawled to the doors and looked through the glass. Jan had gone. She saw the tea rooms – a cottage with a thatched roof and tables and chairs set out in a garden all round the small house. There were people sitting at these tables and girls in long flowery dresses and white aprons were carrying trays with teapots and plates with cakes on them. It seemed a lovely place. *Oh! I must go to the lavatory! I must!* she thought. *But where? Certainly not to the place were all those people would go! I shall have to find a field or a gate leading into a field.* She unlatched the rear doors and carefully climbed out, shutting the doors behind her. She quickly looked round and saw that the tea rooms were surrounded by fields; there were no other houses near by. *Good, good!* thought Bess and she ran, fast, to a five barred gate. She climbed over it and dropped into a field.

Nearly nine o'clock. Jan had glanced at his watch. The light was fading. He was through Truro and would soon be in Falmouth. He was staying at a country house hotel the other side of Falmouth, near Mawnan Smith. What a great name that was; he spoke it carefully, 'Mawnan Smith...' However could a place have been named Mawnan Smith? He repeated it and it became tuneful and he drove along singing Mawnan Smith.

Bess had been asleep, but she never slept deeply, and she was wide awake now and listening to the tunes that came from the front of the vehicle. It was soothing. She was hungry. She hadn't eaten since lunch and then she had only picked at her food. Now, she was very, very hungry. Her stomach made a funny sound. She pressed it quickly, in case Jan became aware of this strange squeaky noise from under the back seat. When, oh, when would they arrive at their destination?' Bess remembered her father saying the word 'destination'.

Jan stopped singing and said, 'Mawnan Smith. Here we are!'

Bess was aware of the Land Rover slowing down and turning right. She longed to look out to see where they were, but she knew that she had to be absolutely still and silent. She tried to make herself tiny. She was clasping Bear to her and his fur was tickling her nose. *I mustn't sneeze!* Her heart was bumping so loud that she felt sure that Jan would hear it!

There was a scrunch of gravel and the Land Rover stopped. She heard a great number of sounds for the next minutes. Voices – 'Hello! Jan Leigh? We've been expecting you. Glad you're safe. Isn't it hot? Hope your journey was OK. I'm Michael Fossey, the owner of the hotel. Do come in. Let me help you with your bags' – and so on and so on, until the voices died away, as Bess realised that the two men had gone into the house.

The Land Rover had swayed and shook but now it was still. Had Jan locked the rear doors? He was always reminded by various people at home about leaving these doors unlocked. They had to be unlocked this time – and, yes, they were! Bess thought hard and fast. What should she do now? Where were they? In Falmouth Town? She didn't think that they were. She could not recall Mawnan Smith. Had she and her father been there?' Her stomach rumbled and grumbled again. She would have to get out, taking her case and Bear, and go and look around. It was dark now. She was able to see everything outside the vehicle, however, as there were lots of bright lights outside the hotel; shining onto large cars and tall tress and rose bushes. It was a beautiful place.

Bess carefully gathered all her belongings, opened the rear doors and climbed down onto the gravel pathway behind the Land Rover. She shut the doors quietly and looked around again. The air seemed chilly. She took out her sweater and put it on. She was very calm on the outside, but her head was full of racing thoughts. She took a deep breath and began to walk down a long, tree-sheltered driveway away from the house. She wanted so much to go into that lovely house, that looked so friendly, find Jan and feel his arms come around her and hear his dear, kind words – but no, she had to be on her own and try to find her daddy.

The driveway was not long and soon she was at the gates. They were tall, black, wrought-iron gates, and sitting on the top of the stone gate pillars were two lions with laughing faces. Bess gazed at them and told them, 'One day I will come back and talk to you, both of you, but not tonight. Goodbye.'

She had to make a decision, to go right or left. The road was empty. There seemed to be more street lamps to the right, so she turned right and walked briskly off towards the middle of the little town…

Chapter Seventeen

*B*ack at The Oak Tree House, the rest of the family was sitting quietly in the kitchen at the round table. They were simply sitting and thinking. Not Sophia and Bibi; Bee had gone to Merlin Cottage with her dear friend, the Sophia Lady! She was staying overnight. A great relief to the others at this moment in time! Not Andrew either. He had been found by Artie, still lying in the grass in the orchard under the apple tree. Artie had brought him back to the house and Hannah had suggested that he had a bath and that she would bring him up some food. He was now in his own bedroom, eating and thinking and feeling a little better. The clock on the wall was ticking steadily and clearly.

Hannah had not mentioned the letter from Bess. Andrew knew that she wouldn't question him. He also knew that he was going to leave and go down to Cornwall to look for Bess. He had made up his mind in the last ten minutes, after Han had left the tray and softly closed the door. He recalled what the old lady had said, 'Andrew, my boy, you have to be brave and strong and most careful when you go to look for Bess. We are ready to help you, if we are able to, but whatever you decided to do, please leave us messages so that we will not be too troubled. There are so many troubles at present. God bless you.'

Andrew didn't even wonder how Han knew that he was gong to find Bess; Han just knew, just as she had known about so many other happenings and would know about more in the future.

Andrew looked at the food. He wasn't very hungry, but he nibbled at some of the favourite morsels that Han had put out for him. He drank slowly, the orange juice that he loved, thinking about his journey tomorrow. *Monday, July 2nd. Shall I travel by train? Shall I hitch a lift? No, no! I mustn't hitchhike! Money?* He picked up his moneybox and shook it. Hmmm, it sounded full and it was certainly heavy. There were only coins in there. He crossed to his desk and opened a secret drawer. *Ah, note money! How many notes?* He would need a lot. He counted up all his money and he had enough. Plans, he loved making plans… Andrew's face broke into a broad smile. He chuckled. 'OK, this is going to be a great adventure. I have a great deal to do… preparations and plans!'

So who *was* sitting at the kitchen table? Nah, Chrissie, Han, Artie. Their heads were buzzing with ideas and their hearts were thudding and sometimes jumping around. But they were all determined not to make the others think that they were overly concerned!

Artie sighed, stood up, stretched. 'I'm just going to take Pippin for a walk. Won't be long.' He snapped his fingers at the sleeping dog. She lifted her head, got up and followed him into the backyard. The kitchen door was open. The evening air was warm and there was a wonderful stillness. The three women looked at Artie. Hannah nodded. Nah and Chrissie smiled. Chrissie was stirring her mug of coffee… round and round and round. Nah put her hand over her friend's hand and the stirring stopped. Again, there was a profound silence. The phone rang, a shrill, piercing noise. Chrissie shot to her feet and raced out of the room. Four ears were strained towards the hall where the phone was. They heard Chrissie say in a tense, tight voice, 'Hello? Hello? Who is it? Oh, Jan, darling! Are you all right? Have you seen Bess? Yes, yes…' There was a pause, it seemed a long pause, while Jan spoke from the other end of the line. Nah began to rise from her chair, but Hannah gestured to her to stay seated and listen. The telephone conversation went on and on. First Chrissie poured out all the news from Gloucestershire; then silences, interjected with short, sharp responses from Chrissie, as Jan told her all his news and thoughts and feelings. Then there was a final goodbye and Chrissie came back into the kitchen. Her face was expressionless. Hannah's name for this look was 'solid'; Chrissie's solid look. Woe betide anyone who ventured near her! Hannah said a very silent prayer. *Lord, please we need you. Here in the kitchen of The Oak Tree House. Could you make it soon… please.*

Chrissie went to the back door and shut it. She said, in a flat voice, 'The night air is getting cold. I'm just going upstairs. I'll be down soon.' And she left the room. Hannah and Nah turned their heads and looked at each other.

Chrissie gazed out of the window of her bedroom, saw colours in the sky, felt the warm evening air on her face. She suddenly shivered and held her breath. She was so confused. She moved away from the window and realised that it was quite dark in the room. She crossed to the bed and lay down, drawing the duvet round her. 'Bess… little Bess… where are you?' Chrissie's voice was just a whisper. Tears started to crawl down her cheeks. 'Bess, oh Bess.'

186

Chapter Eighteen

B ess had arrived in the small shopping area of Mawnan
Smith. It was really dark now, but she could see and
hear people in the pub across the road from where she was
standing. A young man and a girl came out of the pub. The
man was saying, 'I must get some petrol, or else we'll never
get home. There's a filling station just up the road.' Bess
watched them climb into a sport's car. They drove off, then
slowed down about three hundred yards up the road and
turned right, disappearing from sight. She immediately
decided to go to this Filling Station. There would be food
there and something to drink. It wasn't far to walk. Bess felt
wide awake now. She wasn't scared or worried. She had
been thinking about Andrew and Hannah. She could hear
Hannah's voice in her ears, Hannah's words: 'Always try to
be calm, then your brain will be able to work. Ask for help.
Remember, the Lord will be there with you.' Lots of people
would scoff at these words, but Bess had listened and
observed Han and Artie since she had lived with the Leigh
family. She knew that they were very special folk and that
Han had a special friend called God.

So the little girl walked the short way to the filling station with God in her mind and a feeling of safety in her
heart. She pushed open the door into the Shop where you
paid for petrol and, sure enough, there were shelves full of
food and a fridge with cartons and bottles of drink in it. The

young man was in the shop, paying for his petrol. He smiled at Bess when she came up to the counter. The man behind the counter leaned forward and said to Bess, 'You're out late, Missy. What can I do for you?'

Bess said carefully, 'Please would you reach up and get me a sandwich and some orange juice?'

The young man said, 'Ill get them. Which sandwich would you like? Chicken? Cheese and Tomato? Or…?'

Bess replied, 'Chicken, please.' She put down Bear on the counter and opened her case, taking out her purse. She put the purse on the counter and said again carefully, 'Please take the money that you need.' The two men looked at each other. This child was extraordinary, delightfully trusting and so beautiful. The dark eyes looked at them steadily.

The door opened and in came the young man's girl-friend. 'Bob, what's keeping you? Oh…' Her words trailed off as she saw that Bob and the filling station man were bustling around choosing sandwiches and cartons of juice.

'Won't be a mo, Susie. We're just helping this little lass.'

Soon Bess had been given a carrier bag. Her purse was back in the case and Bear's head was poking out of the carrier bag. The two men thought it would be easier for her to carry her case and the other bag with Bear inside it. Bess turned her eyes towards Bob and the other man. 'Thank you for helping Bear and me. I will not forget you. Good-bye.' She moved towards the door. Bob moved ahead of her and opened the door for her. She walked over the threshold and across the forecourt and out of their lives – for the time being, anyway. But they would be involved in Bess' life again quite soon…

Bess turned left when she had come to the road. She was making her way back to the hotel. She had not wondered about which way she should go; she had walked to the edge of the forecourt and turned left. She had to eat soon and maybe she could find a safe hiding place in the hotel's garden, it seemed to be a very big garden. She passed the shops and some small houses. Bungalows, they were. Someone had told her that name. No 'upstairs' like other houses. She saw the big gates again, with the stone lions sitting on top of their pillars, still smiling. She walked back up the drive and stopped. She had glanced through the tall tress that lined the drive. There was a little house in a clearing! It looked like a Wendy House. Andrew had read *Peter Pan* to the children in The Oak Tree House; she knew about Wendy's House. Perhaps the house could become a Bess House for the night! She ran into the clearing. Actually, it was a summer house. There was a door. She opened it and found a room with deckchairs and wooden picnic tables. There were cushions and, amazingly, rugs. Bess put down her belongings and went to look around outside the house. Behind it she found a hosepipe snaking along the ground. She followed its length. It led to a tap! *Good, oh good!* she thought. *Now I can wash and brush my teeth!* Bess had brought all the essentials with her: towel, soap, toothbrush and so on. She ran back to her Little House. She would be safe and warm. She had food and, of course, Bear and God to keep her company.

Back in Gloucestershire, most people were either in bed or going to bed. Hannah and Artie were in The Cottagey House. Hannah was lying quietly in her bed talking to her friend God and stopping now and then to listen to Artie, who was singing in his bath. She was very weary, but her mind was still working, thinking about the next day and this day, Sunday, July 1st. Han had always put the present day to bed before she allowed herself to fall asleep. She balanced the good with the difficult. She would not accept the word 'bad' very often. Yes, there had been problems, troubles, but she was sure that they could be put right. Bess was being kept safe. She was also sure of that. The Andrew story could be quite difficult, but it would have to wait unto tomorrow. Jan had arrived in Cornwall without mishap. She had had a longish conversation with the Lord about Jan's journey. Nah was at The Oak Tree House with Chrissie.

Artie and Hannah had gone back to their home without seeing Chrissie again, but Nah had promised Hannah that she would try to talk to Chrissie before she went to sleep. It was clear that Chrissie was very, very disturbed. It was most important that the 'solid' state that she had gone into was gradually broken down. Chrissie could become profoundly trapped in a deeper depression. *Now, that could be bad*, thought Hannah. Han knew Chrissie better than anyone else in the world.

'Right, I will leave Chrissie in your hands, Nah.' Hannah was speaking her thoughts out loud as Artie arrived, smelling of bubble bath and soap. He chuckled and said in his dear, deep, growly voice, 'I'm certain that those hands will be strong and gentle, my maid. Come now, close your eyes and sleep. We both need rest.' Artie took off his dressing gown, climbed into the large bed and gathered his dear little Han into his arms.

Chrissie had cried herself to sleep. The 'solid' state that Han called her intense fear, had caused her many problems all through her life. It was, of course, a kind of safety barrier. Ever since she was a child, she had hidden herself away behind this barrier, not allowing other people in.

Gradually, she had been able to break it down, but when anything hugely frightening happened, Chrissie's barrier descended. Hannah had helped her whenever she was there. Nah was also able to break through the wall of silence, but she knew that in the end it was only Chrissie herself who could lift herself out of the extraordinary pit. Chrissie had to put herself right in the middle of problems. It was as if her whole being stopped; her mind; her feelings; her body. She usually went away and lay down. Nothing was able to move forward. And, of course, there was the guilt. She realised that she was surrounded by so many people who loved her and would do anything to help her; all she had to do was to go and tell them, to ask them for help. But somehow she couldn't. She felt ashamed and ungracious and useless. This Sunday evening, she had run to her bedroom to hide her shame and guilt, just as she had done when she had been a little girl. The 'solid' state had not happened for a long time. This time she had just lain on her bed and sobbed herself to sleep. Nah found her there when she crept into the room. Nah had intended to talk with Chrissie, to try to gently ease her back into life. Now, Nah just closed the curtains and drew the quilt around the sleeping woman. She bent down and kissed her and tiptoed to the door. She whispered before she closed it, 'Darling Chrissie, come back to us soon.'

Nah was disturbed herself. Who wouldn't be with so much happening? But she must be calm and organised – organised! That was a difficult situation for Nah! However, Nah was at her best in a crisis. She seemed to move into another gear. She stood, leaning against Chrissie's bedroom door and… it was miraculous! Her mind was clear and she knew she would phone Jan, then make sure that Andrew was all right. His light was still on, so she felt sure that he was still awake. Andrew did not need much sleep. She could hear music coming from his room. It was a lovely sound. She allowed herself to be still and listen, and then moved quickly and ran very quietly past the boy's bedroom and downstairs to the telephone.

'You had a good journey then? Oh, how lovely! Were the scones up to standard? And the cream? Greedy man! Jan, tell me your thoughts about Bess. Why do you think she has gone? Where do you think she has gone?' Nah listened to Jan far away in Cornwall. She told him about Andrew. She told him that Andrew was planning something. She would try to get him to tell her – no, it wouldn't be easy – yes, Andrew was a very private person – yes, yes, she would be tactful, she would not ask him direct questions. 'I'll use my brain, Jan darling, I'll be careful!'

They finally decided that Nah would take Andrew to school the next day and have a talk with him. Nah knew that it would be better for Chrissie to stay at The Oak Tree House with Hannah, who was coming up early with Artie. Nah went to bed feeling much more settled in her mind. *Dear Jan*, she thought, *you always have the way of making me feel safe and less frightened*. She fell into bed and was soon deeply asleep.

The sky was grey when Artie drew back the curtains in the living room in The Cottagey House. He opened a window. 'My word, it's warm! It'll rain later… maybe it will thunder.' He called, 'Come along, my Hannah maid! Up you get. We mustn't be late up The Oak Tree Ho. I'll bring you a drink.' Artie took a deep breath. *It seems very still; no wind, so many leaves this year*, thought Artie. 'I wonder who's taking

Andrew to school today...' He spoke out loud, then immediately forgot the thought as he went into the kitchen.

But no one was going to take Andrew to school on this Monday in July. Andrew had left The Oak Tree House. He had left very early indeed. He had made a mental note of the time as he ran silently down the drive, past the tree and down the winding, narrow road that led to the main road. It had been 5.45 a.m.! He had to get the first bus to Stroud to find out about other buses and trains. He was going to Cornwall. He was quite breathless when, at last, he saw the traffic moving along the main road that would take him to Cheltenham and Stroud.

He hadn't had much sleep. He had been writing letters. He had written three, to Chrissie, Hannah and Nah. He had told Chrissie that he was going to find Bess; that he had enough money. (He did not tell her where he was going.) He told Nah that he was very sorry but he would not be going to school for quite a while and would she, please, look after Mum. He was worried about her. Andrew hated it when Chrissie 'took herself away' – that's what he called it. 'Mum, where are you? You've taken yourself away.' He was aware that Chrissie and Nah were soul mates. They helped each other whenever necessary. He hoped that Bess would be his soul mate. He had an instinctive feeling that she could be.

He had addressed his third letter to 'Mr and Mrs Special Lovejoys'. Ever since he was able to speak Andrew had called Artie and Hannah the Special Lovejoys. He asked them to make sure that Joseph, Bibi and Horatio were OK, and that he most certainly and surely would find Bess, and that they would be safe. Perhaps Hannah could have a word with God, so that his journey would not be too difficult. It was bound to be difficult, but not too difficult, please. He would try to bring Bess back by the end of the week. Perhaps Jan would bring them back. Then he crossed out those words because he realised that they would know that he was going to Cornwall! Finally, as a PS, he asked them to check all animalia and keep smiling and laughing whenever they thought it would help. These letters had been left in places where they would be found as soon as the people concerned were up and beginning the day.

Andrew stood by the bus stop. His heart was beating fast, but his mind was clear and he was not afraid. He had a haversack with him, also a sleeping bag inside a bedroll. He was prepared for anything! He had a map, pens and pencils, a change of clothes, an anorak and sufficient money. Well, he imagined that he had only to buy travel tickets and food. He had wondered about where he was going to sleep that Monday night. This had concerned him quite a bit; it still did, but he would not let himself think too much about his problem. He felt hot. It was such a still morning. The sky looked leaden. *Oh, dear! I hope it doesn't rain – not until I'm on the bus, anyway. Where are you, bus?* And as if it heard him, it appeared in the near distance. Andrew peered at the front of the vehicle and read the word 'STROUD'. *Thank you, God! Or was it Hannah who had told the bus to arrive at that moment?*

Andrew heard a voice say, 'Come on, lad! On you get! Don't hang around!' Andrew climbed abroad and the driver asked where he was going. 'Stroud, please, sir.' He was given a ticket and he sat in the seat opposite the driver. The bus moved away and Andrew knew that his adventure had really begun. No going back now. He took a deep breath and whispered to himself, 'I'm coming to find you, Bess!'

🐚 Chapter Eighteen 🐚

Bess had slept well. She opened her eyes and for a few seconds wondered where she was. Then in a flash she knew that she was in the Wendy House and that she was warm and cosy, wrapped in rugs, and Bear was in her arms. She lay there and gradually began to realise that she needed to go to the lavatory. *Oh dear! What shall I do? What time is it?* It was very quiet. The sun was pouring through the window onto her face. She looked at her watch. *Six o'clock. I shall have to move. I wonder if anyone else is up? There are lots of trees… I'll find a spot where no one will be able to see me.* And that's what she did. Then she hurried back and carefully washed and brushed her teeth and her hair. She did not know that she was being watched. A large black and white cat was sitting on a fallen branch of a tree nearby and a rabbit, who had come out to find breakfast, had stopped and was gazing at this beautiful child. The animals had not seen her before. They were not frightened by her. Animals, wild ones or tame ones, were never frightened of Bess. She looked up and saw them and smiled and said, 'Hello, animalia. Now I have three friends. A bear, a cat and a rabbit. Shall we have breakfast together?'

'Breakfast is ready, Chrissie.' Nah was sitting on the edge of Chrissie's bed. She gently pulled back the duvet and touched Chrissie's cheek. Chrissie moved slowly and opened her eyes. Nah thought how beautiful this woman was, just lying there, relaxed and warm. She bent and kissed her. 'Come on, darling girl. Why don't you have a shower and then join me downstairs in the kitchen. Everything's ready. Shall I get you a drink?'

Chrissie sat up and yawned. She rubbed her eyes and

then lay down again. 'Oh no you don't!' Nah grabbed Chrissie's hands and yanked her up. 'Up you get! Artie and Han will be here soon and we have a great deal to do. You've had a wonderful sleep and now we need you. I'm going to open the car; I'm taking Andy to school this morning and then we'll go to see Joseph and talk to Dr David.' And she pulled off the duvet and laughed as she ran along the landing and down the stairs.

As Nah ran along the passage towards the kitchen, she heard laughter and she called, 'Hannah, Artie, good morning. Isn't it hot? Will there be a storm later, do you think? I'm just going to open the car – I'm taking Andy to school after breakfast. Chrissie, hopefully, will be down soon.'

All this was said as Nah ran through the kitchen and out of the back door.

Artie chuckled and spoke quietly to Hannah, 'Well, well! Nah is very alive this morning, she must have slept—' But he stopped as he heard a shriek from near the garages. The two old folk looked at each other and then hurried outside to where Nah was standing, holding a letter in her hand. She didn't seem to notice them and Hannah had to ask her a couple of times, 'What's the matter, dear?'

Nah handed the letter to her and she read it carefully. Finally, Hannah said, 'Artie, please look in the kitchen for another letter. It will have yours or my name on the envelope. It could be anywhere, but I think it may be near the kettle.' Artie began to say something, but Hannah cut him short. 'Please go quickly, my dear. We have another problem.'

She then took Nah's hand and said, 'Andrew has gone to find Bess. He will be all right, but we shall have to be careful when we talk with Chrissie. How is she this morning?'

Nah told her what she knew and they walked slowly back to the house.

One of Andrew's letters had been discovered. Artie was looking for the second. What about Chrissie and her letter? Where had Andrew put this letter?

Chrissie had stayed sitting on her bed after Nah had left the room. She gradually recalled the previous day. At first she felt tight and tense, but she remembered suddenly what Nah had said to her: 'Now we need you.' She stood up, stretched and reached for her dressing gown. She stood looking out of the window. It was so still. Not a leaf moved. It was as if the trees were waiting for…? Chrissie held her breath, then breathed out and moved into her bathroom. She saw the letter immediately. It was propped against her toothbrush mug.

Chapter Nineteen

Jan was humming as he shaved. He was very content, very awake and excited inside. He loved his work and today should be a good day! It was only just after seven o'clock. He had woken early. The sun was pouring in through the window. This was such a beautiful place. He could hear the sea and the birds and now and then the sound of an engine. It could have been a car or a van, but it could just as well have been a tractor. He stood, gazing out of the bedroom window for a long time, looking carefully around, seeing Falmouth Bay stretching for miles and noticing the amazing trees and shrubs in the garden of the hotel. He even saw the garden house, the Wendy House. Perhaps he could see the cat or rabbit or both? He decided that he would ask Artie to help him build a little house like this one for his children back at The Oak Tree House. Bibi would adore it, and Bess might like to play there as well.

He looked away from the house as he saw a small figure run into the wood to his right. He turned back into his room and sighed. 'What a fortunate fellow I am!' he said out loud. He also knew that he was getting hungry. 'Ah, a Cornish breakfast!'

He had plenty of time, as his first appointment at Pendennis Castle was not until ten o'clock. He began to hum again. He so loved being down in Cornwall. Chrissie and he had spent some truly wonderful holidays down there. They had stayed in many villages and tiny seaside places, in cottages that they had found tucked away from the thousands of tourists that invaded the peninsula every year. At last he was here again! Jan dressed quickly and went down to his Cornish breakfast.

He was reading the paper and drinking his third cup of coffee when the young waiter came up to his table and told him that there was a phone call for him. 'Thank you. I expect that will be my Chrissie.'

'No, I haven't seen her. Do you seriously think she travelled with me down here in the back of the Land Rover? Surely I would have known? Well, maybe not, but... Yes, yes, I will look everywhere... I will ask lots of questions and phone you. Chrissie, please keep calm... Bess will be found... she will not be lost again. I love you. Just stay with the others. Give them my love. I'll phone.' Jan replaced the receiver. He stood there, still holding his coffee cup. He had forgotten about Bess. 'Oh, God! Why does so much have to happen to us?'

Michael Fossey, the owner of the hotel heard him say these words as he came out of his office. 'Can I be of some help, Mr Leigh? Are you all right?'

Jan had gone very pale and his eyes were bright and restless.

Michael took the cup from him gently. He went on, 'Would you like to come into my office? We could have a chat.'

Jan said, 'What? Oh, yes. That would be good. Yes.' And he followed Michael Fossey into the office. Michael shut the door. Jan spoke sharply. 'No, please don't shut the door!

It must be open!' Michael was quite shocked at Jan's manner. He opened the door and invited Jan to sit down.

'I would like you all to look everywhere in the hotel and in the grounds.' Michael Fossey was talking to his staff. 'Pete, Nancy? Are you going into Mawnan this morning? Oh, you are. Good. Then will you ask if anyone has seen a little girl...' He began to describe Bess from what Jan had told him. 'She will most probably be carrying a teddy bear. She never goes anywhere without him, I'm told.' The directions went on and on. Jan had phoned home again and had talked with Artie and Nah. Everyone seemed certain that Bess was not very far away from him, somewhere in the vicinity of Falmouth. It was now past nine o'clock and Jan would have to leave for Pendennis. Michael had begged him not to worry too much. The search party was arranged and they would do their utmost to find Bess. 'Who knows,' Michael had said, 'the little lass may be here, having tea when you return. Keep cheerful, old man!' Jan had said that he would try. He was going to the police station first, to report Bess' disappearance. He hoped that he would see the policeman who had first been involved with Bess when she had been found wandering around Falmouth.

No one found Bess that morning, in the hotel or in Mawnan Smith. She was actually on a bus by 8.30 a.m. travelling towards the hospital. She had dressed and tidied the garden house, making sure that it was exactly as she had found it, or as near as she could remember. She didn't have much food, only a few biscuits. She'd drunk some water. Bess had wondered why it had tasted better than the water in Gloucestershire.

She had decided to leave her suitcase hidden under the rugs and cushions in a corner of the little house. She took Bear, of course, and her purse and a warm jersey. Bess had made plans, just as Andrew had made plans. He always told her that, that was 'the best plan' or we must 'make a plan', then everything would 'go smoothly'. So now she was putting her plan into action.

Bess was sitting on a seat on the bus near the driver and she was going to the place where she had last seen her father. She was nervous and it was hot. Bear was sitting on the seat next to her. She touched his head, bent down and whispered into his ear, 'Are you all right, Bear? Are you hot inside your fur?' She seemed to wait for an answer and then she straightened up and looked out of the window as the bus bowled along the road towards Falmouth.

A young woman sitting on the other side of the bus had seen the conversation with Bear. 'Where have I seen that little girl? I'm sure I've seen her recently… couldn't not notice a face like that… or that teddy bear.' Suddenly she recalled the evening before in the petrol station in Mawnan Smith. *Oh, yes! Bob helped the child! What a strange thing. She's on her own again. Haven't seen her in the village before last evening… wonder why she's not with her mam, or her dad, brothers or sisters? Shall I speak to her? No, I'll just keep an eye on her, remember where she gets off the bus.*

Bess turned around and looked straight at Susie, as if she knew what she had been thinking. Susie's heart gave a tiny jump. She smiled at Bess and Bess smiled back, not immediately, after a few seconds. It was as if the little girl was making sure that she could trust Susie. Susie told Bob and her mother, later that night, 'It was as if the child had to be very sure that I was a friend before she gave me her smile – and oh, those eyes! And yet there was a sort of a sadness in them.'

The three letters had been found, opened and read over and over again. Artie, Han, Chrissie and Nah were in the kitchen at The Oak Tree House. It was about nine o'clock now and the table was still waiting for them to sit down and have some food and drink! They had all looked at each other's letters and had discussed them. Now it seemed as if there had to be several quiet minutes for them to think what must be done first. Hannah's mind was clear. Joseph had to be visited. The school had to be told about Andrew's absence. She wondered if Mrs Avery was about to have her baby… Bibi was safe, but Sophia needed a phone call. She felt a wet nose nuzzle her hand. It was Pippin Dog. 'Come on, old girl! You and I will walk down to Merlin Cottage and have a word with Sophia and Bibi. Perhaps you'll work out what's going to happen this morning, my dears… tell me when I get back. I'll only be gone about an hour.' And Hannah took off her apron, picked up the dog's lead and left.

This seemed to galvanise the others into action. Artie said, 'Right, men – oh, sorry, *women*. We must put our heads and bodies into gear and do something practical!' And in minutes Nah and Chrissie were being organised. Nah glanced at Chrissie as she sat down at the table to write out a list of 'to dos'. Chrissie was concentrating hard, plugging in the kettle and then getting the milk from the fridge. Nah sighed.

Chrissie was finding everything very difficult. She had not said much after she had come downstairs with Andrew's letter. She had just handed it to Hannah, who had read it and passed it on to Artie, who in turn had given it to Nah. All four of them realised that Andrew was probably on a train by now or at least on a bus going to Gloucester. Artie had phoned the railway people and they had told him that the boy would have to go to Gloucester station and catch a train from there, which would take him to Bristol, where he would change onto the Cornish Riviera Express, which would eventually take him to Truro. He could then get a bus or another train to Falmouth. It would be a very long journey, but it was possible for him to arrive before teatime.

Chrissie had told Artie to ask if anyone had seen a young boy, by himself. She told Artie to describe him. However, Hannah had gone into the hall where the telephone was and had whispered to Artie, saying that she felt that Andrew should be allowed to make his way to Cornwall. It was vital that he carried out his plan to travel on his own to start the search for Bess. He *knew* that he would be kept safe. So the old man did not mention Andrew to the man who had given him the information about the trains and buses. He merely found out the travel possibilities. He was cheerful when he returned to the kitchen and told the others. He then said that he was going to check the fridge and larder, to make sure that they had enough food for the day. Then he would be going shopping and gathering veggies for the vicar and anyone else who had ordered them. He would take his own car. Nah sighed again. Chrissie said in a small, shaky voice, 'Would you like a cup of coffee, Nah?'

'Yes, thank you darling. Will you have one?'

'Yes, I think I will… and a piece of toast… and you? Will you have a piece, as well?' It all sounded so normal, but Nah knew the effort that Chrissie was making to appear as if she was in control again. She also knew that Chrissie was not in control. Nah cleared her throat. 'What a great idea! We could do with some of Hannah's marmalade. I'll just finish this list. There's quite a lot to do this morning.'

'Hello, Mr Leigh. Now, this is a fine surprise! What brings your down here? Is Mrs Leigh with you… and the wee girl, how's she?' Constable John Pascoe's large round face was wreathed in smiles as he came towards Jan with his hand outstretched. Jan gladly took the hand and looked at the huge policeman with relief. Soon he was sitting in the office drinking tea from a large mug. Everything around PC Pascoe seemed to be big: the chairs, the table, the constable's feet and his magnificent hands, hands that were amazingly gentle as well as being strong and immensely capable. Jan had often watched the gig racing[*] and had envied John Pascoe's ability to wield his oar. The police gig had won numerous races and Constable John was a popular, invaluable member of their crew.

He was not smiling now, however. He had listened carefully when Jan told him about Bess. Then he got up and went to the window, which overlooked the harbour. The sun had broken through the cloud cover and the sea sparkled. There was silence in the room. Then a gull called to another gull. The two men watched as the birds alighted on the window ledge and quietly made throaty sounds. The constable spoke in a low voice. 'We've been unable to find out anything about the whereabouts of the little girl's father.'

Jan nodded. 'Chrissie has been speaking regularly to Inspector Drew. In fact we are becoming quite friendly with him and his family. It is all very odd, very strange. Bess' father seems to have disappeared from – what do you

---

[*] A gig is a large boat, rowed by four, six or eight alternate oars. There are many gig racing clubs in Cornwall.

English say? – from the face of the earth? Chrissie thinks that Bess is here to find him. I have an important meeting in Pendennis in about fifteen minutes. May I ask you to start…'

Jan paused and the policeman finished the thought for him. '…Procedures? Yes, of course, Mr Leigh. We'll start at once. I'll find the file we have on little Bess. Now, try not to worry too much. Away you go to the castle. I'd like to know all about your television film some time. All right?'

Jan told him where he was staying, thanked him and left. Indeed, his meeting was important and he managed to forget Bess and Andrew – he'd also told PC Pascoe about Andrew – Chrissie had poured everything out over the phone earlier that morning.

Andrew was well into his journey. After his initial nerves, he had thoroughly enjoyed himself. He had got a bus from Stroud to Gloucester and had then caught a train to Bristol and that's where he was now, standing looking up at the big round clock on Temple Meads Station. In Bristol! He had enquired about trains to Cornwall and been told that the Cornish Rivera Express would be arriving at Temple Meads at 11.30 a.m. and would leave at 11.45 a.m. The clock told him that he had about fifteen minutes before the train was due, so he decided to go to the buffet and get a drink. He felt very grown up. He had enough money and he could do whatever he wanted to do – as long as he didn't miss the train! He sat at a table that overlooked the platform and watched the various people moving backwards and forwards in front of him. He saw a family, carrying lots of luggage.

They also had haversacks like him. And there were buckets and spades attached to the suitcases. It was a large family: three grown-ups and four children. *Not quite as large as our family*, he thought. *There would be more of us... and we would have a dog!* Suddenly he felt his eyes fill with tears. He had not realised how important they were to him. He jumped to his feet, picked up his haversack and his drink and hurried out of the Buffet. He looked for a telephone box.

The telephone rang in The Oak Tree House. It rang and rang and rang. No one answered it. No one was in the house. Artie was delivering veggies and thinking out lunch. Hannah, Chrissie and Nah were on their way to the hospital to see Joe. Dr David had phoned to say that Joe was appreciatively better and if he continued to get stronger, he would be able to come home on Wednesday morning. That was good news.

'Right,' Nah had said. 'We must go and see Joe, now. He'll do us all good. And what about Horatio? We must find out about him. Han, will you be telling Joe another story about Horatio?'

'Most certainly,' replied Hannah. 'We'll find some other children who may like to meet that pea and hear about his adventures!' They had laughed and set off as soon as it was possible. So the phone in The Oak Tree House just went on ringing until Andrew realised that there was no one in.

Andrew was suddenly aware of a voice on the loud-speaker saying, 'The next train arriving on Platform 2 is The Cornish Riv—' He quickly replaced the receiver and hurried onto the platform. He was becoming panicky! Was this platform he was on Platform No. 2? He saw the family again. One of the girl was saying, 'Mum! Mum, we need Platform 2... this is Platform 1!'

'Come on, then,' the tall boy replied. 'We must go down the stairs!' The large family, all talking at once, was moving away to the long staircase. Andrew immediately followed behind them.

It wasn't far to Platform 2 and they were there just as the train was seen slowly approaching. It was a very long train and many carriages slid past him. He noticed a restaurant car. Then the train stopped and doors began to open. The family clambered on, and he went with them.

Phew! Andrew was really hot now. He found a seat behind a table. It was a window seat. He sat down with a great sense of relief and put his haversack on the table in front of him. He looked at his watch. It showed nearly twenty minutes to twelve o'clock. Good, they would be off soon. He wiped his face with a handkerchief and noticed a small boy watching him. The little boy was looking at him over the top of the seat in front of Andrew. The boy was probably about three or four years old. He had a freckled face and lots of bright red curly hair. They smiled at each other and Andy said, 'Hello, big boy. Are you going on holiday?'

The child nodded and the face broke into a wide grin. Another face appeared. It looked exactly the same as the first one! *Wow! Twins!* thought Andrew. *How lovely.* He would have liked to have been a twin. He said, 'Are you twins?'

The new twin said, 'Yes, we are Ben and Briony Housman. He is Ben and I am Briony. He is a boy and I am a girl. He doesn't say much. I speak for him.'

A lady who also had red hair said to Andrew, 'Now, don't you let these cheeky two be a worry to you, will you? They'll want to know all about you, I shouldn't wonder!' and she smiled at him.

Andrew realised that she was an American lady. He had heard the American accent before, when Kel had come to stay with the Leighs in Gloucestershire. He liked the sound. 'Oh, that's fine, thank you. I like talking to people. Perhaps Briony and Ben would like to come and sit with me? There's plenty of room...' and almost before he had finished the invitation, the two children had arrived, by scrambling over the top of their seats and dropping onto the seats opposite Andy! They lay there laughing. Then Ben poked his sister and they both sat up and stared at Andrew, in silence. Andrew stood up and managed to put his haversack onto the luggage rack above him. The twins watched him. Then Ben poked Briony again and she said, 'What's your name and—'

Andrew said quickly, 'Hey! Hang on a moment! I have to answer all those questions one by one. Now, the first one: my name is Andrew Leigh...' He went on to tell them that he belonged to a family, but he did not tell them where he was going. Thankfully, they didn't ask again as Briony began to ask him lots more questions! The train had moved slowly away from Bristol and was travelling into the West Country by the time Andrew had answered them. He really liked these two fascinating children. He asked them where they were going and they told him that they were going to visit their grandparents in Cornwall. The Grandparents lived near a TheatreontheRocks! Briony ran the words together. 'A TheatreontheRocks!' Andrew thought that Chrissie would be interested in this theatre.

I'm going to enjoy this journey, thought Andrew.

'Horatio and his family sat down to a late tea. What an adventure they'd had!' Hannah stopped and looked at the faces of the children. They were in the day room of the hospital. Joseph was there, sitting as close as he could to Han. His eye was still bandaged but he seemed alert and yet relaxed. There were other children with them, well enough to be in the day room. Two were in wheelchairs, another two were sitting in ordinary chairs, and the fifth on a nurse's lap. Everyone wanted to touch or look at Horatio. He was still in his pod home, but soon he would have to leave it and come into Hannah's hand. She decided that she would ask Artie to design a special house for all the peas. There were a great number of relations!

Joe said, 'Oh Han! Is that the end of the story? Or is there another part tomorrow? Or even later today?'

Hannah replied, having thought fast, 'There'll be another episode – that's the word for the next part of the story, a story that goes on over a few days or a certain time – another episode tomorrow morning. It will finish tomorrow.'

Hannah knew that Joseph would be coming home on Wednesday so this Horatio story needed to finish on Tuesday. The children started to ask lots of questions. 'Can we come to listen? Will you tell us lots more stories?'

'Oh, dear, dear! I can't hear all your questions when you all speak at the same time, can I? Hush, now, and I'll tell you what's going to happen.' She told them that she would be coming to the hospital often and that she would always find out if they were still there. Joe would be with her, all being well. 'Of course, he may be at school again soon...' and so it went on and on. The children seemed so happy. A lot of laughter could be heard as people moved about their business along the corridors and in and out of the wards and rooms. Darling Hannah, she brought such joy to everyone. They felt safe when she was around.

❧

Dr David was telling Chrissie and Nah that they were very pleased with Joe's progress. He felt certain that the boy would be able to go home on Wednesday. He noticed that Chrissie looked drawn and that she was very edgy. She didn't sit still for long. She kept getting up and going to the window to look out. It was as if she was not always with Nah and himself, as if she was somewhere else. The doctor wanted to ask Chrissie if there was something troubling her, but Nah had shaken her head when he seemed about to ask Chrissie a question. He was a sensitive man and realised that this was not the time. He finally said as he rose from his chair, 'I'll see you at about ten o'clock on Wednesday morning, then. Shall I tell Joseph, or would you both prefer to tell him?'

Chrissie didn't reply, so Nah said 'We'll tell Joe, he'll be with Hannah.'

Dr David smiled. 'Of course! The Horatio story time! I'm sorry to have missed it. Maybe, tomorrow. Take care of each other.'

Chrissie turned and spoke quietly, 'Thank you, David. I have heard what you have been saying. I'm sorry if I've been rude.' Her eyes filled with tears. The doctor just smiled and left them together.

'Come on, Chrissie. Let's find Han and Joe, then we can tell them both about Joe's homecoming. How exciting!' and Nah took Chrissie's hand. As they moved into the corridor, they saw Han and Joe walking towards them.

Joe was walking with such confidence. He was talking to Hannah and she put out a hand and touched his head. Then they both laughed. Joe grabbed Hannah's hand and kissed it. Nah called, 'Hello you two. We've some splendid news! You're coming home on Wednesday, Joe.' Joe stopped as he heard the last few words; his face broke into a great smile. He began to run towards Nah's voice. Nah moved towards him and they met. She picked the boy up and gave him a hug. He wound his arms round her neck and buried his face in her.

Chrissie was standing a little way behind them. She turned and walked along the corridor. Hannah called out, 'Chrissie, wait for me, please. I need to talk about Joe's homecoming.' There was no reply.

Hannah said to Nah, 'Nah, will you take Joe out into the garden? I must have a word with Chrissie.' Nah nodded and smiled. She placed Joe carefully back onto the floor and the boy began to tell her about Horatio's adventures.

Hannah caught up with Chrissie as she walked to where they had parked the car. The old lady was quite out of breath when she finally managed to grab Chrissie's hands and make her stop. 'Oh, dear! Now, now, this can't go on! We must sit down, somewhere where it's cool and be sensible and chat... you and I!'

Chrissie looked down at Han and realised that she was very weary. *What a selfish fool I am*, she thought. She bent down and smoothed the hair from Han's dear face. 'I'm so, so sorry, darling little Han.' Chrissie's voice shook and she couldn't say any more, but at once, Han had taken her face in her hands and kissed her.

'Come on, let's find a quiet place. You've no need to say any more until we do.'

'Mum! Hannah! Where are you?' Joe had been calling for quite a while. Nah and he had their elevenses and were searching for the other two.

Nah called, 'Hannah, Chrissie! Would you like a drink?' She was carrying a tray with juice and biscuits on it.

Joe suddenly said, 'Nah, stop! I can hear voices!' Joe's hearing had become very acute since he had been unable to see. 'I think they are in the rose garden. Han, Mum, are you near us?' They heard a muffled, 'Yes, we're here, my dears.'

Nah told Joe to hang onto her skirt, that she knew the rose garden and soon they were sitting with Chrissie and Hannah on the long wooden seat under a wonderful shrub rose bush in the cool. Chrissie was smiling. Nah looked at her friend very hard. Chrissie looked back. They smiled, and threw their arms around each other. Nah whispered in Chrissie's ear, 'You're back! Oh, thank you Lord!'

Chrissie replied, 'I'm sorry. But I was frightened... I didn't know how to cope with everything. Now I do. I'm so stupid—'

Nah cut her off, 'No, not stupid, just a very human being!'

Hannah was drinking some juice and Joe was telling her about Charlie, his nurse. 'Charlie would like to visit us at Oak Tree House and see where you and Artie live and meet the animalia and see my drawings and paintings and—'

Chrissie touched his arm, interrupting him in his excitement. 'Joe, darling, of course Charlie can come to visit us after you have settled in again. She seems a lovely girl.'

Joe said, 'Can she come this weekend? She lives by herself in Stroud. She has a Mini and can get to us. Please, Mum, say she can? This weekend?' The three women were silent. Joe listened in the silence, turning his head from side to side. 'Is there trouble?'

Hannah and Nah looked at Chrissie. She said, 'Yes, Joe, a great deal has happened in the last couple of days, but we haven't enough time to tell you all about it now. Everything will be all right again soon. Jan Dad will make it all right, I know.'

Joe began to speak again, 'Mum, I need to know—'

Chrissie took his hands and pulled him to her. 'I *will* tell you, Joseph, but not now. I'll come back this afternoon. I promise.'

There was another silence. Then Joe spoke. His face was empty of expression. 'I'll wait for you in my room. Please take me back there, Nah.' He had turned to where he thought Nah was sitting. Actually, he was looking at Hannah.

'I'll be back around three o'clock, Joe.' Chrissie's voice was gentle and steady.

Jan, his designer, location manager and the producer of the television film being planned were sitting in the King's Head having lunch. They had discussed the script, locations around Falmouth, Mawnan Smith and the Helford Passage. They were tired. Thankfully, it was cool in the King's Head public bar and Jan began to think about Bess and Andrew. If Hannah said the children would be safe, then they would be safe, but what should be *his* next step? He would have to go back and see PC John Pascoe. Jan wondered what had happened after he had left him. The constable had had about three hours to start his investigations into Bess' whereabouts. Had she really travelled with him in the back of the Land Rover? It seemed absolutely impossible that he had not discovered her. But then, he'd had no reason to look under seats and rugs.

'Jan! Jan, where are you? I'm asking you a question.' It was his producer, Cyril Armitage. Jan put down the glass he was holding and apologised. Cyril continued. 'We've been discussing the Pendennis location for the kidnapping shots. I don't think you've heard one word of what we've been saying!' Cyril was speaking in an amiable way.

Jan closed his eyes and shook his head as if to drive out extraneous thoughts. He said quickly, 'I do have a lot on my mind – should I say, *in* my mind at present. However, these other thoughts must not interfere with us and our plans. Now, please, tell me again what you were talking about, and you will have my full attention.' The discussion was resumed and once again Jan forgot Bess and Andrew.

Chapter Twenty

'Next stop, the hospital.' The driver directed his words towards where Bess was sitting.

She said, 'Thank you, sir.'

Susie also heard the words. She'd been gazing out of the window, having forgotten Bess. Now, she became alert and watched while Bess picked up Bear and her jersey and stood waiting for the bus to stop. Susie noticed Bess was carrying a purse. *Getting off at the hospital stop,* she mused. *Is this little lass going into the hospital? Maybe she's going to visit a sick relative? I wonder how old she is? She looks very young... about seven? Or less? No, surely not! She would never be on her own! Where's her mam? It's all very mysterious...* The bus stopped. Suzie said, 'Goodbye. Look after yourself.'

Bess turned. Was the lady over there speaking to her? She said, 'Did you speak to me?'

Susie was surprised. She had not expected the child to say anything! 'Well, er, yes, I did. Are you going to visit a sick person, in the hospital?' she asked.

Bess said, as she got off the bus, 'No. Goodbye.'

And the driver and Susie watched her walk through the gates of the hospital and up the driveway. Someone near the rear of the bus said in a rather grumpy voice, 'Driver, I have to be in town very soon!'

The driver, said, in a dazed kind of tone, 'Sorry, mate. I was looking at the child. We're off now. Don't worry, we're nearly on The Moor.' The Moor is the name given to the place where the buses stop in Falmouth.

Susie spoke her thoughts out loud. 'What a beautiful little child. I won't forget her in a hurry!'

She heard the driver say, 'No Ma'am, neither will I! Wonder who she is?'

Bess was standing in front of a large, high desk. She could just see over the top. There was a lady sitting in a chair. The lady was talking on the phone. Bess was not listening to the words being said, she was trying to think out what she was going to say. Her brain seemed to be stiff, her throat was tight. She was very frightened. *What would Andrew do? What would Hannah do? Oh, what am I going to say?* She was aware of a voice and words being spoken. Then there was silence. A hand touched her gently on the arm. She looked up and saw a tall lady standing looking at her from behind large spectacles.

'Can I help you, dear? Do you want to see someone in the hospital?'

Bess opened her mouth, but nothing came out. She realised that she was hugging Bear tightly to her. It was cooler inside, but sweat was running down her back.

The voice came again. 'I can't help you if you won't tell me what you want, now, can I?'

Bess tried again and a tiny sound came from her throat. She managed to clear her voice. It was so croaky, *like a frog's*, she thought. This made her smile for a split second and her next words were stronger and clearer. 'Please can you tell me where my daddy is? The last time that I saw him he was here.'

There was silence. The lady said, 'I think we should go and find someone else. I haven't been working here long. What's your daddy's name?'

But Bess couldn't remember. When her father had left her in the casualty department of this hospital the year before, she had gone into deep shock. This shock had caused her to lose her memory and although she was beginning to recall much of her earlier life, she couldn't remember the simplest of things – like names and places. Bess shook her head. 'I don't know his name,' she whispered.

The receptionist, for that's what this lady was, began to think fast. Here was a problem. *I must take the child to the right person, someone who will be able to giver her lots of time, someone who will ask questions in the right way... Ah! I know. Harry!*

This Harry was a kind of a caretaker. He had worked at the hospital for about thirty years! He knew everything and everyone! 'I'll take you to meet a very special man called Harry. He will be able to help you, I'm sure.' The receptionist went on, 'Let me carry your teddy for you.'

But Bess stepped backwards, away from the lady, 'No, thank you. He must stay with me!' Now her voice was clear. 'He's all I have here.'

The receptionist looked at the little girl and her bear. *I'll call Harry*, she thought.

Elizabeth, the receptionist, said gently to Bess, 'I'll give Harry a buzz. He's probably having his mid-morning coffee in his office. Would you like to sit down for a minute?'

Bess shook her head and stayed where she was, in the middle of the large reception area. Elizabeth picked up the phone and pressed something that made a very loud Buzz! Then after a few seconds Bess heard her say, 'Harry. Could you come to Reception? I have someone I'd like you to meet. Yes, all right... bring it with you. Thank you.'

Bess was calmer now. She was looking all around the room. She didn't seem able to remember much about the place. She recalled her father had told her to sit on a large seat of some kind, but she was not sure if it had been here. Elizabeth watched her. She noticed Bess' little thin figure, how small she was, and the way she was dressed. The child looked cared for. She was clean and very tidy.

Harry whistled as he walked briskly along the corridor. He was whistling a tune from *The Sound of Music*. The show was running at the Arts Theatre in Falmouth and he was the stage director. He had worked in the theatre for many, many years. He stopped whistling, 'Doh, Ray, Mee' as he was aware of a tiny figure standing alone in the reception area. She also saw him as he walked nearer and nearer. He looked a jolly sort of man. He had a round, open face and eyes that seemed alive and kind. He said as he came out of the corridor, 'Hello there. Well now, hello Bear. What a grand fellow!'

Bess' eyes opened wide. She said, 'How did you know his name was Bear?'

Harry twinkled at her and knelt down. He put out a hand to Bear. He winked at Bess, then said in his lovely Cornish accent, 'Will you shake hands with me, Bear?'

Bess took hold of Bear's paw and pushed it towards the old man's hand. She said, 'Bear likes you, sir.'

Harry laughed. 'I'm not a Sir, little lass! My name's Harry Hammond. What's your name?'

Bess answered at once.

'Bess. That's a special name, little one. Why are you here? Is there something I can do to help you? Tell you what, shall we go into the garden and show Bear the pond where the fish swim? It's a lovely place, full of flowers and trees.'

Harry looked at Elizabeth and lifted an eyebrow in a questioning way. The receptionist said, 'Oh, that's my favourite place around here! I'll see you later, shall I?'

Bess nodded, but she did not take her eyes off Harry. He seemed a safe person. He led the way out of the reception area and down the path towards some trees. Harry was a shrewd, wise old man. He realised that this child was on her own and clearly needed very careful handling. He also realised that there must be a story here. So once they were out of the hospital he began to tell her quietly about the garden and how he had worked here for a long, long time. He talked in such an interesting way. His words were full of pictures and Bess understood him easily.

They stood looking into the pond. The fish were swimming smoothly about. Gradually, they seemed to know that there were people looking at them and they came to the surface of the water. Their mouths opened and shut. Bess was fascinated. 'Why are their mouths doing that?' she inquired. Harry told her that they always did this when people were near. The fish knew that they might be given some food. There were stone seats all round the pond. Harry went to one of them and sat down. Bess followed him and sat down next to him. There was silence, and then she said, 'I came here with my daddy, but he went away and I haven't seen him for many days and weeks. Can you tell me where he is, please?'

Harry began to hum quietly, then he said, 'Can you tell me more about your daddy?'

Bess told him as much as she could recall, and Harry Hammond listened, sometimes he hummed and sometimes he turned and looked steadily at the little girl. His mind was working all the time, understanding that the child was finding it all very difficult. Her speech, though clear, was quite slow and she had to think about her choice of words. He was also thinking about happenings in the hospital in the near past, but there was nothing about a man disappearing in his memory. He asked Bess, 'When did you and your daddy come to Falmouth for your holiday? A few weeks ago?'

Suddenly Bess remembered that it was not *this* year, but *last* year! She said, 'Last year.'

Harry's mind cleared and he suddenly recalled some of the staff telling him about an incident with a child and a man, last summer. He remembered a young nurse telling him about a child who had been left sitting on a bench for over an hour, waiting, so she said, for her daddy to take her home. She was holding a bear! Harry had been at home the day it had happened. It was his day off. Then someone else had mentioned that they had seen the child sitting on this bench and then she'd gone. Everyone had assumed that the father had come and taken her away after he had seen whoever he had to see. And now the child, Bess, was back again and she was looking for her father! There was a big mystery here. Harry was thinking fast. He must find out more. He needed to know more! But he must be careful. This was no ordinary little girl. He wondered if she had a family. Did she live in Falmouth?

Harry said suddenly, 'Look! Look at the fish… they seem hungry! Would you like to give them some food?' He put his hand in his pocket and took out some crumbs, there was also some fluff.

Bess gazed into his palm. 'Do fish eat fluff as well as crumbs?' she enquired.

Harry laughed again. He laughed a lot! 'Oh, maybe… I just open my fingers and drop whatever I have into the water. Fish just eat it! Here, have a go.'

And he took Bess' hand and shook some of the 'food' into her hand. They spent a happy time, in silence, feeding

the fish. It was a happy time, because they felt so at ease
with each other, as if they had known each other for years.

Without looking at Bess, Harry began to talk. 'About ten
months ago, that's nearly a year, one of the nurses who
work here told me about a gentleman and his little daughter. The father had come to the hospital to see a doctor and
his little girl had come with him. The nurse – Flora is her
name – said that although the gentleman had an appointment – do you know the word "appointment"?' Bess did
not reply, so Harry told her what the word meant. He went
on. 'Although he had this appointment, he did not see the
doc. He was in the reception area one minute and the next
minute he had gone. The same with the little girl. She was
sitting on a long seat one minute and the next minute she
had gone. Also the bear, who had been sitting next to her.
He'd gone too. Now, do you think these folk were you,
Bear and your father?'

Harry rubbed his hands together and the last few crumbs
fell into the open mouths of the expectant fish. He turned
and looked at Bess. She was watching the fish scrabble
around in the water, fighting for the last crumb. Then she
looked up at Harry. She said, 'Yes. That was us. Is this
nurse, Flora here? Could I speak with her?'

'Yes,' answered Harry. 'We'll go look for her. Come on.'

He moved away from Bess briskly, humming another
tune from *The Sound of Music*. Bess picked up Bear and
followed him, running to try to keep up with his long
strides.

Soon they were back inside the hospital, in the casualty
department. But Bess had not noticed the sign saying
'Casualty'; she was too taken up with staying close to Harry.
There were quite a few people sitting, waiting. A nurse
smiled at Harry and said, 'Hello Harry, m'dear! What are

you doing here? You're not a casualty, are you?' She smiled and Harry chuckled.

Bess spoke in a loud voice, 'This is where I was! Daddy went through that door!' and she pointed to a blue door in front of her.

Nurse Tess looked down at her in a puzzled way. Harry said quickly, 'Is Nurse Flora around? Is she busy? We need to have a couple of words with her, it's urgent, m'dear.'

The other nurse, more curious than puzzled now, said, 'Why, yes, Flora's in this room here,' and she called, 'Flora, you're wanted out here!'

The door opened and Flora stood there. She took one look at Bess and gasped, 'Oh, dear Lord bless us! It's the little girl who disappeared last year! Where have you been? And your dad, where's he? We were so worried about you both!'

Harry went to her and mouthed, 'Not now!' He indicated another door and jerked his head back over his shoulder towards Bess. Flora understood and said, in a bright, cheery voice, 'It's good to see you, m'dear. Come into this room where it's comfy and I'll get you a drink and some biscuits.'

The nurse took Bess' free hand, Bear was in the other hand, and manoeuvred her into the room, followed by Harry. Flora said, 'Tess, dear, can you get us some elevenses?' She turned to Bess, who was looking around the room. 'I don't recall your name, m'dear...' She waited, but Bess didn't answer.

Harry said, 'The little lass is called Bess.'

Flora went to Bess. 'Do you know your last name? Your surname?'

Bess shook her head. She had begun to feel very tired. Her eyes were cloudy and her face was strangely stiff. She wished that Jan Dad was here and her Andy. Everything seemed to be going round in circles. The pictures on the wall began to slide about. Bess put her hands over her face, dropping Bear, and she crumpled onto the floor.

Chapter Twenty-one

*A*ndrew was looking out of the window as the train sped along. He was standing in a queue in the restaurant car. The train was moving very fast… it felt exciting. The trees and houses rushed past. He remembered, suddenly, the words of a poem by Robert Louis Stevenson:

> Faster than fairies, faster than witches,
> Bridges and houses, hedges and ditches.

'How true!' He didn't realise that he had spoken the words out loud!

The man behind the counter said, 'What's true, son?'

Andy jumped. 'Oh, sorry! I was thinking aloud. I've a habit of thinking aloud.'

The man smiled. 'You must be getting old, talking to yourself. What can I get you?'

Andrew asked for a sandwich and some orange juice. He had some fruit with him, in his haversack, also some biscuits.

He found it difficult, getting back to his seat. Carrying a paper railway bag with his food and drink made him stagger from side to side, but finally he arrived and he fell thankfully into his seat. Briony had seen him coming and she gave him helpful directions. 'We're here, Andrew! Can you see us? We're waiting for you!' Her mother, whose name was Bunty, appeared, saying, 'No! Briony, Ben, you must not disturb Andrew while he is eating his lunch. Now come over here with us. We're going to have some food. You can see him again later. Please don't argue, just come!' She winked at Andy.

Andy heaved a sigh of relief. He had to write some envelopes. He had managed to write the letters at home, but he hadn't had have time to address the envelopes before he had left that morning. They were letters to Mrs Avery, at school, the Sophia Lady and Joseph. But... food, first!

As he munched, Andy wondered about home. 'What was going on? Were they worried about him? They must be frantic about Bess! No, perhaps not. Hannah would be calm. He imagined Han and Artie organising everyone – everyone? Well, Mum, Nah and...? *Goodness me*, he thought, *of course, the others were not there!* He really must phone The Oak Tree House as soon as possible. When would they arrive in Truro?' He made a note in his head to ask Bunty Housman after their lunch.

He was certainly enjoying the journey. They were snaking along slowly now, with the sea on their left. He noticed lots of birds and the sun was glinting on the water. Children played on the sand. Andrew thought it was so lovely. He wanted to be out with them. Maybe when he had found Bess, they could find the sea and the beach in Cornwall.

The train was slowing down. They crawled into a station. Andrew read the name. 'Dawlish.' He spoke the name: 'Dawlish.' It sounded good. He wondered which county they were in. As the train came to a complete stop, he heard a porter, standing on the platform – or was it the station master? – call, 'Dawlish... Dawlish.' He liked the man's unusual way of speaking, so different to Gloucestershire, but somehow there were similarities. Andrew tried saying the word, the same as the man on the platform. '*Dawrlish.*'

A face appeared around the back of the seat in front, but before any words arrived, it disappeared and he heard Larry Housman, the twins' father, say, 'No! Leave the boy alone!' It was not an angry voice. The words were firmly, positively said.

Andrew was pleased. He looked at his watch… nearly one o'clock. He would write his envelopes and then, maybe sleep? Only a nap. He was a little worried about missing Truro. He knew that the train went on to Penzance. He didn't understand that he had a long way to go yet… Plymouth was the next big station, then across the Tamar Railway Bridge and into Cornwall.

Looking at the letter he had written to Mrs Avery, Andrew wondered when he would be able to go back to school. This was his final term at the junior school. He would be going to a big school in September… a senior school. Jan, Chrissie and Andrew had already had a discussion about schools. The boy liked school very much. He was looking forward to being a senior. It meant that you were beginning to be an adult, or so he thought! Actually, he felt pretty grown up now. You had to be pretty grown up to be in the middle of his adventure, happening at this moment, doing what he was doing. The rhythm of the train's wheels was making him feel sleepy. He repeated, 'I'm grown up, I'm grown up,' over and over, in his head, and then he fell asleep.

Chapter Twenty-two

$\mathcal{B}$ess opened her eyes to find that she was lying on a bed, wrapped in a blanket and Bear was with her. She looked at the ceiling and saw rabbits and ducks and kittens. The drawings were colourful and big. She closed her eyes again. Why was she in bed? Where was she? She made her mind think! Oh, yes! she remembered! The hospital! But why was she in a bed?

'Bess? Bess? Can you hear me? It's Harry. We're all here, Nurse Flora, Tess, me. You fainted, that's all. You were very, very cold, so was Bear, even inside his fur, so we wrapped you both in a blanket and laid you on a comfy bed.' Bess wriggled slightly and thought that the bed was not comfy at all, it was hard! She opened her eyes again and looked for Harry. He was bending over her, smiling his wonderful smile, which made his eyes twinkle and sparkle. He smoothed the hair off her forehead and gave her a kiss. 'So, there you are! Good, good! You're back with us. When did you last eat a meal, I wonder? You are such a tiny, thin little soul. There's nothing of you. When I lifted you off the floor, it was like picking up a feather. Oh, dear me!' but Harry laughed as he spoke.

Bess said in a clear, steady voice, 'What kind of bird, Harry, m'dear?'

Harry was amazed and he felt tears spring into his old eyes and a kind of lump grew in his throat. Who was this child? And why did she touch his heart so? Bess pushed back the blanket and sat up. 'Have you found my daddy? He did not come back for me after he went to see the doctor? He told me to sit where I was, with Bear and that he would come back for us.'

Harry immediately said, 'Go on, m'dear, tell us some more.'

And Bess told them. She described the way she had sat on the seat wondering why it took so long for her daddy to see the doctor and why he did not come back for her. She described the moment when she made up her mind to go and look for him and how she had found her way out of the hospital after she had gone through the blue door. She told them that she had walked and walked until she was too tired to walk any further. She told them about the days of wandering the streets of Falmouth and the beach, which they gradually realised must be Gyllyngvase Beach. It was a most remarkable story. Finally, Bess stopped talking... and there was a profound silence. No one knew quite what to say.

At last, Flora got up from the chair she had been sitting in. Her back hurt. She had been sitting, on the edge of the chair, in a tense, rigid way. Now, she must get this extraordinary little girl something to eat and drink. She patted Bess' cheek and left the room. Harry looked at his watch. Nearly one o'clock. He needed a drink badly! He said in a quiet, gentle voice, 'Would you like to come to my house after you have had some lunch, little one?'

Bess shook her head and replied, 'No, thank you, Harry. After I have asked lots of questions, I must go and see Jan Dad. He will be able to take me home to The Oak Tree House. Please, will anyone be able to tell me about my daddy?' Bess' eyes were full of tears now. She was surprised. She hadn't cried for ages.

Harry looked around, but Tess had slipped out with Flora and the two of them were alone. 'I hope so, but, you see, everybody here thought that your daddy had collected you from your seat and you had both gone off together. They didn't realise that you were on your own and that your daddy had disappeared.'

He stopped speaking. He wondered if this would upset Bess even more. However, she wiped her eyes and said, 'Then who else could help me? Perhaps a policeman?'

Harry thought fast. Yes, he could contact his pal John! Maybe he would give them some clues. But what to do now? His question was answered as the door swung open and Flora came in carrying a tray of food. Bess' eyes lit up. She was very hungry. Flora said, 'Here you are m'dear. Now you dig into this and maybe it will put some colour into your cheeks. I have work to do, so Harry can have his lunch with you in here, there's plenty for both of you. I'll see you later.'

And she put the tray down on the table and scurried out, as they heard someone call, 'Nurse Flora, we need you... where are you?'

Harry chuckled. 'Busy people, nurses, aren't they? Right, tuck in.'

Harry and Bess were unaware that PC John Pascoe had been to see his boss, Inspector Drew, and that they had been looking at a missing person file which was called the John Doe file. John Doe was the name always given to a missing man when no one knew his name. This file had been started when Jan and Chrissie had begun searching for Bess' family, after they had been allowed to foster the child.

A great deal of time and effort had gone into the case by the Cornish Police in conjunction with other police forces throughout the United Kingdom. Nothing was known about Bess' family. There hadn't been any clues as to who she was or where she had come from. It was a mystery and, as yet, no one could solve it. PC Pascoe and Inspector Drew had decided that the constable should visit the hospital once again.

It had been a very hectic morning. After Jan had left for his meeting, PC John had had so much to do that it seemed that he hadn't had time to really take a deep breath! Mondays were often like this.

It was Monday afternoon now, and he had grabbed a sandwich and a cup of coffee and was driving to the hospital to ask even more questions about this John Doe. As he sat in his car waiting for the traffic lights to change to green, a sudden thought shot into his mind. *John Doe... missing. Bess... found wandering. Could there possibly be a tie-up? Could there be?* He put the car into gear and drove on up the hill just as Bess walked through the hospital gates and turned right.

Bess and Harry had enjoyed their lunch and she had told the old man as much as she could remember about the year before. It was about 2.15 now and Harry was not surprised when his young assistant, Bobby, came in and told him that he was needed in the laundry – something to do with a washing machine that had broken down. He was irritated, however, as Bess had been saying that last year her daddy had seemed very unusual for a couple of days before they had gone to see the doctor. He was silent and seemed to have to sit down a lot and hold his head. When she had asked him if he had felt ill, she had had to say the words twice or three times. Then his answer was a short, 'No. I'm all right.' He had also seemed to be 'far away from me'. Bess had said these words carefully and slowly as if she was reminding herself how her daddy had spoken them. All the time the child was talking, Harry had been wondering if the father had an illness, or whether he was beginning to lose his memory. He did not know much about illnesses... maybe he should go to see some of the doctors who worked at the hospital or even his own GP? They might throw some light on the situation... and then in came Bobby!

'Can you come at once, Harry?' the young man had said. 'You're an expert on washing machines!'

Harry sighed and clambered to his feet. It was an effort, but he hadn't done much work today, which was unusual, to say the least, it being Monday! Mondays were notorious days... many things went wrong over the weekend! No, he was not surprised when Bobby arrived with this request. And, yes, he would have to go.

'All right, I'll come now. You stay here, m'dear. I won't be long. Finish your chocolate biscuit.' Bobby beamed at Bess and then she was alone. She liked this little room. There were lots of animal pictures and a few Bears sitting in a box with other toys. She took them out and sat them in a circle with bear. They looked as if they were having a meeting. A meeting! Jan Dad – would he have finished his meeting? When would he go back to the hotel? She made another decision; she must leave the hospital and make her way back to Mawnan Smith! All these decisions! Hannah sighed when there were decisions to be made; Bess remembered how Hannah sometimes said, 'Artie, dear, make a decision for me, will you? My mind's in a turmoil!' Bess was not sure of the meaning of 'turmoil', but it sounded a kind of mix-up inside the head!

'I'm turmoiled! What shall I do, now?' she said out loud.

'Harry will come back. If I go – I *must* go – I'll write him a note!' And that's what she did, and Harry found it when he came in rather hot and breathless.

He was saying, 'Bess, m'dear, I'm sorry it took so long to mend the—' He stopped. The child was not there. He spied a piece of paper on the floor and knelt down to read the words written on it in big letters:

DEAR SIR HARRY,

I HAVE GONE BACK TO MAWNAN SMITH TO MEET JAN DAD. WE WILL COME TO SEE YOU AGAIN.

LOVE BESS. THANK YOU, SIR.

Bess walked up the road and looked for the bus stop. She noticed some people waiting in a queue. *Ah, this must be it*, she thought. It was *so* hot! The sky was an odd colour. The clouds looked purple. She plucked up courage and asked a lady if she could get a bus to Mawnan Smith from this stop. The answer was yes. *Good*, she thought, *I hope the bus comes soon...* and before she actually finished her thought she saw the bus coming towards them, up the hill. The brakes screeched as it stopped. Bess climbed on and sat down as near the driver as possible. He had not seen her move to her seat. She was so small and he was taking money from the other passengers. They moved away at last and Bess put Bear on her lap so that he could see out of the window. They stopped a couple of times to allow the people to alight and it was only after about a mile and a half that the driver turned round and saw Bess. He said, 'Now then, young lady, you haven't paid your fare, have you? You get your money out and you can give it me when I next stop.' Bess nodded and looked for her purse. She couldn't find it! She stood up and looked down the side of the seat. It wasn't there or on the floor. It wasn't anywhere. *I must have left it in the hospital room*, she thought. She was feeling very shaky and was breathing very fast. The bus stopped. A man got on, paid for his ticket and the driver said, 'Right. Where are you going, my dear?' Bess was speechless. The driver repeated the words, 'Where are you going?' But Bess could not tell him. Her throat had closed. The driver looked increasingly annoyed. 'If you won't pay your fare then you will have to get off my bus. I will take you to the next stop and then you must get off. Everyone has to pay for a ticket.' He released the handbrake and the bus moved slowly at first, then it gathered speed and bowled along the road to the next stop. The driver braked and the bus came to a halt. 'Off you get. Make sure that you have money on you when you need to use a bus again!' He sounded grumpy and he looked very, very hot. He mopped his face with a rather dirty handkerchief. 'We're in for a nasty storm, mark my words,' he said. He put the bus into gear and pulled away, grumbling all the while.

Bess stood on the grass verge watching the bus as it wound its way towards wherever it was going. She was scared and her legs felt shaky; so much so that she suddenly sat down. The grass felt cool against the back of her bare legs. She'd not the slightest idea where she was or how far away she was from Mawnan Smith. She began to cry. She cried and cried. Her head ached and she longed to be with Hannah and Chrissie, at home.

But she wasn't at home. She was sitting on the edge of a road somewhere in Cornwall. Bess was so distressed that she couldn't think of names or places! Then she heard a voice. 'I think you should move from where you are, little girl. You're very near the cars. They move quite fast, you know. Where are you going, anyway? I saw you get off the bus. The driver looked rather grumpy.'

Bess listened to the words. When they stopped she looked up and there was a round, cheery-looking face smiling down at her. A large black dog was also looking at her. Bess tried out her voice. Just a croak again. But she gave a small cough and stood up. She opened her mouth and out came two words: 'Mawnan Smith.'

'Oh, right. Good. I can tell you how to get to M Smith.' The words were spoken in short, sharp bursts. The lady went on. 'Down that road.' She pointed towards a long, winding road opposite them. 'No, not a good idea. Bends too much. Better go the straighter way. Through Maenporth. Then perhaps the path. Across the fields. No, you need to ask at the cafe in M Porth.' The lady glanced at Bess who was very still, listening intently. She was fascinated by this lady and her odd way of speaking. All the time the big black dog was gazing at his mistress as if he was listening as well. He nodded his head from time to time!

The lady smiled and said, 'Shall I walk with you to Maenporth? You need to tell me your name.' Bess somehow knew that these two were friends. She nodded. The lady bent down to fix a lead onto the dog's collar. 'Better be safe. T'would be desperate if I lost Dog. Right. We're off!' and so they were, the lady and Dog walking ahead of Bess and Bear.

Bess said in a tiny voice. 'My name is Bess and this is Bear.' The lady answered by telling Bess that her name was Anthea Moreton Jones and that the black chap was Dog. Anthea didn't turn around or give Bess any more directions. She began to sing. It was a deep, pleasant sound, a soothing sound. Bess didn't know the tune, but it made her feel relaxed and her breathing settled into a smooth pattern.

In… out… in… out. Anthea and Dog didn't walk too fast for the child. She found it easy to stay just behind them. Trees hung over the road, like a canopy. Bess had visited a number of churches with her father, and once they had been into a cathedral. The trees reminded her of the cathedral, a wonderful green archway over their heads. Whenever Anthea heard a car coming, she paused and moved close into the hedge, Dog did the same. Bess found herself copying them. She was enjoying herself. It was cool on the road. The trees were shading them from the hot sky. It was quite dark, but never worrying. She looked into the distance and became aware of more light. Anthea said, 'Nearly there. Can you see the light at the end of the tunnel?'

Bess said, 'Yes.' Anthea walked on. The song was different. Bess could not understand the words, she wondered if they were in a foreign language. She liked *this* song as well, and she really liked the voice. Anthea didn't sing loudly, but, oh! it was lovely to listen to! The light in front of them grew and soon Bess could hear the faint sound of… the sea? A soft, whooshing sound… and then she saw the sea! 'Oh, how lovely!' The words tumbled out of her mouth. 'How Lovely!'

Anthea said, 'Yes, lovely. Always hits me hard. Seeing the sea.' Dog made a sudden yap, as if he was agreeing. They stood, looking at the beach, the sea, the rocks. Bess was cool and… happy. She felt a hand on her head. 'Bess, let me show you the two routes you can take to get to Mawnan Smith. First a drink. Over there.' And she pointed to a cafe.

Although Bess was thirsty, she also wanted to stay near the sea and the beach. However, she allowed herself to be guided to the small cafe where Andrea left her sitting at a table, under an umbrella, with Dog lying panting nearby.

The air seemed stifling. She found it quite difficult to breathe. She bent down to stroke Dog. His fur was hot. *Poor Dog*, she thought.

Andrea returned with cold drinks for the three of them. 'Now, don't drink that too fast. It'll give you a belly ache.' Andrea smiled at Bess, then looked at Dog. She went on, 'Same for you, Dog.' But Dog's water had disappeared during the time his mistress had been speaking to the child! 'Oh, well. We can't do anything about this chap, can we? I'll get him some more before we go home. Now. Directions for you, my child.' Andrea told Bess that there were three ways of getting to Mawnan Smith: along the road; across the fields; and by the cliff path. The latter was more sheltered from the heat, perhaps. Did Bess know where she was going when she arrived in M Smith? Bess told her that Jan was staying at an hotel. She tried to describe the hotel. Andrea said that there were about three hotels that answered her descriptions, but if *she* ever needed to stay at an hotel in Mawnan she would stay at the country house hotel on the corner. Bess said that the corner one could be Jan's hotel. After lot's more short, brisk directions and advice, Andrea said that she must get home as she had two old aunts staying with her and it was nearing their teatime. Andrea wished her well, blew her a kiss and was gone, singing as she went back along the road.

Bess sat under the umbrella, listening to the sea and the singing, feeling strangely light-headed. She didn't want to move. She seemed to be legless. She breathed in, deeply, then slowly let out all the air. The cliff path had sounded the right choice. She said, 'Come on, Bear. We must start the next journey.' She thought about her purse. She was not worried about it. She felt sure that Jan would find it for her tomorrow. They would be going back to the hospital tomorrow, of course, to see Harry and ask more questions. Bess spoke again. 'I hope this journey won't be too long, Bear.' And she left the shade of the umbrella and walked towards the signpost that Andrea had pointed out to her when they were resting and drinking.

The path climbed steadily around the side of the bay. Bess thoroughly enjoyed the marvellous views. She heard the voices of children and then the deeper voices of grown-ups. She walked under the branches of trees, heavy with foliage, causing them to droop practically onto the ground. There was dust everywhere. The path was dry and hard. She passed gates on her right. She stopped and looked at the gardens beyond these gates, beautiful gardens. She thought that she would like to live down here in Cornwall and have a small house and a big garden, just like these. Then she felt the first drop of rain. She was leaning on a gate, with Bear balanced on the top rail. The raindrops made her shiver. They were huge drops. There was a great flash of light across the sky and a crash of thunder. The noise was so loud and so sudden that she ducked her head and gathered Bear into her body. 'Oh, dear! A storm… a thunder storm! We must shelter.'

Bess struggled into her jersey and began to move quickly along the path. The rain was falling in sheets now, water bouncing off the hard ground. Bess and Bear were drenched, sodden, in seconds.

The ground was very slippery now. Water was rushing down from the gardens and into the ruts on the path. Bess was only wearing sandals and they were soon full of water. She saw some steps in front of her. She was out in the open again; the tree cover was no longer over her head. She was aware of a wind. It was difficult to stay upright and she often nearly fell. Bess struggled to the top of the steps and tripped. She dropped Bear, but managed to grab him as he slithered towards the top step. 'I must get to the hotel!' Bess gasped. She dragged herself forward on her hands and knees. Bear was filthy by now and Bess' clothes were stuck to her little body. Water dripped off her nose. She saw a large bush on her left and tried to clutch the lower branches. She lay in the mud, hanging on to the bush, not realising that she was lying on top of Bear. Another huge flash of lightning opened up the sky and she gasped and closed her eyes! Her hands were so wet that she lost her grip on the bush. The child began to slip backwards. She felt the lump of Bear under her and rolled over, picking him up. She must stand up! She gathered all her strength and scrambled to her feet. She stood, swaying, and saw that the path straightened out in front of her and there were trees and shrubs hanging over it. She forced her feet to move and she reached the area, which had a certain amount of shelter.

'Oh, poor Bear! You are full of water!' She pushed him under her jersey and started to walk forward, slipping all the time. Her chest hurt. There seemed to be a fire inside it, it hurt when she breathed. Then, without warning, a great gush of water hit her legs and as she crashed to the ground, Bear was thrown from under her jersey. He landed on the ground and rolled towards the cliff and over the edge. Bess was stunned for a few seconds, but she knew that Bear had gone! She shrieked, 'No! No! Bear! Please... where are you?' She pulled herself to cliff edge and looked down. Bear was stuck in a bush. 'I'll rescue you... I will! I will!' Bess leaned out and stretched down to grasp Bear's fur, but her hand kept sliding off his head. He was covered with mud. She leaned out further and felt herself dropping into space...

Andrew was standing on the platform of Falmouth Station. A large clock told him that it was nearly 4.15 p.m. It was raining hard. There was a canopy over the platform and lots of people were standing, huddled against a wall, including him. The storm was gradually moving away and the rain was beginning to ease. The temperature had dropped during the storm and he shivered and pulled his anorak round him. He had slept for a long time on the train, but had certainly enjoyed the experience of being on the Cornish Riviera Express. The Housman family had been very kind to him. The two elder children, James and Jenny, had included him in their card games. He had learnt some new ones and had also taught them a few that they had not come across. They laughed and chatted and the twins watched them. Thankfully they didn't interfere too much, and when they became tired, Larry wrapped them in rugs and they fell asleep in their seats. The time passed quickly and suddenly they were in Cornwall and had arrived at Truro where Andrew had caught another train, which had brought him to Falmouth. He didn't have any problems. He had left his home address and telephone number with Bunty Housman, who told him that they 'would so like to meet his family'. So, what now? He hadn't worked out a clear plan for his time after the train journey. So... what should he do now? His mind was empty.

The rain was still lashing down. Andrew shivered. He wasn't getting wet, but the temperature seemed to have dropped considerably. He was wearing his anorak with a sweater underneath. He moved back to the wall where the other people were sheltering. Then he heard the siren. His mind shot into gear and he knew what he must do. The police; he had heard a police siren! Of course, he must go to the nearest police station! The sky was getting appreciatively lighter and the rain was falling slower now. There was a young woman standing close to him. She was holding a very large umbrella over her head. Andrew moved under it and asked her where the police station was. She told him that he would need to walk up a hill and through various streets and down another hill and... it sounded complicated, but he tried hard to take in the directions. She said that she was going some of the way herself and would he like to go with her? Andrew was relieved. He said, 'Yes, thank you,' and as the storm was moving away, they set off.

Bess could not move. She was trapped, it seemed, in a bush. She was lying, head down, in the branches of a huge shrub-type bush. She wasn't hurt, but she daren't move. She had struggled for a while, but had felt the branches shift. She realised that she was in great danger and she was very frightened. The rain had stopped and the sky was breaking up. The sun was beginning to shine through the clouds at times. Where was Bear? She wondered if he had fallen down the cliff, on to the beach below... or on to rocks? 'Please, please, someone, help me!' The words came out in gasps. Her voice was practically a whisper. She spoke again, and this time the words were stronger and clearer. 'Can anyone hear me? Please help me!' She held her breath and listened. Silence, except for the dripping leaves and... the sound of the sea below her. Bess made an extreme effort and shouted, 'Help me, help me!' She listened again. Nothing.

Anthea opened her front door and called, 'Hello, aunts, I'm back! I say, what a jolly storm! So much rain and the noise! Wow! I'm nearly drowned and so is Dog. Come on, fella, I must dry you off.'

A voice came back from the conservatory. 'Glad you're back, Anthea. We were getting worried.' The voice belonged to Anthea's Aunt Hattie. It was always Hattie who spoke. The other aunt, who was called Hettie, was older and left all the speaking to her younger sister. However, the storm had scared her and she also said, 'We're very relieved that you're back, dear Anthea. The conservatory roof has been leaking.'

Anthea laughed. 'Oh dear! Have you put buckets and bowls down? I must do something about that roof!' She had found a towel, and calling Dog, she went into the conservatory, which led off the living room. It was a delightful place, full of flowers and comfy chairs. It was warm and cosy. The two aunts were seated next to each other, holding mugs of steaming liquid, which smelt like herb tea. Hettie put her mug down and stood up. 'Would you like some herb tea, my dear? It would do you good.' And without waiting for a reply, Hettie scurried off to the kitchen. She was a little lady and she always scurried whenever she moved, just like a mouse! In fact, she had the appearance of a mouse; a small, neat face with a pointed nose and darting, lively eyes!

Hattie looked sternly at her niece. 'You've been gone a long time. Where have you been?' Anthea told her all about the extraordinary happenings and how she had directed the child, Bess, to Mawnan Smith. Hattie listened intently, sipping her tea. Then she dropped her bombshell. 'You let her go on her own? Which way did she go? In this storm! You must be off your head! You must go and find her and bring her back here!'

Anthea was towelling Dog. She opened her mouth to protest, but Hattie went on, 'Well, go on! Get the car out and go and look for the child!'

Hettie had just returned with the mug of tea. She opened her mouth to say something but closed it again as she saw the look in her sister's eyes. Clearly, a crisis was in progress! Hattie continued, 'I'll come with you and Hettie can stay here at the end of the phone in case we need more help! Oh, for heaven's sake, Anthea, get a move on!'

And with these words Hattie jumped out of her chair and left the room. Anthea took the mug from Hettie and downed the tea in one gulp. Hettie thought, *Thank God the water wasn't boiling!* Anthea threw the towel to her Mouse Aunt and rushed from the Conservatory, shouting, 'Aunt Hat, wait! We must think this through – where do we look for Bess? What shall we take?' Her voice trailed away as she ran upstairs. Hettie, left alone with Dog and a towel, said softly, 'Dear Dog, I'm glad you're here. Let me dry your head.'

Anthea and Aunt Hattie were driving along the road that led to Mawnan Smith. They had driven to Maenporth and up the winding hill. Now they were slowly moving past houses and the first hotel. The rain had stopped. It was cooler. The two women had not said much, they had just looked and looked. Anthea had described Bess and Bear. Now, they just had to find them. Aunt Hat looked stern and Anthea understood her concern. She was furious with herself for allowing little Bess to try to reach Mawnan by herself. Anthea was fully aware that she had been very foolhardy. She should have taken the child home with her and then driven her to Mawnan Smith or to the hotel where the father was staying. But, she must not think about herself, she *must* find the child!

Hattie spoke. 'Stop the car, Anthea. We must look on the cliff path. Bess may have taken the cliff path.'

Anthea was appalled. 'The path'll be waterlogged after the storm... it'll be too dangerous.'

'Then we must find help. I have a feeling that Bess took the path after you so stupidly left her!'

Anthea felt terrible, so guilty! 'All right. I'll leave the car in Maenporth and find someone to walk the path with me from where it starts.' She turned the car around and drove briskly back to Maenporth. She was now extremely worried. She was racking her brains to think of someone she knew who would go with her. She couldn't think of anyone in this area of Falmouth. Why hadn't she brought Dog with them? He would have been a great help! *Well, he isn't here, you silly woman*, she told herself.

Hattie called out, 'There's a lad over there, parking his bike – ask him. He looks fit and strong. Tell him you need him. Go on!'

Anthea turned around and saw a tall, sun-tanned young man bending over a bicycle. She sighed, and thought, *Well, can't lose anything, might gain something, I suppose*, and she ran to the young man, saying, 'Can you help me, please? It's very important. I've lost a small child in the storm.'

The man straightened up and looked at this distraught woman. He said in a quiet voice, 'Tell me more... why are you so worried?' He had a slight American accent.

Anthea took a deep breath and poured out her story. The young man managed to take in most of it. He saw how anxious Anthea was and that she obviously needed help. 'OK, OK. Try to calm down and tell me your name... Right, Anthea, I'll help you, of course. You say that your Aunt is sitting in your car. Where is it? Oh, fine.' He looked to where Anthea had parked Aunt Hat. She was waving to them to come over. She was getting out of the car and calling, 'Both of you... I've an idea! Quickly!'

That's a powerful lady, thought the young man and he smiled. *These English Ladies... phew!* He said, 'I'm Brendan.' And he ran to the car and Aunt Hat, who was getting very impatient. Anthea followed him and Aunt Hat told them her idea. 'I will stay with the car. You two must take the path. Look, it starts over there! Keep calling the child – her name's Bess, young man.'

The young man said, 'Brendan, I'm Brendan, known as Bren.'

'Good, good... You, Bren, make sure that Anthea uses her brains... she is slow today – my word, yes! Search the cliff edge. Hurry, hurry, you must find the child as soon as possible... she must be terrified, or hurt or...' But she didn't finish her thoughts.

Bren grabbed Anthea's hand and was running back to his bike. He said, 'I've a thermos of water and some biscuits. You carry them. I'll bring a ground sheet and an extra sweater.' Anthea just nodded. She felt as if she was in another world. However, her mind was clear and she felt very alive and ready for anything. Aunt Hat called, 'Good luck! Phone the cafe when you've found her or whatever – they'll bring me the message. For goodness' sake, get a move on!'

Anthea and Bren ran to the where the path began and made their way carefully along it, calling Bess. Bren kept asking questions. Did Anthea know the path well? How long was it? Were there any tricky, dangerous parts? And so on and so on. He stopped often, called and listened, called again. Then Anthea called, 'Bess! Where are you?' No reply. On they went. The ground was still running with water and it was muddy and consequently very slippery. They both slithered and fell onto their knees quite often. Bren gasped out, 'Hey, we'd better be more careful! Let's slow down... we'll do ourselves some harm otherwise, and that won't help the little girl, will it?' They were hot by now and Anthea was finding it difficult to keep up with this young American. They were at the bottom of some steps. Water was running down them. Anthea called again, 'Bess, dear child, where are you? Please be near us?' She was nearly crying.

The voice they heard sounded pitiful. 'Help me... please, help me.'

Bren grasped Anthea's arm and pulled her close to him. 'Is that her? Bess, little girl Bess? Where are you? My name's Brendan and Anthea is with me. Can you tell us where you are?'

They waited, holding their breath. They heard, 'I'm in a bush, over the cliff. I am so frightened. Please, help...' The words stopped. Anthea pulled Bren up the steps. They saw the marks on the grass, as if someone or something had fallen.

Brendan said in a quiet, urgent tone, 'Lady Anthea, stay here, I'm going to look over the edge. Here, hold these.' Anthea's throat seemed to close up, she couldn't speak, only squeak a strangled 'Be careful!'

Bren dropped on to the ground and inched his way to the edge of the cliff. He hooked his foot round the trunk of a small bush-type tree and his head disappeared over the edge. Anthea thought, *I mustn't faint... my head is going swimmy...*

She heard Bren's voice far away, and the words, 'Bess, are you down there? Yes, yes, I can see you. Don't move! Be still!'

Anthea's throat unlocked itself and the words tumbled out. 'Thank God, thank God! Bess, are you hurt?'

Bren's face reappeared. It was pale and drawn. He said, 'Anthea, you must go and find more people to help us! Go to the nearest house and send them down here. Now, lady, go *now!*'

Anthea dropped the sweater and ground sheet, turned to go, realised that she had the thermos and biscuits and placed them on the ground, saying, 'The water is near if you should need it, Bren.' Bren was amazed how calm she sounded. Anthea's mind was in positive gear now. She had to get more help... She was in charge.

Bren said quickly, 'I must talk to Bess, keep her mind occupied, make sure that she doesn't make a sudden move. The cliff is sheer just below her. Hurry, lady!'

Anthea had been looking to the right of the path. There were houses at the top of gardens. She spoke again as she moved on, up the path, 'Don't worry, I'll get more people... stay with Bess and Bear.' And she opened a gate and ran as fast as she could up to the house. Brendan had heard the word Bear – he was confused! 'Bear? What bear?' He eased his body forward again, the foot still hooked round the tree for safety, and called, 'Bess, Anthea mentioned Bear? Who is Bear? Is he with you?'

The voice that reached him sounded exhausted. 'Bear is my best friend... I don't know where he is.' Brendan's heart missed a beat. Friend? A boy?

'Did Bear fall with you?' He waited.

Finally he heard, 'I think he fell. He may be at the bottom. Please rescue him...'

Brendan waited again. No more words reached his ears. *My God*, he thought, *another child! Most probably severely injured, if not dead.* He heard rustling sounds and voices behind him. Anthea was saying, 'Here we are, Bren... three people from the house up there. Another man has phoned the cafe to tell Aunt Hat. Now we can rescue Bess.' She sounded quite cheerful. Brendan pulled himself back from the edge of the cliff and sat up. He saw four people standing above him, two teenage boys and a woman, who could have been their mother. She was a tall, well-built woman, who spoke to him: 'I knew something would happen one day... that cliff edge is a killer! What can we do?'

Bren replied, 'Make sure that the little girl doesn't move. I'm scared that the bush will break away from the cliff side and that she'll drop. What's at the bottom? A sandy beach? Or—'

One of the boys interrupted. 'There are rocks at the bottom... some sand, but mainly rocks.'

'Dear God!' Brendan's words spoke volumes. He went on. 'I'm based at Culdrose. I'm an American officer over here learning about your ways of doing everything. We shall have to get the emergency services up here from... where?'

The boy spoke again. 'From Falmouth or Truro. I'll go and phone them.' He had gone. His mother said, 'Paul will be quick, he's a good lad.'

The other boy touched Brendan's arm. 'Shall I make myself known to the little girl? Is her name Bess?'

Here's a useful fella, thought Brendan, *so calm! My, these English!* He said, 'Yeah, yeah, but go slowly and get some-one to hold your ankles. Hey, Ma'am, you do that, you help your son.' He got up and went to Anthea. His face was stern and he was obviously very worried. He spoke in a quiet, tight tone, 'I am not sure how long Bess can hold out in the

bush. She seems to be trapped, stuck in the small branches and foliage, but her weight might be dragging the roots away from the soil and stones on the cliff. If this is the case she will go with the bush and...' The man shrugged his shoulders and lifted his hands in a despairing gesture. Anthea's throat locked again. What could she say, even if the words came out?

Chapter Twenty-three

They both turned as they heard the mother say, 'Bess? I'm going to tell you what's happening. My son, Alex is here and he'll talk to you as well. Can you hear me?'

The reply came. 'Yes.'

The mother went on: 'My name is Mary. You are stuck in a bush on the side of the cliff—'

Anthea interrupted. 'Should you tell the child—'

Mary said, 'Yes, she should know.'

Alex was speaking now. 'My brother, Paul, has gone to ring the emergency services – you know, the ambulance and fire brigade. They'll come and rescue you. We'll stay here with you. Who is Bear?'

There was a pause, then Bess answered. Her voice was low and she sounded so tired. The words came in a jerky way. 'Bear is my teddy. He's my special friend. I think he must be hurt…'

Alex was lying on his stomach. He talked to Bess in a quiet, natural way. *Amazing*, thought Anthea. *He's only a child, himself, yet he's so in charge!* Bren was talking with Mary. Anthea couldn't hear any of the words, but the atmosphere was less charged and the wind had dropped. It was still, except for the sounds of drips from the leaves all around them.

There was a lot of activity from the garden and Paul returned, panting. He said, 'I've rung 999 and they're on the way.' Bren was immediately alert. He snapped out, 'Did you describe where we are? In detail? Can they get down on to the path?'

'Yes, yes, of course I told them!' Paul sounded annoyed. 'We've lived here a long time... I know all about the cliff path and how to reach it. What do we do now?'

Brendan was impressed. There were three men and two women all ready to do anything that was needed to keep the child occupied. He would just have to contain his impatience. *God, I hope that bush doesn't shift any more!* He asked, 'Do you know what's underneath that bush? Is the cliff sheer or are there any ledges? How far down is it?'

Alex was resting; Mary had taken over from him and was talking to Bess again. He said, 'The drop is about fifty feet. I think there are some ledges. How are they going to get Bess up? It's dangerous and I can hear stones and bits and pieces falling.'

Mary had raised her voice, 'No, Bess, don't move, don't move!' They heard a cry and groans and tearing sounds as the bush began to move. Anthea screamed and grabbed Alex. Brendan and Paul scrabbled to the edge and saw the whole bush with Bess tangled in the branches come away from the face of the cliff and slowly, strangely slowly, drop out of sight. They heard a dull thud, and then there was a weird nothing. And then, the sirens. No one spoke. Anthea began to sob.

Alex said, 'Don't do that, please don't! She's not dead, I know she's not dead!'

Paul ran up his garden path to meet the firemen and police and suddenly, the path was full of men and Brendan was telling the one in charge what he thought had happened.

Mary had been calling Bess, asking her to answer if she could, constantly talking to the child.

A policeman was telling Bren that he was pretty sure that there were ledges on this part of the cliff. One of the firemen would go over on a rope to find out if Bess had landed on one. He also recalled trees growing out of the cliff-face – maybe a tree had broken her fall.

Anthea and the two boys were told to keep clear of the men. The policeman said, 'Ma'am, get us some cool drinks, please, the lads can help you.' Three less people on the narrow path! Mary was pulled back from her precarious position and made to sit and rest. She was very upset, but she soon recovered and went up to the house to organise trays and mugs. The fireman was being slowly manoeuvred over the cliff. 'Tell us what you see, everything that you see,' he'd been instructed.

The man in charge – he'd told Brendan that his name was Colin – kept shouting to Bess, but she didn't answer. Bren said, 'Let me go down as well, I've done a lot of abseiling. Lower me down a little further along the cliff. Maybe I can see what's going on from another position.'

Colin thought fast and then agreed. 'Hurry up then, we mustn't waste any time... the child may be injured badly... we must try to get her up—'

Bren broke in, 'Or maybe we can lower her on to the beach, or—' And he suddenly realised that they might have to call out the rescue service from Culdrose!

Colin had read his mind. He said, 'Culdrose... yes.' They found a suitable spot about twenty feet away from where Bess had fallen and Bren was lowered carefully over the edge. He was not too far from the other man, who was yelling out descriptions. He was saying, 'I think I can see the child – yes! She's caught up in a tree on a narrow ledge, about twenty feet from the beach. It's going to be near impossible to get her up!'

Bren could also see Bess. The other man was right. They would have to get the helicopter from Culdrose. He yelled up to Colin, 'OK, now listen carefully. Go up to the house and phone the air sea rescue people at Culdrose. Make it snappy, tell them my name.' Then he spoke to the other man, 'We must try to see if Bess is still alive. Tell me your name.'

He heard, 'Tom.'

'OK, Tom. I think you're nearer her than me. Can you get to the ledge and the tree?'

Anthea was listening intently. She mustn't miss anything but often she seemed to be in the way and was certainly not doing anything to help the situation. What would Aunt Hat have done? It came to her in a flash – she even seemed to hear her Aunt's voice. 'Go to the hotel, you silly woman, find the child's father.'

She was running up the garden to the house. No one had seen her go, she wasn't important to them. She passed Mary, Paul and Alex, who were coming down, carrying trays. She called out, 'If anyone asks, I've gone to the hotel to find Bess' father!'

Mary said, 'Fine. Good idea.'

Anthea puffed her way on to the road and stopped to get her breath back. 'Which hotel? Oh, Lord, which hotel?' Bess had not known the name. Better try the first one. She ran along the road and into the reception area. She had no idea what to ask, but out came some garbled words and the receptionist managed to understand that there had been an accident and was there a gentleman and his small daughter staying in the hotel? Oh, dear! Confusion! Confusion!' Nobody could be of any use, so she rushed along the road again to the Country House Hotel on the corner. She was steaming hot by now, but she didn't slow down and finally she arrived in the hall of the hotel.

Michael Fossey was removing some flowers from a table. He watched as a bedraggled human being staggered towards him! He moved aside just as the person collapsed on the sofa. Her hair was loose and stuck to parts of her face. Her clothes were muddy and torn. She only had one shoe. He heard the words, 'Water... I... must have... a drink!'

Michael was trying to take in Anthea's story, but she was speaking fast and having gulps of water in between words. He said, 'Slow down, dear lady! I can't understand all you're asking or telling me!'

Anthea held out her empty glass and said, 'A child called Bess. Her father. Are they staying here?'

Michael shot to his feet, spilling the water he was about to pour into Anthea's glass. 'Yes! Yes! The father is up in his room... he's just arrived back from a meeting!' He turned and ran towards the stairs.

He shouted as he took two steps in his stride, 'Mr Leigh! Mr Leigh! Jan! Quick, Bess has been found!'

He could be heard knocking on a door and then another voice said, 'Thank God! Where is she?'

Anthea heard no more... she had fainted.

When she opened her eyes, she could see faces above her and she felt as if she was floating above the ground. She felt as if she was in another world, a wonderfully peaceful warm place. Someone was patting her hand and someone else was saying, 'Dear lady, wake up, please. We must know more about Bess.'

Anthea was back in her dangerous world again! She tried to sit up. Some strong but gentle hands and arms helped her. She was aware of about eight eyes looking at her! Yes, there were four people staring at her! All most peculiar! Then, her mind cleared and she knew where she was. A tall man spoke.

'Tell us where the child Bess is.' The words were spoken in what sounded to Anthea like a German or Austrian accent. The man's face was set and his eyes were troubled. She told them all she knew up to the time that she had left to come and find him. Jan knelt down and took her hands in his. 'Take me to her. I must be with her.'

Brendan was balanced on the ledge close to the tree that had broken Bess' fall. She was alive. He was unable to touch her, but he could hear whimpering sounds and was pretty sure that he could see her breathing. He didn't know how bad her injuries were. Tom was also there. Bren kept on talking to the little girl. He knew that he must make her listen, must keep her from falling asleep. If she had head injuries or even a mild concussion, she must stay awake.

The message had been sent to the air sea rescue centre and he was certain that they would be with them as quickly as possible, unless they were at another accident. Bren kept on praying inside his head. Time was of the essence. The child needed expert medical attention. Tom took over the talking and Bren wiped his arm across his streaming face.

Above the two men, a great deal was going on. Jan and Michael Fossey had arrived. Jan had been told the situation and Michael was there in case he could be of any use. They had not had time to phone Gloucestershire. Michael had advised Jan not to phone, but to go to the cliff path to find out more. When they knew how the child was, then Michael would go and phone. The atmosphere on the path was, strangely, less frantic now. Nothing more could be achieved until the helicopter arrived. Firemen and police were standing drinking tea and coffee and Alex and Paul were talking quietly to a policeman who had joined them. Mary had gone back to the house to prepare beds in case they were needed. Anthea was at the country house hotel, having a shower and borrowing some clothes and shoes from Michael's wife, Agnes. She was so enjoying the warm water! What a day it had been! It wasn't over, of course, but up to now it had been remarkable, to say the least. *I bet the aunts never imagined that they would be involved in anything like this!* Aunts! Oh, no! She'd forgotten all about the aunts! She shouted, 'Agnes! Agnes, dear! Can you make a phone call for me – to the cafe at Maenporth?' She turned off the water and found that a towel was being handed to her.

'Come on now, Anthea. Get yerself dried and tell me what I have to say when I make this call.' Agnes spoke with the most delightful Irish accent. She had a lovely face. The eyes shone at Anthea. *Dear lady*, Anthea sighed and allowed herself to be gently dried by Agnes, who finally gave her a dressing gown to put on.

Agnes chatted on as Anthea dressed in borrowed clothes. It was such a relief just to listen to the tuneful voice. However, Aunt Hat must be phoned, so Anthea managed to tell Agnes that Aunt Hat was at the Cafe in Maenporth and that she would need to know what had happened and that she should get herself a drink and Anthea would return as soon as possible.

Agnes gathered up the wet towels and said gently, 'Now, don't fret. I'll go right away. You must tell me what *you* are going to do, after you've had a wee drink.' And then Anthea was alone. She looked around the bedroom. It was a lovely, restful room with everything a soul like her could need: books; magazines; writing paper; cards; and all manner of toiletries. The window looked out over the garden and the bay. *Such trees*, thought Anthea.

It was at that moment that she heard the helicopter. She caught sight of it moving fast across the bay. She recognised the colour and the markings. 'Air sea rescue! From Culdrose? Yes from Culdrose!'

Anthea ran out of the room and down the stairs, calling excitedly. 'Agnes! Can you hear the helicopter? I think they've called the rescue people out to get Bess! I must go back. Have you spoken to Aunt Hat?'

She heard the 'ting' of the telephone receiver, and Agnes appeared from the office. 'Aunt Hat has been contacted. Come on I'll take you back there myself. Michael may need me to do something. The hotel will be fine. Come on, now.' And she rushed out of the front door, followed by Anthea.

The helicopter circled the accident area. The crew were in touch with Colin and Tom. They had decided to come in close and drop one of their men with a stretcher. They would need help from Bren and Tom to get the child off the ledge. It wouldn't be easy, as the ledge was narrow. The pilot would have to be very skilful, bringing the helicopter in. However, they had had worse problems before and the child must be moved to hospital. Colin was heard to say, 'Which hospital will you take her to? Treliske? Right. I'll contact them and tell them that you are coming. Take care.'

Bren had heard most of the conversation and he realised that the next minutes were going to be crucial; they must not make any mistakes. He said, 'Tom, I'm going on to the ledge. I think Bess needs to be held. She may regain consciousness and start to struggle. That would be disastrous. Tell Colin and the guy coming down with the stretcher.'

As Tom was carrying out these instructions, Bren moved very slowly nearer the ledge and finally managed to crawl on to it, hanging on to the tree. Bess was wedged in the branches. Her body was twisted, and he dare not attempt to move her. He touched her face and spoke reassuringly all the time. Her eyes flickered at times and she moaned, but she didn't try to move.

The noise of the helicopter was immense. He had never realised how powerful the engines were, but then he had never been underneath a helicopter before. The pilot had come in as close as safety would allow and he could see the man with the stretcher being winched down towards them. The man swung from side to side. Bren thought, *My God, he'll never be able to land near enough!*

But slowly and surely, Bess' rescuer was coming. He saw Tom stretch out a hand to grab a trailing line. He missed it! Tom tried again and he caught it. It was a rope attached to the airman. The man yelled to Tom to pull him in very carefully, and then he was with them. He grinned at Bren and said in a normal, natural way, 'Right, mate. Here we are! Let's be having her…'

The group of people up on the path seemed to have grown considerably. Jan and Michael were watching every moment. Colin was with them. They were all as near to the edge of the cliff as possible, which was difficult as the ground was extremely slippery. Paul and Alex had been doling out drinks and biscuits. The firemen had laid planking on the ground to help make it safer, and a couple of them were now down on the beach below. They'd found Bear.

Mary was in the house when Anthea and Agnes arrived. Anthea had remembered her route from the path to the hotel, and had taken Agnes there. The three women were just going down to join the others when they noticed a car crawling along. 'That's my car! And Aunt Hat is driving it!' Anthea squealed. 'She told me that she couldn't drive! Aunt Hat, Aunt, what are you doing in my car?'

The car stopped and a head came out of the window. 'My dear woman, I've been driving round the houses here for ages. Where have you been? You should have been here to direct me! Gallivanting about as usual, I suppose!' With these words ringing in the ears of the listeners, Aunt Hat climbed out of the car, brushed down her skirt, pulled her jacket straight and marched over to them. 'Oh, it's you Agnes, glad you're here. Are you organising my niece?' She looked at Mary and said, 'Who are you, my dear? Is the child safe? I heard the helicopter. This is all Anthea's fault, you know!'

Mary said quickly, glancing at Anthea's stricken face, 'Nobody's fault. An unfortunate accident. Are you coming with us?' And without waiting for a reply, Mary walked off down the garden path. Anthea followed. She didn't want her Aunt to see that she was crying.

Agnes took Aunt Hat's arm, saying, 'How good to see you, dear. I hope you enjoyed the meal you had at the hotel the other day? How clever of you to find this place, especially as you don't know the area well – or the car!'

Agnes was one of the most tactful member's of the human race! Aunt Hat grunted, but was pleased to be remembered by the hotel owner's wife. Actually, Hat had not met Agnes before, but Agnes had seen her in the dining room with the Mouse Aunt and Anthea the evening they'd come for dinner. The head waiter had pointed out this powerful, eloquent and, yes, elegant lady. For, indeed, Hat was a very handsome, impressive lady. She had been an opera singer of renown and the head waiter was an opera fan, having seen Hat at Covent Garden!

The women were very curious to know what had happened. Unfortunately they all asked questions at the same time! Colin called out sharply, 'Quiet! Quiet please! You must not talk. Bess is being rescued!'

Now, there was absolute silence and no one moved. They could hear voices coming through the intercom, which Colin was holding. They heard Colin's replies and questions and then they heard, 'Take her away.' Every head tilted towards where the helicopter was hovering. They saw it rise up and they saw the airman and the stretcher with Bess in it being winched up into the plane. Then they watched as the air sea rescue helicopter with its precious passengers flew in a circle and away towards Truro and the hospital.

Aunt Hat started the applause. It grew and grew and the faces of the people who had been so aware that little Bess could have been killed were radiant.

Andrew called, 'Thank you for your help.' He watched the lady with the umbrella walk down the street.

She turned and called back, 'Any time. Take care.' Andrew looked up at the sky. The rain had stopped… the storm had passed over. The sun was doing its utmost to shine again. He was standing on the corner of a road that led to the police station. In fact, a police car was driving towards him at this very moment. It was moving fast. It stopped next to him and he saw that the driver looked stern and tense. After he had heard the sirens earlier, he had also heard what he suspected were fire engine sirens. He had forgotten about them as he had walked with the umbrella lady. Now, he wondered if something nasty had happened.

The car moved away from the corner and Andrew started to walk along the road. He'd noticed where the car had come from; it had come from a narrow road beside a building. On the building were the words 'POLICE. DANGER. KEEP CLEAR.'

Andrew looked to see if there were any more vehicles coming, and then crossed the road and went up to the door. He pushed it open carefully. His heart was beating fast. This was his chance to investigate Bess' disappearance…

Chapter Twenty-four

*H*annah was surrounded by children. Joe was with them. Hannah was telling them a wonderful story, all about Horatio and his family, how they had been planted as seeds, how they had grown and when they were first found. Joe thought, *How lucky I am to know Hannah. There is no one else in the world who can tell stories like Hannah!* He felt proud. He could see Hannah every day, could be with her and Artie. He was also a – what would Andrew call him? A splendid person? Yes, a splendid man.

The other children were rapt in Han's words. Horatio was sitting on the palm of her hand and Joe was listening carefully – he must not miss a word – but suddenly Hannah stopped speaking and put her hand over her mouth. She stood up and said, 'Oh! I, I have to go, my dears. Joe, you put Horatio back in his house box. You take care of him.'

And before any of them were able to say anything Hannah had left the room. One of the small children started to wail, 'I want to hear the story, I want—'

Joe felt the big pea sitting on his hand. He put his other hand over the top and began to get up from off the floor where he was sitting.

'Can I help you, old man?' Joe had completely forgotten that he could not see. He turned his head towards the voice. It went on, 'You've met me. My name is Benedict Taylor. I'm another doctor, an eye doctor. Come on, I'll take you to your room.' Joe felt a strong hand cup his elbow and he was gently guided out of the room, which was now very noisy. The children were confused. Hannah didn't normally behave like this. She always finished her story, or at least explained that she would be back with the next part. Joe was very confused. Hannah's behaviour had been so sudden. It had been a shock for everyone when she had stopped and left so rapidly.

Benedict took Joe along the corridor, asking questions about Horatio. He had been sitting quietly on the window ledge of the small 'story' room. He noted how still the children were, how they were totally inside Hannah's words. *A remarkable little lady, this Hannah*, he had thought. He was also shocked when she had suddenly changed – extraordinary!

After their first meeting down by the gates of the hospital, Benedict had seen Hannah a couple of times, but they had only said 'Hello'. He had made some inquires about her and been told that she was a regular visitor to the children's wards, that she was admired and loved and that she had special healing qualities. Benedict had observed Joe without the boy knowing. He had watched Joseph use his pencils and crayons and realised his talents. He knew that Joe would not see again. Benedict had special qualities as well as Hannah. He spent most of his time working with blind children, teaching them how to cope with their blindness. He was going to be deeply involved in Joe's life in the future.

Joe asked Benedict where Han had gone. Benedict said, 'I'm not sure, Joseph. I'll find out. Will you stay here for a short while? I'll be back as soon as possible.' They were in Joe's side ward room. Joe nodded. He wanted to cry, because he needed Hannah. However, he felt safe with this eye doctor and he liked his name: 'Benedict'. It was a good sound when spoken. He spoke the name.

'Benedict. I'll be OK, Benedict. Come back soon. Please find Hannah.'

Benedict touched the boy's cheek and left, saying, 'I'll be as fast as I can. Think good thoughts.'

Hannah knew that something was very wrong, very seriously wrong. She had felt her whole body change. It was as if a great surge of energy had entered her head, which shot through her veins and into her bones. Her mind was absolutely clear and she was being told to telephone The Oak Tree House immediately.

'Hello, hello? Chrissie, did you phone me? No, you were just about to... well, I beat you to it. What's going on?'

Chrissie told Hannah all she knew about Bess. Michael Fossey had got in touch with her and had told her everything. Chrissie was mind-blown! At the end of the conversation Agnes had come onto the phone and said, 'Can you come, Mrs Leigh? Jan and Bess need you to be here. Is there anyone who could come with you?' Chrissie made herself think calmly. 'Hannah, yes! Hannah!' She told Agnes that she would start driving within the half hour and that she would be with them before midnight, hopefully. Agnes said, 'God speed, my dear.'

Hannah took a deep breath when Chrissie had finished. 'Yes, of course I'll come with you. Please tell Artie to prepare my suitcase. Will you make other arrangements? Bibi? Sophia? Nah needs to stay. She should be here for Joseph. I'll go and tell him. Will you meet me outside the front door of the hospital? Thank you.'

Benedict watched Hannah as she replaced the receiver. The old lady was sitting on a chair with the phone in her lap. He saw her close her eyes and heard her say, 'Dear Lord, be near. I will only do what you tell me to do. I know what I have to do first.' Hannah put the telephone on to the table and seemed to pull together her mind and thoughts. She saw Benedict watching her. She looked up at him and said, 'Ah, Benedict Taylor. Good, good. I'll need you to run around for me. I'm going to see Joseph. Will you come?'

Joseph had put Horatio back in his house box, which Artie had made for him. Joe had very slowly felt around his room. He had become familiar with the positions of the furniture and his own possessions and as long as they hadn't been moved by a cleaner or a nurse, who were unaware of the necessity of objects and furniture being always in the same place, he was able to move smoothly and confidently.

He was talking to Horatio when Hannah and Benedict arrived. 'You'll be fine, Horatio. You need to rest, after you have fed your relations. I'm going to draw you. Green.'

Charlie came into the room. She had caught Joe's words as she walked along the corridor. 'What are you looking for, Joe?'

Joe turned towards the voice, the lovely Scots accent. He replied, 'A green crayon. I'm going to draw Horatio and his house and family. I need lots of colours. Will you help me find them?'

Charlie laughed. 'Yes, I'd love to help. I'll just go to the kitchen with these dirty cups and saucers. Your coloured pencils are in your bedside cabinet.' Joe was the other side of his bed but it wasn't difficult to feel his way round to the cabinet, and that's what he was doing when Hannah arrived. He was chatting away to Horatio and was unaware that Han was in his room until she spoke. 'Joseph.' Joe froze. Hannah only called him 'Joseph', when she was worried or upset. His heart missed a beat. Hannah continued. 'Joseph, I have to tell you something important. It might scare you but you need to take it in and really, really think.' Charlie ran into the room. Hannah spoke again, quickly. 'Ah, Charlie, good, we need you.' Hannah told them that she and Chrissie were about to travel down to Cornwall and why they had to go. She told them as much as she knew about Bess and Jan and the fearful happenings.

Then there was silence. A heavy silence. Joe spoke first. 'What will happen to me? Will I be able to go home? Where's Andrew?'

Hannah repeated, 'Andrew! Oh dear God, I'd forgotten Andrew! Now, where on earth can he be?'

Benedict came into the room… he'd heard the last words. Cheerfully he said, 'Andrew? Oh, he's in Falmouth at the police station. He's phoned home. He's fine!'

Charlie looked from one face to the other. She was amazed. 'What going's on!' Ever since she had met this family, these people, amazing things had happened – and she was involved!

Hannah thanked Benedict and began to speak again, but Benedict interrupted her. 'Excuse me, Hannah. I've just had a word with Dr Miles. I've told him what's going on. He thinks it would be a good idea for Joe to go home tomorrow morning and he's suggested that Charlie goes with him. I gather you have a few days' leave, Charlie. Joe, would this please you?'

Joe whispered, 'Yes, yes.' Then his voice was back and the next 'Yes!' was very loud!

Charlie was stunned. Not so long ago she had been wondering if she would ever see The Oak Tree House and

be able to visit The Cottagey House. She was delighted with
the idea of looking after Joe! 'Och, yes, yes! I'd love to go
home with you, Joe! That's a great idea! I can be there when
you all return. Will Nah be at The Oak Tree House?'

Nah! Yes, Nah! thought Hannah. Bibi would need Nah.
Benedict smiled his beautiful smile and said, 'Right, what
next, Hannah? Any more phone calls?'

Hannah patted his hand and smiled back at him. 'Yes.
Merlin Cottage. Mrs Sophia Grant Beauchamp. Come
outside and I'll tell you what you have to say to her.'

Charlie, left alone with Joe, went over to him and took
his hands. She knelt down so that she was on the same level
as the little boy. 'Joe, how exciting! You're going home a
day early! It was arranged for Wednesday and I was thinking
that I would not be seeing you after Tuesday and now I
shall be seeing you for lots more days and nights – and
you'll be seeing me!'

She gently pulled him into her arms and gave him a long
hug. Joe was very hot. He had been in and out of so many
feelings in the last ten minutes that he felt quite exhausted.
He felt his body slump against Charlie, and he let himself
be held. He was aware of her perfume. In fact, he knew
Charlie was around by her perfume. He said, whispering
the words into her ear, 'You smell lovely, Charlie,' and he
snuggled into her neck.

'Don't worry, Hannah darling, Nah and I will work out
Bibi's well-being!' laughed Sophia. 'Bibi has had an extremely busy and tiring day. She's fast asleep surrounded by
animals. She has such energy! No, I'm fine… not too
tired… I've had a large brandy and am about to eat my

supper. Are you all right? Take my love and prayers with you... pass them onto Chrissie and please, please don't worry too much! Give me the Falmouth hotel's phone number... yes, yes, I have it, thanks. Goodbye now... safe journey.' And Sophia put down the receiver. She thought, *Wow! What a life! Will it ever settle? Probably not – probably not meant to! Well, it's good for us to be so deeply involved in living!* And she walked briskly into the kitchen.

Nah was helping Chrissie to pack some essential bits and pieces for the journey. She called, 'What's the state of the petrol tank in the sports car?'

The answer came from the other end of the corridor. 'Sorry, I don't know – could you check it for me?' Chrissie sounded very wide awake and alert. Her voice was steady and strong.

'All right, after I've finished packing this case. Have you got your toilet things etc.?'

Chrissie called back, 'Just fetching them. Leave the case, darling. Check the petrol, please.'

Nah ran downstairs and into the yard behind the house. The little white sports car was bathed in evening sunshine. *It looks smug*, Nah thought, *as if it is the most important and essential car ever made!* The petrol gauge showed a half tank. Chrissie came out of the back door carrying cases, rugs and a basket with a thermos flask and sandwich tins in it. She was breathing heavily. 'I think I've got everything! Thank you for all you've done, Nah. I must go now, Han will be waiting for me.' Chrissie had been putting the luggage into the boot and onto the back seat as she spoke. Nah told her about the petrol situation. Chrissie said, 'Right, I'll pop into the filling station on the way to the hospital – thanks, darling. Bye now. Take care of yourself. Are you going to talk to Artie and Sophia? I'm so relieved that Andy is safe. What a time this is, isn't it? Maybe we'll all laugh about it in years to come.'

Chrissie threw her arms round Nah's neck and hugged her close. 'I love you so much,' she said rather shakily. She pulled away, wiped a hand across her eyes and climbed into the car. Nah closed the door and blew her a kiss as she watched her friend drive away and out of sight. 'God, keep her safe, let her drive safely.' Nah took a deep breath and walked very slowly back to the house and the telephone.

Chapter Twenty-five

*A*rtie was singing loudly as he prepared the supper for Hannah and himself. In fact, he was singing so loudly that he didn't hear the phone ringing. He hit a high note and stopped to take a breath for the following part of his song, then he heard the phone! *Who's phoning?* he thought. And he went through various names as he walked to the telephone in the hall. He picked up the receiver and said. 'Chrissie – oh, sorry, my maid! Are you still at the hospital? Han, Han, speak slower! I can't catch what you're telling me.' There was a long silence as Artie listened to the words at the other end of the line. There was a chair next to the table where the phone was housed. He stretched out a hand and held on to the seat as he lowered himself on to it. His face was becoming set and it had lost some of its colour. Finally he spoke. 'Yes, I understand. You have to go with Chrissie. Right. What do you want me to do? Have my supper? My dear girl—' Clearly Hannah had interrupted him.

Artie sat nodding his head and saying periodically, 'Yes, yes… I see… I understand. Yes, I'll pack some clothes for you… and all the essentials. What did you say? Oh, yes, give the suitcase to Chrissie to put in her car… yes.' There was another time of just listening and then he said, 'God bless you both. Ask Chrissie to phone me when you stop for a breather. I love you, dearest little Han.' Artie took a large hanky from his cardigan pocket and blew his nose. He heaved himself out of the chair and made his way back to the kitchen. He wasn't singing now. He looked at the food and the bottle of wine on the table and slowly shook his head, saying, 'No, no wine this evening… it'll keep until my Hannah returns, until the lot of them return. Then we'll celebrate.' He picked up the plate of sandwiches and took them into the living room. 'I'll have a glass of ale.' Artie's voice was low and shaky, not a bit like the usual Artie.

Then the front door bell rang and he heard Nah's voice. 'Hello there, Artie. Thought you might like to come with me to Sophia's place to talk about the Cornish adventures.' Artie turned and Nah saw the tears on his cheeks. She flew to him, took the plate and the glass and having placed them quickly on the table, went back to him and held him in her arms. Nah was the same height as the old man. She rested her cheek on his and just stood there as he sobbed. She said gently, 'Come on now, darling. Let's lock up and go to Merlin Cottage. Shall we walk? It's not far.' She put the food and drink into the fridge and they left arm in arm.

Sophia welcomed them cheerfully and soon they were munching her sandwiches and drinking hot chocolate, which Sophia had insisted was much more comforting than ale or whisky. Artie had begun to relax, though Nah realised that he was still very concerned that Chrissie and his beloved Hannah had rushed off into the night. Cornwall was a long way from Gloucestershire! He didn't like that sports car either. It went too fast and it was so near the ground. However, Sophia's living room was cosy and the chair he was sitting in was very snug. He was beginning to feel sleepy. Nah shot a glance at him. His eyes were drooping and he looked peaceful. She got up and went over to Sophia, indicating that they should go into the kitchen to talk. Sophia nodded and they left the room, quietly closing the door behind them.

'What do we do about Bibi?' asked Sophia.

Nah said, 'She can come to me at The Oak Tree House tomorrow. Joe is coming home tomorrow as well, with Charlie, his nurse. It's all fixed up. Bibi can help with Joe. It'll be good for her to think about someone else. She can be an important, essential helper!' Nah chuckled.

Sophia's eyes had stretched in astonishment.

'She can be helpful, you know, Sophia. I don't stand for any silliness from that delightful little girl. She is so intelligent. Don't you find her bright?'

'Oh yes. She's quite phenomenal at times!' Sophia said decisively. 'You're right, of course, she'll be very useful. How does Joe get on with her? Does he like her?'

Nah nodded. 'Hmm. He wasn't with her, often, before his operation. He spent most of his time with Andrew and Hannah. Bess worried him and he seemed wary of Jan. Artie gets on with everyone, Joe is always happy to be with Artie. Charlie will be invaluable. I gather that a doctor called Benedict Taylor will be visiting Joe. This Benedict will start teaching him how to manage his blindness—'

The telephone rang. Sophia shot to her feet and rushed to the answer it. 'Sophia here... ah! Chrissie! Where are you? Near Bridgwater? Artie's with us... he's asleep. Here's Nah.'

Sophia handed the receiver to Nah. 'How's Hannah? Oh, fine... I expect she's enjoying the car!' Hannah had always found Chrissie's sports car exciting. Nah went on: 'The weather's good, anyway. Phone us again... No, we haven't had any more news from Jan or anyone else down there... Oh, you phoned The Cottagey House first... It's all right,

Artie is with us, sleeping in the living room!' Nah laughed.

Sophia went back to the kitchen. Nah went on in a quieter voice, 'Just drive carefully, you're both very precious. Make sure that nothing else happens, won't you? Love you, bye.' Nah smiled and went to the kitchen to continue her conversation with the Sophia Lady.

Andrew was sitting on a bench, holding a mug of sweet tea and listening and watching as police, both men and women, hurtled around. There was something enormously urgent going on. He'd gone into the building and seen a desk in front of him, but when he had tried to tell them why he was there, he had been told to wait on the bench and asked if he would like a mug of tea. He was clearly in the way and they hadn't time to deal with his problems. He had attempted to find out what was going on, but a large policeman had said, 'You stay on the bench, son, and drink your tea – we'll be with you as soon as possible!' Though, actually, the policeman had said, 'We'll be with you ASAP.' Andrew knew what these letters meant, so that's where he was: on the bench, drinking tea. However, he made sure that he was registering everything that was happening. It all had to be remembered so that he could tell the others when he saw them.

A policewoman was on the phone close to him. He could hear every word she was saying. 'There's one fire engine and two police cars at the incident… Yes, a young girl has fallen over the cliff just beyond Maenporth. I can't give you any more information at present. Phone again a little later. Goodbye.' Andrew thought, *Wow, so that's what I heard earlier. Sirens, police cars… fire engine. Gosh, hope the girl's safe.*

A man, not in uniform, came out of a room on Andrew's right. He spoke to the WPC. 'Was that the press? You didn't tell them too much, did you? Be careful – we don't want them on the scene. There's no room on the cliff path for that lot.'

PC John Pascoe came through the front door. He was out of breath and very hot. 'I've just been talking to Harry Hammond at the hospital. He tells me that he's been with a little lass called Bess. She's been in trying to find out about her father. He apparently—'

Andrew jumped up, slopping tea over himself. 'Wait, wait, did you say Bess? That's my Bess – where is she?'

The man in the suit spoke. 'It's all right, son, nothing to do with you, stay there.'

But Andrew would not be quiet. 'Please listen to me. Bess is missing – I've come all the way from Stroud to find her. Is she here?' he persisted.

John Pascoe felt himself go cold. Harry had shown him the purse that had been found – Bess' purse. He'd opened it and there was an address in it, The Oak Tree House, then a name he couldn't read – it was all smudged – and then the word 'Stroud'. Who was this boy? Who was the girl on the cliff?

Andrew went on speaking. 'Bess would have a teddy bear with her, he's called Bear. She has to have him – have you seen them?'

The WPC, who had naturally overheard all what was being said, shouted, 'A bear? A teddy bear? The man on the phone said something about the child's teddy – that the bear had been lost over the cliff.'

All eyes turned towards her. A split second went by, then the man in the suit moved fast, saying, 'What's your name, lad?' Andrew told him. The tall man went on. 'Is your father called Jan and is he a film director?'

Andrew blurted out, 'Yes, yes! Where is he? And Bess – is she hurt? What's happening?' He was nearly crying now and the man, who Andrew learnt later was Inspector Adrian Drew, realising that the boy was Bess' brother and that he was needing a great deal of reassurance, led him into an office and shut the door firmly behind them.

Inspector Drew pulled a handful of tissues out of a box and handed them to Andrew, saying, 'Now, son, blow your nose, gather your mind and we'll have a quick talk. There's lots that you should know and there's lots I have to know from you. All right?'

Andrew gulped and did what he was told.

Michael and Jan had driven in near silence to Truro. They arrived at the hospital quite quickly, although it seemed like hours to Jan. Michael drove as fast as he could, but the route was dangerously twisty and he felt that he mustn't do anything to risk another accident. The helicopter had arrived much earlier and Bess was now being taken care of by a team of nurses and doctors in the A and E department. Jan was allowed to go and see her. She lay on the bed covered in tubes with a doctor examining her carefully. In a strained voice, Jan said, 'Will she be all right? Are there serious injuries?'

The doctor nodded his head at one of the nurses, who came over to Jan and took his arm. She spoke very quietly, 'Please come with me, sir. I'll tell you all I know.' She led Jan to a pleasant room. She noticed his stricken face. This nurse had talked to hundreds of relatives of badly injured people and she was a sensitive soul.

'Bess is unconscious, but we've been told that she was conscious at times when she was on the cliff and had been talking coherently. It seemed that she lost consciousness when the American was with her, before the rescue team managed to lift her onto the stretcher. As yet, we've found no broken bones or deep lacerations. It may just be intense shock. It will be necessary for us to do lots of tests. Would you like to contact your wife or anyone else?'

Jan stood looking down at this woman. Her words seemed to be running around his brain. He kept hearing 'intense shock... intense shock'. Like Joseph. Oh, why was all this happening to them, to their family? He sat down heavily and was aware that the nurse was offering him a mug. *Tea*, he thought, *always tea!* He was so tired. He took the mug automatically, but his hand was shaking and he found that the nurse was kneeling, holding his hand that held the mug. 'Sorry, I'm sorry...' The words fell out of his mouth, and then he began to sob.

The nurse took the mug and placed it on a low table. She came back to him and said, 'That's good, Mr Leigh. Cry as much as you can. Have you a hanky? Ah, fine!' Jan had dug out a hanky from his pocket. 'No one will come in here. When you feel steadier, ring the bell near the door and I'll bring you more news of the little girl.'

'Wait, wait!' Jan gulped and managed to say, 'Please, make sure that Bess has Bear – please.'

The nurse didn't understand, but she said, 'Yes, I will,' and she left Jan.

Back in the urgent place, as Andrew called it later, she went up to the bed and looked for a teddy bear. No, there wasn't one anywhere to be seen. She whispered to another nurse who was looking at one of the machines, 'Did a teddy bear come in with Bess?' The other nurse shook her head and shrugged her shoulders.

The doctor was on the internal telephone. 'The child will have to stay in. I need a bed for her.' The doctor glanced towards the nurse and beckoned her to come over to him. He continued the telephone conversation. 'Yes, it's urgent! I wouldn't have contacted you otherwise, would I?' He sounded annoyed. 'Please find me a bed… we'll need it very soon!' And he hung up. He moved back to Bess, saying, 'How is she now? Any movement? Has she stirred at all? Her breathing seems consistent… keep talking to her. Nurse, were you enquiring about a teddy bear?'

The nurse had followed the doctor, making sure that she was not in his way. She knew this man well. He was a very good doctor, but needed everything to happen at once. She told him quickly and succinctly about Jan and the teddy bear. 'Find out more about this Bear. Ask Mr Leigh why it's so important.' The doctor was watching the machines and then Bess. The nurse went back to Jan who, by now, seemed to be much calmer. He was walking round the room, looking at the pictures on the walls. His mind was racing. He must find out if Agnes had managed to get in touch with Chrissie. Was she on the way down to Cornwall? So many thoughts – so many questions that needed answers!

The Nurse came in and said, 'Mr Leigh, could you tell me more about this teddy bear? Could he help Bess in any way?'

Jan sighed and sat down. 'Yes, I'll tell you.'

Chrissie was driving steadily, aware that Hannah was asleep. They were over the Tamar Bridge and into Cornwall. They'd stopped a couple of times to have a drink, but not for long and the journey had been free from problems. Chrissie loved driving her little car, and, thankfully, it was going well. She felt sure that they had to be in Truro as soon as was humanly possible. Her stomach kept turning over when she thought about Bess and she wished that they could take off and fly! But she had to be patient and calm. She had a very, very precious passenger.

Hannah stirred and opened her eyes. She yawned and then said in a sleepy, croaky voice, 'Where are we, dear?'

Chrissie squeezed her hand and said, 'In Cornwall, darling. We should be in Truro in about an hour and a bit, all being well.'

Hannah smiled. 'All will be well. It's not so far now then, is it? Good. You do drive well… I wish I'd learnt to drive when I was younger. I would have loved a car like this!' And Hannah stretched out her legs as if to feel the pedals. 'Yes, I would have driven fast!' She laughed.

Chrissie chuckled and said, 'I can just see you in a sports car, Han, with the roof down and you wearing a scarf! You would have been stunning! I think you should have a go when we get back to Gloucestershire. Would you like to?'

Hannah said, a little tentatively, 'Well… yeeeess.' And then out came, 'Why on earth not? Yes! Thank you. Will you teach me?'

Chrissie was only surprised for a moment: she had known Hannah all her life. Hannah had guts. She patted the old lady's hand and spoke with enthusiasm, 'Of course. I'd enjoy that enormously.' They smiled at each other and lapsed into silence. Their minds were overflowing with thoughts. Bess, naturally, and Jan, Andrew, Artie – oh,

Everyone and everything! The light was fading rapidly. Soon it would be dark. Chrissie switched on her lights and began to concentrate hard. They must keep going at a steady pace. She needed Jan and she knew, without any doubt, that he needed her.

Nah was having a bath, and listening to some very tuneful music on the radio. She and Sophia had decided that Bibi should stay at Merlin Cottage until Tuesday morning. The two women had thought it would be dangerous to disturb the child, she just might stay awake if she was moved back to The Oak Tree House! That's why Nah was having a wonderful bath. She lay in the hot, steaming water, sipping a glass of whisky. She felt content and beautifully warm. She had talked to Andrew and had heard that he was about to be taken to the hospital in Truro, in a police car, driven by an inspector. Andrew had sounded so excited! He appeared to be enjoying himself, although she had also realised that he had been, and still was, extremely worried about little Bess. She had phoned the hospital and had spoken with Jan. He'd told her about Bess. She was still unconscious, but stable. The problem at this time was the whereabouts of Bear. Jan was positive that Bear would help Bess to regain consciousness, but no one seemed to know where he was. They were unable to have a long conversation; Jan had to go. Nah didn't really know why and that was a little worrying, as he hadn't phoned her back. Oh well, there was nothing she could do up in Gloucestershire, so she'd run a deep bath.

Artie and Pippin were walking up the lane to The Oak Tree House. The dog trotted at Artie's side, cocking her ears when the old man spoke to her. 'All right, old girl? We're going to visit Nah, see if she's safe. She's on her own as well as me – it was good that you came down to see me. You must have known that I was unhappy without my old Han. You doglets know it all, don't you?' He fondled the dog's head and Pippin looked up at him and smiled. She was a great smiler! Golden retrievers seem to have the knack of turning up their mouths to make it look as if they are smiling. Pippin was a comforting sort of animal.

They turned the corner in the lane and saw a large, old estate car swing though the open gates of The Oak Tree House. Artie stopped. Who on earth was calling now? *Oh, he thought, I know that car: it's Fred from Scotland. I remember. He's coming down to look at a pony. And he's here now.* Artie called to Pippin, 'Here! Wait for me, girl!' Pippin had run on ahead and was barking madly as the old ramshackle car trundled up the drive to the front door. Artie called out, 'Is that you, Fred? Are there more of you?' He hoped that Fred was on his own, that the other members of his nutty family were still in Scotland.

The car had slid to a halt and the driver's door swung – or should I say, groaned? – open! A very large man scrambled out.

'Hello, Artie, my dear old man, how are you, great to see you, and Pippin Dog!'

All these words were spoken so fast that Artie only caught a few of them. Fred shook Artie's hand ferociously and bent down to speak to Pippin, who had recognised a friend. Her tail was wagging so joyously that she kept falling over.

Fred straightened up and said, 'Where is everyone? Why aren't they out here giving me a Leigh welcome?' He looked at Artie and suddenly Fred became still and when he spoke again, the voice was quiet. 'Tell me what's happened, old friend.'

Artie, having regained a certain control after the shock of seeing Fred, said, 'It's very good to see you, sir. Yes, we do seem to have a fair amount of problems. The others are all spread around the country and – but we should go inside and tell Nah that you're here. She's around somewhere, I'm not sure where…' Artie's voice faded as he walked towards the back door, which he knew would be unlocked.

Fred watched the old man and his head went into another gear. *Problems*, he thought, *indeed there must be!* He took a battered old holdall out of the car and followed Artie to the kitchen door. Whenever he had arrived before at The Oak Tree House, a large number of people of all sizes and some animals had seemingly fallen out of the house and the welcome had been immense. But today, well… He went into the kitchen and dumped his bag on the floor. Artie was filling the kettle and he was talking to himself, not realising that Fred was in the room. 'Shall I tell him everything, Han, me dear? I'm so befuddled in my old head. I need you here…' and he sighed deeply.

Fred walked across to the Aga cooker and put a hand on Artie's shoulder. 'Let me make the tea, old friend. Tell me where to find the necessaries. Sit down and tell me what you think I should know. Have you found Nah? No? Well, no doubt she'll be in when she has to be.' He patted Artie's shoulder and gently pushed him towards the chair by the fire.

Artie didn't argue. He just went as he was bid and sat down. He told Fred where the others were in a simple way, but he made it all quite clear.

Fred took in the information as he pottered about the kitchen getting the milk, sugar and biscuits, as Artie interspersed his narrative with instructions. Fred was stunned by the remarkable stories that he was being told. So much had happened in such a short time. Poor souls! He was fully aware of the amount of organisation that had gone on and, indeed, was still going on. Thank God there were extra folk around who were obviously willing to help!

Artie had stopped speaking and was wiping his face with a large hanky. Fred needed to know more details; Artie had only given him the general outline of events. He must find Nah, she could fill in the gaps. He asked Artie if he took sugar. There was no reply, so he put two teaspoonfuls in; Artie looked as if *he* were in shock. *Poor old fella*, thought Fred. 'Drink this before it goes cold, old friend. I'm going to find Nah.' And he left the kitchen.

Nah was having a lovely time. She had wallowed in her bath for over half an hour, listening to the radio and singing along with any tune she knew. She was towelling herself down when she heard a tap on the door. Fred had come into the hall and listened for any telltale noises. He heard music wafting through the old house… it was coming from upstairs, so up he went, following his ears. The bathroom – ah!

Nah said, 'Is that you, Artie? I'll be down in a jiffy… I'm just drying myself. Are you all right? The phone hasn't rung, has it?'

Fred called softly through the door, 'It's Fred, old girl… now don't fall over the towel. I've come down to see a pony… I'm hoping to buy it. Artie's in the kitchen having a cuppa. I need you to fill me in with all the ghastly goings on!'

Nah was amazed! *Fred here in Gloucestershire! He's just the person we need – miraculous!* The door opened and Fred saw a figure swathed in a pink towel looking very warm and with eyes wide with amazement. Nah threw her arms around him and the towel began to slip.

'Hold it,' said Fred, 'the towel's going!' Nah grabbed the towel to her and planted a damp kiss on his cheek. They both burst into laughter. Nah and Fred were great friends and they had been through many problems involving Chrissie and Kel. Nah was suddenly aware that she had nothing on but a towel. She squealed, 'Fred, I'm sorry! What a fearful sight I must be!' Actually, Nah had forgotten that she was wearing a shower cap – she always looked amazing in her shower caps!

Fred reached up and whipped it off her head, allowing her dark hair to shoot in all directions! 'There,' he said, 'that's better. Now I can stop laughing! Come on, old girl, get yourself in to a decent state. I'll be in the kitchen – hurry, hurry!' And he patted her hand and ran downstairs. Nah smilingly replied, 'I'll be with you very soon!' And she disappeared back into the bathroom.

When Fred went into the kitchen he found Artie fast asleep in the chair by the fire. Of course, the fire was not lit; it was still very warm. Fred went over to the old man and gently took the mug. Artie looked so peaceful, it would be a pity to wake him. Fred placed the mugs and plates on the draining board and tiptoed out of the room. He'd reached the bottom of the stairs when he saw Nah appear from her bedroom. He whispered, 'Artie's asleep.' He pointed towards the music room. Nah nodded and they both went in and closed the door quietly behind them. 'Now,' said Fred, 'tell me all.'

Chapter Twenty-six

*B*ack at the hospital in Truro, a careful search was going on... for Bear. No one seemed to know that one of the firemen had found him on the beach.

Bess was still unconscious. A nurse had been left to monitor her. This nurse had immediately noticed how beautiful the little girl was – the bone structure, the fine skin. She'd also noticed Bess' hands. The fingers were long and slim. They moved now and then, imperceptibly, but they certainly moved. The nurse sat by the bed and gazed at Bess. *This Bear? Could he really help her? I wish he could be found*, and she stifled a yawn.

The Doctor returned. 'Any change?' he enquired.

The nurse shook her head. 'Not really. I noticed her hands move... the fingers twitched.'

The doctor smiled, 'Good, good. She's not far away. Wish they'd find this bear.'

Andrew and the inspector were driving up the hill on the outskirts of Truro. It was twilight now and the trees were becoming silhouettes against the sky. Andrew was having trouble keeping his eyes open. They had not said much to each other. This Inspector Adrian Drew was a solid sort of man, and Andrew felt safe with him. He didn't feel it was necessary to talk.

Adrian Drew was deep in thought – there were many! He had liked Jan Leigh from the first time he'd met him. He had seen a couple of television films that Jan had directed. They had been impressive, sensitive and full of truth. Adrian had also realised that there was a certain look of sadness in Jan's eyes. Jan was a very good-looking man, but the eyes held secrets. Adrian had also registered the deep concern and love that the man had for his family; they were clearly immensely important to him. This child, Bess, was an enigma. He hoped that she was not going to die. He glanced at the young boy sitting next to him. Andrew was looking straight ahead, through the windscreen. His eyes drooped, but he was forcing them to stay open. *Poor little fella*, thought Adrian, *I must talk to him later about his remarkable journey*. Andrew had told the Inspector barely anything, just why he had left Gloucestershire.

'About two miles and we'll be at the hospital,' Adrian's voice cut into Andrew's mind. His heart jolted. Gosh, he would soon be seeing Bess. He was frightened. What would he see? Would she be injured? Her face? Her body? He realised with a shock that he hadn't been given any detailed information about the state Bess was in! Should he ask the inspector? No, he didn't trust his voice… He began to tremble. Adrian noticed and put out a hand to Andrew. Andrew found himself grabbing it and holding on desperately.

They were waiting at a mini roundabout. The indicator was flashing. Adrian withdrew his hand and the car turned left and accelerated. The man said, 'Andrew, you need to be strong again. Can you cope? The little girl could be badly hurt, but on the other hand, she may be less injured than you think. Let's just get there. Do you believe in God?' The words came out so simply. Adrian was concentrating on the road ahead, he didn't turn his head.

Andrew said, 'Yes. Do you?'

Adrian smiled and said, 'Certainly. Shall we think some prayers?'

Andrew took a very deep breath and nodded. There was a quietness in the car for the rest of the journey, until it swung into the drive leading up to the front door of the hospital. Adrian parked the car and said in a strong, gentle voice, 'Right, lad, let's go and see this Bess of yours. Follow me.'

Bear was lying under the seat, in the cab of the fire engine, that had been sent to the road above the cliff path earlier in the afternoon. It was now mid-evening. The firemen who had manned the vehicle were in the canteen back at their fire station having their supper. There was a great deal of chatter and joking going on. The fire crew were good buddies. One of them was saying, 'What a mixture of people on that cliff path this afternoon! Did you know any of them? What about that Anthea lady? The way she spoke – short bursts!'

An older man looked up from his plate of toasted cheese. 'I know that lady. She's a singer. She's got a deep voice – my wife and I heard her sing at a concert in our local hall not so long ago. She's smashing. We met the aunt she had with her today – now, there's a character! I gather she was an opera singer and still works now and then—'

A younger man interrupted. 'I can't be doing with opera – can't understand the words.'

Someone else broke in. 'Yeah! Like your rave, pop music!'

The conversation moved from one topic to another and then the firemen began to get up from the table and move away. The older man called out, "Ere, Toby, it's your turn to clean the engine. Be here early tomorrow, please. Goodnight all.'

The canteen became silent again. No men, just the women washing up and they were not speaking. Sounds of cutlery, crockery and water. Toby went to the fire engine and made sure that it was locked securely.

Anthea and Aunt Hat were in Mary's bungalow. Mary had felt so sorry for them that she had asked them to stay to supper with Paul, Alex, herself and her husband Ralph. Aunt Hat had said at once, 'Thank you. Anthea and I will be delighted to accept your invitation.' She had glared at Anthea, who did not have the energy to argue. However, she did point out that the mouse aunt would be on her own with Dog. Mary had suggested that Anthea should phone to tell Hettie that everything had calmed down, 'and would she like Anthea to come and fetch her?'

The mouse aunt had jumped at the idea. She had run out of conversation with Dog and was quite distressed because the phone hadn't rung since Hat had left the car. In fact, she was sitting with the telephone on her lap when Anthea rang her from the bungalow. After Anthea had said, 'Goodbye. I'll be with you in about ten minutes,' she turned to Dog and said, 'It's all right, Dog. Anthea is coming for us – I must hurry, hurry,' and the tiny mouse-like lady scuttled upstairs to get changed.

Anthea was relieved to be able to drive on her own without Aunt Hat bellowing instructions in her ear. She had had the most remarkable day – and all because she had spoken to that beautiful child who looked so lost! She needed her own space to think about what had happened.

The journey was not long, so she hadn't finished her thoughts when she arrived at her house. Dear Aunt Hettie was standing on the doorstep dressed in her Sunday best, wearing the most becoming hat. Dog was sitting in front of her. His ears pricked and his tail began to thump as he heard the sound of the engine; he recognised Anthea's car. He was a very intelligent beast. He'd missed her – she seemed to have been away for ages! Aunt Hettie waved and she looked as if she was bouncing up and down. Anthea stopped the car and got out, saying, 'Hello, darling. Have you been all right? In you get. The others will be waiting for us. This Mary and her family are awfully pleasant. I don't know what we would have done without their help.'

They bowled back along the lanes with Anthea telling Aunt Hettie as much as she could. Poor mouse aunt was quite confused with all the details! However, she took in as much as she could. Perhaps Anthea would write it down for her some time – what a story! She was feeling hungry. She had certainly not bothered about getting herself any food whilst she had been waiting news of the adventure.

They arrived at the bungalow and Anthea introduced the mouse aunt to the family.

Mary said, 'Of course, we haven't told you our surname, have we? It's Curtis. As you can see, Ralph is blind.' Naturally, Aunt Hat and Anthea had immediately realised this when they were first introduced. Anthea wondered how he coped, but after watching him at the supper table and the way he carried the dishes into the kitchen, she fully understand that he was very confident inside his dark world. It was Aunt Hat who said later, 'Anthea, Hettie, did you notice the way the boys and Mary kept making sure that the furniture was not blocking Ralph's path through the room and out to other parts of the house? I wonder how long he's been blind? I do admire him! Wonder if he has a job? We must ask them all to lunch. I'll ring Mary in a couple of days – we're going back to London next week, aren't we? Yes, they must come over before we go!'

Chapter Twenty-seven

$\mathcal{J}$ oseph woke up. He'd been dreaming about Horatio. For a few seconds, he couldn't remember where he was. He turned over, realising that this was not his Oak Tree House bed – it was so hard! The hospital, or course! He was still in his side ward. He was restless, he couldn't get comfortable. Finally, he sat up. What day was it going to be? Tuesday? Yes, Tuesday. He was going home a day early – of course, how marvellous, and Charlie was coming with him! Joe had insisted that Charlie must tell him everything that happened to each member of the family.

That had been when Charlie was sitting with him as he ate his supper. He had tried hard not to ask too many questions, but he *had* to know about Andrew, Chrissie and Hannah, Jan Dad and Bess! Charlie could tell him quite a lot about everyone except Bess. She wasn't at all sure about her facts and she didn't want to frighten Joe. He had fed himself bravely, but he kept dropping food on to the bed. He cried at times. Charlie had been advised to let him do as much as he could for himself, but it was difficult stopping herself feeding him. She longed to take him in her arms. However, when finally the meal was finished and she'd cleaned him up and changed his bed, she was able to give him a big hug and tell him how well he'd done. He'd seemed very wide awake and had asked for Horatio. Charlie put the huge pea into Joe's hand. Joe balanced him on his palm. He was certainly the largest pea Charlie had ever seen. He'd left his pod now – indeed, he was showing the first signs of becoming shrivelled. Nevertheless, he was a handsome pea.

Joe had asked her to tell him a story, but it was not long before the boy's eyes began to droop and he was asleep, Horatio still sitting safely on his palm. Charlie carefully picked up the pea and put him back in his box house. She was pleased that Joe had finally dropped off, as she had to make preparations for Tuesday's departure to The Oak Tree House. Actually, she always called it 'Ho' now, not House – she thought it sounded splendid. She expected the Ho to reflect the people who lived in it, and she wasn't disappointed!

Joe wondered what time it was. Was it still the middle of the night or was it the morning? He remembered that there was a bell at the pillow end of his bed. It was on a long string or something... at the end there was a small knob that you pushed and you could hear the bell ring in a room nearby. A night nurse might come to see him and he could start asking questions again. And then, a clear thought shot into his mind. It was as if he could actually hear Hannah's voice, as if she were in his room! 'I should have asked Joe if I could bring Horatio with me – he could help Bess get better!' Horatio! His extra special pea! That was his job; to make people feel better, as long as he was with Hannah! Joe put his hands over his ears and listened intently. The voice didn't come into his head again. He knew what he must do, though – he must get Horatio's box house and tell him that by hook or by crook the box must go to Cornwall. But how? *How?* Joe slithered off his bed and slowly put out his hands to feel where he was.

He moved away from the bed and was gradually edging

his way across the room, when he heard a voice. It was Amanda's voice. 'What are you doing out of bed? Get back at once.' The words stung into his brain. He was suddenly very frightened. The voice came again. 'Go on! Do as you're told or I'll make you—'

Joe heard another voice. His head was muddled... he didn't recognise the new voice at once.

'Hey! What's going on? You shouldn't talk to the child like that, nurse. Look how confused he is. I think you should leave.'

Joe heard the woman make a strange moaning sound and then he felt a firm, warm hand on his. The larger hand held his smaller one and the next thing he knew was that he had been guided to the chair by the side of his bed and that he was sitting in it. The voice came again and this time he knew that it belonged to Doctor Benedict. 'What were you trying to find, Joe?' Benedict asked.

Joe was trembling all over, even inside his tummy! He got out the words, 'I'm so frightened... who was that voice? I think I've heard it before... I don't like it... I don't—'

Benedict broke in to Joe's words. 'It's all right. That was Amanda. Yes, you have met her before. She works on the children's ward. She is rather unhappy at the moment and she sounds scary, but you're safe. Now, let's get back to the time before Amanda came in... what were you looking for?'

Benedict's voice had a cool, calming effect on Joe. He let out the breath inside his shaking body and gradually made his brain think back. 'I remember... I was going to the window ledge... Horatio is there, in his house box. Hannah must have him – for Bess – he'll help to make her better. Charlie told me that Bess is inside a deep sleep, like I was. Horatio and Hannah will bring her out of this sleep. She'll wake up again, I'm sure of that. Could you wrap the box and post it to the other hospital? Or perhaps Charlie could do it?' Joe had made a supreme effort to get all these words out. His inside was still trembley, but he realised that Horatio should go as soon as possible down to Cornwall.

Benedict's handsome face was beaming. *This family!* he thought. *This family is full of amazing surprises*. He stood up saying, 'OK! Come on, Horatio, you're off on an adventure! I'll find a special padded envelope for the house box, Joe. Then it'll be safe. Sometimes parcels are thrown around by the Royal Mail! I'll make sure that it gets away in the next hour. I'll send it First Class Parcel Post… it should arrive in Truro tomorrow morning. Will that satisfy you?' He came back to Joe and put the house box into his hands. Benedict continued, 'You'd better tell Horatio where he's going and why. He'll need to know.' Benedict thought, *Now I'm becoming like all these marvellous Leighs and Bests! Wow!*

Joe opened the house box and felt for Horatio. He took him out and put him close to his face. He appeared to have forgotten that Benedict was still in his room. He began to whisper to the pea, which was sitting in his usual place; on the middle of Joe's palm.

Joe didn't know it, but it was morning and Charlie had arrived to give him his breakfast. She was standing in the doorway, holding a tray, mouth open, fascinated by what was going on. Benedict turned and saw her. he gestured to her to leave Joe alone and he indicated that they should move out of his room for a while. Joe was engrossed in his conversation with Horatio and didn't register that anything else was happening. Yes, it looked just as if he and the pea were having a conversation! He whispered to Horatio and then lifted his hand to his ear, as if he were listening to Horatio's reply.

Charlie said, in an awed tone, 'My, that was impressive,

doctor! I'm glad I arrived when I did. I passed Amanda in the corridor – she looked very grim. What a strange lady! She scares me too… can't think why the powers that be allow her near the children. No one likes her, you know.'

Benedict sighed. 'There's something deeply wrong with that lady. How much did you hear?'

'I didn't hear what she said to Joseph, but I heard all you said to him.' She glanced back through the door at Joe, who was still talking to Horatio. She went on. 'Joe's so much stronger, but the shock will last for quite a while, won't it?' Benedict nodded. Charlie looked concerned. 'Will you be coming to The Oak Tree House to see him? You know that I've been asked to go there to look after the little lad until the crisis settles in Cornwall. I'm looking forward to it enormously! We're hoping to be taken to the house by one of the hospital cars before lunch today.' Her bright, cheerful face was shining.

Benedict said, 'I'll pop in around teatime, OK?'

Charlie looked pleased. 'Good. Now then, Joseph, my lad, breakfast!' And she went into the room. Joe looked up and said, 'Doctor B, here's Horatio. He's happy to go to Cornwall. I've told him that he needs to be near Bess, with Hannah. They'll be able to talk to Bess and then everyone will come home again… I miss them.' Joe's eyes filled with tears.

Charlie said quickly, 'That's smashing, Joe! Now you and I are going to have breakfast. I've some of your favourite food here.' She lowered her voice. 'I've found some of *my* specials as well!' And Charlie laughed her tinkly laugh.

Benedict found that he was always smiling when he was with this nurse! She was infectious! He took Horatio from Joe and put him back into his house box. He decided that he must get to know Charlie – he found her most attractive!

But now he must make sure that this special pea started his journey. Joe was adamant that Horatio was necessary in Bess' recovery. 'I'm off now,' he said in an energetic, bright voice. 'First stop, the post office. I'll buy the padded envelope there so that I won't waste time; I'll get the parcel posted quicker! Goodbye, see you at home later on – I look forward to seeing you – both!'

He added the 'both' looking directly at Charlie, who looked up from taking the breakfast dishes off the tray. She said, 'Fine. See you then. Bye!'

Amanda was in the cloakroom. She was standing in front of the big mirror that stretched across the wall behind the washbasins. She was staring at herself. Her face was ashen, her eyes wild. Her hands gripped the edge of the basin as she leaned forward so that her face was practically touching the glass. She was holding her breath. Two red patches appeared on her cheeks and then she hissed, 'Why, oh why? Why did you die – why did you leave me?' She repeated these words over and over again, until her voice became a croak and her legs were unable to hold her up any more. She slid to the floor. No one came in. No one knew about her baby, the baby who had died.

Jan was looking down at Bess. He felt such love for the child. She was so helpless, so frail. He'd been allowed to spend the night at the hospital. He'd been given a room especially kept for relatives of very sick or injured children. He hadn't slept much, but at least he'd been able to rest, to

Chapter Twenty-seven

lie down. Michael Fossey had returned to his hotel, of course. He'd told Jan that if he needed him, or Agnes, he should phone at any hour. Jan was quite overcome by the amount of kindness he and his family had received from the Fosseys – in fact, from everyone he'd come in contact with during this fearful time. He sat down on the chair by the side of Bess' bed and gently touched her hand. It was warm and smooth. She had such lovely skin. He touched her forehead. Yes, it also was warm. She was breathing steadily, quietly, but she didn't respond to his touch or to his voice when he spoke to her. 'Bess? Please, please get well again. I will never leave you – I will always be here for you. Let me be your daddy now. You could be my little girl, our little girl. You belong to us, to all of us. You can be part of us all. Would you like our name? Will you be Bess Leigh?' Jan's voice began to shake, he couldn't go on. He just sat holding Bess' hand, gazing at her face. Then he thought, *Bear! Bess must have Bear! I have to find him!* Where should he go? Who should he ask? Perhaps someone who had been on the cliff path?

He turned around quickly and nearly collided with the nurse who had talked to him the previous evening. 'Ah, Mr Leigh, I've been looking for you. Would you like some breakfast? Perhaps you would care to join me. I'm off home soon, but I thought, maybe you would like company.' Jan thought fast. He could do with a drink and something to eat; he was very hungry. Perhaps he could discuss the bear problem with this lady… she was very kind.

He said, 'Thank you. I would very much like to join you for breakfast. Bess will be all right?'

The nurse smiled at him. 'Oh yes, Bess will be fine. The doctor on duty will be with her soon and lots of nurses are aware of her condition. She's in good hands. My name is

Naomi Carter, please call me Naomi. We'll go to the staff dining room, shall we? It'll be quieter there.'

Jan said, 'Naomi, has Bear been found yet? He's extremely important... Bess is never without him. She communicates with him – he must be with her!'

They were walking briskly along a corridor towards the smell of fried bacon and coffee. Naomi said, 'I searched everywhere for this bear last evening. Unfortunately he hasn't been located. Where was the last time that he was seen? Have you any idea?'

Jan shook his head. 'No, but someone who was on the cliff path yesterday when the accident occurred might remember seeing him. I think I must telephone the hotel where I've been staying since Sunday. Michael or Agnes may recall something. There were so many people around – police, firemen, others, a family, I recall, who lived in a house close to the path – maybe they would know.'

They'd arrived at the staff canteen. Naomi said, 'I'll order some food for us – tell me what you would like. The telephone is over there.'

Naomi pointed to a phone booth on the far side of the room. Jan muttered a 'Thank you' and was gone. He hadn't told her what he would like to eat or drink! Naomi gave a little understanding smile and thought that toast and coffee might suit.

'How is everything at the hospital?' Michael was in his office. 'Yes... yes... I see... I understand. What? Bear? Whose bear? Oh, Bess' bear! No, no, I've no idea... Agnes might know... Wait, she's here...'

And Michael handed the receiver to his wife.

'Hello? Ah, Jan... Bear? No, he's definitely not here. Maybe Anthea would know... yes, I'll telephone her for you, then ring you back. Please don't worry too much...

Have you had any food this morning? Oh, you're about to have something, good! Off you go, now! Give me your phone number... Yes, yes, I'll phone Anthea at once then contact you with her news. Goodbye.'

Agnes replaced the receiver and said, 'Michael, do you have Anthea's number?' Michael began to shake his head. Agnes said in an exasperated voice, 'Well, go and find it, quickly!'

Michael sighed and got up. He was very tired. 'All right, all right, I'm going. Try to be patient with me, Agnes, my head is still whirling round – I didn't get much sleep last night...'

'None of us did, and I'm sure that Jan and the others were awake most of the night as well,' was the curt reply. Michael swallowed another sigh. Agnes was a powerful lady when roused! He went to find the telephone directory, saying, 'Tell me Anthea's surname again... I can't remem—'

Agnes cut in with, 'Moreton Jones!'

'Oh, yes, of course – Moreton Jones... More... Here it is!' He wrote down the number and hurried back to Agnes. 'You phone her, my dear. I need to check if Chrissie and Hannah are OK.'

Chapter Twenty-eight

I haven't told you about Chrissie and Hannah recently, have I? They had arrived safely in Truro at about ten o'clock. Hannah had suggested that Chrissie should phone the hospital before they drove there. The old lady had noticed how tired Chrissie looked – it might be wiser for them to go straight to the hotel. Jan had arranged for them to stay in Mawnan Smith with Michael and Agnes. Chrissie had found a call box... Hannah could see her talking... she seemed quite calm and she smiled now and then. *Good, thought Hannah, maybe everything is quiet at the moment. Thank you, Lord.* She heard footsteps and opened her eyes to see Chrissie coming back.

'Well? How is Bess?' Han felt remarkably relaxed.

Chrissie settled herself behind the steering wheel and said, 'Jan says that she's still unconscious, but the doctors are pretty sure that she'll slowly regain consciousness over night, or perhaps tomorrow.'

Hannah broke in quickly, 'That's fine. I think we should drive to the hotel – has Jan given you directions?'

Chrissie patted Han's cheek, 'Yes, darling... we're going to the hotel. We'll see Bess and the others tomorrow morning – that's what you wanted, wasn't it?' and she bent over and kissed Han, then continued, 'We need to rest soon. Are you hungry? Agnes has prepared something for us. It'll take us about twenty minutes or so to get to Mawnan. Oh, by the way, Andrew's arrived at the hospital. He came with Inspector Drew, in a police car. Very exciting! He was rather disturbed at first, when he realised that Bess was not able to look at him or speak to him. However, the inspector managed to persuade him that she was really not far away and that it would be better for everyone if he spent the night with him and his family; he could be back at the hospital early tomorrow. So, Andy's all right, Bess is being cared for and Jan is staying at the hospital. He sounds rather distant. I know him, he needs to be on his own. I'm beginning to understand his alone moments...' Chrissie stopped speaking.

Han glanced at her and waited in silence for her to speak again. 'Are you all right, Han darling? Shall we go?'

Hannah said, 'Yes, yes, I'm looking forward to bed!' She squeezed Chrissie's hand, which was lying on the gear stick. They smiled at each other, a knowing little smile.

They were sitting in their bedroom, sitting in big, comfy armchairs. It was warm and cosy. They had eaten a very tasty snack and had drunk a glass of whisky and a mug of coffee. It was quiet and peaceful. Chrissie yawned deeply and dragged herself out of her chair. She was in her nightie and dressing gown. She'd had a shower before Agnes and a young waiter had appeared with the food trays. Hannah was still dressed. She'd talked with Agnes whilst Chrissie was in the bathroom, finding out as much as possible about the day's events. Agnes immediately felt at home with both the women. She had realised very quickly that Hannah was a special mortal. They talked together as if they had known each other all their lives.

Agnes had told Han all about the people who had been on the cliff path, everyone who had toiled away for hours trying to rescue Bess. Han had listened in silence, never interrupting, just nodding or shaking her head now and then. She stored the names of the folk in her mind. They would need lifting up to God. He was with them in this room – He was always with Han, and the presence was practically tangible now. Han had noted the time: 11.30 p.m.

She stifled a yawn, but Agnes had gimlet eyes and immediately got up from where she was sitting, saying, 'Ah! You're a very weary lady! I'll leave you now. Sleep peacefully. Have you both everything you need?' Chrissie and Han nodded. Agnes didn't wait for words, she just blew them a kiss and moved briskly to the door. 'Goodnight then, God bless!' And she was gone.

Han sighed. 'We're so fortunate – what lovely people. Come along, me dear, into bed with you! I'll just wash and brush my teeth. Thank you for the safe journey.' The old lady kissed Chrissie and disappeared into the bathroom, humming a tune. Chrissie climbed into her bed and snuggled down. She was exhausted, yet strangely relaxed. She closed her eyes and fell asleep within minutes.

Toby whistled as he hurtled down the hill towards the fire station. He always cycled to work in the early morning – and it was very early: about 5.30! He'd watched the sun rise through the kitchen window as he drank his first mug of tea. *What a day it's going to be*, he thought. The sky was cloudless and his heart was light.

Toby was an early morning chap; he just loved being out on his own at this time of day. Hardly anyone else around and he could potter along the lanes on his bike or rush down hills without being bothered by too many cars. This morning he was very happy. He was in love! In fact, Toby was getting married at the end of this week – Saturday, the seventh of July. He laughed out loud and yelled to the birds, 'Hello, you birds! Tell Beatrice I love her, love her to bits!' He laughed again and pushed down on the pedals. The bike shot forward and he saw the fire station grow bigger. The bike stopped with a squeal of brakes and he slid off. He stood absolutely still and listened. Nothing. Then a thrush began its morning song of praise. Other birds joined in and Toby grinned. He parked his bike and went into the station. The night staff were still there. There were 'Hellos' and grins. The staff were a friendly lot, they worked well together. That was because their boss, Reg Trelawney, was a great boss. The men liked him, admired him. Reg's wife had died about a year ago and he had nursed her from the time she'd become sick. He was a huge, gentle man and he believed in treating people with sensitivity and understanding. Mind you, he was also a tough, fair man, he couldn't abide any form of cruelty or meanness.

Toby chatted for a few minutes to his friend Alf, who was going off-duty, and then he gathered the cleaning gear and went to the engine. It looked rather dusty, but as it had rained the day before, the outside didn't need washing – that was a relief! He opened the cab door and climbed up. It was very messy, with paper and bits and pieces strewn everywhere! Toby recalled the previous day when they had driven to the road above the cliff path. The fellow driving the fire engine had gone as fast as he could. It had been a hairy journey – there were so many bends – and anything loose in the cab had been thrown around. *Thank God we didn't hit anything on the way or get caught up behind other vehicles*, Toby thought. He always marvelled at the way fire engines and police cars seemed to travel without mishap. Of course, he'd heard of accidents involving the rescue services, but there weren't many. Amazing! And yesterday they had managed to rescue that small girl. What a relief! He sighed and wondered how she was, if she was going to be all right. He had noticed how beautiful she was.

He had wanted to help the American man, but Reg had sent Tom down. That had been a disappointment, but Toby realised that Tom was older and more experienced and there had been no time to argue – not that he would have said a word; he trusted his boss completely. No, Toby had stayed on the path, obeying orders and making sure that he carried them out to the best of his ability. He had been congratulated on his attitude and alertness by Reg, and this made him glow inside. He'd only been in the fire service for a short time, in fact, this was his first big job since he'd finished his training.

He picked up the papers and tidied the cab, finally bending down to look under the seat. There was Bear, lying on his back with his feet in the air! 'Oh, goodness me! What are you doing here? Oh, yes! Tom must have chucked you into the cab.' Toby carefully picked Bear up and rubbed some of the dirt off his face. Bear had sand and bits of seaweed on his fur. His right arm was twisted and his left foot looked bent and useless. Toby thought carefully. He remembered hearing Tom say that he had found a teddy on the beach below the cliff path, but he couldn't remember hearing what had happened to this ted. This chap must be *the* bear; the one that was so important to Bess! Toby still had a number of bears at home; they had been important – they still were important! Bess *must* have this fellow, and as soon as possible. He must take him to the hospital. But he was on duty until the middle of the afternoon – that might be too late. God! God! what should he do? He made up his mind. He would cycle to the hospital. He was an impulsive young man – sometimes he just had to do whatever he thought was right, but it got him into a lot of trouble.

Truro? It was such a long way to Truro from Falmouth! Cycle? No, that was daft! He would ask one of the other men who were slowly coming on duty. He looked at a couple who were nattering intently as they walked passed his engine. He didn't know them. His pals – his crew – would not be around until later on. What should he do? His mind was confused. He knew that Bear had to be with Bess and he must be the person to take him to her. A train – of course, a train!

He jumped down from the cab and ran to the canteen, having pushed Bear inside his jacket. The sun was high in the sky now and he was hot. He called out to one of the girls who was wiping down a table. 'Please tell the boss when he comes in that I've gone to the hospital in Truro with Bear – please, don't forget!'

Toby raced back through the door, nearly knocking over another member of the morning crew. 'Hey! Look out, young fella, what's the hurry?'

Toby managed to get out a sort of apology as he ran to his bicycle. He jumped onto the saddle and was off.

Toby sat with Bear on his lap. The train was chugging slowly – at least it seemed slow to the young fireman – towards Truro. He had persuaded the guard to put his bike in the guard's van and to allow him to travel in the van with it. The guard was perplexed. This young man seemed very worried. He was obviously on an extremely important mission. With a bear!

The guard was an older man without much sense of humour. He didn't understand the young people of today, but he'd never come across a young fireman like this one, sitting on the floor of his special area. The young man had insisted on staying with his bicycle and he was now trying to clean up a very dirty, bedraggled looking teddy bear, who should have been thrown away!

This guard was really a retired guard; trains did not have guards any more! However, this one was so totally immersed in trains that his employers had given in when he practically begged them to let him continue to work for them. 'In any capacity,' the old man had said. So here he was, working the Truro to Falmouth line. There were more passengers now in July. Cornwall was filling up rapidly with tourists from all over the world.

Gerry the guard kept looking at Toby. What on earth was this young fireman –Toby was wearing his uniform – doing with an old worn out teddy bear? Poor Gerry, he didn't have much imagination! He was a serious man – in fact, a rather dull man – but he was fascinated with this situation in his van… he had to know. So he asked and Toby told him – well, he told him all he knew about the little girl who had been rescued. Gerry suddenly found that his mind had become alert and he realised that he had to be involved in getting Bear to Bess.

'Right, my lad, I'll help you. We're about to stop to pick up passengers. I'll go and phone the hospital and tell them that you are on your way with Mr Bear – no, don't argue! It's clearly a matter of great import.' Toby grinned and nodded. His throat had gone all tight and he felt his eyes pricking. *What's the matter with me?* he thought, *I haven't cried for ages.* Even his words were jumbled. Gerry was looking out of the window and the train was slowing down. There was a long whistle and the train came to a halt. Out jumped Gerry the guard. He was off, running down the platform. Toby was still wondering about the events that had gathered him in; he didn't give a thought to the fire station back in Falmouth or anything else to do with his job. He looked at Bear sitting on his knee. The animal had a surprisingly intelligent face. Although he was decidedly old and worn, he was still a bear of great character. The face seemed to smile at him, as if to say, 'You're doing the bestest thing that you've ever done in your life up to now! I have to be with Bess.'

Gerry was back, out of breath and panting, but his old, lined face was beaming. 'Let me get the train going, then I'll tell you all,' he gasped, between closing the door, leaning out of the window, waving a green flag and coming back into the van. He sat down on a pile of sacks and took a deep breath before he spoke. 'I rang the hospital... told them about you and Mr Bear... the lass who answered seemed overjoyed. Apparently people there have been searching for this animal – he is vital to your rescued child.'

Gerry stopped to breathe deeply again. Toby said, 'Thank you. I'm glad they know we're coming. When will we arrive in Truro?'

Gerry said, 'Soon, soon, my boy. I'll come to the hospital with you.'

Toby was quite shocked at this remark; he had his bike, how would Gerry get there?

Gerry appeared to have read his mind. He spoke quickly and with a kind of excitement. His eyes were shining. 'I'll ride pillion, behind you. I used to do that with my brother – yes, a long time ago, but I bet I can still do it!'

Toby was dumbstruck. What a great old fellow this was! He didn't say 'No' to Gerry, but he did wonder about the hills. *Oh well, we'll meet them when we have to*, he thought, *we'll manage, I'm sure!*

And they certainly did manage. Gerry knew a taxi driver who took them up the steepest hills and they rode the rest of the way. Toby's bicycle had a basket on the handlebars; Bear travelled in the basket and Gerry rode behind Toby. Toby's legs were strong and he pedalled like mad. The hospital loomed in front of them.

They were bowling along quite fast now, they were through the gates and at the front doors in seconds. Toby braked and felt Gerry's body lurch forward into his back, which made the bike wobble. Toby lost control and the two men and the bear found themselves on the ground with their machine on top of them. Two nurses were walking up the drive behind them. There was a shriek from one of them, whilst the other said, 'Oh my! What a bump! It's all right, we're here!' Gerry lay on the gravel feeling extraordinarily light-headed. A pretty young nurse was leaning over him asking if he was all right and what was his name. He heard himself say, 'I'm Gerry.' Toby sat up and picked up Bear, who had dropped out of the basket and was lying on the ground. He struggled to his feet and said loudly, 'Gerry, Gerry, I'm going to find Bess… stay with the nurse!'

Gerry found that he was beginning to giggle inside himself. Yes, he'd stay with the nurse… he didn't want to move… it was most peaceful, down on the gravel with this young lady holding his hand and smiling at him.

Toby had scraped his hands and there was blood on them. He felt it trickle down his fingers and now Bear had blood on his furry body. He ran up to the reception desk and said, 'Bess. Do you know where she is? The little girl, rescued from the cliff yesterday? I've found Bear, she—'

He was cut off by a man's voice saying, 'Yes, I know where she is... give Bear to me!'

Toby looked up and saw a tall, fair-haired man with a white, sad face looking at him, holding out his hand to take Bear. 'No!' snapped Toby. 'I don't know you. I'll give Bear to Bess – I found him.'

Jan withdrew his hand and began to walk quickly towards the lift, saying, 'Very well, follow me, *now!* As fast as you can!'

Toby jogged after the tall man and they were in the lift before Jan told the young man who he was. He asked Toby where he had found Bear and in fits and starts Toby told him the whole story. Jan looked at this hot, untidy fireman in front of him, leaning against the wall of the lift. He had a tanned, handsome face and his eyes were green and shining. His clothes were torn and bits of leaves and twigs were stuck to the trousers and shirt. Then he looked at Bear. Poor Bear! He was a pitiable sight. His fur all damp and dirty, with drops of Toby's blood stuck to it. His arms seemed twisted and that foot! *Chrissie will need to mend him*, Jan thought. But never mind, he was with them. Bess would have him and then, please God, she would come back to this world!

The lift stopped and they were running down the corridor and into a long ward. Jan led Toby to a bed that seemed to be surrounded with people. Actually, there were only three other people there... Hannah, Chrissie and Andrew. They had arrived earlier, having made contact with each other. Inspector Adrian had phoned Jan and Chrissie had phoned Jan and they had all driven to Truro and met in the hospital. The inspector had left them in the care of Sister Naomi, who had answered all their questions and had then taken them up to see Bess. She lay there, her eyes closed, breathing regularly as if she were fast asleep. Hannah bent down and spoke quietly into her ear. She straightened up and smoothed the child's face and then her hands. Bess did not move and her breathing did not alter. Andrew was standing, holding Chrissie's hand. He began to sob... not loud sobs, but they were coming from deep inside him. Jan knelt down and took him into his arms, holding him close. The boy's body was shuddering. Jan whispered, 'Bess will be back with us soon. Believe this, Andrew, believe it!'

Toby was standing a little way behind the family. He was a tall young man and could easily see Bess. He had never seen a more beautiful child. He took a deep breath and Hannah heard it and turned round to look at him. The old lady's face broke into a wide smile and her eyes shone up at him. 'You have Bear! Oh, well done! Will you give him to Bess, please? Just lay him down on the bed by her... let her realise that he is here – she'll know.' Hannah moved to Toby and gently pushed him forward. Chrissie, Jan and Andrew watched in silence as the young man moved to the bed and placed Bear next to Bess.

Bess was seeing pictures. Hundreds and hundreds of pictures. Houses, animals, people, faces... she was aware of eyes and mouths. The pictures became very bright and then they faded as they left her mind. She seemed to be floating down... where was she going? It was a lovely, peaceful feeling... floating. Her body was light... it was as if she were being held up by lots of strong, soft hands... she was being carried through the air. Where was she going? She began to hear sounds... then she heard her name. 'Bess. Bess, Bear is here with you. Open your eyes and you will see him. He's lying beside you... move your hand and you will be able to feel him there.'

My hand, Bess thought the words. *Hand... hand...*

Chrissie watched Hannah. The old lady was standing staring down at Bess. She was mouthing words... Chrissie felt the amazing silence grow around them. Andrew was holding Jan's hand and Toby just stood and watched each face in turn. He'd never in his whole life felt such love. Yes, he felt the love that was being transferred from each of these people. It seemed to be flowing in the air in the room. He dragged his gaze from the boy and looked directly at Bess. Her face had changed.

It seemed smaller, tighter, and her hand was moving. The fingers flexed then straightened. They touched Bear, touched his damp, dirty fur... felt for his paw. Then they heard a whisper, 'Bear, dear Bear.'

It was Andrew who reacted. He jerked his hand from Jan's and shot forward to kneel beside the bed. He whispered urgently, 'Bess! I'm here as well. It's me, Andrew! Look at me!'

The others held their breath as a smile spread slowly, oh, ever so slowly, over the little girl's face as she opened her eyes and looked at Andrew. 'Hello, Andrew.'

Everyone else seemed to breathe out at the same time! It was Hannah and Toby who spoke at the same time: 'Thank you, Lord.' Toby was stunned, he'd never said 'Thank you, Lord' before! Well, he'd said it to himself, but he'd never had the courage to say it out loud!

Jan had moved to Bess. 'Darling, darling little Bess! So you've come back to us!'

She reached up and touched his wet cheek, brushing the tears away. Her face was quite expressionless, then, she smiled. It was like a light being switched on behind her eyes. 'I've been in another place, Jan Dad. It was not a bit scary, just new and full of faces and quietness. I needed to come back, though... I needed to see you all again.'

Chapter Twenty-eight

Bess was looking at Chrissie and then her eyes moved on to Hannah. She smiled at both of them. Then she looked at Andrew. Stretching out her hands to him, she spoke: 'Andy, I knew you would be here. You must have had a long journey. Did you enjoy it? Will you take me on the train? Will you take me with you all our lives?'

Andrew couldn't use his voice, it was stuck in his throat. He was still kneeling by the bed. Bess put her hand on his head. It felt cool and he felt safe and brave again. 'We'll always… be… together, Bess… I love you, you see…' He couldn't go on. Bess moved her fingers through his hair and just smiled. Then she saw the tall figure of Toby standing watching her.

She gazed at him in silence, then he said, 'I'm Toby, miss. I found your bear in the cab of our fire engine. I'm sorry he's so dirty and smelly – I can put him in the washing machine if you like.'

Bess began to laugh. The Leighs and Hannah had never heard Bess laugh before! It was the most marvellous sound, not loud but tinkly, like a bell. Her face was alive and she suddenly sat up and hugged Bear to her, the laughter dying as she buried her face in Bear's messy fur. Everyone was amazed, they felt the relief flow through them. Bess seemed so grown up and certainly amongst them. She finally said, 'Bear smells of seaweed and sand. It's lovely. No, I will wash him – he would hate being in a washing machine! Wouldn't you?' And then, looking at Toby, she said, 'Thank you for bringing him to me.'

Toby told his Beatrice later that day, 'She is the most beautiful little girl that I've ever seen. Shall we ask all of

312

them to our wedding on Saturday?'

Beatrice, being a sensible soul had said, 'Yes, that would be lovely, but they may have to go back to Gloucestershire.'

He'd told Beatrice – in fact, he'd told everyone he came in contact with – the whole story of the rescue, the people he had met, Bess, Bear, Andrew.

'The young boy told Bess that he loved her! D'you think children can love each other? Funny!' He told them about Gerry, the train guard, the nurses, the doctors – oh yes, Toby had had the most remarkable adventure!

Chapter Twenty-nine

It was now Tuesday evening. Jan, Chrissie, Andrew, Bess and Hannah were at the hotel in Mawnan Smith. They were sitting in Michael and Agnes's own private sitting room. Bess had a new dress and cardigan and Bear looked clean and happy. Agnes, with help from Hannah, had done a splendid job cleaning the animal. Bess had slept the whole afternoon. She did not know that the washing and brushing was going on. She was thrilled when she woke to find Bear looking spruce and shiny. He had new trousers and a shirt. He looked immensely pleased with himself.

There was a friendly atmosphere with lots of laughter and many, many stories about the weekend's events. 'It would make a great film, Jan,' Michael had said.

Jan shook his head; it was all still too close in his mind. He had been terrified, as frightened as he had been when, as a young lad he had escaped from the Germans in Austria. He wanted to be back in The Oak Tree House with his family. He wanted to be alone with Chrissie.

Hannah stood up, glancing at her wristwatch. 'Jan, dear, are we driving home tomorrow?'

Chrissie answered for Jan. 'Yes, darling. We'll start about ten o'clock. We can go to the hospital first, to take some thank-you presents to the doctors and nurses. Is that all right for you, Jan? Do you have to see Cyril again?'

Jan said in a quiet, weary voice, 'We'll leave as soon as

possible, Chrissie. I have to go to bed now. Goodnight and thank you all, yes, all of you. I shall never forget your kindness, your love.' He left the room.

Hannah said quickly, 'Come along, children. I'll help you get ready for bed. Would you like a story? A special Hannah story?'

Andrew and Bess said, 'Yes, please Han!' together.

And the room was empty, except for Michael and Agnes. They looked after the retreating figures. Agnes sighed. 'What a lovely family! Come along, m'dear... time we stirred ourselves. I could do with an early night myself. What is the time? Oh, that's good. Only nine thirty. Would you like a nightcap?'

Michael nodded. 'Hmm. I'll read the paper for a while. Thank you, dear Aggie, for all you've done. What a couple of days... I expect it'll all be in the local papers tomorrow or later in the week.'

Not only was it in the papers, but a television crew turned up the next morning and there were interviews with everyone concerned and lots of filming!.

In the end, the Leighs left Mawnan just after lunch, and when they arrived at the hospital in Truro, another surprise awaited them. There was a parcel there, addressed to Mrs Hannah Best. It was Horatio in his box home! Andrew and Bess were so excited. There was a letter from Dr Benedict accompanying the pea, stating that Joe had insisted that he sent Horatio down to Cornwall, so that Hannah could help Bess and maybe some other children as well.

The rest of the afternoon was taken up with Hannah, Bess and Andy going into children's wards and rooms with Horatio and Han, telling them stories about the pea. He was a great success, but they had to leave for Gloucestershire. The journey would be long and they really should get back before midnight.

Chrissie and Andrew were in the sports car and Jan, Hannah and Bess followed them in the Land Rover. They changed round during the journey and it seemed to take a shorter time than they had imagined. The children and Han slept now and again, though Andrew denied it. 'I was only closing my eyes – I wasn't asleep, you know!'

At last they were driving up the lane to The Oak Tree Ho. *Thank God, we're home*, thought Chrissie. They knew that Fred would be there as he had phoned the hotel the evening before, and as the two cars crawled up the drive, the occupants saw two large figures standing together under the trees on the front lawn.

'Artie! Artie! My dear man!' called Hannah. The two figures moved quickly to greet them and soon three weary grown-ups and two sleepy children and one Bear were in the kitchen surrounded by luggage and lots of chattering. Little Bess had coped with the journey bravely, but now she looked very pale and she was not speaking. Hannah realised that the child must still be suffering from shock and would need careful nursing, so Bess was carried up to her room by Uncle Fred, who had given Han such a hug and a large wet kiss when she had finally got out of the Land Rover! In fact, Fred had lifted the old lady off her feet and had held her close to him, whispering in her ear, that she was *his* nan and why hadn't she been up to Scotland to see them? They missed her – and she *must* come soon!

Fred carried Bess so carefully. She was as light as a feather. She seemed to curl into his arms. Bear was snuggled into her body. Her eyes watched his face as he moved to the stairs. He looked up and his heart jumped. There, standing at the top, was Joseph. On his right side was Nah and on his left, Charlie. He stood there, straight as a soldier. His eye was still bandaged, but not as heavily as the day before. He had arrived home early Tuesday afternoon with Charlie. It was a time that Charlie would remember all her life; in the years to come she would tell her own family, her own children, over and over again about the joy that poured out of the blind boy as they drove nearer and nearer to the house at the top of the lane, and the great oak tree that stood guarding the front gates. Joe knew where they were as they passed through the village. It was uncanny, like a miracle – Charlie used these words: 'Joseph kept telling me that the Church was on the right just round the corner and over there is Merlin Cottage, where the Sophia Lady lives – he actually called out, "Hello Sophia Lady!" as we drove past the wee cottage! I didn't really believe that he was right, but I asked Mr Best and he told me, "Yes, the lad's a clever fellow" – he must have somehow sensed where he was… uncanny!'

Dr Benedict had kept his word and had visited them after lunch. Charlie poured out the words in such a way that the young doctor could only sit and wonder. Joseph had talked non-stop to Nah until he had worn himself out and had had to go to bed and sleep. But this was not a bad thing for now, here he was, full of amazing energy again, standing waiting to greet little Bess as she was carried up the long, elegant stairway in The Oak Tree House. He heard Fred's feet coming nearer and nearer. Bess heard his words, his voice.

'Bess, Bess! You're safe and you're here with us. Did you go into another place, like me? Will you tell me where you went? Please let me touch you!'

Joe's voice was low and seemed to vibrate through Bess' mind. She was exhausted. She had closed her eyes so she did not see Joseph being lifted up by Nah; she did not see how Joe stretched out his hands to feel for her face, but she felt the hands touch her face, her eyes, her lips. Such soft, yet strong fingers.

She smiled then and she heard Joe laugh. Then he whispered, 'Oh, it is you, little Bess! We must get to know more about each other. I'm blind now, but I can see everything in my head. Tell me about Horatio. Is he—'

But Nah cut into his words. 'Not now, Joe. Bess is very, very weary. She must sleep. Tomorrow you'll be able to see her and talk with her. Say Goodnight.'

There was a minute pause, then Joe said, 'Goodnight, Bess, see you in the morning.'

Fred winked at Nah, and Bess was taken to her room. Her body felt warm and she snuggled deeper into Fred's arms as he walked down the corridor. *I'm home*, she thought. *I'm in my home with my Leigh family. I belong with them.*

The large house had welcomed everyone. It was humming with people again. It didn't like being empty; it was meant to be full – it had been built for families. It was late now and a silence had settled on the rooms. The bedrooms were occupied. An extra bed had been put up in Joe's room for Charlie and, of course Nah was there in her own bedroom. The Oak Tree House was her home too. Hannah and Artie had gone back to The Cottagey Ho, but they would be up again early the next day.

Chrissie lay in bed next to Jan. She had been saying 'Thank You'. Inside her head the words repeated themselves: *Thank you, thank you, Lord*. She strained her brain.

What day is it? The end of Wednesday, July 4th. Dear God, dear God! We've been through hell and you've brought us back here. We're all safe, all of us!

Jan shifted in his sleep. He turned towards her. Chrissie touched his cheek and his lips parted for a split second and he sighed. He was restless. She loved him so much that her heart ached. He looked drained and the bones showed under the fine skin. *My darling man*, thought Chrissie, *Bess will be ours now. She has accepted us as her family. Be peaceful. Tomorrow will be a good day. Tomorrow will be the first day of a new life.*

Back in Cornwall all the folk who had been involved in the Bess adventure were also resting. They had been through a most remarkable experience and their lives would be different from now on. All of them had had been touched, changed by this child, Bess – indeed, *these children*, for Andrew had made a deep impression on everyone he had come in contact with. All these folk would play an important role in the future of the Leigh family and their closest friends, and the Leighs and Nah, the Bests and Fred and his family would play their part in the lives of the Cornish folk for many years to come.

Chapter Thirty

$\mathcal{T}$ oby and Beatrice were married on Saturday, July 7th at a tiny church in Budoc, near Mawnan Smith. The whole of the Leigh family were invited and they all attended. What a day that was! A day full of happiness, joy and laughter. Gerry the guard was there and Anthea and Dog, the fire brigade and the police – lots and lots of them! The firemen formed a guard of honour for the bride and bridegroom as they left the church. Even Pippin went. She and Dog became firm friends. Agnes had been clever and had been in contact with Anthea and others. The aunts postponed their return to London – Aunt Hat refused to go home! She told Anthea and the mouse aunt that she would not go home until after the weekend if the Leighs were coming down to Cornwall again.

Agnes had found out about the people who had helped with the rescue of Bess and had arranged with Alf, Toby's friend, and Reg Trelawney, the fire chief, that they should all be invited to a reunion on Sunday the 8th at the hotel. It was a wonderful weekend. A convoy of cars had left The Oak Tree House on Friday, 6th July, including Fred in his battered old vehicle. Charlie was with Joe. She kept pinching herself to make sure that she was awake and that it was all real. She had been totally accepted into the fold. Andrew and Bess travelled together with Pippin Dog in the Land Rover, with Jan, Charlie and Joe. Chrissie drove her sports car with the front seat and boot laden with presents. Nah, Hannah and Artie travelled together and Sophia had Bibi with her. The women thought this was the best plan. Bibi was happy and generally controlled when she was with the Sophia Lady. What a cavalcade it was! They didn't hurry the journey – they made the most of it, stopping now and then at country pubs and tea cottages.

They arrived in Mawnan Smith in the middle of the afternoon. It was a fine, sunny day, not too hot and Michael and Agnes greeted them. 'Come in, you're all most welcome!' Agnes called.

The Fosseys had decided that they would not accept any other guests at the hotel that weekend; actually, there were only about four other people staying. They had been told about the special visitors from the Gloucestershire village and the Falmouth folk who had helped in the rescue of Bess, and why they were there. You can imagine what the atmosphere was like during the next few days! Agnes and Michael had also invited their close friends from around Mawnan Smith to various meals.

Friday evening was wonderful. The children were allowed to stay up for dinner and even the dogs were given special food. Yes, Dog was there, with the aunts and Anthea. He was wearing a splendid yellow bow, which made his black coat look even blacker. Pippin followed him everywhere – love flowed between people and animalia!

Hannah and Chrissie finally managed to persuade the children to go to bed. Bess was still very frail. Her lovely face became ashen and Andrew had whispered to Hannah that maybe Bess should go to her room? And should he take her? Hannah patted his cheek, saying that she would look after Bess.

Naturally, Bibi was fast asleep upstairs, she'd been wide awake all through the journey down to Cornwall and, thankfully, for everyone's sake, she'd just shut her eyes and fallen into a deep sleep as soon as her head had touched the pillow!

Joe was remarkable. He seemed to thoroughly enjoy being with the grownups! He talked to each person, asking their names and touching their hands and faces. Charlie never left his side; she guided him from person to person, they even walked around the garden. Jan watched the two figures as they slowly moved among the shrubs and trees. He was so thankful, so profoundly aware of the goodness that surrounded his family. He found it very difficult to talk, tears kept pricking his eyes and his voice was shaky. Chrissie stayed close to him as much as she could. So many people wanted to talk to her and she had many questions to ask.

The evening came to an end and it was quiet again. Bedroom lights gradually went out and all was silent. Tomorrow would be the wedding and more people to meet and talk to. Hannah and Artie lay in the large, comfy bed. They held hands and said their prayers. Artie was utterly amazed. He'd never experienced such a week. Fred had asked question after question earlier in the evening. Fred had insisted on coming with them; he'd phoned Fiona and told her that he would be away longer because of the happenings. He needed to be with Chrissie. They had always been the best of friends. They loved each other dearly – always had, as children. Fiona understood her husband. He was constantly surprising her with his impulsive decisions. She liked it, it made their marriage exciting! Mind you, she insisted on knowing where he would be and that he phoned her regularly.

Fred was kneeling by his bed, talking to God and Fiona, sending thoughts over the hundreds of miles to Scotland. He looked forward to the wedding enormously. What luck that he had arrived at The Oak Tree House when he did!

The little church at Budock was packed. The vicar had been notified that he should expect extra guests – he was thrilled! He was a most gregarious man. He just hoped that they would all fit into his church. They had! Now, they were all in the churchyard, cheering Toby and Beatrice as they walked underneath the firemen's guard of honour. Joseph and Charlie stood, hand in hand. Charlie had given Joe some rose petals, real ones. He was holding them close to his nose… the scent was so strong.

'Joe, Joseph! They're coming down the path, throw them… *now!*' and he threw them and heard Toby say, 'Oh! what a lovely smell! Bea, look, real rose petals!'

Joe felt his face being kissed and heard a gentle voice with a strange accent, 'Thank you, thank you. Stay with us. Let me have your hand. Tell me your name… Joseph, will you walk with us?'

Charlie gave him a tiny push forward and Joe was suddenly holding two hands, one large and the other small. He realised that he was between the bride and bridegroom. He felt important and quite safe. He called out, 'Charlie! All of you! Can you see me? I'm here!'

Chrissie called back, 'Joe, you look great! You're going to have your photograph taken, smile now!'

There was a great deal of laughter and every face was alive with happiness. Charlie stood watching little Joe, with the tears running down her cheeks. She was aware of a large white handkerchief being thrust into her hand and saw a big, untidy man looking down at her. It was Fred.

'Here, you'll need this. What a marvellous day, eh? Aren't we fortunate to be here?' And Fred laughed, a huge, rolling laugh. Charlie blew her nose and laughed too.

There was cheering and clapping and then they all began to move to the cars. The reception was being held at the local rugby club. Toby played for the first team in the winter. They didn't all go to the reception; just Toby and Beatrice's invited guests. The hotel crowd gradually made their way back to Mawnan. Sophia, Bibi and Nah were the first to arrive at the hotel. Bibi was very high, very excited. She jumped out of the car and proceeded to dance and sing along the terrace and into the garden. The two ladies sighed and Nah closed her eyes. Phew, what energy the child had! She just needed a shower and a rest.

Sophia chuckled, 'It's all right, Nah darling, you potter off and have some private time. I'll look after Bibi. I'll ask Charlie to cope with her when she comes back. Go on!' Nah heaved another sigh – of relief this time – and disappeared inside the hotel.

The rest of Saturday proved to be relaxed and easy. The children went to bed early and slept, some adults, too. It had been a good day.

Chrissie and Jan walked down to the small beach and sat staring at the sea as it moved over the shingle and into pools and over rocks. They were at peace. The horror was beginning to recede and they were beginning to feel that their lives would be able to move forward again. They didn't speak, they just looked and stayed very close to each other. It was as if time had slowed down to a trickle and they were slowing down with it.

Hannah and Artie were sitting in deckchairs, under an umbrella, in the orchard that ran behind the house. Artie was asleep, but Hannah was wide awake. She was smiling and her eyes were twinkling. She was enjoying this place immensely. There was no wind, just a cool breeze now and then. So beautiful, she thought. *And we have another day... or two? Sunday, tomorrow. We must find a church in Mawnan...*

Bess stood on the terrace. Andrew was close to her. He

was holding Bear. The young boy was so happy. He tried to describe the feeling to Hannah in later years. It was not easy to put these feelings into words. Bess had given Bear to him; the first time that anyone else had held Bear. Now they stood together looking out over the garden of the hotel. It was full of people, the special people who had come into their lives in the past days. It was a week since Jan and Bess had travelled in the Land Rover down to Cornwall; a week since Andrew had made his train journey – seven days! Andrew felt a small hand creep into his. He looked at Bess. She was smiling up at him, holding his hand tightly. It felt strong and a strange warmth flowed though his body.

Bess spoke in a quiet, reassuring tone. 'Andy, this is a remembrance day. We will talk about it when we are grown up. Maybe we'll tell our friends about it, but only you and I will understand that this day is our day.'

The little girl turned away and began to walk towards the steps that led to the great lawn. Andrew moved with her and Jan, standing in a group of people, caught sight of them as they walked, hand in hand, towards the summer house. Bess was chatting away and Andrew was nodding and laughing. He watched them break into a run, and he saw Andrew throw Bear into the air and catch him as the two children disappeared from sight amongst the trees. Jan's eyes filled, once again. He sniffed and cleared his throat. *I really must pull myself together*, he thought. *What's the matter with me?* But, he knew, without being told!

'How did you manage to find all these folk, Michael?' asked Chrissie, incredulously.

Michael replied, 'It wasn't difficult, actually! We had many phone calls from many people who had been involved with the rescue. Even the police got in touch!'

Agnes heard her husband's words, as she passed them, carrying a tray of drinks. 'It was quite extraordinary! The phone kept on ringing and I invited them all… isn't it marvellous?' She moved on, calling out, 'Anyone for another glass of wine?'

Anthea and the two aunts were deep in conversation with the Curtis family. Aunt Hat just stretched out a hand and took a glass from the passing tray, thanking Agnes and then continuing her sentence. The Curtises were enthralled with Hat's descriptions of her debut at Covent Garden when she was a young singer. The two boys were involved in music and they found this formidable lady absolutely fascinating, as she certainly was!

Harry Hammond was showing Bob and Susie Pringle and Susie's mother, Agnes Trevone, the huge conifer trees that ran along the side of the kitchen garden. Yes, Bob, Susie and Aggie Trevone were there. Aggie always read the local paper from cover to cover and there was a long article about the cliff rescue. She knew the Fosseys quite well and had phoned to ask for more details. They had been invited and they'd arrived wearing their Sunday best. Well, it was Sunday and this was an occasion, wasn't it? Aggie was delighted that she had the same name as the owner lady of the hotel. What a time they had! They talked to the police inspector and the fire chief; they were introduced to a film director – and the food! The food was a topic of conversation for weeks to come! I don't need to describe everything, or everyone, I just leave it to your imagination. It was a truly unforgettable day, a day full of joy and gratitude and laughter and radiant faces.

🐣

And then it was the end of the summer. The month of August had slipped away and September brought golden days which were getting shorter. The leaves on the great oak tree were beginning to change colour and Andrew noticed that there was a rug of leaves on the ground under the branches.

Life had gradually settled down into a pattern of everyday jobs and visits to Bristol and Cheltenham with various members of the family and circle of friends. Bess had had a slight setback after their return from Cornwall, but Dr Benedict had assured them that this was only delayed shock and had advised them to just be careful with the little girl and she would be fine, as Charlie and Hannah knew exactly how to care for her. Horatio's adventures helped. The stories happened every day and more and more people listened to them. Han was such a clever storyteller. She asked Artie to make her a large notice board and she pinned up the time and place of the stories. They were in different places and at different times, of course: this made it even more exciting! Joseph was Han's helper. He had made models of Horatio out of plasticine and clay and he took them in a box to every location. He set them out on a tray. He managed to do most things on his own, but Charlie was there to help if he needed assistance. She had become part of the family. Benedict had persuaded her to leave the hospital and accept the offer of a job at the Oak Tree Ho with the Leighs. Benedict and Charlie were in love! Oh, yes! They were engaged to be married. Wow, what a summer! This thought ran through the minds of everyone.

And now it was time for Andrew to start a new chapter of his life: senior school. He was scared, but he was also excited. He had a new uniform and new pens and pencils and new sports gear. *And* Bess was going to his old school! Mrs Avery had had her baby, a round, jolly little boy called

Sebastian! She would still be head mistress and Seb would be with her at school. 'Very good for the children to have a baby around... they'll be able to learn all about babies, won't they?' The education authority was not as sure as this delightful lady, but they didn't argue, so Master Seb Avery was there on the first day of term, much to the surprise of teachers and children!

Bibi had gone. Laura, her mother, had finished her theatre tour and had come to stay with the Leighs in August. She was going to visit her parents in America and would naturally take Bibi with her. There were sighs of relief from all around, but oh, how they missed her! She was such a character! However, she would always come back, whenever Laura had a job that meant that Bibi would be better off with the Leighs. Nah had been offered a good, ongoing role in a new television series. She was in rehearsal in London, living in her own lovely little apartment near the River Thames. Andrew had stayed there and he loved it. He loved London! Nah took him to see everything he wanted to see. He asked her if Bess could come with him next time and Nah had hugged him and said, 'Of course she can!' But now there were new schools to get used to, for all three children! Joseph was also going to a new school, a school for blind people. It was in Bristol, but he would be living at home. Charlie or Chrissie – whoever was around – would drive him there and back. He was also going to spend some time in October with Ralph Curtis down in Cornwall. Ralph would help him with his blindness. The Leighs and the Bests would go on living for many, many years. There would always be wonderful times – times full of wonder. They would have problems, like all of us, but their faith and their immense capacity for thinking and caring would help others and consequently themselves.

I have shared the summer of 1988 with you, their summer.
I could share more… maybe I will.

Postscript

I need to tell you that Hannah became deeply concerned about Amanda Jenkins. Do you remember Amanda, the nurse who was so desperately distressed? Hers is a most heartrending and tragic story and Hannah vowed that she would try to help her. 'Hannah and Amanda Jenkins'... but that is another story...

Printed in the United Kingdom
by Lightning Source UK Ltd.
115879UKS00001B/2